I0651945

A
Scarcity
of
Virgins

A
Scarcity
of
Virgins

JOANN CATANIA

IGUANA

Copyright © 2021 JoAnn Catania
Published by Iguana Books
720 Bathurst Street, Suite 303
Toronto, ON M5S 2R4

All rights reserved. No part of this publication may be
reproduced, stored in a retrieval system or transmitted, in any
form or by any means, electronic, mechanical, recording or
otherwise (except brief passages for purposes of review) without
the prior permission of the author.

Publisher: Meghan Behse
Editor: Lee Parpart
Front cover artwork and design: Anthony Catania

English translations of *Divina Commedia* and *Madame Bovary* by
JoAnn Catania

ISBN 978-1-77180-510-0 (paperback)
ISBN 978-1-77180-511-7 (epub)

This is an original print edition of *A Scarcity of Virgins*.

Tempted,
We accept passion's wild ride
To an unknown place
As essential as a heartbeat,
As evanescent as the wind
Blowing through fingers
That cling to a stranger
With the certainty
Of the disillusioned.

Halfway through the journey of my life
I found myself inside an unknown wood
As from my straight and narrow path I strayed.

A delicate flower with the chill of night
bends and closes all her petals tight,
but opens them again, kissed by the sun,
as did I, although I might not dare,
but so much ardour pulsed inside my heart,
that I began as one who had been freed:

— Divina Commedia, *Dante Alighieri*

It was the first time Emma had heard such words spoken to
her, and her pride, as one relaxing near a heated stove,
softened completely in response to the warmth of his language.

— Madame Bovary, *Gustave Flaubert*

To Bruno, my number one supporter

PROLOGUE

Winter 1987

The operating room is surprisingly large and brightly lit and walled with windows on one side as if they are expecting spectators. Faceless bodies, garbed in green, send muffled, dispassionate conversation floating up to the high ceiling. Against my skin, I feel rough cotton, hard stainless steel. My legs feel cold. The stirrups bite into my bare skin. Too much exposure. I ask for leggings.

"Alright now, Rita, I want you to count backwards from one hundred." The voice seems to drift in from far away.

I hear the words, but I ignore the anesthetist's instructions, and when I finally feel I'm succumbing, I struggle and push the mask away. Stronger hands, more determined, press it back onto my face. At the end of the operating table between my spread knees, behind a mask, I see the doctor. Wearing white. A white jacket stained with dried brown smears and splatters of blood, like fly specks. Something not right about it. Something. In his hand, a flash of metal much wider than any scalpel. As I'm losing consciousness, I see it is a meat cleaver.

The anesthetic wears off prematurely, before the procedure is completed. I awake, my mouth dry and tasting of parsley.

Above me, a flurry of green masks, and hands fluttering, and objects passed — a rubber hose, a plastic vial, a syringe.

Groggy, I ask: "Is it over?"

"Just about, just relax now."

"Was it a girl or a boy?"

"We couldn't tell."

"IT WAS FOURTEEN WEEKS OLD, DAMMIT — YOU COULD TELL!" My voice sounds very loud to me. Possibly I have screamed this.

"A girl."

"A *girl*," I repeat to myself as they jab another needle into my arm. Just before falling again into unconsciousness, I recall reading in a newspaper article, that in China, where only one child per family is allowed, a father had pushed bamboo splinters into the head of his baby girl so they could try again for a male child...

CHAPTER ONE

Spring 1986

1986 Beaujolais Nouveau.
    This lively red wine displays notes of raspberry with a hint of apricot...

Reading the words aloud, I type the French translation on my manual Underwood: *Ce vin rouge vif présente des notes de framboise avec une touche d'abricot...*

A couple of years ago, when the price of electric typewriters plummeted because computers became affordable to the masses, I said "an electric typewriter" when Victor asked what I wanted for my birthday. But Victor didn't think I needed one for a translating job that was only part-time, so he got me earrings instead. Diamond studs. Probably wanting to appear magnanimous to his teaching peers at social events. It *was* generous of him, so I couldn't very well complain. And anyway, I like the slight resistance of each manual key under my fingertips; it seems to make each word more deserved.

I had thought at the time to take a night course in journalism at the local high school, with the goal of eventually doing some freelancing from home. But Victor wasn't keen on my studying at night — nor the fact that, eventually, the writing would take me away from home, to do the interviews, and so forth, and the thought of having to drive to the interviews by myself, possibly in the middle of the night, to God-knows-where, made me chicken out about the idea. Then, the job of translator coincidently came my way. The job — *jobba* — as my father referred to it, was to translate, into French, descriptions of the wines produced on the Niagara winery where he worked tending the vines. Until his death last year, he worked at Cardinale Estate Winery for thirty-nine years, since first immigrating to Canada. The Cardinale brothers, who own the winery, were looking for a French translator for their various wines, the French translation being a requisite for the Canadian market, and my father had vaunted me to his employer as the perfect candidate for the position.

Victor had, surprisingly, acquiesced and given my newfound employment his blessing.

I was hesitant at first to accept the translating job, but it turned out not to be terribly demanding — a few hours of my time while the kids are at school — and requires no more knowledge beyond my book French; it has been eighteen years since I studied the subject, along with Spanish, as part of a double major towards a Bachelor of Arts degree from the University of Toronto. That's where I met Victor. "Maria Rita," I'd answered, when he'd asked my name.

"Maria Rita," he'd repeated. "Can't it just be one of the two names?"

"Well, Rita, if you like," I said. "We already have about a dozen Marias in the family circle."

Victor wanted to teach, and he was taking one of my French courses as a minor. At the start of the course in September, he'd sat beside me because it was the only seat available in the class. But he picked the seat next to me each time he returned to class, even though there were others vacant.

We were already engaged when we both graduated the following year, and even before that, he'd made it quite clear that what he wanted was a *stay-at-home* wife and mother to his children — when they eventually arrived. "*Our* children," I had corrected, dreamily, as we sat in the front seat of his father's blue Cutlass on a balmy summer night in the vacant parking lot by Lake Ontario, our usual spot. We listened to the rippling waves, their crests argent with moonlight, and it all seemed terribly romantic to me. In other cars, parked a considerate distance from each other, couples did more than just kiss chastely as Victor and I did. He wanted his wife virginal on the wedding night, and my religious scruples would never have allowed me to go beyond kissing, in any case.

I take several gulps of the too-cool coffee in my mug and remind myself that my deadline to submit the translations to Cardinale is tomorrow, and I certainly won't be able to get any work done tonight.

Enjoy with meat or chocolate fondue ... Déguster avec une fondue à la viande ou au chocolat...

Le chocolat — masculine. *La viande* — feminine. In French, nouns are either masculine or feminine. And letters are too — at least in my mind. "A" is feminine — a woman with a wide skirt. "B" — masculine: turn it sideways and it becomes a man's most precious possessions — his jewels, *les couilles, os colhoes, le palle, los cojones.* "C" — feminine, obviously; any man would tell you that ... and so on, masculine and feminine, down the alphabet. "O" is, definitely, feminine — "O" is the shape of a woman's mouth when a man enters her in pleasure, or in pain, like on the wedding night. "O" is the shape of a woman's belly when she becomes pregnant, which might follow the pleasure — or the pain. "O" is the opening of the birth canal to bring into the light another life. "O" is the "o" in w-o-man. Woe-man...

***

From the back of the house, the sunroom screen door opens with a loud click and a waft of cold air pours into the dining room. Pushing my chair away from the antique, burled-oak table that serves as my desk, I start to get up and call expectantly, "Micah?" at the same time glancing at the glass-domed anniversary clock on the sideboard and realizing it's too early for school to be out.

"No — Maddy."

"Oh, Maddy, it's you," I say, sitting back down.

Maddy never knocks, just walks in like she used to do when we were kids. I catch a glimpse of today's power suit — a showy red jacket with shoulder pads covering a body-hugging black dress that most men would call sexy. A far cry from what she looked like the first day we met, when Maddy, then a stringy eleven-year-old, traipsed over from two houses down and greeted me at my front steps with a metallic smile that revealed full braces. "Hi, I'm Maddy," she'd said. "What's your name?" That was twenty-seven years ago. We've been best friends ever since.

"I'm starved. You got anything for me?" she calls from the kitchen, her words accompanied by the squelch of the refrigerator door.

"There's a pan of brownies I made yesterday."

"With chocolate icing?"

"Yes," I tell her, with an appeasing tone I would use with the twins and even the two older ones, "with chocolate icing. What are you doing around these parts?"

"Had a demonstration on Thorncrest Road." Her words are muffled as she walks into the dining room chewing on a chocolate brownie. "Oh, my God, these are good … are they from scratch?"

"Of course."

"You *have* to give me the recipe."

"I got it off the cocoa tin," I tell her. "Don't tell me you've developed an interest in cooking?"

"Fat chance. I'll get Stef to make them."

This seems more plausible. Stefan has always done the cooking whenever Victor and I have been invited to dinner. He's always given Maddy the freedom to blossom in her career. "So how did your demo go? Was it a good day for Mary Kay Cosmetics?"

"Of course — Thorncrest Village — ritziest area in west Toronto, don't you know."

I do know. It's only a few blocks from my house, and sometimes, after dropping off the kids at school, I take the longer route home just to drive through the neighbourhood and admire the mansions. I like to imagine the house I might have chosen to buy, if Victor hadn't insisted on our Tudor. Maddy looks as tall and striking as ever, even more so now that she has followed the lead of her fiercely competitive rivals. She now goes to her sales demonstrations decked out in designer clothing and plenty of costume jewelry, aping the company founder, except that Mary Kay's diamonds are real. At the moment, though, her impeccable appearance is marred by a blob of chocolate icing stuck to the corner of her mouth. She flicks her tongue out, like a frog zapping a fly, catching the sweet chunk with the tip of it and taking it into her mouth. The smell of chocolate mixed with the musky scent of her expensive perfume vitalizes the tired air of the room. I stop typing so I can talk to Maddy.

"You working?" she asks.

"Yes. I have to get this translation done before the kids get home. Then I have to get the food ready for tonight. And if that isn't enough for me to worry about, Victor invited his principal and his wife over for dinner tomorrow night."

"Poor you," Maddy says. She sounds sympathetic, although I'm not sure she fully appreciates the stress Victor's invitation will cause me.

Dragging a chair away from the table with her clean hand, Maddy sits back and slips off her shoes. "These things are killing me," she says, kicking aside a pair of shiny red, patent leather shoes with dangerously pointed toes and long, lethal stiletto heels — *come fuck me heels,* Maddy calls them. She likes to come out with this kind of scandalizing remark just to see my reaction. Had we not met early in life, I sometimes wonder whether we would have become friends at all. We have very different philosophies, very different lives. We look very different, too.

"I don't *get* how you can eat that stuff and not get fat," I say, slightly disgusted. "I can't eat what I bake without packing on the pounds." It has always been true. Maddy could eat the whole pan of brownies and never gain an ounce, while I seem to gain weight just by breathing in the smell of anything baked.

"Sex," Maddy says, "that's how to stay slim. You burn three-hundred and fifty calories each time."

"Uh huh," I nod, unconvinced. Maddy has clawed her way to top salesperson in her area, winning both the diamond bee *and* the pink Cadillac. I sometimes wonder whether there isn't something strangely masochistic about having a best friend who so flagrantly outshines you in so many ways.

"So, what time's the confirmation tonight? That's so sweet of Alison to ask me to be her sponsor."

Trust my twelve-year-old to make the right choice when there are gifts involved. "You and I and Alison have to be at the church at seven to get instructions. Victor will come later with the other three."

"Is it a Mass with Communion? If it is, I have to go to confession."

"That bad, eh? You don't have to *take* Communion, you know."

Maddy smirks and takes another bite of the brownie. "But I want to — I like the taste of Communion wafers."

Recently, I read an article about the wafers in some business magazine I looked through at the hairdresser. The article described how they were made. It was only a matter of two ingredients, really: flour and water. They'd even given the recipe. "You can make them at home, you know — the Communion wafers."

"Really? I thought they came from heaven," Maddy says dryly.

"No — Greenville, Rhode Island, actually. It's been a family business for the last seventy-five years. They pretty much have a lock on the Communion wafer market. They even sell them at Walmart in the States."

"Hmm," Maddy responds, showing scant interest and contentedly biting off another large mouthful of brownie. "What did you do to your arm?"

"Oh, *that* — Victor got a little frisky in bed," I laugh, tugging at the cardigan draped across my shoulders and covering the ovoid marks that have now turned the colour of ripe Sicilian eggplants. It was nothing, really — Victor had simply grabbed my arm when I'd turned my back on him in the middle of an argument. He *did* apologize, and the truth is, I bruise easily.

CHAPTER TWO

Wednesday night. The confirmation celebration has ended with most of my relatives having attended. Victor's parents had not come, much to Alison's disappointment. But they sent a gift via Victor — a card with twenty dollars in it, which Alison has already slated to go towards the Sony Walkman she's been wanting. When we've said goodbye to the last of the relatives, I return to the kitchen where the sweetness of cake and *cannoli* and the warm scent of espresso linger in the air. The kids, with school in the morning, have already gone to bed. Victor suggests, "Leave everything and clean up tomorrow."

I glance at the sink full of dessert plates and a counter covered with coffee-smeared cups and take him up on his offer.

I *am* dead beat. But it's Wednesday night, the mid-week lovemaking night. I lie on my half of the double mattress while Victor's pale and almost hairless body moves against mine, like an ice skater propelling himself forward, rhythmic, sure. Even though he has just showered, the scent of lavender and bergamot escape from the damp creases of his neck. *Brut* — a Father's Day gift from the kids. Though faint, the stale, sickeningly sweet smell is nauseating. I suddenly feel unable to breathe and turn my face sideways towards the bedroom wall commonly shared with the twins. Whenever the boys shift around in their sleep, the bunk beds on the other side hit the wall with a resounding thud that sounds so much farther away than the next room, creating a sense of remoteness, isolation. I focus my attention on the framed print that hangs in the centre of the common wall, hoping Victor doesn't notice I'm drifting. The print is a limited-edition Bateman, secondary market — expensive, but already worth double what Victor paid for it. In the dim, diffused light of the Tiffany lamp, the print is a mixture of earthy ochre and gray shadows, interspersed with splotches of white. *Coyote in Winter Sage.* I squint; the picture comes into focus enough to pick out the coyote, but not the discarded beer can I know lies hidden among the grasses — an ecological reprimand by the artist. The animal is frozen in its noble stance, its muscular body covered by a luxuriant golden coat, the fur so real, I can almost feel it, silky between my fingers, the effect, I have read, painstakingly obtained by the artist's use of a single-haired brush. Such patience.

"Give me your mouth, Rita."

I turn towards Victor. In his excitement, he covers my lips roughly, sucking hard, hurting me. I can feel him trying to get his tongue between my teeth, but I resist. His breathing quickens. He lifts himself on the palms of his hands and sucks in air — short, shallow breaths, vain gulps, like a fish out of water — while his face contorts in pleasurable voiding of some searing internal slag. Immediately, he collapses on top of me, his body limp, his breathing laboured as after a sprint. I rub his neck gently and as his breathing slows and he becomes motionless, I realize he is asleep.

***

"Victor!" I pound lightly on my husband's shoulder. "Victor! Get off. I want to sleep too." Languidly, accompanied by a long, deep sigh, he rolls to his side of the mattress. Lifting the rest of my body, I pick up the nightgown discarded on the night table and, grabbing a Kleenex, cup my hand between my thighs and slide my legs over the side of the bed until my toes touch cool hardwood. Lifting the rest of my body, I walk ape-like to the bedroom ensuite. I turn on the taps in the tub, adjusting them until the water is lukewarm, so close to my own body temperature that all I can feel is a silky pressure against my wrist. I've already showered earlier, so instead, I squat in front of the faucet, take a bar of soap and lather my upper legs, my fingers tracing the raised keloids stretching like thick cords along my left upper thigh where a birthmark had been removed years ago. I have never been comfortable with my own nakedness, having cultivated self-consciousness from birth.

While pregnant with me, my mother had craved fresh figs. But, although my father searched high and low throughout the Italian markets in the city, there were none to be found. My mother resigned herself to the fact that her baby would be marked. I was born with a brown, scabrous growth — a raised nevus the shape of a man's hand that covered my thigh and extended like groping fingers into the crease along my groin; in the heat of summer, it festered and became offensive. At the playground, wearing shorts, kids taunted me. *"Rita shit her pants! Rita shit her pants!"* At the age of nine, when I came home crying, my parents finally agreed to have it surgically removed. But the scars remained.

Having completed my perfunctory bidet, I grasp the rolled edge of the tub and climb out; it's one of the high, old-fashioned types with clawed feet, which had impressed Victor so much when we'd viewed the house that he hadn't minded the chipped enamel or, later, the expense of having it resurfaced. This is Victor's house — his choice, his dream. No — not so much the house as the area. *The Kingsway.* The agent was a small, gray-haired man, fiftyish, who wore the guilty expression of a kid playing hooky. "You have to keep in mind the most important consideration in real estate. Actually, it's three considerations," he'd corrected, with a grin too impish considering his age. "Location! Location! Location! You're gonna have to pay for the location!"

In spite of the price, Victor had gone ahead and bought his century home in the Kingsway, complete with gumwood, leaded windows, and turreted alcove in the living room. The prestige of living here had overridden many deficits, including disintegrating plumbing, inadequate electrical service, and a basement that was no better than a root cellar. The previous owner had poured concrete over the basement's dirt floor, but the mustiness remained. On top of everything, the basement flooded each spring, and the water stunk horribly. I have spent hours down there with a bucket and mop sopping up smelly sewer water in the dark. But — it was the right *location*.

While I'm drying myself, wedging the towel between each of my toes, I hear Victor stirring, apparently awake again, and quickly slip into my nightgown. Even though we'd both been naked in bed only minutes ago, I prefer to cover myself from Victor's eyes. He enters the bathroom and says, "I have to pee," his words stretching out into a yawn as he lifts the lid of the toilet. Picking up a hairbrush, I move in closer to the vanity mirror and run it through my hair.

I often wonder what attracted Victor to me. When I first met him, he was tall but slightly built, with narrow shoulders and hips. He had a pleasant enough face, tanned from an outdoor job with the Toronto Department of Sanitation, which paid better than most summer jobs; his eyes were light blue and gentle, and his gold-red hair crowned his head like some Nordic god. I, on the other hand, had dark, slightly slanting eyes, which appeared unremarkable behind thick-lensed glasses, and a complexion that was prone to acne; on top of that, I always carried a little extra weight, especially on the hips. But Victor wasn't put off by any of that, christening me his "little Sicilian peasant girl."

No doubt I was attracted to Victor by qualities I myself lacked: his confidence; his positive way of moving and talking and thinking; the way he never doubted that he was as good, and probably better, than the next person; his certainty that he would succeed. He was a rock of Gibraltar and I had *needed* someone to lean on.

Victor's head appears above me in the mirror as he reaches past me to wash his hands. Each time our faces come together, in a mirror, in photographs, I'm startled by the incongruity: his sparse reddish hair and baby-pink skin, my thick, chestnut-brown hair and tawny Mediterranean complexion that, next to his, appears almost green. He suddenly focuses his attention on the top of my head, which he can view handily, being almost a foot taller than me. "I see some gray hairs," he announces almost triumphantly.

"Have you checked out your own head lately?" I retort defensively. "Just because your hair's lighter and they don't show as much doesn't mean they're not there." But we're both getting older. The skin on our faces used to be so tight, it glistened. In our wedding pictures, the photographer's lights *bounce* off our cheeks into the camera. Now our faces look slightly wilted, as if the skin has become a half size too big for our facial bones. Victor has developed deep creases around his eyes and fluid-filled pouches underneath them, which, along with his receding hairline, make him look older than his forty years — older than *me*, although his mother had warned him that *Mediterraneans* aged early.

Mrs. McEachern — I still call my mother-in-law that, and my father-in-law, Mr. McEachern. They live not far from us in an impressive centre hall Georgian, meticulously maintained by a cleaning lady who comes twice a week. The first time my parents were invited to the McEacherns' home, they sat timidly on a tufted loveseat, their coarse fingers caught in the small holes of the Rosenthal teacup handles. They had come from houses that were little more than hovels with compressed dirt floors and crumbling stucco walls. Sitting in the back seat of our used Chevrolet as my father drove us home after the visit, I could see my parents' taut bodies relax and hear them both breathe a sigh of relief.

Victor dries his hands, then folds the towel neatly and places it back on the rack. "Don't forget to put guest towels out tomorrow for the Farrells' visit. Maybe buy some new ones. I noticed the ones in the powder room are pretty shabby."

A shiver passes through me, as though a window has suddenly been opened in the room, although the ensuite window is shut tight. I've been cringing at the thought of having the Farrells over again. Frank Farrell, the principal at Victor's high school, is burly and bald-headed and opinionated, and he laughs so loudly that, the last time he was over, he scared the dog, who headed for cover underneath the couch. He will be accompanied by his trophy wife, Judy, beautiful and blonde, naturally — though not *naturally* blonde — who had formerly been a secretary at the school. Victor invites them once a year, thinking it wouldn't hurt to suck up to the boss in an attempt to get the vice-principal position that will soon become vacant with Fergus Malone retiring.

It's ludicrous, whenever the Farrells visit, how uncomfortable I can be made to feel in my *own* home, even though I mostly sit and listen, hopefully with some semblance of interest.

Sometimes I even attempt to enter the conversation, although I know little about the education programs they are always discussing. Still, if it's a topic that I have some knowledge of, and if I can drum up the courage, I have, at times, attempted to join the conversation by interjecting: *Isn't it true that — ?*; *In my opinion — ; But don't you think — ?* Maybe I speak too softly, or maybe I just don't manage to get the timing right — whatever it is, my brief dispatch of words is usually overlooked and just hangs foolishly in midair.

"Have you decided what you're making yet?" Victor asks.

"I thought maybe veal parmesan. They like Italian."

"Veal parmesan is fine as long as you use milk-fed veal."

"Why does it have to be milk-fed? Do you realize how they raise those poor calves? It's cruel!"

"It's the only way you can be sure the meat won't be tough."

"Well, you'll have to go to Santini's then. Two pounds I think should do it. You can pick it up tomorrow on your way home."

"Can't tomorrow. I have a meeting after school. I'll be late getting home as it is."

"But nobody has milk-fed around here." My words have a pleading tone that I know Victor hates. I hate it too.

"So — go to Santini's."

I bite down on my bottom lip, gnawing at it uncertainly. "I've never driven there by myself."

"Take Bloor to Jane, Jane to St. Clair — it's easy, Rita."

Easy for *him*. "It's supposed to snow tomorrow, and didn't you have the snow tires changed to summer ones last week?"

"Yes, but it's only a forty percent chance of snow — heard it on the news driving home."

I sigh in exasperated acceptance. It seems ridiculous, I know. I've had my licence for twenty years — longer than we've been married — but I rarely drive further than a few blocks from home. I've never driven the highway — you might as well ask me to fly to the moon; whenever it comes to highway driving, Victor always drives. In fact, Victor has never allowed me to drive when we're *both* in the car. But there it is: I'm afraid to drive the highway and I'm not the only one. Plenty of the women I know have never driven the highway. "Alright, I'll try to go to Santini's," I say, resigned.

"Coming to bed?"

"In a minute. I want to check the kids."

***

I open the bedroom door and step out into the hall, guided only by the dim glow of a nightlight plugged into the wall. Our upstairs is divided into two wings, each wing three steps higher than the stairway landing; one wing is the master bedroom and ensuite, the other, the kids' three bedrooms and the main bathroom that they share. At the top of the landing, looking straight down the remaining ten steps, is Victor's study, where he prepares his classes each night. It is a unique feature of the house: the front of the study facing the stairs is a combination of gumwood panelling to a height of three feet, while the remainder is gumwood framed sections of bevelled glass, including the door, which has bevelled glass inserts. It allows Victor, when he sits at his massive oak rolltop desk preparing classes, to monitor the comings and goings of both floors.

Crossing over to the bedrooms of the other wing, I look into the children's rooms, lit minimally by the weak glow of the nightlight. I stop first at Micah's door; a bullet-shaped metallic object on his night table catches the light and flashes silver at me: his ghetto blaster. Micah is fourteen and the oldest, but even so, I hold my breath and listen, a habit since the kids were babies, fearful for a moment of hearing nothing; when I catch the even cadence of his breathing, I exhale. Alison's room next. I see the mound of blankets moving gently up and down; she sleeps on her stomach with her backside up. She's twelve now, almost a teenager; fine reddish hairs have begun to appear under her arms. She has Victor's colouring. Tonight, she became a soldier in the army of Christ — or so she was told by the Bishop conferring the confirmation. I have mixed feelings about all that, but Victor adheres to religious tenets regardless of the religion. He converted to Catholicism before we married and was quite happy to be released from the "abstaining from alcohol" part of his Episcopal Methodist upbringing, developing quite a liking for the stuff, even considering himself a wine connoisseur. As far as the kids go, I suppose I want them to have options and make their own choices about religion when they're older.

From the doorway of Joshua and Jamie's room, the sound of the twins' breathing is repeated like an echo in the room, identical in sound, but not in unison — like a choral round. I return to my own bedroom after this, my regular evening ritual.

The bedsprings creak a lament as Victor rolls over. I slip under the covers, wriggling into a comfortable position. "Don't use mozzarella for the veal parmesan," he instructs me. "It's too runny. Use Jarlsberg."

"Alright."

"The Farrells were crazy about that French silk pie you made the last time."

"You want me to make it again?"

"You mind?"

"Not if it will snag you that vice-principal position you're after."

"Very amusing." He pauses as if to ruminate on that. "Oh — listen, I wrote down the name of the wine on a pad by the fridge. A *Beerenauslese* — I checked in the wine bar and we already have a nice, crisp French Chardonnay to go with the veal, but a sweet wine will complement that pie nicely."

"What's wrong with Cardinale ice wine?"

"Rhine wine will be more impressive. The liquor store on Bloor will have it. It'll be a good twenty bucks, but don't worry about that."

"What a shame we couldn't have brought more wine back from Europe." My tone makes it sound sarcastic. It was *meant* to be.

Victor misses it altogether, or deliberately overlooks it. "Yeah," he answers sleepily.

Turning away from him, I pull the covers up over my chin. My father used to do the same when he slept, covering his face up to his nose, even at the end when he was in palliative care at the hospital. I had sat by his side as long as I could. But Victor was adamant that we should go ahead with the European trip we had planned months before, for who could say how long my father would last, and what could I do for him, anyway, if I stayed? It was a three-week trip, and Victor had managed, at least, to buy some wine before we were called back during our last week, suddenly, not unexpectedly. The airline, fully booked, had accommodated us, for compassionate reasons, up front with the stewardesses. The wine went with us, five bottles altogether: two French burgundy, two Rhine white, one German ice wine. The ice wine, the one Victor most looked forward to opening, had gone "skunky" by the time he uncorked it several months later, and I'd felt — though not without some conflicting quivers of guilt — an almost perverse satisfaction in watching him pour the whole bottle down the sink.

A yelping from downstairs dissolves the veil of sleep that was beginning to descend on me and rouses Victor from his half-sleep. "That damned dog! It's almost midnight. Are we ever going to get any sleep tonight?"

"I'll go."

"Well, hurry up. I can never get to sleep until you come to bed."

In the dark, I feel around with my feet for my fuzzy slippers, then pad through the hall and down the stairs to the kitchen. Whining softly, Gigi jumps up on me, the matted, gray hair of her forepaws tickling my legs. "What's the matter, girl? You gotta go out?" The whine becomes more urgent, and I open the back door that leads to the sunporch, then the sunporch door to the backyard. An icy draft bites at my ankles as Gigi brushes against them in her urgency to get out. We have already had a couple of weeks of spring-like weather, but today it has turned miserably cold again. The night air smells of frost, and splinters of ice float down from the sky, landing on my face and instantly melting into mini rivulets down my cheeks. *Please don't let it snow. I've got to go shopping. I've got to take the car.* I'm not sure whom I am asking for this favour. Shivering, I close the sunporch door; inside, my breath creates a white mist in the frigid air. My in-laws have the right idea, taking off with their golf clubs on Boxing Day and not returning until the grass needs cutting again. So does almost everyone else on the street; they are mostly retired couples, financially secure, liberated from children and responsibilities, free to travel at will to Florida, to anywhere. Except for Mrs. O'Brien next door who has been a widow for as long as we've known her and stays home with her cat.

Where had that dog gotten to? "Gigi, come on girl, here girl." A rustle of last season's dried leaves, and Gigi appears out of the darkness and comes scampering up the steps. "Get inside where it's warm, old girl." Gigi *is* old — and *fat*. One of my brothers had brought her home as a pup, then abandoned her to the care of my reluctant but vigilant parents. No one would guess that she is part miniature poodle. Too much spaghetti — my mother couldn't see the harm in feeding a dog spaghetti. I offered to take Gigi after my father died, my mother not wanting the nuisance of having to take the dog for daily walks, which had been my father's responsibility. My father *died*, and Victor and I had been gallivanting through Europe, rooting out rare wines. Never mind. Don't think. Bed.

The dog settles into her corner of the kitchen, beneath the antique pine coat rack that Victor has refinished. I lock the back door and, from force of habit, check the basement and front doors as well, to make sure they are locked. Upstairs, Victor is sleeping soundly. As I gravitate towards the feverish warmth of his body, I wonder how he'd managed to fall asleep without me.

CHAPTER THREE

Through the window over the kitchen sink, I look out into the backyard. A nausea, reminiscent of morning sickness, bubbles up in my stomach. The grass is covered with white again. Up to yesterday, there hadn't been a speck of snow leftover from the winter, not even the gray, honeycombed ridges of gritty ice that linger along the driveway curbs where the snowplows dump high mounds after a snowfall. Purple and yellow crocuses had already started to come up along the side of the house, where the earth, still frozen deeper down, was becoming spongy on the surface, but there is no sign of them now. There has to be a foot of snow out there!

"Wow, snow!" Beside me, Jamie lifts himself on tiptoes to see outside. "Can we make a snowman after school?"

Distractedly, as I turn to the stove to stir the oatmeal, I answer, "We'll see. Are your brothers and Alison up?"

"I think so."

Joshua appears and asks, "What's for breakfast?"

"Oatmeal. You can have cornflakes if you want." I know how much he hates hot cereal. Jamie and Joshua are fraternal twins and don't resemble each other at all. Jamie is the only one who really looks like me — the same longish nose, the same slightly slanting eyes. *Scurciatu,* my mother says — made from the same skin. On the stairs, footsteps thunder, sounding distant, muffled by carpeting: Micah, with all of his fourteen-year-old gangliness, comes into the kitchen. "You're going to break your neck one of these days, Micah. And wear a belt with those pants, they're falling down." He pulls a face and goes back up. "Jamie — put Gigi outside, please, she's going to make me trip." Falling into the daily routine, no longer able to dwell on my apprehension concerning the day's tasks, I feel more at ease. While the oatmeal bubbles on the stove, I set the table: bowls, spoons, cinnamon, brown sugar, a cut-glass pitcher of milk, a plastic jug of orange juice. By the time I've finished, the oatmeal has thickened. Micah is back down, and from the bottom of the stairs I summon the rest of the family: "Victor, Alison, breakfast." Alison and Victor appear, dutifully, and take their places at the table.

"Dad — guess what?" Jamie says, excitedly. "Mom said we can make a snowman after school."

"Did you say that, Rita? Last time he got soaked, then he got an earache and kept everybody up all night."

"Jamie, I said we'll see."

"I want to make one too," Joshua wails.

I sigh in exasperation and take refuge in my bowl of oatmeal.

"The Farrells are coming at seven-thirty, Rita, don't forget."

"Can we make a snowman, Mom, can we?"

"We'll see after school. Maybe it'll warm up," I add, before Victor can protest again. Instead he says, "Tank's empty. You'll have to gas up."

I drop my spoon, heavy with oatmeal, into my bowl. "Oh, Victor, couldn't you do it before you go. The stations around here are all self-serve now, and I've never done that before."

"For God's sake, Rita, it's very simple. You drive into a gas bar, you get out of the car, you pick up the nozzle, unscrew the cap of the gas tank, and stick the nozzle in. When the tank's full, you go and pay the attendant at the booth."

Not to show my agitation, I leave the breakfast table and go down into the basement in order to dig out boots and toques and mitts that I had stored away in a plastic bin in the belief that winter had ended. How could I be so stupid! This was Toronto. It was practically tradition having an April snowstorm each year. The basement smells musty; I glance suspiciously at the floor along each ancient fieldstone wall, looking for signs of powdery lime residue, which signals water seepage. No water yet, but wait until the snow melts — there'd be a flood.

***

Amid the squeaking of the boys' polyethylene jackets as they jostle each other in the back seat of the station wagon, I pull cautiously out of the driveway. The roads aren't bad; the snowplows have been out. I drop the children off at school, congratulate myself for having succeeded that far, and head east along Bloor. There is salt and sand on the road; I go the speed limit and feel surprisingly confident.

At the liquor store, a cherry-faced clerk with a bulbous nose dotted with blackheads sells me a bottle of Beerenauslese 1985 for twenty-seven fifty. I carry it carefully back to the car, put it on the seat next to me and drive on. Victor will *croak* when I tell him the price. On the Rhine, he would have paid five, six dollars for it. Our *European* holiday. We had waited eighteen years for that trip, booked it eight months in advance, lined up, as babysitters, my brother and his wife. It had taken so long for me to summon the courage to actually get on a plane for the first time. So ironic. *I shouldn't have left my father.* The guilt keeps returning, over and over. Just before the trip, wasted and weak, his cheekbones pressing sharply against his skin, my father had insisted on having a party to celebrate my parents' forty-fifth wedding anniversary. What gift do you give a dying man? He'd sat, drained of energy, on the couch, wrapped in a thick blanket my mother had knitted for him because he was always cold, his grandchildren scrambling on and off his knees, being reprimanded by my mother. "*Nonno* is too tired right now." But although he bravely attempted a smile and a few words to us, he couldn't manage to hold back a soft, continuous moaning, like the sound of a toiling machine, and I could read on his face shame for not being able to endure silently. The relatives stood at a respectful distance, feigning joviality. His scalp, nearly bald from radiation treatments, made him seem someone other than my father. Except for his eyes: dark brown with a slight slant, I recognized, but for the glint of pain, my eyes. Victor had been insistent. He argued we had waited eighteen years for the trip, and that was true. Still, we'd taken my father to the hospital by then, where he lay in a drugged stupor, so that when the time came, he could slip from life unknowingly. "You can't help him, even if you stay," Victor insisted. "He could go on like that for months."

I should have said: *I'm not going, Victor. You go. I'm staying with my father because I know he's dying.* I should have said that at the airport. My lips formed the words minutes before boarding the plane. Instead, I said weakly, "I don't feel right about this, Victor."

I spot a gas station and stop. Carefully following the instructions on the gas pump, I fill up, then go inside the store to pay. An elderly, turbaned clerk accepts my cash and smiles at me in a fatherly, approving way, as if he's guessed it's the first time I've pumped my own gas. I smile back, half expecting him to reach over and give me a pat on the head. "Have a pleasant day," he tells me as I head for the door.

I feel buoyed as I get into the station wagon and resolutely continue my unwelcome errand. To my relief, the traffic is light along Bloor, and even lighter when I reach St. Clair. This is an ugly stretch of road: rail yards flanked by sagging fences, crumbling factories, desolate little stores interspersed among aluminum framed semi-detached houses with porches covered in phony grass carpeting — a confusion of mixed zoning. Further on, the stink of decaying meat heralds the stockyards with its network of holding pens and slaughterhouses and meat packing plants, which always depresses me because they remind me of the German concentration camps in war movies.

Just past the stockyards, the streetcar tracks begin. They gouge the road just where I want my wheels to go. Partly because of that and partly because of the greasy slush that covers the road now that the day is warming a little, I have some trouble controlling the car. My hands grip the steering wheel; I can feel this morning's oatmeal, which is supposed to stick to your ribs, compress instead into a tight ball in my stomach. A constricting band of tension tugs painfully at the roots of my hair, as if the strands are being held tightly back with an elastic band instead of lying loosely inside the upturned collar of my jacket. When I hit the brakes at a red light, the car starts to skid. For an instant, the loss of control paralyzes me; helpless, as though I am a detached observer, I watch the car glide, as if airborne, diagonally into the opposite oncoming lane, and I feel for a split second the euphoria of flying — mind and body, flying. The next second, I am pumping the brakes hard, pumping, pumping, until the station wagon spins round and comes to a stop on the other side of the white line of the intersection, in the opposite direction of where I should be driving. But at this moment there are no cars around me on either side of the road, as luck would have it! I'm safe! It was a close call, but I'm safe! My heart is beating excitedly; my body seems light, my face tingly. I feel tremulous and grateful and, strangely, exhilarated.

***

In the parking lot outside Santini's, a half ton pickup with a shovel attachment is clearing away the snow. I take the only empty space in the area already plowed, beside a mound of snow that is growing higher with each dump of the snowplow. The small lot serves not only Santini's, but also a strip of stores joined together like colourful postage stamps: a hairdresser, a travel agency, a Mac's Milk store, a bakery, a Chinese restaurant. I head towards the store sign that has *Santini's Choice Meats* painted in bright red lettering, flanked on one side by a steer head wearing a blue ribbon and on the other by a can of Unico oil.

The glass door at the entrance to the store resists my pull, its opening baffled by an overhead pressure release. Inside, the shiny black-and-white checkerboard floor, the chrome, and the glass all mirror each other. Surprisingly, it's already crowded with customers this early on a Thursday morning. From a plastic dispenser that resembles a horizontal apostrophe, I tear off a pink ticket that sticks out like a tongue. It reads: 25. The box on the wall behind the counter says NUMBER BEING SERVED: 21. The warmth relaxes me, erasing the tension of the ride; I can feel my muscles loosening. Unbuttoning my jacket, I inhale the familiar aroma of spicy salamis, peppered prosciuttos, and sharp Romano pecorino cheeses. Everyone is waiting patiently, shifting from one foot to the other, clutching their pink tickets, checking them each time a number is called. Most are middle-aged housewives, Italian mostly, it appears, dressed in fabric coats with mink collars or imitation fur jackets and ankle boots with rabbit fur pom-pom ties. Though there is one frazzled young mother who is chasing after a preschooler who is sticking his fists into a barrel of olives, while the baby, packed papoose-like in a denim carrier against her chest, jounces up and down. Once, the floor had been covered with sawdust, but not anymore. My three brothers and I used to write letters in it with our toes, like sand on a beach, while we waited patiently for our parents to make their purchases. Kids aren't patient anymore. I can't shop with mine. Too demanding, spoiled, fidgety. No sawdust to play with.

Behind the counters, meat clerks with dark mustaches and white jackets speckled with blood reach inside glass doors towards meats of various hues separated one from the other with strips of plastic grass: pale chicken legs, breasts and wings, liver the colour of dried blood, burgundy roasts, pink pork, stringy gray brains and entrails, white-skinned rabbits. At the far end of the counter, an endless variety of cold cuts. Above the clerks' heads, thick, oblong provolone cheeses and triangular prosciutto hams hang from the ceiling like male and female genitalia. But of everything here, it is the boiling hens that intrigue me most with their tough yellow skins, leathery legs and sharply clawed feet. They are split open at the breast, revealing, like a buried treasure, golden yolks in graduating sizes, the largest about the same size as when you crack open an egg, then smaller and smaller until they are no bigger than a pea, each one veined with a network of fine, scarlet lines. Great in the soups my mother made. The eggs cooked first; my mother would scoop them out with a slotted spoon and let my brothers and me eat them before the soup was ready. You would never find chickens like these in supermarkets, packaged in Styrofoam trays, hermetically sealed in cellophane.

It's getting warm now, and my feet begin to feel itchy inside my fleece-lined boots. I wiggle my toes. The digital numbers on the box against the wall say: 23. Good. There are business cards displayed in little holders on top of the glass refrigerated cases; the cards have the same steer head as the sign outside, minus the can of Unico oil. The address, hours of business, and telephone number are printed on the card, and I pick one up so I can call ahead with my order next time. Then I won't have to wait. I slip the card in my purse for future reference. The numbers on the wall change to 24. My turn next. Someone nudges in beside me. A blonde. Victor had once said that blondes are more attractive than brunettes. "Why did you marry me, then?" I asked. Maybe it was true. *Is it true blondes have more fun?* the old TV jingle used to ask. In high school, most of my classmates thought so, bleaching their hair diligently once a month — the Prom Queens and Eaton's reps, almost without exception, blonde. Like me, they would all be entering middle age now, probably still dyeing their gray hair blonde. I glance surreptitiously sideways at the woman; what astonishing blue eyes she has! Her lashes, darkened with mascara, aren't clumpy like when I put it on, enhancing the blueness even more. Blonde hair, blue eyes; sunshine and sky. Victor might be right. My plain brown hair and brown eyes are earth, not the unreachable beyond. And, as if nature hasn't been generous enough to the woman, she has a flawless complexion. Like Gloria Halton's. In grade nine health class, Miss Hawkins, who was also the gym teacher and one of the few lay teachers in our convent school, made Gloria stand so everyone could see what she meant by peaches and cream complexion. "Girls," she said, "with

Gloria's complexion, only a light shade of lipstick is required. With sallow colouring and oily skin, a darker shade is a must. Would Rita stand as an example?" In the next row, Maddy sat with her fist in her mouth, her eyes slits of indomitable amusement. Even best friends can be cruel sometimes.

"May I help you."

I am about to speak when I realize that the clerk's toothy grin is not directed at me, but at the blonde.

"Half a pound of ground chuck, please."

I feel hot blood flow up to my face. *It's my turn!* Come on — say something, dammit! The words are on the tip of my tongue, but it feels as thick and lifeless as the beef tongues on the other side of the glass. Inside me, the adrenaline rouses my heart into an erratic thumping; it vibrates against my chest like a jackhammer on asphalt. Talktalktalktalktalktaltalktalktalk. Too late. The clerk is already wrapping the small mound of meat. *Half* a pound of chuck! Once I heard of a *canary* who ate meat. Maybe *she* had a pet canary!

The clerk hands the package to the blonde with a smile so broad it exposes his gums, pink as an open gash, beneath his black mustache. Without waiting to be asked, I stick the pink ticket under the clerk's nose. "Two pounds of milk-fed veal," I demand, then, catapulted by my adrenals, add, "And you should have asked that lady for her number — I was supposed to be before her."

The clerk eyes me calmly, as though he is quite used to dealing with hysterical housewives. "Sorry ma'am, no milk-fed today."

My heart picks up its pace. I feel my face burning, and the whole room with its counters and shelves and people, pressing in on me, taking up my space, my air. What will Victor say? I have to think. There are other meat stores around here — it's the stockyards, for heaven's sake. Maybe one of them will have milk-fed. But just in case… "Give me two pounds of the regular, then." I can feel myself breathing still much too quickly, only half filling my lungs with air. Everything seems suddenly too brightly coloured, each object, each person, etched with a bold, black line. Just as suddenly, they begin to dim. My own body is becoming unsubstantial, light as air, numb, as if its living spirit has left it and is hovering a short distance above it. Now I can't breathe at all. Panicking, I stamp my feet on the floor, trying to bring some feeling back to my body. People are staring at me. I can hear the clerk call out vaguely from behind the scale, "fifteen sixty-eight," as he hands me a cylindrical package of red-brown paper. Grabbing the package, I hurry to the checkout, where I drop sixteen dollars on the counter, and, without waiting for my change or a bag, I escape through the glass doors into the open air.

**

Outside, a bright sun is dulling the glazed surfaces on concrete and asphalt, penetrating the ice underneath and turning it into frothy bubbles, like an Aero chocolate bar. I take several slow breaths. There — my heart is slowing down. Calmly now. Alright … Quality Meats … just a block and a half from here. Maybe they'll have milk-fed… My purse is still open; I zip it up, fling the strap over my shoulder, and march to the car holding my body very straight. I feel fine now, a little humiliated, perhaps. I get into the station wagon and set the package next to the wine, then, taking a long, resolute breath, turn the ignition key and step on the gas. The car starts, then stalls. I press the gas pedal three times, then take my foot off the gas and turn the key, like Victor had shown me I should do when a car refuses to start. The motor turns, then dies. I pump the gas pedal again, vigorously this time, and at the same time, turn the key. It starts and continues running. I turn to back out but realize my view is obstructed on the driver's side by the snow mound, which now looks more like a mountain; it has grown and is now higher than the station wagon. My hands are sweaty, the steering wheel slippery beneath my fingers. If I hesitate, the car might stall and not start again. Then I would have no recourse but to call CAA, and they might take over an hour to come, which means I would not have enough time to go to Quality Meats and get back in time to pick up the twins from kindergarten. Leaving the car running, I step out and peruse the parking lot. Seeing no cars, I quickly get back into the car and, looking directly behind me, step on the gas and back up quickly. I catch sight of the red van a split second before impact. My body pitches forward, then lashes back, constrained by my seatbelt. The rear window on the driver's side disintegrates into a wealth of diamonds. The flat-faced front of the van and the tail-end of my station wagon have joined together in a tangle of metal.

A door slams. A man whips out of the van. I half-open my window in preparation for his approach, bracing myself for the onslaught. When I look up a few seconds later, a maroon leather jacket with hands hidden deep in the pockets stands on the other side of the driver door; it takes a step backwards. The man inside it has a dark, unshaven beard. On his head, greasy black curls extending down his neck. Unkempt. A derelict. Maybe a drug addict. He is glaring at me, stepping back and forth in an excited little dance.

"Christ, just look at this mess!"

Inside the station wagon, I sit stunned, my beige duffle jacket and black polyester pants shimmering with glass. "I'm sorry," I say. It comes out in a squeaky child's voice.

The man inside the maroon leather jacket shakes his head, then turns to study the damage more closely. "Jesus," he says and shakes his head again with each new angle of inspection.

"I'm sorry," I repeat more loudly, with my head out the window so it will carry.

The maroon jacket walks back towards me. The jacket's owner, taking his hand out of the pockets, winces and reaches up to rub his neck as if it were stiff. "Christ," he says again. "Well, we'll have to call a cop and do a report." His voice is gruff, gravelly, but not loud and not angry, as it had seemed at first — just matter-of-fact.

"Did something happen to your neck?"

He rebuffs my concern and doesn't answer. He goes back to his van and returns with a piece of paper and a pen. "Here," he says, handing them to me through the open window, "write down your name, telephone, insurance number, licence plate ... all that stuff. I'm going in to call the cops and tell the boss I'll be late for the eleven o'clock shift." He disappears behind the giant mound of snow.

I take this opportunity to get a handle on things. Everything around me seems so different, so unreal. My station wagon, his van, unwieldy weights of painted metal and chrome, seem to be floating in space. Am I really sitting here covered in glass? My eyes fall on the paper-wrapped meat, the bottle of wine that has rolled off the seat — the wine! I grab the slim bottle and frisk it quickly up and down. All in one piece! I can't believe my luck. Why was I worrying about the *wine* when the station wagon...! I should have looked more carefully ... I should have backed out slowly, an inch at a time. Such a fool!

How am I going to break it to Victor! I feel as though I might be sick right here in the car. I open the station wagon door and drag myself out, my legs feeling like rubber bands, my body numb and disoriented, as if I have woken from a deep sleep in daytime. Suddenly, my legs buckle under me and I find myself sitting on the ground watching — half in amusement, half in disbelief — my glasses go skittering across the asphalt.

"Hey, lady, are you alright?" The driver of the van hurries towards my, grabbing my arm to help me up.

"I must have slipped." I take hold of the car door for support, while he goes after my glasses, which have slid under a parked car several spaces away.

"Here," he says. "They're not broken."

"Thank you, you're very kind." My hands are shaking when I put them on, and things seem not to be in focus even after I do.

"Maybe you'd better sit down … just a minute," he says. He brushes glass from the seat with delicate strokes, so he won't cut himself, then prods gingerly, purposefully, in the cracks where the two sections of seat join, in order to remove more of the crystalline chunks.

I watch, mesmerized. He takes my arm again and helps me into the car. I notice now that he is younger than he had at first seemed; his deep voice, with the grittiness of a smoker, had seemed that of an older man, but I can see now that underneath several days' growth of beard, his cheeks are tight and smooth, his slightly bulging eyes sparkling with youth. From the way he says *seet* instead of *sit*, I surmise that he must be Italian, Spanish maybe?

"I gotta get my papers from my truck," he says. "I'll be right back."

After a few minutes, I start to feel ridiculous sitting in the car like an invalid. "Get a grip!" I tell myself out loud. I get out of the station wagon and, after confirming that I have my sea legs back, walk around both vehicles to do an assessment of the damage: to the station wagon, a broken tail light, rear fender damage, a dented side door, and a shattered side window. To the van: a broken front grill and front fender damage; more seriously the entire right corner of the vehicle is crumpled like a discarded box of Cracker Jacks. This is going to severely affect our insurance premiums, I'm quite sure. I circle the rest of the van but see no further damage. It is a jazzed-up version of a work van, a conspicuous Christmas-red colour, with a ladder at the back, but no luggage rack. What use is the ladder, then, I wonder? On each side of the van, close to the back, are two small windows of red glass in the shape of teardrops or drops of blood. It has a vanity licence plate that says: MEAT ME.

The driver of the van comes out of his vehicle. "You broke my good luck charm," he says as he approaches me. He is looking down mournfully at a miniature plastic statue he is holding, the kind I've seen in souvenir shops — ridiculous caricatures of people extolling a variety of careers with identifying plastic banners saying WORLD'S GREATEST TEACHER — or doctor, or actor, or golfer — even mom or dad. This one says: WORLD'S GREATEST SOCCER PLAYER. The head had been lopped off. "It was on my dash," he says morosely. "A friend of mine gave it to me. I play soccer in an amateur league."

I take this as an admonishment. The final straw. Tears threaten; I feel as though I have swallowed something enormous and it has caught in my throat. Struggling for control, I bite my bottom lip hard. "I'm very sorry," I say, looking at the headless statue. Turning away, I slide my fingers under the rims of my glasses and surreptitiously wipe my eyes.

"Hey, lady," he says, speaking more gently than before, "don't worry about it. These things, you know, they happen. It's not your day. It's not my day either. Not my *week*." He gazes meaningfully towards Santini's, presenting me with a profile of his face. The whites of his eyes, which are large and bulge just a little from their sockets, are veined with thin red blood vessels, like the yolks of the boiling hens; his eyelids droop slightly, giving him a sleepy look. His cheek bones are high and I notice that, although his nose is quite ordinary straight on, it is exceptionally handsome in profile, neither too big or too small, not crooked or hooked, nor too pointy like mine; what I would call a perfect nose for a man. The moisture is evaporating from my eyes; I begin to shiver.

"I'm a butcher," he says, nodding in the direction of Santini's.

A butcher — of course! — the licence plate, MEAT ME. Yes — I can picture him behind the meat counter in a white jacket dotted with blood. Probably I've seen him at Santini's before.

"They're laying guys off," he continues in a cheerfully resigned tone. "They gave me two weeks' notice yesterday. When unemployment reaches twelve percent, everybody's buying hamburger."

I nod my head sympathetically, thinking about the blonde with the canary. "I'm sorry," I say, for what seems to be the dozenth time.

He rubs his neck again, as if to loosen a kink. I can't think of anything else consoling to say. Silent, we both look at the ground instead of each other. Moments later, the police arrive.

Chapter Four

"What time's Maddy picking you up?" Victor looks up from his breakfast, a shiny shellac of syrup coating his lips. Buttermilk pancakes, scrambled eggs, and bacon — that's what he expects each Sunday after Mass. A few times I've tried to go fancy, with Grand Marnier French toast, or eggs *en cocotte,* but it only put him in a bad mood and I had to listen to his grumbling all through breakfast. He never tires of the same breakfast each Sunday. Just as he never tires of his other favourite, Caesar salad — my version, which I have perfected over many years. Realizing that he expected me to make it day after day almost without exception, and afraid of forgetting an ingredient when I sometimes prepared it in haste, I'd finally written it down on a slip of paper and taped it, handily, to the inside of one of the kitchen cupboard doors. He'd still have me make Caesar salad every living day, but I put my foot down about that. Don't get me wrong — I like Caesar salad as much as the next person, but *every* day! I just got tired of washing all that romaine, so I cut it down to three times a week … like sex. Sex and Caesar salad, which had been an almost nightly event in the first years of our marriage, dwindled down to three times a week. Which sometimes feels like three times a week too many, if you ask me. Especially the sex. The enthusiasm wanes after a while; it's only natural after you start a family. How can you be in the mood for sex when your kids are throwing up in the next room? And with four kids, someone is always throwing up, or burning up with fever, or wanting you to lie in bed beside them because they had a bad dream. But Victor is oblivious to that; his wants always come first and some of our worst arguments stem from his persistence. I just don't see lovemaking as something that should be regimented or negotiated.

"She'll be here about eleven," I say, pouring three blobs of batter into the pan for a Mickey Mouse-shaped pancake for Jamie. Only the boys are home this morning. Alison slept over at a friend's, though I wonder just how much sleep she actually got, recalling what overnighters at Maddy's had been like. Maddy would sometimes invite me and a few classmates from the convent school we all attended to her house for a sleepover. Our high school had been a private school run by nuns; it looked less like a school and more like a castle, and I had only gone there on Maddy's insistence, even though my parents could ill afford the tuition. But I had gotten a part-time job, which, combined with the financial assistance my father was able to give me, got me through to graduation. We would stay up all night at the sleepovers, never growing tired of talking about our respective hoped-for beaux, who, for the most part, didn't even know we existed or, if they suspected we'd set our caps for them, avoided our carefully planned, *coincidental* confrontations like the plague.

"Maddy'll probably be late," Victor declares. His words sound stuck together. He swallows, then picks up a napkin to wipe the stickiness from his mouth. "I think you should call and remind her. She's so unreliable."

The edges of the Micky Mouse pancake are turning golden; bubbly craters begin opening up in the middle of the uncooked batter; with the deftness acquired over eighteen years, I flip it quickly without letting the batter run, and watch it puff up nicely. "It's not a dental appointment, Victor. It's a Mary Kay demonstration and Maddy's giving it, for heaven's sake. It can't *start* without her. And don't forget, it's a potluck afterwards, so I'll be late. I left you a tuna casserole to warm up for supper."

"The sooner she starts, the sooner it'll be over."

"Well, you should be glad she offered to drive me, since the car's in the shop, or you would have had to take me."

"Yeah, and *who* put it there?"

Obviously, he hadn't forgiven me yet. Not just about the accident with the car, which amounted to more than a thousand dollars' damage, but also about the dinner for the Farrells, I would bet, since it hadn't exactly been a rousing success and likely didn't score any points towards Victor's promotion to vice-principal. Yet at Mass this morning, I had felt, somehow, absolved. I pretend not to hear and tip the pan, letting the perfectly browned *Mouseketeer* slide easily onto Jamie's plate; marvellous stuff that Teflon, but who could tell, maybe years from now they'd discover it caused cancer. Always something to worry about. The aluminum pots my mother used for years, they are saying now, cause Alzheimer's disease. Rita Hayworth has it; they did a feature on her in the paper. That gorgeous lady — someone had to look after her like a baby and she was barely sixty.

I carry the plate over to the pine breakfast nook that Victor built himself from reclaimed pine and refinished along with the six maple chairs that were part of a lot he'd bid for at an auction; the remaining two chairs are in the garage waiting to be refinished too. He loves country auctions, the power of his dollar over someone else's. He is always on the lookout for antique Canadiana — stuff his ancestors might have used when they'd first arrived in this country a century ago. Most of them are pine or maple that has been painted many times, over many decades, and sometimes have two or three different coats of colour, one on top of the other. He has all the patience in the world in stripping them down to bareness, staining them with his favourite Puritan pine stain, and lovingly waxing them just enough to enhance the patina created over generations. Sometimes I go along to the auctions, watch him flush with excitement in his bid to get what he wants. *She's a good-looking table, ladies an' gen'lemen. Who'll give me a hundred dollars for her?* Everything they sell at the auction is *female.*

I quickly gather up the breakfast dishes and carry them to the sink, noticing how cheerful the yellow buttercup design on the rim still looks after eighteen years of use; oven-to-table ironstone, they are the everyday dishes of my trousseau. The pattern has barely worn. Amazing how things last longer than people, get recycled, renewed and exist on, but not us.

"They called yesterday from the body shop..." Victor says with his mouth full of pancake, something he would normally reprimand the kids for. "Forgot to mention it. Car won't be ready till Wednesday. The kids will have to walk to school till then."

A rebuke. When I had told him about the accident over the phone, he hadn't sounded angry, only concerned whether I was alright. Later, when he looked at the damage, he'd muttered something about "women ... behind the wheel." The station wagon is the family car. Victor has his own car — the Mercedes sedan, which he justified buying because he said it was a safe, well-built car for a family, but after the twins were born we couldn't all fit anyway, so he is the only one who drives it.

When everyone has left the table, Victor says, "Think I'll go and see about finishing those other two chairs." He gets up and takes his jacket off the coat rack next to the door; it is blue leather, his university jacket, with 6T6 sewn on the left arm in felt letters, once white, now a dingy gray, and BSc for his degree sewn on the right in matching letters. I remember walking proudly next to him across the university campus. My brothers and I had fulfilled my parents' dream of *each* of their children obtaining a university degree, but they agreed with Victor that once married, a woman didn't need a career if she had a husband who could support her.

"Anybody coming?" Victor asks as he opens the screen door to go out.

"Me!" Jamie jumps up, grabbing his own jacket from the coat rack. Another one of Victor's projects, he has installed the coat rack, much against my wish, in the kitchen where cooking smells can cling to coats. I refuse to hang my coat there and hope my children's coats don't have an offensive vegetable soup and grease smell. Hard to tell, though; people get used to their own smells; each house with its peculiar odour — vague mixtures of smells from cooking, people, pets; blindfolded, I would know whose house I was in. Except my own; it's as if you get so used to the smell of your own house that you cancel it out. To verify, I sniff and smell only pancakes.

The screen door of the sunporch hisses snake-like as it closes slowly behind Victor and Jamie. It is followed by an identical hiss from the door to outside. I watch my husband and son make their way to the garage. I start rinsing the dishes and putting them in the dishwasher. From the window, I can see them enter the garage at the very back of the yard. It had been Victor's only complaint after we bought the house: when it snowed, the driveway seemed endless. But there is no snow now; it has all melted again, causing, as I had feared, a basement flood, though thankfully not a major one, with a mere inch of water covering the floor. I'd mopped it up in less than an hour. An act of penance I felt I deserved.

This morning's sermon extolled penance and obedience as a means of gaining eternal life. Not having been raised Catholic, Victor, surprisingly, is adamant about our attending Mass each Sunday. Secretly, I had begun to draw away from religion after university, once I had been introduced to the unconventional thinking of philosophers and authors who planted in me the seed of skepticism; everything I'd been taught from childhood seemed so questionable. Miguel de Unamuno's simple rationalism so much more acceptable than the strained logic of the French Jesuit, Pierre Teilhard de Chardin. What happened to all that knowledge, I sometimes ask myself? Stagnating in the dark, mouldy recesses of my brain while I wrestle with pancake syrup on breakfast plates and feel guilty for smashing up the family car, and possibly, just possibly, jeopardizing, with one failed dinner, Victor's career. *Mea culpa, mea culpa, mea maxima culpa.* Still, religion has its place. The self-flagellation is particularly useful. Somehow, I'd managed to pull off the dinner after the accident, but barely. My hope of finding milk-fed veal dashed, when I'd gotten home, I'd pounded the veal from Santini's to within an inch of its animal soul. It had ended up tasting like mechanically deboned chicken. But the Caesar salad was passable — at least Victor enjoyed it — and the pie tasted fine, though it was far too runny. Thankfully, at least, Frank Farrell had realized that he was being served a really good bottle of dessert wine. Victor hadn't said anything about the dinner afterwards, but this omission only verified his displeasure. *Mea culpa.* (Strike the breast.) *Mea culpa.* (Strike the breast.) *Mea maxima culpa.* (Strike the breast hard.) Latin — cold, hard, archaic, with its regimented declensions and conjugations, was definitely more suited to religion. The Pope should never have modernized Mass and allowed it to be celebrated in the vernacular.

I rinse the syrup off the last plate, file it in a slot of the dishwasher and snap the machine shut. After setting it to *Light Wash,* I go upstairs to change for the Mary Kay demonstration before Maddy arrives.

***

Strawberries decorate the kitchen of Eleanor's house: they are imprinted on the wallpaper, glazed onto the ceramic backsplash, painted on the bread box and canisters, woven into a mat in front of the sink; magnetic strawberries affix messages to the fridge, appliquéd cloth strawberries border tea towels and oven mitts, plastic padded strawberries twirl from a mobile in front of the sliding kitchen doors. Eleanor has offered to host the makeup demonstration at her place, partly because her twenty-eight hundred square foot house offers more space than anybody else's, and partly because it is her turn to have the yearly gathering of our small group from high school. The group includes Eleanor, of course, who is a primary school teacher; Roxanne, whom I have always considered the most attractive with her even, cameo features, although she's gained a considerable amount of weight over the years and now, pregnant again and soon due, is heavier than she's ever been; Kayla, with her velvety, mahogany complexion; Antoinette, tiny, jovial, and perennially thin; and Pamela, whose blue-black Japanese hair still reaches her waist. Although our last names have all changed, we continue to refer to each other, nostalgically and with humourous defiance, by our maiden names.

Right from grade nine, when the strangeness of a new school intimidated, we were a group that had formed haphazardly at a lunch table and each day after that, finding the familiarity comforting, had continued to eat together. Besides these five, and Maddy, I have few other friends. Only Maddy lives reasonably close to me, but usually she is busy with her demonstrations. As for the others, except for this yearly gathering, a Christmas card, and the odd telephone call to impart a tragedy or announce exceptionally good news, we scarcely keep in touch.

"I love your house, Eleanor — I think ranch-style bungalows are great, but they're not building many of those anymore, at least not in the city," I tell her as I take out teacups and saucers from her china cabinet. We had arrived, Maddy and I, a half hour before the others were expected and I was helping Eleanor set up the tea service in the dining room.

"Well, there's more space out here in Bramalea. Besides, Bob's practice is here, so it works out much better than living in the city." Bob, Eleanor's husband, is a chiropractor, so Eleanor, who in school had walked hunched over, clasping her books to her chest, now walks and sits and moves holding her back very straight, almost as a form of advertisement for her husband's practice.

"You like Bramalea?" I ask. Twenty-some years ago when my parents had thought about getting a bigger house (who knew why? — perhaps to bribe my brothers and me, almost full-grown then, into spending more time at home), Bramalea had seemed like the end of the earth. The world was shrinking. It hadn't taken more than twenty minutes to get here the way Maddy drove, always as if someone's life depended on it; ironically, *she* has never had an accident.

"Sure — I like it. There's everything here now — it's really built up."

"*Our* street is so dark. The road's so narrow, and then there's all those huge maples closing it in even more. I wanted to buy new, but Victor wouldn't hear of it."

"Yes, but those old houses have character. They're so quaint."

"If you had to bail out my basement, you wouldn't call it quaint."

Eleanor laughs and tears open a package of party napkins to set out on the table, just as the doorbell rings. "Here comes the gang. Rita, be a doll and finish folding these napkins, will you?" She passes the napkins over to me and hurries to answer the door. The napkins have a vine motif interspersed with tiny wild strawberries.

***

When the news and gossip have been exhausted, everyone moves into the kitchen, where, instead of dishes and cutlery, each table place setting consists of a pink plastic box whose lid opens and becomes a mirror. The rest of the container has diverse grooves into which Maddy has poured goos of various hues.

"Okay, everybody, let's get started. Find your name tag. I've varied your makeup according to your complexion."

The doorbell rings again, and a bleached blonde, with the narrowest hips I've ever seen on a grown woman, walks in, apologizing for her lateness. "Girls, this is Cindy, my neighbour." The woman's heavily kohled eyes look huge, doll-like, innocent — Goldie Hawn eyes. Looking for her name tag, the woman finds it directly across the table from me.

The makeup in my box is a buff-coloured blob that closely resembles the contents of a baby's diaper before it starts eating solids.

"You got something for facial hair?" Antoinette asks. "After my operation, I got this terrible moustache." Bringing her fingers to the corners of her mouth, she pretends to be curling the ends of it. She has always been the group clown, her jokes self-deprecatory. Now, following a hysterectomy for uterine cancer that has left her sterile and childless, they have taken a bitter tone.

"Antoinette, don't be silly," Pamela says. "You look *mahh-vellous*."

"Well, thank you, *dah-ling*. I'm glad to know what's left of me looks *mahh-vellous*."

Into Antoinette's hand, Maddy dumps a pile of warm, wet face cloths. "Here, hand these out for me," she says, obviously trying to change the morbid direction in which the conversation is going. She then instructs everyone to wipe off their existing makeup, taking care not to scrub too hard.

Besides a little lipstick, I have none to wipe off; I rarely wear makeup, rarely have occasion to need any since Victor and I go out so little. I take off my glasses and, getting close to the mirror, wipe my face, recognizing, but not really accepting, the plain, olive-tinged visage that stares back at me. In this mirror, my nose seems especially long; my mouth, which I consider my only redeeming feature — not too big or too small, with a pronounced Cupid's bow — looks dried out and pale. My eyes with their slight slant look sunken, darker, smaller than usual. Each mirror tells its own story, the reverse of what it sees, jealousy in its reflection. Next to me, I am shocked to see, in spite of her jokes, how much older Antionette looks since her operation, her cheeks flat pockets of flaccid skin; she is about a year older than the rest of us, but not more. Feeling guilty about this surreptitious scrutiny, I lower my eyes.

"Now use the astringent," Maddy instructs, "wiping gently from the centre of your face so you don't harm the elasticity of the skin." The foundation, she instructs us to apply, "in dots, here and there," smoothing it outwards towards the hairline. Walking around the table, Maddy monitors our progress. "Rub in a little more foundation to hide the pockmarks," Maddy whispers into my ear.

"Thanks, pal." I am actually quite sensitive about the scars inflicted by adolescent acne and feel genuinely embarrassed. Certainly, Maddy has never suffered the stigma of acne, in her teens eating as many French fries and drinking as much Coke as she wanted. I had spent hours at home washing my face, dabbing on ointment, never knowing, in my adolescence, the taste of chocolate or fried foods. Yet my face had remained disgustingly speckled and unsightly as fly paper.

"You wanna be beautiful, don't you?" Maddy cajoles.

Casting Maddy a sardonic smile, I dip my finger into the chalky goo and inch in closer to the mirror, dabbing it on my face. Sometimes I'm not certain whether Maddy's comments are in jest or a bit of a put-down. I concentrate on applying the powder blush, which has a hint of shimmer and promises a "natural-looking radiance."

"By the way, girls," Maddy says, "you can order any of the makeup separately, but it's much better to use the products with each other for a smoother effect. The complete kit costs sixty-five dollars." As the *pièce de résistance,* she pulls out of her travelling case, a portrait of the great lady herself, Mary Kay, and props it up on the table. "Can you believe she's over eighty years old?" The woman in the portrait looks ravishing, impeccably coiffed, her complexion flawless. "Of course, she has the proof airbrushed," Maddy admits.

"I wouldn't mind looking like that at my age," Cindy, the neighbour chimes in, her voice juvenile and high-pitched. Her mouth reveals peg laterals, pointed as fangs. "I just turned thirty the other day and I can tell you, *that* was a trauma."

"Thirty! What are you complaining about?" Antoinette scoffs. "I'm forty — that's already mid-life according to the statistics."

"Forty," Cindy retorts disdainfully, "God — how can you live with yourself?" Her comment, though thoughtless, is likely not meant to be deliberately cruel, since she has obviously no knowledge of Antoinette's recent hysterectomy to remove a malignancy.

"Oh—" Antoinette shoots back, "I guess it beats the alternative."

Feeling uncomfortable now, I begin to wish I could excuse myself from this pathetic tableau of women trying to cling to their youth, desperately seeking beauty, of which, admittedly, I am a part.

"Say — guess who came to one of my demonstrations a couple of weeks ago?" Maddy breaks in light-heartedly.

"We give up."

"Denise Perdue."

"That name sounds familiar," Roxanne says. "Who's Denise Perdue?"

"Being pregnant for the fourth time is having a detrimental effect on your memory, Roxanne. She used to go to school with us," Eleanor fills in.

"That's right, remember — she used to sit at the corner table with the rich girls. Petite, short blonde hair, big blue eyes — cute. After Christmas she developed this voracious appetite, stuffing her face like there was no tomorrow."

"Oh, I know who you mean now," Roxanne says. "Her uniform kept getting tighter and tighter in the front, and if school hadn't ended when it did, it would have burst at the seams."

"She was going out with some hockey jock who played for an American team and was never around for the proms, so she always had to take her cousin."

"Yeah — he was around even less when she started fattening up."

"How come I didn't know anything about this?" I ask, surprised. "I remember Denise as a nice, quiet girl."

"You were too innocent, honey," Maddy says.

"I wonder how it happened? I thought Catholic girls didn't allow anything below the waist." As she says this, Eleanor has one eye closed, as if she were winking in jest, though actually, she is smoothing mauve shadow on one eyelid.

"Do you really think Catholic girls were different than any other girls?" Pamela asks.

Eleanor, her other eye closed now, says, "Yeah — I think we were less promiscuous in general."

"In general, *everyone* was less promiscuous in our day."

"Our day—" Antoinette sniffs, "You make it sound like it was a hundred years ago."

"Well, you might think so, the way morality has turned around in two decades," Roxanne says, clearly disgusted. "Do you think any of the brides walking down the aisle today *still* wearing white gowns are *virgins?* Been making it since they were teenagers, most of them, and absolutely *all* of them have been living with the guy they're marrying and just decided, what the hell, might as well get all the goodies. Greedy little things."

"We weren't *all* virgin brides in our time, either," Pamela says. "Look at Denise Purdue. Someone else ended up marrying her, taking the kid and all."

"Well, just for the record," Roxanne says, on the defensive, "I want you all to know that *I* was a virgin on my wedding night."

"So was I."

"Me too."

"Okay, okay," Maddy, says. "Everyone who was a virgin on her wedding night, hold up your hand. You get a free sample of our newest perfume. Anyone who didn't allow anything below the neck before marriage gets two samples. Rita, you get *two*."

CHAPTER FIVE

"So how much was the damage?" Behind the wheel of her pink Cadillac, Maddy sits relaxed and confident, merging into the oncoming rush of highway traffic as effortlessly as drinking a cup of tea. She has amassed enough sales the previous year to merit the luxurious vehicle and drives it proudly with just a hint of ostentation.

"What?" I ask. I am looking past the apartment buildings in the distance, trying to catch an unbroken stretch of sunset; the sky is streaked with pink and mauve, promising good weather. "Oh, you mean the accident — one thousand and sixty dollars."

Maddy whistles. "I'll bet Victor was fit to be tied."

"Actually, turns out the first accident's a freebee. So Victor's not out of pocket, but the premiums will increase."

"Mine are always going up."

"Speeding tickets?"

"Yup. But I never bother to pay them. One of these days they're going to come after me." Fidgeting in her purse, Maddy pulls out a pack of cigarettes and a pink lighter. She slides out a cigarette, transferring her attention in measured shifts from the road to the package. "I guess I should consider myself lucky that it's my first accident. You know how nervous I always am behind the wheel. I'm still shaken up about it all."

Clamping her cigarette between her lips, Maddy gives the lighter a flick and inhales. "I have an idea that will help you unwind. Let me take you for a drink. I know a place that has male strippers!"

"Are you crazy! Victor would *kill* me."

"Don't tell him."

"Maddy — *no!*"

"Alright, fine," Maddy says, taking a long pull on her cigarette. She never smoked until recently. Other things about her have changed too. She seems more confident. What else? Something. Too vague for me to name. She'd been so timid in school, never missing a day of attendance; in knee-high snowstorms, she was the only student who showed up, fearful of being reprimanded for truancy.

"Let's go to a restaurant that has Happy Hour and have a couple of drinks, then." She taps her cigarette ashes into the car ashtray, and asks, "What do you say?"

"Well ... Victor knows I'm with you. I didn't really say what time I'd be home ... and I did leave a casserole for him to warm up..."

Maddy flashes me one of her mischievous smiles harkening back to childhood and flicks her unfinished cigarette out the window.

"Refresh your lipstick, girlie. Let's go have some fun."

***

The restaurant is a fair distance from Eleanor's house, halfway to downtown. The walls outside are covered in barnboard for a country look. At the front door, there is a sign that reads: Happy Hour: 4 to 7. Inside, the restaurant is dimly lit. We follow the hostess through a maze of rough-hewn boards and ceiling ties with hanging plastic pots of Boston ferns and Swedish ivy. On the walls, there are taxidermized moose and deer heads, and rusty hunting rifles, the kind that might have caused their demise. A waitress with denim cut-off short-shorts and a white, low-necked peasant blouse takes our orders. Maddy has gin and tonic, and I have Dubonnet on the rocks with a twist of lemon, feeling just a little disloyal to Cardinale Estate Winery, my part-time employer. I scan the surroundings with misgiving, not sure that I should be here with Maddy. A half-moon-shaped, white-and-gray speckled granite bar is almost completely obscured by an equal number of young men and women. Most of the women are standing alone, looking indifferent; some are chatting to the man next to them, others to another woman — probably a friend they had come with — wearing exaggerated expressions of animation, as if they are carrying on the world's most interesting conversation. The men's eyes follow, with unconcealed scrutiny, each new female who passes by the bar. Next to the bar is a dance floor with a few conspicuous couples dancing to a slow Michael Damian song, which I recognize only because Alison plays it over and over at home. They hang heavily on each other and move around slowly with bland, joyless faces, as if they are token dancers recruited by the management to induce others to come up on the floor.

At the table next to us, two girls are seated, one with reddish hair and a little on the plump side, the other a tall, willowy girl with waist-long blonde hair, wearing a red silk blouse and black leather pants. Both look in their early twenties. Though I'm not consciously listening, I can't help overhearing their discussion: should they move from where they are sitting and go over to the bar where there are more people but no seats, or remain where they are? I glance again at the willowy blonde. So pretty. Why didn't she already have a boyfriend and not need to come to places like this?

"Is this a singles bar?" I ask Maddy, hoping it *isn't.*

"I guess you could call it that."

I feel instant panic wondering how I'll ever explain this to Victor, but before I can express my apprehension to Maddy, the waitress returns with our drinks. Mine has a fuzzy speck floating on one of the ice cubes, and in the dim lighting, I can't tell if it's animal, mineral, or vegetable, but it appears inanimate. "There's something in my drink," I tell Maddy.

"What?"

"I'm not sure."

"You want me to tell the waitress to get you another one?"

"No, it's alright."

Maddy pulls out her cigarettes and her pink lighter from a brown suede handbag that matches her shoes, a wry smile crinkling one corner of her mouth.

"What's so funny?" I ask.

"We've changed roles, you and I, you know that? I mean who was the one who had to ask for directions if we were lost, or call up to order the pizza, and oh — go into the drugstore to buy Kotex while little Miss Chicken Maddy waited outside with toilet paper in her underwear?"

I laugh. "I *remember* that. You were thirteen years old and you'd just started your period — I'd had mine a year and was a veteran already."

"I wanted to be like you, did you know that, Rita? So mature and responsible. And I was always a little jealous that you made the Honour Roll every year and I didn't."

"But you made the powder puff hockey team and got to go to the boys' schools to play. I could barely skate."

Maddy smiles and nods, pensive.

There was something special about a friendship rooted in childhood. Who else can you share your memories of growing up with? Who else can understand the longings and fears and heartaches of adolescence? I take a sip of my drink, careful not to tilt the glass too much in case I disturb the something on my ice cube. It clings tenaciously, so I take another sip. "Do you really think we've changed roles?"

Maddy shrugs. "It was inevitable. You're home all day with the kids. You don't have to go out and challenge the world."

"Oh, I don't know, last week I had to tell the paper boy to stop stepping through the shrubs."

Maddy's laugh is a strange mixture of chortle and hiccup. Maybe she's right, though. I *do* depend on Victor — for almost everything. I *have* lost confidence in myself; so many things intimidate me now. Why, just knowing I had to drive to Santini's last week made me so anxious, it kept me awake half the night. I've never driven the highway, rarely driven more than a few blocks from home. I have to admit, home is the only place I feel safe. And if I go anywhere, it's because Victor takes me there. What would I do without Victor?

The two girls at the next table get up, apparently having arrived at a decision; picking up their drinks, they make their way through the dancing couples on the floor towards the bar where they immediately start attracting glances.

"What's new at home?" Maddy asks.

"Alison wants me to sew her a dress for a school dance. She's very fussy and thinks only I can make her the dress she wants that doesn't make her look fat. She's *not* fat, but she says the boys are teasing her. You know how boys are at that age."

"She's already going to dances!"

"She's almost thirteen. It's not really a *dance,* dance. They're going to have a band, so they're calling it a dance. I don't think thirteen-year-old boys are much interested in dancing."

"You wanna bet? It's all different now, Rita. They have sex education in the schools."

"I know that."

"We had the *blue book.* Remember? We used to sneak it out of your parents' closet. It had all those illustrations. Our first look at the male anatomy — and our own probably, since the nuns were always warning us not to mess around down there … 'and girls, be sure to always use a washcloth when you're cleaning your private parts.' Can you believe that crap?"

I laugh. "The *blue book* — how could I forget? *Sex and Birth Control in Marriage.* The way my mother went to so much trouble to keep it hidden, you'd think it was the worst pornography ever written. In English, no less. My parents must have gotten it from their Anglo family doctor." The book, as I recall, was a slim volume of instructive and very clinical material for married couples. I had come across it by chance one Halloween when I'd been rummaging through my mother's closet in search of a costume for the school party. I was twelve; the book had been a revelation for both me and Maddy. Whenever my parents went out, we would sneak it from its closet hiding place and look through it together. Maddy was right; sex education had been the *blue book* and a smattering of information gathered here and there from other kids, most of it inaccurate. "I didn't even know what a period was when I got mine. When I found blood in my underwear for the first time and ran to my mother, my mother said it meant I was a *signorina* now — she also told me that it wasn't anything to worry about, that I could expect this to happen every month, and that I shouldn't tell anybody. But above all, that I must *never* get near boys. For almost a year after that, I was *terrified* each time a boy bumped into me in the cloakroom, convinced he would make me pregnant and I would have a baby. You were the only one who could appreciate my terror, knowing even less than me. Remember how you promised I could move in with you and you'd help me look after the baby, since I was convinced my parents would kick me out of the house if I got pregnant?" We both have a hearty laugh, but I'm so grateful my own daughter never has to have that experience. "You ever going to have kids, Maddy?"

"Maybe. I don't know. I know the biological clock—" she wriggles two fingers on either side of her head to indicate quotations "—is running out. I'm just not sure. I've been doing so well with Mary Kay, I hate to slow down."

Maddy had married three years after me, when everybody else, it seemed, was married already, although she'd had several short-term boyfriends. Stefan was twelve years older than Maddy, an accountant for a large firm. I still couldn't see what had drawn them together, Maddy so vibrant, Stefan so passive, even though, physically, he was a burly, outdoor-loving Finn; he was quiet, far too quiet for Maddy. "How's Stef, anyway? He still going out of town a lot on business trips?"

"Fairly often — he's fine. I'll have to have you over sometime for dinner, just you and Victor."

"Sounds great. It's been ages since anyone's cooked for me." The drink is beginning to take effect, loosening my knees and making me feel very warm; I've almost finished it, and the foreign object still remains anchored to the ice floe. If it's a bug, it surely drowned happily. I'm beginning to feel relaxed — more relaxed than I've felt in days. We order two more drinks, the same. Looking over at the bar, I realize the willowy blonde isn't there anymore. I search the dance floor for a red blouse and leather pants and find them pressed against a young man, shorter than her, with a thick black mustache and a large, hooked nose. He is rubbing her back up and down, wearing a half-cloaked expression that brings to mind a word I remember from my Baltimore Catechism — *covet*. His body is angled back slightly and his pelvis gyrates barely a fraction of an inch from hers; she slips her knee, rhythmically, in and out of the upside down "v" formed by the spread of his legs.

The waitress returns, putting new coasters down on the table and placing two dewy drinks on top of them. I take a few sips and when I look over at the dance floor again, I see the couple kissing — French kissing, was it still called that? — both of them fitting their tongues cannibalistically into the mouth of the other. Had they even had time to ask each other's name?"

"Hey, Rita."

"What?" I answer, reluctantly detaching my attention from the couple on the dance floor whose behaviour I find quite mesmerizing.

"Those guys at the other side of the restaurant sitting in the corner booth — they're looking at us."

Trying not to make it obvious, I glance in the direction Maddy was indicating. I see pillars and plants and a variety of heads, but I'm still not wearing my glasses, so I really can't see clearly. "Why would anyone be looking at us? We're probably the oldest ones here?" I say with a giggle. The alcohol is already affecting me. I take several more swallows and giggle some more, without really knowing why.

"Well, *you're* certainly a cheap date," Maddy says with a laugh. "But no — I mean it. The one with the curly hair is looking at you."

"You're crazy, Maddy."

"Oh, you think so — well here he comes ... and with a *friend*." She crosses her legs, letting her skirt rise above one knee, and takes a puff from her cigarette, exhaling the smoke in a slow, measured rhythm.

The two men stop at our table. One is a tall youth with slightly protruding eyes and wavy black hair; he is narrow-hipped but wide at the shoulders, with thick, muscular arms that create the irregular bulges in the short sleeves of his knitted Polo shirt; he is carrying a maroon leather jacket across one arm. "I thought it was you," he says. He pronounces the "ought" in thought like "oat." *Thoat.*

"Hello. How are you?" I respond, recognizing the young man from the accident. But he looks different, his hair is in loose curls, instead of tight and greasy like the last time I saw him. It gives him an entirely different aspect, more youthful. He is clean shaven, revealing his prominent cheekbones and angular jaw. His eyes are large and deep brown, luminous in the muted lighting.

"It's a coincidence seeing you here."

"Yes, well, my friend and I are just having a little time away from our husbands. How's the neck?"

"So-so."

"I really feel terrible about what happened."

"What can you do," he says, shrugging his ample shoulders.

"Oh, excuse me — this is my friend, Maddy. I'm sorry, I can't remember your name. I have it written down at home."

"Valentin ... Valentin Marino." He introduces his friend, as well, both men shaking hands as is customary for Europeans.

"Did my insurance get in touch with yours?" I ask, catching too late Maddy's disapproving expression.

"They got in touch."

"Will you fellas join us for a drink?" Maddy asks, changing the subject.

"Thank you, but we were just leaving to meet some friends," he says. "Studebakers — new place — you heard of it?" he asks as he puts on his jacket and zips it all the way up. Maddy has and says so, tells them it's a *cool place*. I haven't. Why would I? Victor and I haven't been to a dance club in almost two decades. "Well, nice seeing you again," he adds, nodding towards me. "You ladies have a nice evening."

We wish them the same, then watch both men slip between the dancers on the floor and disappear into the crowd. When I turn to look at Maddy again, her expression clearly shows disappointment. "Why did you say that about our husbands?" Maddy asks.

Taken aback, I stare at Maddy, puzzled.

"If they know you're married, it limits the conversation. What if they'd decided to sit and have a drink with us? All you'd be able to talk about is your husband and kids. You'd be *obligated* to talk about them. Let me explain something: there is nothing wrong with a little varied male companionship now and then. Life is dull. You get tired of each other, everything becomes so familiar."

"Maddy, aren't you and Stefan getting along?"

"Sure, but I like it when a man pays attention to me. It makes me feel attractive, desirable still. Stef doesn't make me feel that way anymore; he's past looking."

"He doesn't have someone else, does he, Maddy?" I ask, hoping the answer is no.

Maddy pulls a cigarette from the pack. Her fourth since we've been here. Her sixth since we left Eleanor's. She puts it in her mouth and goes to light it, changes her mind, puts the lighter down and holds the cigarette unlit between her fingers. "Not that I know of."

"You don't have someone else, do you?" I ask warily, again hoping the answer is no.

"Not at the moment," she admits, with deliberate nonchalance.

I feel my jaw muscles slacken, in response to Maddy's admittance and possibly from the added effect of the alcohol.

"Are you trying to tell me you've had ... an *affair*?" Even whispered, the word sounds so slick on my tongue, it makes me shiver.

"Oh, I just knew you were going to get all judgmental about it. That's why I've never told you." She lights her cigarette and takes one long, desperate puff, as if it's delivering life-giving oxygen instead of deadly chemicals.

"Well, who?"

"It doesn't matter." But then she continues. "Would it shock you to know there's been more than one?"

It does, but I try not to show it.

"But there's only been one that I ever got serious about; the others were just antidotes, I think. He was married ... had kids ... decided to stay with his wife. I really think I might have left Stefan if he'd asked me to. Her eyes are becoming glossy and her voice is beginning to sound croaky, as if she is forcing it out, like someone is trying to choke her as she is speaking.

I can see her pain is genuine, and even though I feel for Stefan, my loyalty has to lie with my best friend. "I'm sorry, Maddy." I want to reach over and touch her hand, but it seems too private a gesture for such a public place.

Maddy sniffs loudly but seems eager to relieve herself of this secret. "You know that convention I went to in Acapulco two years ago? He was there on business, staying in the same hotel. You know when you're far away from home and you meet someone from the same country, it's like you're practically related." Her voice doesn't sound like she's choking anymore, changing into what seems almost rapture. "He was from Kingston — sweet, so funny. Every weekend that he could get away, we would meet halfway."

I try to appear calm, although inwardly I feel as numb as I had after the accident. I swallow a large mouthful of Dubonnet and feel a liquid heat trickle down to my stomach. I can picture Maddy behind the wheel of her pink Cadillac, that enraptured look on her face, *tried* to picture her in the arms of this faceless stranger. Maddy, revealing all of herself to this faceless man, letting him look at her and touch her in places that we had always kept secret, even as children, from each other. The thought both shocked and excited me; I felt repugnance and fascination. I look at her slightly stunned. "How was it?" I ask.

She's not the least bit hesitant in answering such an intimate question. "Wonderful."

I stir my drink with the swizzle stick that's spearing a twist of lemon peel. I pass no judgment, in fact, feel slightly in awe of her.

"And after it was over?"

"It hurt — rejection always hurts."

"And the others?"

"Nothing like him. Nothing serious. But endings still hurt."

I study my drink, checking to see if I've stirred up anything extraneous, but this time the ice cubes are clear. "Why do you do it, if you get hurt over and over?"

"Keeps me on my toes. Like pinching yourself to make sure you're alive. It's a new beginning each time; there's so little of that the older we get. I don't go looking for it — it's no good if you go looking for it. I don't come by myself to places like this." She indicates the rest of the room with a sweep of her cigarette. In profile her chin points prettily, her nose upturns slightly — Rita Hayworth rejuvenated. "If the opportunity presents itself, if the feeling seems right, I let it happen."

"What about Stefan? Aren't you being unfair to him?"

"He's away half the time, and when he's home, he's always working late into the night — he has no time for me, or else he's too out of it from boozing it up. I'm a very *physical* person. I *like* sex. I can *come* over and over again and still not get enough."

I feel my face suddenly warming. Unable to meet Maddy's eyes for fear she'd read my genuine embarrassment for her candidness, I look away towards the dance floor where the music has gotten louder, and the yeasty smell of beer and alcohol coming from behind the bar, more intense. The tall girl with the red blouse and her shorter young man are still at it. I watch them swaying almost drunkenly to the music. Suddenly, they stop. Holding hands, they walk over to her friend, the plump redhead who is still standing at the bar looking bored. The blonde says a few words to her, picks up her purse that her friend was guarding, then heads towards the entrance at the front with her new man. I can't help but wonder where they're going — his place, hers? It wasn't the seventies anymore; two decades had gone by and the music wasn't the Beatles. That's the way it happens these days, so I'm told, casual one-nighters quite common, and now I can believe it. Maybe *this* girl was a very *physical* person. "How does it feel?" I ask sheepishly, continuing to look in the direction of the dance floor, still not ready to look Maddy in the face."

"How does what feel?"

"You know … an orgasm."

"You don't *know*? Are you trying to tell me you've never had an *orgasm!*"

Alarmed, I face Maddy, whose face is frozen in an expression of disbelief. "Will you keep your voice down!"

"You've *never* had an orgasm?" Maddy repeats, lowering her voice this time.

"Not that I've noticed."

"Rita — it isn't something you'd miss! I don't believe it, after — what is it — fifteen years of marriage?

"Eighteen."

"After eighteen years of marriage — and four kids! They might as well have been *virgin* births. The *virgin* Rita. Doesn't Victor care?"

"It's not *his* fault. He's done everything right."

"Oh, honey, get help. Get a therapist, a sex surrogate, something. Life's too short." She smashes her cigarette into the ashtray on the table and looks around the room as if to search out prospects. Wearing her mischievous smile, the same smile she had worn once in grade nine when, as novice students, she had talked me into spying through the third-floor nuns' quarters. She was curious to see if they really slept on stone beds instead of soft mattresses (they didn't). The plan was to use disorientation as our excuse if we were caught, since we were new to the school. "Hey, I've got an idea. Those two guys who came over to our table tonight, why don't we go after them and find out if they want to share a motel room, see if a little wild excitement doesn't do the trick."

"Maddy, you're disgusting." But I giggle, nonetheless, and notice that the second glass of Dubonnet in front of me is nothing but ice cubes. The upside-down numbers of Maddy's watch look unclear; I bend closer to read them: 9:30. "Yikes, look at the time. Victor's going to *kill* me," I tell her, retrieving my purse from where I'd left it under the table. "Let's pay and get going. I promised I'd be home in time to put the kids to bed. And I still have to make the lunches."

CHAPTER SIX

The lights are off downstairs when Maddy drops me off. Victor has already gone up. I go in through the sunroom, careful to lock both doors after me, then check the basement and the front doors as well, in case Victor has forgotten to lock them. I find Victor in the bedroom ensuite brushing his teeth. "Well, it's about time. Where have you been?"

I quickly start brushing my teeth too. "Maddy took me out for a drink," I tell him.

"Oh," Victor says, surprised. "Where?"

"Just a restaurant where they had Happy Hour."

"Two women alone in a bar, Rita — what's the matter with you?"

I point to my mouth, which is full of toothpaste suds, making it hard for me to talk. "*Maey knew da plape,*" I say, through the suds, then pause to spit. "She'd been there before — it wasn't a bar, just a restaurant."

"I don't like it, Rita. That Maddy, she's always got crazy ideas."

"I don't see anything wrong with it. You go sometimes with Bud, or some of the other teachers after work."

"But two *women* — maybe you don't read the paper? Didn't you hear about that woman who disappeared last week? All they could find was her empty car in a parking lot. The police think she was abducted."

I do read the paper. It's always been one of the highlights of my day, especially when the children were babies and I was confined to the house day after day, week after week, endlessly, it seemed — the local paper was my only link to the outside world. I *had* read this particular news item and wondered how a woman could drop her child off at nursery school, then mysteriously disappear. I judiciously change the subject. "Did the kids go to bed okay?"

"*Yes*," he answers in a slightly hostile tone.

"They eat?"

"They *ate*."

"Oh, *my God*, I forgot to make the lunches."

"Well, you'd better hurry. I want to get to bed." Victor follows me down to the kitchen in his pajamas to get a drink of water. "So how *is* Maddy, anyway?"

"Fine. The usual — loud, crazy. More sure of herself than I've ever seen her. She's really doing well, making as much as Stefan. Seems happy." I debate whether I should tell Victor what Maddy told me. There was nothing that I knew that Victor didn't also know; even secrets I promised not to repeat to anyone automatically excluded Victor. But I couldn't tell Victor *this*. I busied myself buttering slices of bread and spreading them out on the counter like a game of solitaire.

"She's a wild one, that Maddy, unpredictable. I don't like you hanging around her."

"Victor, she's my best friend. What do you mean *wild*?"

"What would you want to go out drinking for? Coffee, I could understand."

"It was something different, that's all. I don't know why you're making such a fuss."

"I don't like it." He walks over to the sink with a glass and turns on the tap. When he finishes drinking, he says, "I'm going to bed." He rinses his glass and puts it upside down on the drying rack. "Hurry and come up," he tells me. "I want to go to sleep."

***

At the bottom of the stairs, I hesitate, my palm frozen on the smooth globe of the newel post. My mind seems confused; I cannot remember why I am here, how I got here. I feel cold and tug at the open sweater that hangs on my shoulders like a tight-fitting cape. It is the pink cardigan with pearl buttons and fancy beading around the scalloped collar that I loved so much as a little girl. Draped across my back, it's too small and scarcely blocks out the chill. The house is dark. There is something I've forgotten to do. I am in danger, my children, my husband, in danger. Panic seizes and holds me like a high voltage electrical current. A cool draft — coming from where? — chills the back of my neck. Still, I must act. I turn hesitantly towards the kitchen where beams from a weak source bathe the floor with dull light. Slowly, cautiously, I follow the vague phosphorescence, stepping into the puddle of light spilling from the partially open basement door. How many times have I warned the kids to keep the basement door locked! *Things* live down there: rodents and centipedes and black spiders with bulbous bodies. Things. Move quickly, hurry, slam it shut, turn the lock on the knob. I move towards the door, but something impedes my movement, a terrible lassitude, an oppressing force. My hand — reaching desperately, stretching, straining, so that my muscles ache from the effort — is scarcely making any headway towards the knob. My eyes are bolted to the shiny metal globe. The knob! The knob! I have to reach the knob!

Just as I'm almost there, I see a wrinkled arthritic hand slip through the open crack of the door, the fingers crawling like a spider's legs across the white painted door frame; blue veins pop worm-like from the transparent parchment skin. Suddenly, the door is flung open. Panting from exertion, a grizzly old woman executes the last of the basement steps. She is bent over, ancient, atrophied — a phantom in a black dress, her wretched body that of a crow, a vulture, a black widow spider. Her white hair is pulled severely back in a bun from a leathery brow; the rest of her face is a shrunken, decayed, dried apple; her cheeks are sunken, as are her eyes — black pearls deep in her skull. Her nose hooks downward towards her chin with a wrinkled depression in between — her mouth. Black lisle stockings, like the kind my grandmother still wears, cover her bird thin legs. But she is *nothing* like my *nonna*; she is the antithesis; she is an anomaly of life itself. The smell of urine, of decay, of dust and damp earth seep out from beneath her skirt. I am nauseous with disgust. My stomach threatens to hurl up its contents and precipitates a flow of saliva from one corner of my mouth, a luminous silver thread that turns viscous and light pink like early menstrual blood. The phantom reaches out a quivering hand towards me as if to unburden itself. NO! My revulsion converts to anger, hate, mobilizing my strength. I grab the hag by the arm and pull, pull! swinging her this way and that way, hard; she is weightless — dried skin and brittle bones, merely, within my Herculean grip. I ram her body against the door frame again and again and again.

Aaaaagh ... Aaaaaagh ... Aaaaaagh....

"Rita!"

I jerk bolt upright, opening my eyes. Something is pulling at my elbow. I see blackness, only blackness. I am dying, I am dying! My heart has stopped. My hand flies to my neck, feeling for a life sign, the carotid's familiar throb, finding it. Yes, now I can feel my heart fluttering wildly in my chest, bounding terrifyingly out of control. Tachycardia, brought on by a panic attack. *Remember, remember* what the doctor said: harmless. These attacks are harmless — merely a symptom brought on by my own fear of experiencing the symptom — though it's hard to believe it while my heart convulses crazily within me. I want to escape my body, its vulnerability, its mortality. Slow down, *dammit*, slow down! My body feels as though it's on fire. I tug at the buttons of my flannelette nightgown, pulling it open at the neck.

"Rita, relax, you're hyperventilating."

I see Victor's face in front of me as my eyes adjust to the darkness. With my open hand, I fan back and forth creating a breeze. Breathe. Hold. Exhale. Breathe. *Ahhhh* — there…

"Any better?"

"A little." I lie back on my pillow as the darkness relents its constriction.

"What was it, another dream?"

"Yes … sorry I woke you."

He rubs my arm dutifully up and down, his concern mitigated by his drowsiness. "You okay now?" he asks sleepily.

"Fine. Go back to sleep."

He gives my elbow a few more solicitous strokes before his hand goes limp and his breathing becomes weighted with sleep.

I lie awake in the darkness. The same dream again. Why did dreams repeat themselves? This one was recent. One other had been recurring since childhood: I am cowering in a ditch or hiding among bushes or running behind a brick wall, and there is shooting, always shooting, but so far, I've managed to escape the bullets. Maybe I've lived a previous life and been shot dead during World War II. I *am* a post-war baby. Are souls so speedily reincarnated?

I am wide awake now, had had trouble falling asleep in the first place. Maddy's admittance had shocked me more than I had let on. Maddy had been intimate with other men. And yet she'd been a virgin on her wedding night, just as I had. Had she found blood the next morning? I had looked and looked without being able to find even one drop on the stark white sheets of our marriage bed. I tried to imagine myself lying beside someone other than Victor. A ridiculous thought. Who'd want to look at the horrible scars on my thigh, the stretch marks on my abdomen, my breasts that had lost their firmness from nursing four babies. My pubic area I find particularly ugly, not that I've ever compared. I was terribly embarrassed the first time a man looked at it. Not Victor — it was the gynecologist I'd gone to see before we were married to make sure everything would go smoothly, that I wouldn't disappoint. The doctor had been past fifty, bald on top with a clump of gray hair pressed against each side of his head above his ears. Without warning, while my legs were up in the stirrups, he'd use two fingers and stretched and stretched. "It's alright," he'd said, his head between the arches of my bent legs, his fluff of hair pressed against my knees, comforting as cotton batting on a wound. "I want to stretch the opening so there will be less discomfort your first time." How had he known? I didn't make a sound, though surely from the tenseness of my body, he must have realized he was hurting me. Afterwards, he'd patted my knees consolingly. "You're fine," he'd said, in the same assuring voice you'd use with a child to convince him his hurt wasn't real. Something else he'd asked me to do. Naked, after getting off the examination table, he'd told me to jump up and down while he watched, while my breasts bobbed this way and that.

Was this a usual part of an examination? I didn't know. I was already a grown woman, but I didn't know. When I stepped outside his office, my eyes were tearing, though I wasn't sure whether from pain or from humiliation. I hadn't questioned. Would I question now? How can we protect our daughters when we ourselves remain silent and ignorant?

Victor's breathing is becoming more profound, cadenced with light, even snoring, as he sinks into a deeper level of sleep. I usually fall asleep after him and have become accustomed to his uncomplicated sleep pattern. Even when we were first married, I remember lying very still as he slept, my head on his chest, rocked by the up and down movement of his breathing, lulled by the even beating of his heart. The apartment was always too hot; we slept naked, something that was new to me. When his hold on me slackened, I would slip out of his arms, away from the sticky heat of his body. My nipples tingled; I wanted them touched. Inexperienced as I was, I must have known there should be more. Sometimes I whispered his name in his ear but he never woke up, he slept so soundly. Instead, I lay listening to the noises around me, outside, behind the walls, beyond the ceiling — the honk of a car horn, the ding of a closing elevator door, a telephone ringing on the other side of the bedroom wall, and above, the squeaking of springs practically every night, accompanied by muffled moans and gasps filtering through the ceiling drywall. On our wedding night we'd both been virgins and it had been a very clumsy first attempt. Victor had become frustrated and ordered me to *"Do something, do something!"* As if I knew just what it was I *could* do. But things became easier as we became familiar with each other. We'd settled into a routine — no — more of a schedule that Victor made up that he insisted we adhere to, and he would rarely accept an excuse for any deviation from it without an argument.

Victor still said he loved me fairly frequently, in between his moodiness and irritability. Once, shortly after we were married, I tested him in order to assuage my insecurity. "You love me, but do you think I'm pretty?"

"Pretty enough for me."

"But not as pretty as Maddy — *objectively* speaking?"

"Maddy's very pretty."

"But *objectively* speaking — prettier than me?"

"I guess so."

"But if you really *love* me, how could you think she's *prettier*?"

"You told me to be objective! Look, you're what I want. I married *you*!"

Well, I'd asked for it, I admit. And, of course, Maddy *was* more beautiful. But didn't love trump all? Wasn't beauty in the eyes of the beholder? Maddy was comfortable with her looks, and why shouldn't she be? A slight embellishment from Mary Kay and she became Rita Hayworth's twin. Her body was toned from regular aerobics; its compact interior had never expanded to the limit to encompass another life. No wonder she was so at ease with the world, at ease with the two young men who'd approached us tonight at our table. *Will you fellows join us for a drink?* Why hadn't I noticed before, this new boldness about her? What a coincidence seeing the driver of the van again. He didn't seem to hold a grudge. Funny how coincidences really do happen, even though when you see them in a movie or a TV sitcom or something, they always seem so contrived. But in real life, that's just the way they happen sometimes. He'd looked so different with his face shorn of its stubble, his cheeks glossy, like mine and Victor's were on our wedding day, his hair, loose curls — the kind of curls my mother said you would get by eating orange rinds. My mother was certain of that, just as she was certain that a bowl of water, a few drops of oil, and some salt, assembled with an ancient incantation, could remove the evil eye. Valentin Marino — his first name seemed Spanish but his last name sounded Italian; my parents had *paisani* with that last name. Did he have a mother who fed him orange rinds when he was little?

Victor's snoring is becoming more stertorous with each breath. I'm unable to fall asleep and lie there listening. A snore. A pause. A long pause. My breathing stops along with his. Panicking, I shake his arm roughly, making him splutter and gasp for air.

"What? What is it?" he asks, disoriented, shocked out of sleep.

"You were snoring. I can't sleep when you're snoring. Turn onto your side."

He did. Better. The sound of modulated breathing. The scarlet digital numbers on the clock radio brand the time into the darkness: 2:27. When I was little, I used to make a game of trying to keep track of the exact moment I fell asleep to see if I could remember the next morning. Somehow, sleep always came elusively, unpredictably, erasing memory. Like death.

That horrible dream! How I hate that basement; it's the cause of my recurring dream. If only Victor would agree to move the washer and dryer upstairs, there would be no need for me to go down. What if we converted the sunporch into a laundry room? It wasn't much use really except for storing lawn furniture in the winter, and *that* could go in the basement. We could insulate the walls, put down new flooring... What would it cost really? — lumber, drywall, fiberglass batts, a roll of linoleum. What else? — a dryer would need heavy duty wiring, and that was expensive, plumbing too. I groan silently. Maybe if Victor got the vice-principal position ... or why couldn't I work like Maddy?

Maddy did well selling cosmetics. But Maddy was beautiful. *Rub in a little more foundation to hide the pockmarks... A spot of blush on the bridge of your nose will shorten it.* Maybe they wouldn't buy from me — they'd look into their pink mirrors and see my face instead of Maddy's.

I can feel my eyelids getting heavy, and I fight off the weight. There are still things that I want to think about. The sunporch — I'll talk to Victor about it tomorrow. Perhaps, if Victor is willing to do some of the work himself, and if I help him out, laying down the flooring, maybe, or putting up the insulation. Maddy has a main floor laundry room; we should look at it next time we visit. Maddy ... *unfaithful* Maddy ... Maddy hurrying to meet her lover behind the wheel of her Cadillac. Flying. Maddy had wings. Maddy was beautiful. Why wasn't I beautiful? I feel my eyes closing, my thoughts becoming jumbled. Maddy — flying through the air in a diaphanous pink gown that billowed in the wind — was that Maddy's face, or *mine*? — flying through the air into the arms of her lover. What does he look like? I can see him quite clearly, surrounded by billowy pink cloth, his sinewy arms, his fresh face, his hair — his *hair!* — her lover had orange rind hair...

CHAPTER SEVEN

Inside Santini's, the tang of rancid meat mixes with the sharp smell of vinegar and Lestoil. It is closing time. Young girls in white cotton jackets are shining the glass and chrome of the meat counters with soft cloths. A young boy with a pink baby face and the beginning of facial hair is painting watery semi-circles back and forth across the floor with a mop. It is ten minutes before the store's eight o'clock closing time. There are no customers. Behind the tall glass counter, a clerk is scooping leftover bits of ground beef in a stainless-steel tray together into a pile. It's rare for me to go shopping this late at night; in fact, I don't recall ever having done so before by myself. But the station wagon wasn't ready until late in the day instead of early afternoon as promised, and the fridge was empty to the point of drawing complaints (there's nothing to eat!), which gave me both the impetus and an excuse to go out this late in the evening. I tell Victor, "I'm going to get a few things I forgot to get last time I went grocery shopping." Victor's parents are coming for dinner tomorrow, Sunday, and I deliberately delayed picking up a roast.

Victor nods, disinterested, his attention focused on the playoffs he is watching on the television. He knows that the Loblaws is just a block away on Bloor and open until ten.

"Can I come, Mom?" Joshua asks.

"No, you stay and get ready for bed. I'll be back before it's time to tuck you in." I plant a kiss on his head and leave.

The supermarket is surprisingly busy. I can feel myself getting agitated in the long line at the checkout and I almost decide not to complete my errand, after all. But I manage to overcome my hesitation and soon find myself driving along St. Clair once again, passing by the Canada Packers. In the darkness, the column of smoke rising from the tall chimney stacks floats like vertical cumulus clouds and fills the air with the stench of burning offal. The holding pens, empty, convey a sense of terror and desolation, and I very nearly lose my nerve again and wonder if I shouldn't just turn around and go home. But I can see the gift-wrapped box sticking out of my purse, and I am almost there, in any case ... and so I keep on going and park once again in the parking lot which still has remnants of the snow mountain.

"Excuse me ..." The clerk has sleek black hair and a bushy mustache that completely covers his mouth, the kind that would need a mustache cup when he drinks, to keep it dry. "Can you tell me if Valentin Marino is working tonight?"

"Valentin — yeah, he's in the back. I'll get him." He disappears through some doors marked EMPLOYEES ONLY.

A quivering uncertainty returns as I recall the last time I was here, the panic attack, the accident. But I've come this far, planned to be here, and the fact that there are no customers around makes it all the easier. And I do need a good roast for Victor's parents' visit. I move further along the counter towards the beef roasts and examine what remains behind the glass: not much selection.

"Hello." Valentin is standing in front of me, his white jacket blood-smeared. I'm physically jolted by the sight of him; he seems to emit a powerful energy that makes me jerk back a step. He is smiling in recognition, perhaps in amusement, a few days' growth of beard darkening his face again, except where a triangle of taut, hairless skin shines above each cheek, looking vulnerable next to the stubble.

"*Me* again," I say sheepishly."

"How are you?"

"I'm fine. How's the neck?"

"Not sure. It seems to be getting worse." He moves his neck back and forth, wincing. My insurance is going to pay for physiotherapy. There is a slight space between his front teeth that I hadn't noticed before; too narrow to be lecherous, the gap gives him instead a pre-adolescent innocence. He puts his hands together on the top of the display case at eye level and, leaning in, stares straight into my face. His hands are coarse-skinned and hairy on the back, his fingers bulky, as if overdeveloped by excessive manual labour.

"I can't tell you how terrible I feel about the whole thing."

"Don't worry 'bout it — a friend of mine is going to do the body work on my truck for free so I can use the settlement cheque for other stuff. I'm going to need it now that I'm being laid off. You actually did me a favour."

"Oh, okay," I say stupidly — the only thing I can think to say.

"Can I get something for you?"

"Well, yes. Have you any decent prime rib roasts left? There's not much to choose from in the display."

He turns, disappearing behind the EMPLOYEES ONLY door, and minutes later returns with two roasts, holding them high in the air, one in each hand, like a scale of justice. They are dark burgundy around the edges, well-trimmed, with delicate zigzags of fat coursing through the deep red centres — just the right amount of marbling. I choose the one in his left hand. He places it on the scale. "Fifteen dollars and thirty-eight cents, is that okay?" I nod and, after a ruckus and a pause, the machine spits out a white ticket that he slaps onto the hefty paper bundle.

I take the bundle, balancing it in the crook of my arm. "And..." I say, trying to hold on to the roast while at the same time reaching into my purse, "*this* is for you." The gift I proffer is wrapped in lilac paper splattered with purple flowers; the lady at the gift shop close to my house where I bought it insisted on wrapping it special, since I told her it was a gift. I now wish I had followed my first instinct and given it to him in a plain paper bag.

"What's this?"

"It's for you."

He unwraps the parcel carefully, cautiously, as if he were unsheathing something dangerous, then pulls out the statue. Across the front pedestal the words WORLD'S GREATEST SOCCER PLAYER anchor the ridiculous caricature. He smiles, a pleased smile, it seems, his slightly bulging eyes widening and revealing the whites with delicate red veins. Shaking his head, he says, "Thank you, but you didn't have to do that." He laughs and shakes his head again, his laugh sounding somewhat like a snort, so that I can't be sure whether he is genuinely pleased or whether he thinks me ridiculous.

"I really feel bad about it, seeing how it was a gift from a friend and a good luck charm." It *was* ridiculous, I suddenly realize; I could replace the object but not the sentiment attached to it. He must think me an oddball. "Well, I'd better get going," I say, turning to leave, not wanting to appear any more foolish than I already have.

"Listen — I get off in a few minutes. Can I buy you a coffee? There's a Tim's a couple of blocks from here."

"That's very kind, but it's not necessary — really." The young girls polishing the glass counters are staring at me, and I want to run out of the store.

"I *insist*. Wait for me out front. I'll be out in a jiffy." *Jeefy*, he pronounces it.

After paying for the roast, I walk out of the store with the bulky load. Outside the door, I wait, uncertain. The spring air smells fresh, without the stench of decomposition that earlier in the week seeped up through the muggy earth quickened by the melting rays of the sun, but a cutting breeze blows coldly against my face like a reawakening slap. What was I doing standing at the front door of a meat store waiting to go and have coffee with a *stranger*? What did I know about this man, really? His name, telephone number, licence plate number — not even a *number*, words: MEAT ME. What if he was a rapist-murderer? A woman had disappeared, her car found abandoned in a mall parking lot. Police still hadn't found a trace of her, a quiet housewife according to her neighbours, who dropped her son off at a nursery school and, inexplicably, vanished. Maybe she'd agreed to go for coffee with a stranger. Why worry about offending someone when it's a matter of life and death. This is his last week at Santini's. If I get in my station wagon and drive away, I will never see him again. I can hear a voice in the back of my head, plainly audible; it says: *don't go.* I reach in my purse and dig furiously along the bottom, listening for the jingling of my car keys as the contents shift from side to side. My fingers feel their jagged edges just as Valentin comes flying through the door, one arm already through his maroon jacket, the other poking blindly, searching for the hole of the other sleeve. "Nice out," he says. He seems boyish, bursting with exuberance.

I lose track of my keys.

"I can't wait for summer. Winter doesn't agree with me. Come on, we'll go in my truck," he says, walking ahead, expecting me to follow. "No point in taking two cars."

I hesitate, my feet unwilling to move from their spot on the concrete walk, as if they are obeying the voice in my head and not me. The meat is dead weight in my arms. Everything around me, the stores, the road, the parking lot, and cars, seem stilled, suspended, a twilight zone. I want to linger longer, to study the situation, but there is no time. No man other than Victor has ever asked me to go for coffee. Asserting itself, the voice at the back of my head is shrill: *DON'T GO!* A cup of coffee, after all — what could be the harm? Walking ahead of me, Valentin turns, surprised to see I am hesitating.

"I — I was thinking," I stammer, searching for something to release me now that it is already too late, "maybe I should leave this roast in my car."

He springs towards me suddenly, startling me. "Let me take that," he says, slipping the bag with the roast away from my grip. "We'll leave it in the truck. It'll be alright."

Now I feel naked, vulnerable, my weighty armour taken away from me. Instead, I grab hold of my purse and clutch it tightly, as though fearful of a purse snatcher. He continues walking backwards, looking intensely into my eyes, talking nonstop: "My truck's over here. My friend's going to do the body work — I already told you, didn't I? — first vehicle I've ever owned, paid eight thousand for her, used, of course, customized her myself. Had an idea I'd do some travelling with her, use her like a camper, live in her for a while..."

Trucks were *female* I note, although still in a stupor.

He rattles on rapidly, walking backwards still, staring still, as if the spell would be broken if he ceases eye contact and, liberated, I would dart off like an unsnared rabbit. Am I bewitched? How else to explain the fact that my legs are moving towards this strange man, a possible rapist-murderer? Now we are standing in front of the red van with the teardrop windows that look like drops of blood. He unlocks the passenger door, slides his hand under my elbow and helps me in, then places the roast in the compartment between the two front seats — captain's chairs, I believe they're called: crushed velvet, red, with padded armrests and high backs. He slams my door shut, then goes around the front of the vehicle to reach the driver's side, while I surreptitiously glance back at the van's interior. Lit by the florescent lights of the storefronts, I can make out at the back of the van the custom features he's been talking about: a closet, an actual mini bar with a tiny counter and sink, a bed — a *double* bed — neatly tucked across the back, flanked by two ornate balusters. I've heard of customized vans, seen signs stuck on bumpers: *If this van's rockin', don't bother knockin'.* And until now, I had thought it amusing. *Oh my God, what have I gotten myself into?* I hear myself saying this aloud in a panicked whisper, then hear the voice in my head: *RUN!* I could do it still. It wasn't too late. Crank the handle, open the door, *run!*

The door flies open on the driver side. Valentin climbs into his seat and asks: "Coffee or a drink?"

"*No!* — I mean coffee, coffee's fine."

He puts the key into the ignition without looking, looking at me with a somewhat puzzled expression. The van starts and we head out of the parking lot. As we pass the family station wagon, I wonder if I'm abandoning it forever.

***

The air in the Tim Hortons smells of toasted coffee beans and is moist from the steam of drip coffee. A sugary sweetness hangs in the air surrounding the glass case where the iced donuts are displayed. Leaning an elbow on top of the counter where a clerk awaits our order, Valentin asks, "How do you take your coffee?"

"Regular."

"Two coffees, one regular, one double double."

The girl behind the counter is young — sixteen, maybe seventeen. The scarlet flush of adolescence burns under her freckles; her light reddish hair, tied back in a short, stubby ponytail, hangs from the back of a chocolate-coloured Tim Hortons cap, exaggerating even more her Susie Q turned up nose. I step aside so Valentin, who is staring, can get an unobstructed view of her. Instead, he turns to me with the same scrutinizing look as before. "You look different without your glasses."

My face heats up instantly at the unexpected comment, not knowing his exact meaning. I *have* been playing around with the Mary Kay makeup kit Maddy delivered earlier in the week, and I have spent some time experimenting with the eyeliner and mascara so that my eyes appear larger, and the gloss Maddy has instructed me to smooth over my blotted lipstick does give my lips a nice sheen. But I don't actually know what he means by "different" and assume he's referring to fact that I'm not wearing glasses. I'm wearing my contacts, which Victor made me purchase some time ago, but have rarely worn. "Sometimes I wear my contacts when I go out," I tell him. "I guess that's why I look different. Besides, the lenses on my glasses got all scratched in the accident and I have to get a new pair," I add, not wanting him to think this outing was anything special.

The girl behind the counter comes back with two steaming paper cups, smartly slapping on two brown lids and marking them with a white grease pencil. Valentin notices that she's gotten the order wrong and brings it to her attention. "That was one regular, one double double," he tells her, "not one regular, one no sugar." Snarly, she takes one coffee back, giving a little sigh of exasperation. "That'll be a dollar-forty," she says when she returns with the replacement.

"Please … let me … now that you're out of a job."

"But I invited *you*."

"*I* insist this time." I clumsily grapple in my purse for my wallet and pull out a dollar bill, then go after the change; two nickels, I grasp easily, but the three dimes prove more challenging, getting trapped in the tight corners of the change pocket. It seems to take forever for me to fish them out and I can sense the girl's impatience without looking. When I finally manage to lay the money down, she snatches the dollar bill, then briskly sweeps the change off the counter into her open palm without saying thank you. Valentin picks up the coffees and heads to an empty booth in the far corner. "Nice server," he says.

I miss the irony and agree, "Yes — she's cute."

"Not *my* type. I'm not too crazy about her personality, and anyway, I don't go for redheads … I like blondes."

"Ah, yes — gentlemen *prefer* blondes," I affirm with a little laugh. The coffee is good and hot and relaxes me. I feel more comfortable now, less fearful, even happy to be here. Valentin isn't saying much as he drinks his coffee and, for some reason, keeps fixing his gaze on my mouth, making me wonder whether a poppy seed from the supper dinner rolls remains lodged between my teeth, even though I'd brushed them before going out. "So, you're going to be getting physiotherapy for your neck?"

"Yeah," he answers, becoming more animated. "For three weeks. I'm going to have to wear one of those cervical collars."

"All because of me," I say, truly contrite.

"You didn't do it on purpose. I'm out of a job, anyway. It'll give me something to do while I'm on unemployment. And I have some neck issues from playing soccer in any case, so it might help me. Maybe it'll keep my mother from pestering me to get things done around the house," he says with a laugh.

"You've played a lot of soccer?"

"Back home I did, yeah. I was part of a semi-professional team, but my coach said I was good enough to play for a professional team — *Primera División,* and he was preparing me for that, when I screwed up my knee. It's better now, but I'm not fast enough anymore to play competitively. I just play for fun now, locally, on an amateur team."

"That's a shame."

"Well, what can you do? There's a saying in Spanish: *nadie me quita lo bailado.*"

I harken back to the Spanish I'd learned years ago in school and translate back: "*No one can take from me the dance I have already danced.*"

"That's right. You speak Spanish?"

"Not very well."

"What I mean is, I've had a chance to play in some important games — some exciting games — and no one can take that experience away from me."

"Where are you from," I ask, "originally?"

"Guess."

"Well, you speak Spanish, but your last name sounds Italian."

"Spanish mother, Italian father," he explains. "My father was a paid soldier in the Spanish military during the Basque civil unrest when he met my mother. They got married and he stayed. I grew up in Barcelona."

He pronounces the name of the city in the proper Castilian manner — Bar-*thay*-lona — the way I'd been taught in my high school Spanish course by Mother Catrina, our eighty-year-old teacher. She would spray us with spittle each time she spoke any Spanish words containing the *theta* pronunciation — the soft Cs and Zs, which, according to legend, had been adopted centuries before in Spain out of respect for the king who spoke with a lisp, in order that he might not feel self-conscious.

"I'm named after my paternal grandfather, Valentin — you know, like the actor, Valentino. It's pronounced *Vah-len-TEEN* — with the accent on the end — most people don't know how to pronounce it. I'm guessing you're Italian too?"

"Sort of — Sicilian, actually. The rest of Italy doesn't seem to think that's Italian. Born here though."

"Do you speak Italian?"

"Well — *Sicilian*." A dialect so rustic it was scarcely used anymore, even in Sicily, except by the very old and the illiterate. I had made this discovery on our trip to Europe when Victor had agreed we could visit my parents' hometown as a concession for forcing me to take the trip, knowing I'd wanted to stay home to be with my dying father. But Sicilian was still spoken *here*, in this city — there were pockets of Sicilian speaking immigrants all along St. Clair and Dufferin. My own family and relatives had continued to use the dialect as if they were still back in their mountain hometowns. I had taken Italian as a minor in university. The Florentine professor had mocked me severely each time I'd accidentally slip in a word in dialect: "*vacca signorina! vacca!* Ha, ha, ha — *mucca invece*," he'd corrected, much to my humiliation. I'd dropped the course mid-term. My father and uncles all speak a passable English, so I only have to speak Sicilian to my grandmother who is in her late eighties, and my mother and aunts, who still speak no English after forty years in Canada, having always remained at home and lived in Italian neighbourhoods since they had immigrated. In Canada, you could get away with *never* learning the language.

"How old are you?" Valentin asks bluntly.

"I'm thirty-eight, been married for eighteen years, mother of four," I answer without hesitation.

"That's a lot of kids."

"And you?" I ask, since he's been so bold as to ask me the question.

"I'm twenty-six. No ties. No kids — as far as I know. I like the free life. My mother is enough of a responsibility — she's a widow. My brothers are all married and moved out. Had a little sister who died of leukemia. Now I'm the youngest." He reaches into the pocket of the maroon jacket he's hung on the back of his chair and takes out a package of Craven "A"; partially pulling out a cigarette from the red and white package, he holds it out to me like a proffered gift.

"No, thank you, I don't smoke." He takes it for himself, lights it, and continues talking, taking over the conversation, going into more detail about his family. They had emigrated to Canada in 1975 due to the civil unrest, much later than my family who had come forty years ago. In between pauses, as he pulls on his cigarette, I glance around at the people sitting in the booths next to ours — couples mostly, married, not married, dating, who knew? — most wearing blue jeans, including Valentin. I am wearing a beige turtleneck sweater that feels hot and sticky inside the coffee shop and matronly black polyester pants; I own only one pair of baggy blue jeans that I wear for housework.

"I was fifteen when we came to Canada," he continues. "Didn't speak any English. I stayed home the first couple of years memorizing the dictionary and taking night courses at COSTI. And watching *Sesame Street* — that's how I improved my pronunciation — listening to Big Bird and

Ernie." (*Air-ny*, he pronounces the puppet's name.) He laughs his snort-laugh, and I laugh too.

I listen, enthralled by his sharing of these mundane details, as if he were telling the most riveting story, and I'm sincerely eager to know more. "So how do you like being here?"

"It's good, except for the winters — all that snow! The first time we had a snowfall, I ran outside and danced around in it — ruined my leather moccasins — I didn't know it would be wet!"

"Did you think it was cotton batting?" I laugh. "So, you live with your mother. How long has she been a widow?"

"Five years — my father worked in construction. He was killed in an accident at work — a concrete truck backed into him. He was pinned."

"How horrible. I'm so sorry."

"It's been a long time now. But since my brothers left, I've had to stay at home and be the breadwinner."

"Don't you have a girlfriend?"

"I've had a few. Nothing serious. Right now, I'm a free man."

I'd entertained the idea that he was a virtuous young man, a devoted son, staying home and looking after his mama, until the right someone came along. Good Lord! What business of mine is it, anyway? But now I'm filled with curiosity. How many girls had he been with? Had they been casual or serious relationships? Long term or one-night stands? I think of the girl in the red blouse, dancing mouth to mouth, pelvis to pelvis. Where would *he* take her afterwards? Not his place with his mama at home. He would have to go no further than the nearest parking spot with his self-contained seduction pad on wheels!

The coffee is cooling off; I have drunk less than half of it. Valentin moves the ashtray from the middle to the side of the table and rests his hand beside it; his fingers are no more than an inch from mine. They are rather short for a man, but thick and strong looking. They remind me of my father's fingers. I feel a magnetic pull towards them. I have the urge to touch them, just to see what another man's fingers would feel like.

"How's your friend? he asks.

"Maddy?"

"Right — forgot her name."

"Fine, as far as I know. I'll tell her you asked about her," I add with slight sarcasm — but *why*? Maybe he thought she was a *cougar* — wasn't that what they were calling women who preyed on young men these days? I tone my voice down. "She's quite busy with her Mary Kay demonstrations."

"Who's Mary Kay?"

"Someone who realized that women long to be beautiful and got rich on the idea."

"I'd like to be rich."

I give him an approving smile. The butcher with aspirations. What did he aspire to? His own meat market like Santini's, a whole chain of meat markets, citywide, countrywide? "Do butchers get rich?" I ask.

"Not by being butchers. I'd need to marry somebody rich. When I get some money together, I plan to start investing in real estate. I got friends who made a lot of money that way."

"And when you've *made it,* what will you do?"

"Then I'll give up butchering. Not get pushed around anymore. Be respected. That's the most important thing in life — to be *respected.*"

"And rich."

"Why not?"

Looking at my watch, I notice it's almost nine thirty. I've been so engrossed in the conversation, I'd lost track of the time. Loblaws closes at ten. Victor would be wondering, if I wasn't home by then. "I have to get going," I say. "Please, could you drive me to my car?"

***

Back in the van, I settle myself into the captain's chair and, unzipping my purse, begin immediately searching for my car keys to underline the fact that I intend to go *straight* home. Valentin glances at me questioningly but turns on the interior lights for me so I can find them. I breathe a sigh of relief when shortly afterwards we drive up beside my parked station wagon, which is the only car still in the parking lot. He turns off the motor; soft music flows from several recesses of the van.

"How do you do that — play music when the motor's off."

"It's got its own juice. You like my van?" he asks, unlatching the captain's seat and swiveling to face me. He clicks some switches and the interior lights up, allowing me to see. "A friend of mine did the electrical." I see that the walls and ceilings are padded with a red Naugahyde in a diamond design. The floor is carpeted in a matching royal red. "This is a bar," he says, getting out of his chair and opening it to show me. "Nothing in there right now." He opens the closet, which has a shirt and a pair of pants hanging inside. Valentin is taller than the height of the van, and he stoops slightly as he walks towards the back, then sits on the edge of the bed between the two ornate columns. "This is really a couch, but it converts into a bed."

"Very convenient," I answer dryly. Why wasn't it a couch now? I jiggle my keys nervously. "Well, I'd better get going. I have to get back to put my kids to bed."

A sweeping lunge brings him back to the captain's chair. He turns off the interior lights. In the remaining light, which comes from the lampposts and the headlights of passing cars and the still-lit signs of the storefronts, I see that his eyebrows are knitted together in concentration, the slightly bulging orbs of his eyes fixed on me as though they are trying to solve a puzzle.

"Thanks for the coffee," I say.

"You paid."

"Well, thanks for asking me. I enjoyed the conversation."

"I haven't thanked you for the gift."

"You did."

"I mean I haven't thanked you properly." As he moves towards me, panic seizes and paralyzes me; I envision a snared rabbit, a station wagon abandoned in a plaza parking lot, an all-points bulletin with my name on it. Clasping my head between his hands, he combs his fingers back into my hair, pressing his thumbs behind my earlobes. I taste coffee and cold saliva. Petrified by surprise, I sit frozen, my body numb, until too many seconds have passed, and it would be ridiculous for me to protest. A mistake. He grasps the back of my head more firmly, massaging my skull with his fingers, and brings his mouth back to mine; his lips feel warmer now, with a tender moistness that is not unwelcome.

"Please," I say, pushing my hands against his chest, "I think you must have ... I must have ... given you the wrong impression. I'm sorry." My cheeks are burning. I'm feeling breathless and confused, but curiously *not* afraid. "I don't know what you must think of me." It occurs to me that he might have sized me up when he met me at the bar with Maddy and come to a reasonable but *wrong* conclusion. Or that, perhaps, he interpreted the gift as more than a compassionate gesture because he lost his job, because I'd added to his trouble.

"I think you're a nice lady," he says, easing himself back in his chair, with a smile that seems partly bold and partly ironic, so that I am not sure whether he *meant* what he said or *what* exactly he meant by it.

With apparent insouciance, he swivels the chair to face forward and starts tapping the steering wheel with his hands in rhythm to the music coming from the speakers, glancing sideways at me from time to time during the performance. He wasn't taking any of this seriously. I press my lips together thoughtfully. "Can I ask you a question?"

"Ask away."

"How many girls have you made love to?"

He gags on the question, exhaling a sound that resembles a horse snorting … *prrhhh,* then shrugs. "How do I know — ten, fifteen, twenty — I don't keep score."

I stare at him in astonishment; this man had made love to perhaps twenty women — too many to keep track of the number. How could you make love to someone and not remember? "Do you know how many men I've made love with? I want you to guess."

"I don't know."

"One. My husband — and only after we were married. I've never even been kissed by anyone other than my husband — until a minute ago." Another snort-laugh, a puff of air, exhaled. On his face a look of amazed disbelief, as if he's stumbled on something totally out of place, like the time I was driving the kids to school one morning and a pheasant had crossed the road in front of the car, amazing us with its bright red head, blue-green neck feathers, and copper body plumage. He looks away, out the window, then, opening it, reaches out towards the branches of a crabapple tree growing next to where the van is parked. Breaking off a twig, he offers it to me; it is heavy with unborn blossoms. "For you," he says.

His fingers brush mine and I feel an unexpected electricity, a warm tingling. "Thank you," I say, not wanting to seem ungrateful. I trace the slender stem with my fingers, stroking the spade-shaped buds, purple and plump and bursting with spring, anxiously awaiting the warm weather to bud. He watches me, silent, as I pluck nervously at some of the buds, shredding them in my palm, exposing their inner secrets.

"Here," he says, finally breaking the silence, "you'd better let me take that." Cupping his hands, he offers them to me so I can drop the fragments of buds into them, then holding his hands tightly together as if scooping up water, carries them to the window and, opening his palms, lets them drop; he brushes his hands together to clean them off, making little clapping sounds of applause. "There," he says, "a street-cleaning job for someone."

Bending to once again unfasten the clip of his chair, he swivels it back to face me. Our knees touch. "Now ... put this down," he says, taking the twig from me, "and give me your hands." He reaches out to me, grasping at first only my fingertips, drawing in my fingers gradually until my whole hand is enclosed in his. An electric current generates from his touch; I feel it travelling up my arms and down the rest of my body. Leaning forward, he kisses me harder, longer than before, his kiss cool and liquid at first, then warming with the prolonged contact. A spell has been cast, magical, inexplicable; nothing else could justify *this*. One hand releases mine, strokes the back of my neck, the ball of my shoulder, slides downward and clasps my breast. I freeze. This was insanity! Suddenly frantic, I struggle free, grab my purse, then the roast, and, without knowing why, the crabapple twig. "I have to go," I say, quickly unlocking the passenger door and climbing awkwardly out of the captain's chair.

"I'd really like to see you again," he calls after me.

I shake my head. "*No* — this is crazy. I'm married, I'm older — this is crazy."

"Call me," he insists, "at the store. You have the number. I'll be there another week."

"No."

"Just to talk."

"*No*, I'm sorry."

I slam the van door, then, with some difficulty because my hands are shaking, finally manage to unlock my own station wagon door. After starting the car, I back out of the space, and, without looking towards the van, I tear out of the parking lot as though I am being chased by the devil and all the fiery tongues of hell!

CHAPTER EIGHT

It was perfectly clear what I should do, although losing something always makes me feel uneasy, as if I've lost control of my life. I arrange the roast and some peeled potatoes in an enamel roasting pan and set it inside the fridge, ready to pop into the oven this afternoon, two hours prior to Victor's parents' arrival for Sunday dinner. Last night, it wasn't until I had driven into my driveway (*found* myself in my driveway, to be exact, since I couldn't consciously remember having driven home, although surely, I must have stopped on reds and gone on greens), that I'd noticed the missing earring. How different and strange I'd felt. Surely, I must have *looked* different. Victor would *know*, I told myself. Looking into the rearview mirror, I had expected to find a shocking transformation, yet all I noticed was a slight flush on my cheeks, a feverish gloss in my eyes, and, on my left ear, the missing diamond stud. Victor had bought me the earrings as a birthday gift; they were real, a third of a carat each, and he had made quite a show of presenting me with the extravagant gift in the presence of both our immediate families. If I failed to wear them for some special occasion, he always noticed, chastising me and reminding me that he'd spent a fortune on them, and he *meant* for me to wear them. I feel guilt and remorse for my negligence but can't honestly say I regret last night's experience. The wonder and irreality of it lingers still, blighted only by the loss. The earring could have fallen anywhere: in the parking lot or the donut shop, in Valentin's van or the station wagon, although, last night, I'd searched carefully with a flashlight that Victor keeps under the front seat for emergencies and found nothing. Before going into the house, I'd removed the mate and slipped it into my purse.

I'd found Victor asleep in front of the TV, his face stony in the reflected blue-green light of the tube; although I'd planned to tell him I had been delayed, driving around trying to find a local drug store that stayed open after hours in order to buy my preferred brand of sanitary napkins, it hadn't been necessary, after all. The kids were already in bed, and after quietly putting away the groceries, I went upstairs and slipped into bed, while Victor still slept downstairs. But what to do about the earring? I didn't have to tell him yet, I decided. Instead, lying in bed, I wanted to replay everything that had happened — every word, every gesture, every touch, like a favourite taped movie, except I, Rita, was the star! I was far too excited to fall asleep, although I pretended to be when Victor eventually came to bed. I stayed awake for the entire night, playing and replaying the tape of the movie in which *I* had been the leading lady.

But this morning there is a tightness in my throat, strangling me. I feel ambiguous tears spring uncontrollably to my eyes. From fear? From happiness? I'm so confused. My eyes start to tear up as I slice onions for Victor's favourite creamed onion accompaniment to the roast, and I pull a Kleenex from the box over the fridge. Would it be so terrible if I called Valentin at the store, just in case I'd lost the earring in his van? He'd think I had left it behind intentionally and get the wrong message. And what were the chances that I had lost it there? I toss the sliced onions and a knob of butter in a frying pan and start stirring them over medium heat to caramelize. Teardrops fall from my eyes and barely miss becoming part of the creamed onions. The contents of the pan appear wet and wavery from the wetness obscuring my vision as I add the flour to thicken the mixture.

The doorbell rings. Joshua tears out of the family room to answer it, with Gigi yelping excitedly at his heels, as I hurry to the sink to wash my hands and wipe my eyes.

"Hi there Joshua — or is it Jamie?"

It's Maddy. Does she see the children so seldom that she can't even tell them apart? Joshua and Jamie are fraternal twins and there are obvious differences. "I'm in the kitchen, Maddy," I shout. Heels click dully on hardwood, down the hallway towards the kitchen; I can only hope Maddy isn't leaving puncture marks on the oak strips with her metal tipped stilettos. "Well, I don't believe it!" I say as light-heartedly as I can. "This is rare, seeing you two weekends in a row. Don't you usually have a demonstration?"

"They cancelled last minute. Here — I brought those samples of the new perfume I promised you."

"Thanks."

Alison walks into the kitchen tethered to a Sony Walkman and optimistically, since the temperature today is still hovering in the sixties, wearing shorts. She lifts one earphone momentarily to say hello to Maddy.

"*Look* at this kid!" Maddy says, "She's so grown up. Another couple of inches and she'll be as tall as you, Rita."

Alison smiles self-consciously, revealing gleaming metal, her lips dry and pushed out. After each orthodontic adjustment her mouth is excruciatingly sore, and I have to press soft wax against the bands to cover the sharp edges that scrape her lips and gums. Who devised these instruments of torture? Were these things necessary in order to be loved by a man? Alison had wanted them. Beauty at all cost; I had agreed to it.

Alison lowers the earphones so that they hang around her neck like a necklace. "Mom — I can't find my Michael Jackson tape. Micah borrowed it and now he doesn't know where he put it."

"I saw it in the family room on the bookshelf next to the ivy plant. Tell Micah when he borrows something, he's *got* to give it back."

"Michael Jackson — is that all these kids are listening to these days? I see kids walking around like zombies with these things attached to their heads, getting brainwashed. I heard of a group that tapes subliminal messages backwards into their songs. How do you *play* a song backwards?"

"Well, it's your fault. Your confirmation money contributed to the purchase of the Walkman." I'm laughing, but secretly, I do fear encroaching influences that threaten to take control of my children, and I feel frightened and helpless against them. "Well, if Michael Jackson has any subliminal messages, we've had it — he's what I hear all day long these days." I slide into the kitchen chair next to where Maddy is sitting.

"You don't look so hot, Rita. Why are your eyes so red?"

"I was peeling onions. But I couldn't sleep last night, either."

"I know what you need — a good workout. I'm just on my way to my fitness club. Why don't you come? I have a free pass you can use."

"Victor's parents are coming for dinner — the roast is ready to go in the oven, and the side dishes just have to be heated up, but I don't think Victor would want me to go."

"You just leave Victor up to *me* and go upstairs and change."

***

The women's change room smells of baby powder and steam. We stop at Maddy's locker to change. I remove my skirt and blouse and quickly pull on my jogging outfit.

"You're going to be awfully hot with that," Maddy warns. She is slipping into a low-backed leotard over her panties and bra. Neither one of us has ever seen the other naked. There were no shower facilities at Holy Grace Convent School. We changed in the dark basement hallways outside our lockers, always wary in case the old, lecherous janitor might appear suddenly, as he so often did, quickly shucking our navy wool uniforms and replacing them with a cotton skort and blouse. The skort was a short skirt with attached bloomers — the pleated style looked particularly ugly on full hips like mine. After gym class, when we changed back into our uniforms, the coarse material against our heated, sweaty bodies pricked as though it was woven out of a million microscopic pins.

Maddy and I lace up our jogging shoes and join an aerobics class that has just begun. We start by running around the gym at a brisk pace. I start to feel good after a few laps, my body springing against mind, against air, against gravity. In the centre of the circle, the instructor commands us to change direction. Maddy, always the athlete, is high stepping with no problems, but I can already feel myself running short of breath. Looking over at Maddy, I loll my tongue to indicate exhaustion. Maddy laughs, running effortlessly, and winks me in the direction of a large woman running a few yards in front of us. Her buttocks are huge boulders that bounce and quiver with each enormously exacting movement of her thick legs. I cast Maddy a disapproving look of reprimand; the poor woman is making such a determined effort.

The instructor brings the running to a halt. Olivia Newton-John blares on the loudspeaker, exhorting us to get moving … mimicking the head guru in the centre, everyone stretches and bends and stretches again; hands reach for the ceiling, then touch the floor; legs strain, bending in and out, jabbing the air. Standing again, we are forced to endure more leg extensions and knee bends and body rotations until we are finally released from the gym, which is considerably spicier than when we entered, the air acrid with a peppery odour of sweat.

In front of Maddy's locker, we change again, down to our underclothing, then, modestly wrapping a towel around ourselves, reach underneath the towel to pull off our panties and bras, like magicians pulling scarves out of a hat. After that, we head for the showers. I notice with relief that they are private stalls. Maddy steps into the first empty one while I note, on further inspection, that the stalls have *no* doors. I pick the one at the far end, slipping off my towel and hanging it hurriedly on the hook outside the opening to the cubicle before stepping inside and turning on the water. I begin to wash, exposing my back to the opening; I've always felt that the back of person's body is so much less private and vulnerable than the front. The water, turned on fully, is comfortingly hot; I close my eyes and feel it beat down on me forcefully, almost painfully, like little slashes of a tiny whip. Yes, this was what I needed — blocking out memory with physical exertion, pain even. I rub the bar of soap under the shower spray until it's covered in suds, then slide my soapy hands around my neck, under my chin, behind my ears, my fingers tracing each earlobe, soft as a rose. Is that what Valentin had felt? Valentin's hands behind my ears were soft, and, oh, so gentle his touch, generating warmth and electricity. I would encapsulate these few treasured memories and keep them as my own secret trove that I could unearth whenever I wished. It was enough. It was more than I could have ever wished for or imagined.

I turn off the water and reach for the towel, drying myself quickly, then slip it around me again before stepping out. I notice Maddy's shower stall is empty. At the opposite end of the shower room, a girl stands naked, obliquely facing me, one leg up on a bench, her back arched, her spine bumpy as a chicken neck, as she bends down to dry her ankles with a towel. Her wet hair drips water down her back and has the strange taupe colour that blonde becomes when wet. She is slender and toned, so that in bending, there are no bulges around her middle. Her buttocks are round and firm, her legs, lean and long. She puts down her towel and walks past me, unselfconscious in her nakedness, exuding perfumed steam, the body of a nymph from Bouguereau's paintings. How wonderful it must feel to love your body, to rejoice in its perfection, to compare and not feel lacking. Fascinated, I watch her walk over to the hair blower mounted on the wall, press it on and lift her breasts — full, yet firm, with pale nipples and areolae — upward with splayed fingers, as though posing for a *Playboy* centrefold, in order to dry the creases underneath. Her hair, long and silky, blows gently back off her shoulders. I think if I could look like anyone, I would wish to look like her.

Maddy is already dressed. I hold my towel in front of me with my teeth in order to modestly slip on my underwear and change into the rest of my clothes. We both move towards a mirror with a string of light bulbs overtop. In the mirror, Maddy's cheekbones protrude elegantly from her face, a multi-level landscape; my cheekbones are less pronounced, less interesting. I take out my lipstick and am about to paint my lips with Mary Kay lipstick when Maddy stops me.

"Pencil your lips in first," she tells me. "You have a very pronounced Cupid's bow — you should make the most of your best features — accentuate the positive. And put on some eye shadow and blush — remember stroking outward. You bought the stuff — experiment with it!"

I don't bother telling her that I had already done some experimentation the other night when I brought Valentin his statue.

We stop at the Orange Julius bar on the way out. Maddy orders pineapple mango, but I can't decide between coconut or strawberry banana.

"It's only a drink, not life and death," Maddy says, getting impatient.

I order coconut but regret it as soon as the words are out of my mouth. It's bound to be bland. We take our drinks to a small circular white table with a slender base widening at the bottom like a wine glass. When I take a sip of mine, I realize that my suspicion was right: the drink is flat and tasteless. My eyes mist up all at once. "I shouldn't have ordered this," I say, blinking away the wetness, so Maddy won't notice, as I leer into the milky liquid in my glass as if it were the sole culprit in my present state of confusion.

"Something bothering you, Rita?"

With the opportunity of revealing my secret, my heart speeds up, but settles down again as soon as I decide against it. "I don't know. I just seem to have trouble lately making up my mind about things. What is that — a sign of immaturity?"

"Actually, no. According to the psychologist who spoke at one of our seminars, not being able to choose means you're scared to death you're going to miss something."

"Is *that* what it means?" I take another sip of my drink, barely tasting it.

"Well, only if you *think* you are. You make your own reality. Don't you read Jane Roberts? Everything that happens to you happens because you want it to happen, even if it's just a subconscious want, up to and including your own death. Take that horrible train collision in February — twenty-three people killed. Each person was making a statement by his or her death. Subconsciously, they had made the choice to die in that crash."

"What are you saying? If I got in my car and it crashes into another one, it would be because I *wanted* it to?"

"Subconsciously, it is, according to Jane Roberts' books. Do you read her?"

"No. When did you develop this sudden interest in reading? I've never known you to complete an entire novel."

"True, I usually just read the *juicy* bits. I don't have much time for reading. I just happen to think that clairvoyance is so interesting."

"What about fate?"

"Fate? You make your own fate. According to Jane, at least."

"You make your own tragedy, you mean."

"Or your own happiness."

Getting up, I pick up my unfinished drink and carry it to the nearest waste can, pushing the flap and dropping it inside. "Well, Victor's parents are coming for dinner and if you don't take me home right now, Jane Roberts will be right, and the *reality* that I make for myself will be Victor *killing* me."

CHAPTER NINE

By Monday morning, the loss of the earring has taken on a critical, almost frightening, level of importance, and I have a sick feeling in my stomach knowing I will have to deal with the matter. It hadn't taken long for Victor to notice I wasn't wearing the diamond studs when I'd dressed for the dinner with his parents. I told him I had lost one earring somewhere around the house. I would find it, I assured him. He'd had no opportunity to grill me further because just then his parents arrived. But I could tell by the tight-lipped expression that he maintained throughout the meal, and the fact that he didn't once look me directly in the face, that he was pissed — *very* pissed. His face got redder and redder throughout the dinner, and I could almost hear the anger churning inside him. It was probably the first time I was actually sorry to see his parents leave to go home.

"Well, good luck finding it. You might have dropped it anywhere — in the garbage, inside a heating vent, down the sink drain ... you'll *never* find it." His anger surpassed any other outburst that I could recall. He'd pulled out the scotch right after his parents left and had knocked back several shots. He called me stupid and ungrateful and said he regretted ever buying me the earrings. "I spent a fortune on those things. I can't believe you'd be so careless." I turned my back on him again, and he grabbed me roughly, thinking I wasn't registering his words; and now there's a little archipelago of bruises on my arm. I had once seen one of my uncles, during a family gathering, get very angry with my aunt and slap her hard across the face. He had had too much to drink and she was reproving him. I had never seen my father lift a hand to my mother; I never saw him call her names, or even yell at her, for that matter. They had heated discussions at times, disagreements, but I never witnessed any physical or verbal abuse. For the first time, I thought Victor might actually hit me. It was not as though Victor had never made a mistake, never lost anything or done something foolish. I never blamed him, never called him names — what good was that? It would only compound the problem. But I had felt humiliated, his speaking to me this way in front of the children, who cowered in the living room, wide-eyed and fearful, unused to this level of anger from their father. Finally, the older ones gathered up the two little ones and quietly took themselves upstairs to bed, as the yelling continued for some time, during which I did not defend myself for my stupidity, since I had no defence. I promised Victor I would retrace my steps and look more carefully tomorrow. This seemed to appease him for the time being, at least, and he poured himself another scotch and went into the living room, hunkering down in the wingback chair to watch TV.

I'd quickly tidied up the dishes and gone upstairs, Victor following shortly after. He'd wanted to make love, which I felt I owed him; but how can someone feel any desire given the circumstances of the evening? To Victor, there was obviously no correlation between the two, and I, as required, did my wifely duty.

***

As soon as I drop the kids off at school, I go back home and scour every inch of the car, even say a prayer to St. Anthony, patron of lost objects, convincing myself it can't hurt, but I find nothing except the dried twig of the crabapple branch I had left on the station wagon passenger seat. I stroke it thoughtfully and am reminded of the bedding plants Victor has purchased and asked me to plant yesterday. I didn't have time, having gone to aerobics with Maddy. Perhaps planting them before he gets home tonight will help me get back in his good graces.

It is a fine day for gardening, and even though I'm sick about the loss of the earring, the warm sun heartens me. I collect a hoe, a hand spade, and gardening gloves from the garage, wave to Mrs. O'Brien who is also gardening in her yard, and bring everything to the front of the house. I walk briskly back for the flats of annuals that Victor buys each year: red impatiens, yellow marigolds, and gray-leafed dusty miller. Their vivid colours help considerably to brighten the front of the house, which is a dark Tudor style with multiple front gables and a façade of black, rough-hewn timbers and red brick. The front door fanlight and some of the windows have stained glass, which obscures the brightness of the sun seeping in; the interior light is further reduced by the ancient sugar maples on the street, which keep the front yard in constant shade, so that plants don't really thrive, but the front yard desperately needs that splash of colour, so Victor persists in bringing home flats of flowers and foliage every spring, which he expects me to plant.

Swinging obliquely with the rectangular end of the hole so that the sharp corner edge points downward, I chop the earth of the front flower beds into large clumps, then break it up into loose soil. When I've worked the beds on both sides of the front door, I use the rake to smooth the soil into a rippled brown blanket. I dig small holes with the hand spade in even rows. Starting with the impatiens, I take a box, tapping it on the back until each plant, anchored to its compact cube of peat and vermiculite, pops out, then place one plant in each hole, pressing the earth firmly around it. I don't bother putting on the gloves; I like the feel of the earth between my fingers, cool and crumbly as biscuit dough.

Cool. So cool and *liquid*, Valentin's kiss, but his hands were warm, heat emanating from his fingertips — heat and electricity. I never imagined that just touching hands could be so sensuous. My fingers brush a leaf of dusty miller covered with fine white hairs. I stroke its velvety surface, trying to bring the sensation back of Valentin's fingers behind my ears. His fingers *stroked* the back of my ears. Was it possible…? Could my earring have come off…? I had resolved that Saturday night's insanity was a blip that should not have happened, could never be repeated, and must be forgotten, but what if…? The chances were slim, but Valentin might have loosened the backing of the earring when he touched me and it might have come off. Tonight, when I tell Victor I still haven't found the earring, there will be another scene. *What if…?* It's possible.

I go inside to wash the earth from my hands, then take my purse from the front closet and dump the contents on the floor, spreading them out: a comb, a lipstick, a pack of Kleenex and some bunched up used ones, car keys, a cheque book, a lengthy receipt from Loblaws, my wallet, and, hidden under the wallet, a white business card with a steer head and *Santini's Choice Meats* printed on it. Open 8 a.m. to 8 p.m. Closed Sunday. The address and telephone number follow. Quickly, before I lose my nerve, I dial the telephone number with sweaty hands and trembling fingers, my heart galloping in my chest.

***

"You even found the back part." The butterfly, I believe the proper name for it is, though I'm not sure enough to call it that. With one finger I move the earring around in the palm of my hand, an amulet, by magic rematerialized.

"I couldn't miss it — it was lying on the seat, so shiny."

So are his eyes — does he realize? — they sparkle with youth. His face is shaded by a charcoal beard that belies the youthfulness of his eyes. He seems pleased, I think, to see me. I am giddy to see him, and grateful for his having found the earring. On the phone, I had doubted him and asked for proof — *describe it* — in case he was toying with me. Why had I doubted?

I had come to Santini's during his lunch break as he'd instructed. He told me he'd put the earring for safekeeping in the locked compartment of the van closet and asked me to follow him to his truck. This time the van felt familiar, cozy almost. He had converted the bed to a couch and, kneeling next to it, he'd flicked through his keys until he'd found the right one to unlock the drawer. When he'd handed me the earring, I could scarcely believe my luck.

"Come, sit," he invites me, patting the couch next to where he is sitting.

I do. The couch is comfortable. "Thank you — thank you for finding it, I'm so grateful, thank you."

"Put the earring in your purse," he says, "in case you lose it again." His voice has a deep, fatherly tone. I slip the earring into the zippered pocket of my purse, and immediately afterwards, he gently takes my hand, studying it, his touch conducting the same electrical flow as before, not imagined, a tangible thing.

"What do you do for a living?" he asks. "You've got dirt under your fingernails."

I laugh, embarrassed. "I was gardening." I left in such a hurry after he'd confirmed on the phone that he had found the earring, that I'd done only a perfunctory washing of hands. He continues holding on to my hand, and I don't pull it away. I just stare at it, objectively, as if it isn't part of *me*, but someone else's — some lucky woman whose hand was being held tenderly by a young, handsome man.

"Are you in a hurry to get back?" he asks. "I have an hour. Why don't I take you for a sandwich? My treat this time. I'm still getting paid for this week at least."

"A sandwich?

"Yeah — I know a place where they make great veal sandwiches. Veal on a bun with tomato sauce and peppers and mushrooms — you'll like it."

"I don't know." I have to go to Birks to order an engraved silver cup for my niece, who's being christened in a few weeks. But I don't have to pick up the twins until three today, since the class is on a field trip, and I could order the cup another day. Against my better judgement, I agree.

We drive away in his van, and he glances at me sideways. "I like your sunglasses."

"Thanks."

"They make you look like Jackie Kennedy."

I burst out laughing. "Not *quite*." But I accept the compliment with pleasure.

The car behind us speeds up, passes, and cuts Valentin off, causing him to break suddenly. His muscular arm shoots out in front of me, acting as a protective barrier, preventing me from being flung forward, even though my seat belt is fastened.

"*Hijo de puta*," he spits out, annoyed, then looks at me and asks, "Are you okay?" His English is good, but it seems, when it comes to swearing, his first language comes more naturally, I note with amusement.

"I'm fine."

"They should put guys like that in jail."

"Or you could challenge him to a duel, like Don Quijote, tilting at windmills. Have you ever heard of Don Quijote?"

"Of course. You can be my Dulcinea," he says, looking sideways at me, smiling.

"Isn't she a toothless hag?"

"Not in the eyes of Don Quijote." He gives me another playful sideways glance, taking his eyes off the road for a second.

What would happen if there had been a serious crash, I wonder? How could I ever explain being *here*. I am cognizant of the risk but, at this moment, scarcely care. We arrive at the sandwich shop without any further mishaps. It's a tiny store wedged between residential housing. Inside, the air is fragrant with pan-fried breaded veal and simmering tomato sauce. Valentin orders two veal sandwiches — veal sandwiches being the *only* item on the menu. The owner wedges two crispy breaded cutlets between a crusty bun and smothers the veal with fried onions, green peppers and mushrooms, and tomato sauce on top, then wraps them in foil and hands two fat packages to Valentin. "Do you want some olives?" Valentin asks. "I'll get some olives," he says, before I can even answer. He orders two Brios and a scoop of olives that the owner wraps in a square of aluminum foil and twists together at the top. I observe everything, *bouche bée*, in astonishment, never having seen food sold in this manner; the only food I have ever eaten outside our own home was either at a sit-down restaurant or a take-out like MacDonald's, not a little hole-in-the-wall of someone's house.

We take the food back to the van, and after pulling out a table that materializes ingeniously from underneath the couch, Valentin spreads the food out for us. "Am I supposed to eat this whole thing?" I ask, opening the foil and releasing a mouth-watering aroma of tomato sauce and fried veal. "It's huge," I say, laughing.

"Eat what you can — I'll eat the rest." He takes the small packet of foil and unravels it, disgorging the little mountain of plump green olives condimented with chili peppers and oregano. He makes conversation in between bites, telling me about all the different jobs he's held since coming to Toronto — quite a variety of jobs, it seems, from upholsterer to carpenter to landscaper, and finally butcher after two years of on-the-job training. I can't eat more than half of my sandwich and Valentin is happy to finish it, oblivious to any sharing of germs.

"I don't think I'll be able to move after a meal like that," I declare.

"Relax," he says. "I don't have to go back for another twenty minutes. Here, lean against me."

I barely hesitate to take him up on the offer. I feel so languid, leaning back against him, my head cushioned by the thick chest hair underneath his shirt, which also peeks black and curly from the unbuttoned part at the top. On his clothes, I can smell the clean lemon scent of detergent and a hint of tobacco smoke. How awake each sense seems to be! How new each feeling! Where is this going, I wonder? It is something I should put the brakes on immediately, I know that, and yet I know with certainty it's something that will never come again. I feel as though I've given free rein to a force that is no longer within my control. Chastely, at first, he kisses the top of my head, then, lifting my chin, finds my mouth, slowly pressing, molding, sucking, like a muscle being flexed and unflexed, but without tension, without hardness. A cloud of pleasure presses around me; I am *floating*, floating away. His tongue probes with darting movements each contour of my mouth. At the same time, I become aware of a light tugging at my blouse; with measured slowness, he is easing it from inside the waistband of my slacks. This strikes me as comical, and I begin to giggle hysterically. Nonplussed, Valentin stops what he's doing, an expression of bafflement on his face. "What?"

"Am I really not supposed to notice what you're doing, or just pretend it isn't happening?" I calmly push his hand away and smooth my blouse back down, tucking it back into my slacks.

He cocks his head, looks at me, perplexed, as if I'm a puzzle to which he's trying to find the pieces that fit together. "You're a strange woman. Don't tell me that you haven't done this before?"

I recall sitting with Victor in a parked car, the chaste kisses, the imaginary stop sign that lit a warning whenever the kissing became too intense. "No, I haven't done *this*. My husband never touched me until we were married." How quaint and clichéd that sounds. "In fact, I was a *virgin* on my wedding night." I imitate his snort-laugh. "Pretty old fashioned, huh?"

Instead of the sarcastic response I expect, he looks rather serious. "Some people think that way," he says.

I brush my fingertips absent-mindedly along the ribbed velvet upholstery fabric of the couch. "Can I ask you something?"

"Another one of those questions?"

"Sort of. Those twenty or so women you made love to — did you love them?"

He snort-laughs. "Maybe it wasn't that many — maybe half that many — I'm no lady-killer." He ponders his answer. "It was just sex."

"*Just* sex. But how can you be so *intimate* with someone you don't love, maybe only met that very night? I couldn't do that — I couldn't be with someone that way unless I loved the person, unless I knew the person loved *me*."

"Well, you feel *something*. A closeness — it's automatic when you have sex with someone."

Automatic. Like the washer, or the dryer, or the toaster, doing its job swiftly, efficiently, mechanically. Intimacy had become automated. "Okay, but what about practicality? Don't you worry about catching something, or getting a girl pregnant?"

"I've been one of the lucky ones."

"Do you have a girlfriend now?"

"No," he says, then qualifies it. "There's someone I go out with now and then, but we're just friends."

"What does that mean?"

"It means I'm not going to bed with her, if that's what you want to know. I'm not inter*est*ed to sleep with her," he says, placing the accent on the wrong syllable of *interested*.

The euphemisms amuse me: go to bed with; sleep with; make love to — really meaning nothing other than the physical act.

"She's had a few meaningful relationships and is just getting over one. She's not inter*est*ed in another one right now."

"*Meaningful relationships*? The first, the second, the third — is there a quota to how many *meaningful relationships* are allowed before a girl gets a reputation of being loose?" I ask, quite seriously.

He shrugs. "Like I said, we're just friends."

"I'd like to be *that* — just friends, with you."

My fingers continue stroking the ribbed red velvet of the upholstery, feeling its bumpiness. "What did you do all this for?" I ask, indicating with a stroke of my hand the extensive customization surrounding me.

"I told you, I wanted to do some travelling with the truck, use it like a camper."

"What else do you do with it?"

He cocks his head, reflecting for a moment, then responds candidly, hoping that he's found a puzzle piece that fits. "If I told you I've never made love to anyone here before, I would be lying."

His response is honest but goes down like castor oil. Why did I ask? My face heats up. I look away for a moment, studying the fixtures on the padded walls — dim light bulbs encased in rectangles of plastic gold filigree — *gaudy*, it was all *too* gaudy.

"Is that what you went to all this trouble for — to impress your conquests?"

"No. It's comfortable, don't you think? Lie down, try it."

"No, thanks."

He puts his arm around me and bends his head to kiss me, but I turn my head away. "Why won't you let me kiss you? You did before. Are you *tizzing* me, or what?"

"*Tizzing.* That's *te-e-asing.*"

"*Te-e-asing*, whatever. Why can't I kiss you?"

"I told you, I'd just like to be friends."

He releases me and sits at the edge of the seat, his head bent and his hands clasped together between his knees. "I see."

"I mean, what would be the point? I'm thirty-eight and you're twenty-six."

"So — is it my fault my mother had me late? Look, maybe there won't be a pot of gold at the end of the rainbow, but we can still have something nice together." As if in need of reinforcement, he reaches in the breast pocket of his shirt and pulls out a cigarette from a pack of Craven "A". With the cigarette clamped between his lips, he slaps his pockets until he's found by touch what he's looking for — a Zippo lighter — and lights his cigarette. A puff of smoke fogs his face and dissipates to the four corners of the bedroom compartment.

I don't know how to respond to his last statement. "I should go," I say. "I'm really glad you found my earring. I'm really grateful."

"Would you do me a favour then?"

I look at him uncertainly. "What?"

"Would you write a letter for me? My English isn't perfect and I need a letter for my insurance company from a witness to the accident. I really need the settlement now that I can't work because of my neck. My unemployment insurance won't last long and my mother — well, I gotta help her out. The creditors are calling all the time."

"Why, yes. Tell me what you want me to say."

"Just explain how the accident happened. I need the letter by next week. But I won't be at Santini's anymore. I could meet you somewhere else." He pauses to think for a moment. "Do you know the park down the road from Santini's? There's a soccer field there where we practice and play our games. We could meet there next Saturday, around noon."

"Alright, I can do that. I'll meet you on Saturday."

"Thank you." He presses me towards him, holding the cigarette in the air between two fingers, so close to my scalp, I can feel the heat of it in my hair. His lips cover mine, and he kisses me long and hard. "Friends can kiss," he says.

But his kiss is far from friendly. Hot and wet, it feels magical, melting, delicious — even with the slight bitterness of smoke.

"You have a beautiful mouth. Let me taste your tongue."

I let him. We kiss long and hard and are both breathless afterwards. He strokes my cheek. "I know you're going to think this is crazy," he says dreamily, "but I have this feeling … I just feel that if we'd met before you were married — well, I guess it wouldn't have been possible anyway, I would have been too young — but if we'd met under completely different circumstances, I really think you could have been the *one*, that we could have made it all the way."

Pressed against him, my laugh vibrates against his shoulder.

"You're laughing at me."

"No. I don't think it's funny. It's just … it's not something I would ever have expected you to say. It's such a *touching* thing to say."

He releases me and lies down on his back across the couch, staring intensely, but blankly, at a point in the padded ceiling. "Were you really a virgin when you got married?"

"Of course."

"I've never been with a virgin before." His eyes, with their slight bulge and long-lashed eyelids, are wistful and bright.

"You mean not one of those girls you slept with was a virgin?"

"There are no virgins," he says disdainfully. "Every girl you go out with has *been* with someone else — unless she's fourteen years old. You can't even be sure when you go out with a girl that she hasn't been with someone else that same night. I met a girl once who was coming on to me at my friend's café where I was playing poker with some guys. We spent the evening together, were intimate, and then she tells me she'd had a fight with her boyfriend and broken up with him that same day. She didn't waste any time. Maybe she'd already been with someone else before me and was comparing, who knows. I wish I'd stayed a virgin until I was older. I was thirteen my first time."

"Thirteen," I say, shocked, thinking Micah was already older than that at fourteen, and to me, he was still a baby.

"I never expected it would happen like that. I thought maybe, seventeen, eighteen. There was this lady who lived across the street from us. She was maybe forty. She liked to drink. Her husband worked nights. She invited me over for a drink of soda. She started kissing me, touching me. I was tall for my age, looked older than I was."

"But you were just a child," I say, shocked.

"I don't have any regrets. It's made me appreciate older women."

"You make me feel ashamed. I think I should go."

"I'm *not* thirteen years old anymore." He shrugs. "Once you hit adulthood, why should age matter?"

Perhaps this was something to ponder, but for what reason, I wasn't sure. For now I had my earring and a present to get for my niece's christening.

CHAPTER TEN

I catch sight of the red van with its teardrop windows, the ladder going nowhere, the licence plate MEAT ME, even before I turn into the parking lot of the park. I stop next to the van and smile at Valentin, noticing the plastic statue I'd given him hanging from the rearview mirror. I park the car and hurry towards him as he stretches an arm from inside the van to open the passenger door for me. He is wearing a blue and garnet coloured T-shirt with a *Fútbol Club Barcelona* logo. "I like your shirt," I tell him.

"My team — *Barça*," he says proudly, pinching the shirt on two corners and stretching it out to display the logo emblazoned on the front.

"Nice. Here's your letter," I say, holding it out to him.

"Thanks."

"Aren't you going to look at it — see if it's alright?"

"Maybe later."

I stand outside the open door as he looks at me intently without speaking, perhaps searching for a puzzle piece, until I become uncomfortable and break the silence. "It's a beautiful day."

"Yeah. Would you like to go for a walk? I know this park pretty well. We play soccer over there," he says, pointing to a neatly manicured grassy field enclosed partly with wooden boards and partly with chain-link fencing, a soccer net at each end. "There's a pond further in."

I try not to appear too eager, although I'm happy to see him again. "I guess I can spare an hour."

We lock both vehicles and take a narrow asphalt path that follows a small stream meandering behind some houses whose backyards incline severely towards the water and are heavily wooded with a variety of deciduous trees and shrubs. Valentin reaches for my hand and wraps his baby finger around mine so that we are connected ethereally by this one small appendage. This simple, spontaneous gesture delights me. We reach the pond, which looks green and glassy, the air surrounding it smelling of fish and frogs and whatever other amphibious creatures might live in its waters. A family of ducks floats by, the mother followed by a string of little ones, the perfect silence suddenly broken by a loud *quack!* from the mother duck, warning her ducklings to stay in line. The air is perfumed with crabapple blossoms that are now in full bloom. Yellow daffodils and red tulips have sprung up in prepared beds along the path. The sky is brilliant blue without a single cloud; birdsong escapes from among newly-leafed maples and oaks. This is too perfect to be real, I tell myself.

We reach the edge of a wooded incline, thick with stunted trees and vagrant shrubs and patches of wild daisies. There is a narrow footpath leading downward stamped into the dry earth. We attempt it, and I immediately regret having worn my flats with the hard, shiny soles, but my snug blue jeans look so much more attractive with the flats than with clunkier running shoes. My feet start to slide as I follow Valentin down the slope. "Hold on to me," he says, taking the lead.

I scurry after him, my feet accelerating with each step ahead of my body. Stones and pieces of gravel break away underfoot and roll noisily down and I almost lose my balance. He turns and links his hands under my buttocks, lifting me up with his strong arms, as easily as a child. When we reach the bottom, he presses me hard against him and swings me around.

I begin to giggle hysterically. Never in my adult life have I done anything like this, acted like this. "What about your neck?" I ask, alarmed.

"It's fine."

"I could use this against you, you know. Tell your insurance company that you're not as damaged as you let on."

"I'll just have to shut you up, then … like this…" He lets my body slide down along his, kissing me when our lips level, then lowers me the rest of the way until my feet touch the ground, and kisses me again.

"This isn't me," I say, breathless. "I don't know who it is, but it isn't *me*."

"Let's christen the new you," Valentin says. "What should we call you?" He ponders, looking around, then bends down and plucks a daisy from a clump growing nearby. He threads it through my hair in behind my ear. "In Spanish we call this flower a *margarita*." He bends down once more and gathers a fistful of the dusty clay at the foot of the slope. "To christen you," he says.

"But it's supposed to be holy water."

"We only have dust." Through an opening in his fist, he lets the dust sift through in a thin stream over my head. "I christen you … *Margarita*…"

Laughing, I shake dust from my hair and feel reborn.

***

We cross the bridge that passes over the stream, hands linked, saying little until we find a perfect place to sit among some golden forsythia shrubs, their blossoms already fully open. In among the shrubs, the thick trunk of a Sunburst locust shoots upward, its fern-like leaves shining saffron in the sun, the tree's long-limbed branches bent and almost touching the ground. Underneath the densely-leafed branches, it is a private world, just nature and the two of us.

Valentin sits on a grassy patch at the foot of the tree, his back against the tree trunk, then pulls me down to sit on his lap. When he cups one of my breasts with his hand and moves to kiss me, I offer no resistance. No resistance, either, when he unzips my jeans and reaches a hand inside. I can barely breathe, am barely conscious of what is happening. With eyes closed, his lips never releasing mine, I hear the sound of unzipping repeated, then a momentary struggle with unyielding denim, a repositioning of our bodies and too soon it is done. It is *done*. My body rejoices in celebration of our joining; the voice in my head screams in admonition: *it is done. You have now officially been unfaithful.*

CHAPTER ELEVEN

"I baptize you in the name of the Father ... and of the Son ... and of the Holy Spirit..." The water is poured three times over the baby's head as she howls in indignation, her cries rising to the vaulted ceiling, reverberating through the choir loft and back down through the incense-scented air, to join the ripple of laughter from the assembled relatives and proud parents of the three babies, each decked in white and being held in their godmothers' arms. I have been given the honor of being one of them, and it is my duty to hold the infant over the baptismal font as the priest pours the holy water. When he's done, he wipes the baby's head with a cloth and continues administering the sacrament, to the renewed protests of my niece. Oil on the forehead, salt on the lips. My part completed, I hand the baby back to the mother and take my seat in the pew beside Victor.

Another grandchild my father would not know. He's been dead almost two years now, yet his genes live on in his children and grandchildren. *That* was how you lived on. And in people's memories — for as long as they remember. Not in a fantasy place of perfection from which you could look down and observe the lives of mortals. Yet, why is it that I feel like they are watching, the dead? Had my father been able to see how on the day of his funeral I'd desecrated his memory? *Copulated*, at Victor's insistence — that's all it was. Like animals. Flies, even. Doubling up, anywhere in the house. Or birds. I had seen a couple of crows from the kitchen window once, the male hunkered over the female, his wings flapping to balance himself, his backside moving back and forth; the female's head twisted to look back at him, her beak wide open in unuttered cawing. What was she feeling? Pleasure? Pain? Not thoughts for church, these. In chapel, at the convent school during mass, my mind would sometimes wander, and forbidden thoughts enter my head. Why? Precisely because they *were* forbidden. *Do not think of a pink elephant.* Christ on the cross, tortured, torturing my adolescent conscience; hands, feet, thorn-crowned head, bleeding, naked, the pathetic swatch of cloth — loin cloth, loosely draped, no bulge. The man behind the cloth, the organ behind the cloth, mustn't, mustn't imagine. *Corpus Domini Nostrum.* Pulsing, erect, a man, though I had never seen, only imagined. *Domine non sum dignus.* Soul so recently confessed. Oh my God, I am heartily sorry … *Don't think of a pink elephant.* Turn away, concentrate on the statue of the Blessed Virgin on the side altar, dressed in celestial blue, eyes turned heavenward, hands clasped in prayer, feet crushing the serpent's head.

"Do you renounce Satan?" the priest asks the godparents of the next baby he is now baptizing.

"We do."

The priest repeats the entire ritual as before, then begins again a third time for the final baby. In other churches, too, the ritual is being repeated over and over — different churches, different priests, different voices, but the same. Holy, Roman, Catholic, Apostolic, and Universal Church, which obviously meant nothing to the Vatican guards who had barred me from entering St. Peter's Basilica because I was *sleeveless*. Victor had been allowed in. Inside, near-naked statues and flagrant frescoes. No sense to it. I'd wanted to go in and say a prayer for my father who was lying in a hospital bed at Toronto General close to death. Why? I'd even gone to confession for the first time in ten years just before the flight — in case the plane crashed. Ridiculous, hypocritical. I knew it and I had gone anyway, wanting my soul to be sinless, to be pure and shining, erased of wickedness. What is the condition of my soul now, I wonder — is it full of wickedness and sin, now that I am loving Valentin? How could love *ever* be a sin?

Beside me, Victor asks if I'm going to take Communion. I say, "Forgot to fast, had something to eat this morning." So he goes without me. It's a lie. I have no appetite. My stomach confirms this on cue, by growling loudly, so that I'm sure it can be heard several pews behind me. I cover my abdomen with one hand, as though I have shamefully exposed a private part of myself. I can feel a satisfying flatness there, a firmness that hasn't been there since before I became pregnant with Alison. On either side of where my hand presses, my pelvic bones jut out like blades under my skin. Today, for the ceremony, I'm wearing a dress which hangs loosely on my body. My weight has dropped drastically in just a few weeks. Eating has become unimportant. I mostly wear blue jeans now — tight, hip-hugging jeans that make me feel like a girl. The baggy polyester pants I used to wear when I went out, I've given to Goodwill.

***

Several cameras flash. My brother Joe has invited all the relatives to his daughter's christening — my grandmother, aunts, uncles, cousins, their wives, husbands, and children.

The gang's all here. Taking photos, chatting, laughing, commiserating — my mother commiserating more than the rest, displaying the rawness of her loneliness, resigning herself to being so the rest of her days. Her dinners at home are meagre, since it's no longer necessary to prepare dinner for her husband each day, as she used to do, and whenever I drop in, the kitchen is no longer redolent with comforting smells coming from simmering sauce and roasting meat. She had come to Canada forty years ago, and in those forty years my mother has never worked outside the home. She'd been a wife and mother — a good one. When she'd gone out of the house, it had always been with my father. Her world had extended no further than the nearby plaza that was walking distance and whatever stores existed there, and the Catholic church a few blocks further.

Wearing an apron, Joe, the proud Papa, was passing around a tray of pizza my aunts had made. When had I ever seen him, or my other two brothers, wearing an apron when we all lived together in my father's house? Now, I've even seen him doing dishes for his wife, something unheard of in my mother's kitchen. His wife, Iry, was Danish and hadn't a clue how to make pizza, although she made tasty open-faced sandwiches of thinly sliced rye bread, thickly buttered, with towering layers of cold cuts and lettuce and cheese. Strangely enough, not one of my brothers or cousins, or I, for that matter, had married an Italian, much to our parents' disappointment, though they had warmly accepted the alternative choices. My grandmother, my aunts, and my uncles communicated in gestures and a few in broken English with their daughters- and sons-in-law. My father had been the only one to make any real effort to learn the language, having gone to night school, and yet I had been ashamed to accompany my parents on parents' night in elementary school and hear my father address the teacher in his halting English, each word punctuated with a gesticulation of his darkly cuticled, calloused hands.

Joe approaches me bearing a tray piled with pizza. The smell of tomato and oregano and melting cheese usually starts my mouth watering but repulses me today. Where did my appetite go?

"Come on, Sis. Eat up."

"No thanks."

"Come on, you're getting skinny."

"No, really, I can't. Maybe later." My insides growl with hunger, but I can't eat. Now I know where the expression *lovesick* comes from. In spite of my lack of appetite, I feel *wonderful,* full of energy. I had bought myself a pair of jogging shoes — pink and white Adidas — and use them most days. Those superfluous ten pounds, garnered by four births, had dropped off effortlessly. Joe puts the tray down on a nearby table and sits down in the chair next to me. Reaching in his back pocket, he pulls out a package of Craven "A" cigarettes. Seeing them, I feel a pang of longing for Valentin. "Have you always smoked that brand?" I ask, staring at the package as if it were some rare, exotic talisman.

He looks at me questioningly, squinting from the smoke of the cigarette he just lit. "Quite a while. Why?"

"Just wondering." I feel dazed, in a trance. I can't take my eyes away from the cigarette package he's holding in his hand, silly as that seems.

"Anything wrong, Sis?"

"No — no, I'm fine. It's hot in here, that's all. It's making me sleepy." I feel relaxed, actually, very relaxed, some kind of somnambulism that makes me feel detached from everything that's going on around me. All I want is to be left alone and not have to make conversation. To have the luxury to escape in my mind to the new world I have discovered, where only I and Valentin exist. Inside my head is a private, beautiful world, where I can travel to, where no one can follow, and I am always eager to return to it.

"You want me to open some windows?"

"No — no, that's not necessary."

He turns and strikes up a conversation with Victor who is sitting in a chair adjacent to me, looking bored. Joe is a research scientist, and he starts talking about his work, which Victor seems to find mildly interesting. "Right now, we're working on the H1N1 vaccine for that flu that's going around lately, trying to find a treatment. It's actually a strain of coronavirus that goes all the way back to the Spanish flu — seventy-five years ago — can you believe that? And we *still* haven't got a handle on it. It's really giving us a run for our money. At the lab, we refer to this virus as 'the Bitch,'" he says, laughing.

I smile at him, wryly. So — life-threatening viruses are also *female*. "I'm going to go over and talk to *Nonna*," I tell them.

***

At the opposite end of the living room, the baby has started to squawk, bringing picture taking to a halt. Iry takes the baby away to nurse her, leaving my grandmother and aunts sitting in a cluster with the other women of the family. My grandmother's cataracts have progressed in the last year, and I have to get close before she recognizes me. I speak to her in dialect, the only way I have ever spoken to her, and to most of the other relatives. But more loudly, since her hearing loss has become more profound. "*Comu si, Nonna*? How are you feeling?" The Sicilian doesn't come as naturally to me as it once did; I have to fish around for the words, often bastardizing them.

"Maria Rita — *figghia mia*," my grandmother says, reaching for my hand, "Come and sit next to me."

"*Comu pozzu essiri? Comu 'na vecchia.*" My grandmother answers, "How else can I be? Like an old person." I smile at her, noticing the creases in her face that are filled with Johnson's Baby Powder.

She strokes my hand with her long fingers, knobby with arthritis. My grandmother's life had been just as restrictive as my mother's. Nonna is eighty-nine years of age, and she has always lived with her eldest daughter, my aunt Giuseppina, who never married; she has outlived her husband and son and is in reasonably good health still. In forty years, she has never once ventured out the door on her own. Still, my grandmother has always seemed more daring than my mother, her daughter-in-law. My mother never wore makeup in her entire life, yet my grandmother powders her face with baby talc and rouges her cheeks with a damp piece of red tissue paper every time she goes out. She has always had more gumption than any of her daughters, my mother's sisters-in-law. Three times she's been on her deathbed with pneumonia and survived. She can talk unabashedly about pregnancy and childbirth, things which to her are natural, while my mother and aunts have always been ridiculously secretive, using childish euphemisms to impart news of a pregnancy: *la signora* so and so is going to *buy* a baby. In her youth, my mother and her sisters had been forbidden by their father to go to school beyond the fifth grade because classes were mixed, with boys and girls in the same room. They had been forbidden to wear sheer stockings, which revealed their legs, or lipstick or perfume, or even to cut their hair short. When they came to Canada, the first chance they had, they'd rid themselves of the old-fashioned buns they were forced to wear at the nape of their necks.

My grandmother looks at me appraisingly. "But you look well, Maria Rita. I see a sparkle in your eyes." She lowers her voice conspiratorially. "It comes to a woman when she has a secret inside her. But you can tell me — are you expecting another baby?"

"No, *Nonna*," I laugh. "Four is enough."

"Four babies is nothing," she insists. "Even I had seven, and that was few for the time. Two of them died, *figghiceddi*, my poor little ones. I had five girls and only two boys," she goes on to recount. "But your grandfather didn't mind, *bon'arma*. Other men, when they came back from the *campagna*, didn't even bother getting off their mule when they heard their wife had given birth to a girl; they turned right around and went back to the fields. When I was expecting, how he looked after my cravings!" My grandmother's face lights up and looks vibrant. "Mostly, I craved the stems of young artichokes — dipped in oil with salt and bread. I couldn't get enough of them. Your *Nonno, bon' arma*, kind soul that he was, used to bring them back for me from the mountains where they grew wild. To the little ones, he used to bring prickly pears, and figs, and persimmons when they were ripe. Remember, Giuseppina?" she asks her daughter, who nods. "How he loved his children. The poor woman across from where we lived, her husband used to beat her when she got herself in *that condition*. Remember, Giuseppina, how he used to beat her?"

My aunt nods but looks very ill at ease.

"Poor woman, *mischina* — she used to stuff *puddisinu* — parsley — inside herself to get out of *that condition*. One time it made her so sick, she almost died."

"*Mamà!*" my aunt reprimands, "why are you telling Maria Rita these things from so long ago. They aren't pleasant things to hear. Can't you talk about something else?"

"Did you say parsley?" I ask.

"Yes — *puddisinu*. It's what the women used then. Some of them had ten, twelve children and nothing to eat."

"It happens unexpectedly sometimes," my grandmother persists, "that a woman finds herself like that, *'ncinta*, without even suspecting it. The men — they don't know how to wait," she says, then draws me closer and whispers in my ear. "They can be '*na camurrìa*. Only women know patience."

I don't know the meaning of '*na camurrìa* and I ask one of my aunts, *Za* Lina, who is married to my mother's brother, *Zu* Franco, and is quite a bit younger than him. Of all my aunts, she is the most modern, I've always thought, because she reads risqué photo magazines with black-and-white pictures of actors whose spoken words are printed in balloons hovering above their heads, and because she is my only aunt who speaks some English. "*Ma*, you *no* know?" she says, surprised, gathering the fingertips of one hand together into a point, artichoke-like, in front of her chest and pumping her hand up and down in a common Sicilian gesture of disbelief. "'*Na camurrìa*," she says, laughing, "it meana a biga paina in da ass."

CHAPTER TWELVE

Summer 1986

On laundry day, separating the whites from the colours, the underthings from the rest, I find at the bottom of the hamper a shirt I'd worn on one of my meetings with Valentin. We have managed to meet every few weeks for the last two months. It is less than two weeks since I have seen him. It seems a year. Gathering the shirt into a ball, I press my face into it and inhale, hoping to discover there a trace of sweat, of cigarette smoke, of musk — that indiscernible scent I would recognize, even with my eyes closed in a room full of others, as Valentin's.

The phone rings. Leaving the clothes scattered on the bathroom floor, I rush to answer it. *"Buen día, preciosa."*

His voice in the morning is the true rising of the sun. I depend on it now. I had approached the relationship with reservations, always with the intention of fleeing before there could be any serious damage. But it's already too late. I have fallen into a trap from which there is no escape without severing a part of me, and that would be too painful. But the cage is comfortable after all.

I go about doing my housework just as before, polishing silverware that is seldom used but merely sits oxidizing in the breakfront, waxing Victor's cherished antiques — the burled side tables, the walnut dry sink, the scrolled oak escritoire. Each morning, I drift restlessly from room to room, half-heartedly making beds, picking bits of fluff off the carpeting by hand rather than vacuuming so I can hear the phone ring. I dare not leave the house to shop for fear of missing Valentin's call. All these things have become secondary.

Preciosa — he thinks me precious. *"Buen día."* I pronounce the words stiffly, self-consciously. It has been years since I've practised my university Spanish. "How's the neck?"

"Good — I'm feeling really good today." His voice holds an early morning huskiness that mellows later in the day, but never leaves it. A pleasant grating. Music played on sandpaper. It seems to encompass, as well, all the other senses; I feel as though I can touch and taste and smell and feel him through the connecting telephone wire, which has become my lifeline, the source of each day's nourishment. He always calls from home, his mother chirping in the background, oblivious to his conversation.

"Did you go to therapy this morning?"

"I went. It must be helping, I'm playing better. Coach is playing me tonight. *Our* park. I was hoping you could come and watch. We're playing the Royals, an English team."

Our park, the one where he'd christened me Margarita was *our* park now. "We're going away." My stomach lurches with the telling. I have known for a while about the holiday and worried, each time I thought of it, that this disrupting vacation would spoil our cherished routine.

"Where are you going?"

"On a holiday. Just for a week. A lodge up north in the Bruce Peninsula. It's on a small lake. We're renting a cabin there. We go there every year. The kids really like it."

"Oh." It is neither an expression of disappointment or displeasure. "When are you leaving?"

"Tomorrow. School got off yesterday, and today's my husband's last day of work. But he teaches courses in the summer, so we have to have our holidays now before he starts his classes."

"I see." He begins a distracted vocal doodling into the phone, a rhythmic *doo-doo-doing* — *sotto voce,* so only the d's click to the tempo of the beat. "Any chance I could see you tonight?"

"Tonight? I don't think I can — I have to pack — we're leaving in the morning."

"I really wanted to see you. And I had something to tell you." I feel a shiver pass through me. "What's wrong?" I press the phone, our bedroom extension, hard against my ear, but cannot mould myself into its rigid flatness; it is one of the contemporary styles with touch tone that one of Victor's classes had given him as an end-of-school gift. My eyes fall on a dark blemish on the oak strip flooring of the bedroom. Before we had moved into the house, and while it was vacant, a squirrel had found its way into the house and been unable to get out again. It had died and decomposed in front of the bedroom window, leaving a black stain that Victor, when he'd redone the floors, had sanded and sanded as much as possible without leaving a gouge. But the stain had seeped deeply, and now it remained a grim memorial preserved under three coats of urethane.

"*Tell* me Valentin, I want to know." Bad news, I remind myself, usually comes via the upstairs phone, as I'm focusing my attention on this mottled blemish; my brother's wife has miscarried in her third month; my uncle has fallen on some ice and been taken to the hospital with a broken hip; my father keeps throwing up from the chemotherapy and did I think, my mother asked, that some bay leaf tea would help? Now Valentin would tell me that he has found someone else, that this pubescent game must end, that he wouldn't be calling again. How can I exist now without hearing this voice that I've become so dependent on?

Again, he sighs. "If I weren't such a coward—"

"Valentin?"

"*Baby* — what are we going to do?"

Baby — she couldn't imagine Victor *ever* calling her that. "Valentin, what's wrong?"

"I think … I think … I've fallen in love with you."

I close my eyes, blocking out everything but the resonance of the words he has just spoken. My gaze deflects off the black spot on the oak floor to the open window where maple leaves, like open hands, are swaying gently in the summer breeze, tenderly caressing the air. My mouth gapes, wordless.

"Do you care about me?"

"I *do*. I *love* you. I really, really *do*." My words are a wonderful unloosening, my head reels as if I'm inebriated. I exhale in beatific relief. Valentin *loves* me! I am euphoric. My heart does a little dance, skipping a few beats from too much happiness. But still, I ask, almost too demandingly, "Are you sure, Valentin? About how you feel?"

"Ninety-five percent sure."

Outside the window, a sudden gust of wind sets the maple hands into a palsied trembling as I consider, ninety-five percent. "But you have doubts?"

"I just need time. It never happened to me this way before. I can't believe what I'm feeling. I really miss you." He sounds almost desperate; my heart does a gleeful somersault. "Why don't you try and make it tonight? Just for a short while?"

"I wish I could. I don't know."

"*Mom!*" Jamie has sought me out.

"Hold on a sec." I cover the mouthpiece of the receiver with one hand. "What is it, Jamie?"

"I'm thirsty. Can I have chocolate milk?

"Yes. Tell Alison to help you pour some in a glass, so you don't spill it." He scurries away happily. "Sorry," I say back into the phone.

"I wanted to ask you something else. Only if it's possible, only if you can. I can't think of anyone else to go to."

"What is it, Valentin?"

"My mother needs me to help her out with the household bills — groceries, utilities, all that stuff. But I haven't been working, so — no money coming in. And you know how long those insurance settlements take. I hate to ask, but would you be willing to lend me a thousand bucks to tide me over until my insurance claim is settled? They're threatening to turn off our hydro."

I desperately study the bits of information my brain is relaying to me in an attempt to gather together a possible solution. I do have some cash that Victor gives me to cover weekly expenses, but it rarely adds up to a thousand dollars. Shamefully, I remember Alison's confirmation money, which she has deposited for safekeeping in an account on which we are joint, since she is too young to open one in her name only. Between the two accounts, I'm sure I could manage to come up with the total amount he needs.

"Alright. I could meet you for a few minutes to give you the money. But I would have to get right back."

"Come to the fence at half-time, in about an hour. The soccer field at *our* park."

"I'll be there."

***

"Can I use the car?" The hood of the station wagon is up; peering inside, Victor is carefully examining the bowels of the engine, prodding gingerly at the greasy conglomeration of metal cylinders and rubber tubes. Joshua stands next to him, watching.

"What for?" Victor says distractedly as he unsheathes a long slender rod and wipes it with a cloth.

"I need to go to the drugstore to get some things — band-aids and Solarcaine and calamine lotion — you know — what we usually take. We're all out of that stuff."

Bending over the motor, Victor turns his head to look at me. "New top?" he asks.

"Yes, I got it for the trip to go with these capris."

"Just let me check this oil," he says, inserting the long thin rod into the motor's entrails, then extracting it and examining it with seriousness. "Oil's okay. You can take her, I guess."

"I wanna come with you," Joshua whines.

"I'm only going for an hour. Why don't you get some of your toys together for the trip?"

"I wanna *come*."

I barely hesitate in giving in to his request for fear of causing suspicion. In any case, I wasn't really expecting to spend any time with Valentin.

I go to the cash machine at the bank first and take out five hundred dollars from Alison's joint account, which, along with the housekeeping money, adds up to a thousand. At the drug store, I buy all the items I'd mentioned to Victor, plus a roll of Certs and a bag of chips for Joshua.

In the car, I turn on the radio, which is playing a song by the Eurythmics. As I half-listen to Annie Lennox singing about words of endearment coming from her lover, I replay in my head Valentin's words. *Preciosa,* he'd called me. And *Baby. I think I've fallen in love with you,* he'd said. How long have *I* been in love with him? Always, it seems. *Lovers* — we truly are *lovers*.

"Look, Joshua," I say as we drive into the park, "there's a soccer game going on here. You play soccer sometimes. Want to stop and watch for a bit? I think there's a playground on the other side too." I feel breathless from mere words. There are shouts and yells of excitement from inside the playing field, which is partly surrounded by a tall wooden fence on the side where we are parked, concealing the players. All I can see are the spectators in the top stands. I catch sight of Valentin's van in the parking lot, though. My body is shaking from just knowing I'm in close proximity to him.

"Yeah, let's watch," Joshua answers enthusiastically.

We go around to the back where there are bathrooms, a snack bar, a ticket booth, and several entrances. I realize I have to buy tickets to see Valentin and ask for two from a gray-haired woman with an extremely tight perm. "Kids are free," the woman says, handing me one ticket and change. With the leftover money, I let Joshua buy a chocolate bar. At the entrance to the stadium, someone tears my ticket and gives me the stub. We follow a passageway that consists of two triangular concrete walls that lead to the spectator stands. It is half-time. I pause to scan the benches at the edge of the field, searching for Valentin, too desperately, so that my eyes will not focus on any one player, then looking over each one more slowly, I recognize him. He sees me and comes over to the chain link fence that separates us. I hand him an envelope with the money. He squeezes my fingers through the metal. "Thanks. I really appreciate it." The whistle blows. "I gotta go. I'll call you." He releases his hold and returns to his team, the pressure on my fingers lingering deliciously.

Joshua and I walk back towards the stands. "Let's watch for a bit," I tell Joshua, "while you eat your chocolate bar." Eagerly, I take Joshua's hand and lead him into the section where I catch drifts of speech in Spanish. We take a seat high up, next to the triangular wall of concrete, so we have an unobstructed view. Entranced, my gaze locks on Valentin and follows his every move. When else can I, unknowingly, feast my eyes on him as greedily as I like?

I watch him run, bare knees high, smile, to see him pause during a break, to pull his socks up. His shorts and jersey are garnet and gray, the colour of the Barcelona club. The furious running begins again; he lowers his head slightly and bends his thick muscular neck, like a bull preparing to charge, as his forehead meets the ball straight on. More running, hopping, passing, skirmishing with a player of the opposite team. The game resembles an aggressive, accelerated ballet. I feel pride, excitement, ecstasy; he is my idol, I am his groupie.

Joshua, having finished his chocolate bar, is climbing the angled rail that follows the triangular concrete wall, straddling it, bumping his behind up and down on it as if he is riding a horse. "Joshua, get down," I warn, sliding over on the bench to where he is. "What if you fall? You'll hurt yourself." I grab him by the hand and lead him back to our spot on the bench.

"I'm hungry."

"You just finished a chocolate bar, and a bag of chips before that."

"But I'm still hungry."

A shout from the field. Something has happened; I am missing the game. I rummage in my purse and pull out the Certs. "Here," I say, ripping open the roll, "have a mint."

"I don't like that kind."

"It's all I have."

He takes the mint, grudgingly.

Goal! A roar rises from the crowd around me. Valentin's team has scored. The players run to embrace each other, on their faces, wide grins of intense pleasure. Valentin beams. The other team, retaliating, becomes more aggressive. Scores. The gray and garnet of Valentin's team intermingles with the blue and green of the other. Players jostle and block with torsos and limbs as they compete for the ball. Valentin's leg shoots out, snagging an opponent's. On the ground, the player, grasping his bent knee, writhes in pain. The remaining players of both teams disperse, back away, watch. Valentin looks on with indifference. The team trainer, a short-legged man in a yellow and black jersey, resembling a bumblebee, comes running onto the field carrying a bucket of water, which he splashes with a rag on the leg of the injured player. Meanwhile, a referee dressed in a black-and-white striped polo shirt and black shorts stands by Valentin making notes on a pad, like a policeman giving out a ticket. He hands Valentin a yellow card. From the indifference on his face, it appears Valentin feels no remorse.

A child screams. A chilling staccato burst of crying like machine gunfire. My heart contracts, my blood turns frigid. I scan the benches for Joshua. Not there. *Dear God!* I run to the rails. Joshua is lying on his stomach on the concrete floor on the other side of the wall, his head raised and streaming with blood. I leap from bench to bench, lacing through empty spaces in the crowd, veering around the triangular wall. Joshua is standing up now, still screaming. I grab him and hold him for a second to reassure him, then search desperately for the pack of Kleenex in my purse. I wipe the blood from his face in search of the source and find it: an open, inch-long gash on his right brow. Holding the Kleenex against it, I apply pressure. The tissue becomes instantly saturated with blood. My knees are rattling against each other.

"Don't worry, Joshua, Mommy's going to take you to the hospital. They'll fix your cut there. It'll be alright."

My head is swimming as we make our way back to the station wagon. I keep replacing the Kleenex with a new one that becomes instantly soaked in blood. I apply pressure, five minutes by the clock, and to my relief the bleeding slows. "Joshua, listen to me carefully. I want you to press this Kleenex hard against the cut, okay. I'm going to drive you to the hospital and the doctor will fix it all up. Press hard now," I tell him again as I start the car.

Pulling out of the parking lot, I drive quickly, keeping one eye on the road and one eye on my son. He would need stitches. Three, maybe four. I shouldn't have taken him here. Selfish. I am a selfish, negligent mother. I should not have come. No one could ever be as important to me as my children. My lover could never replace my son. Selfish, negligent, horrible mother. I will stop seeing Valentin. Only my family matters to me. I love my family. I love my son. He's being so brave, making scarcely a sound, pressing his small hand against his forehead. The hospital is only ten minutes away if I don't hit a series of red lights and, so far, they've all been green. Joshua will get stitches. He will be alright. And I will never see my lover again.

At the hospital, an amicable, fresh-faced intern with gold-rimmed glasses takes Joshua away, then brings him back a short while later. Joshua is happily sucking on a lollipop, a bandage covering his brow. In seven days, the intern tells me, I can remove the stitches myself with a pair of sterilized scissors. He's been a brave boy. The scar will be pink for a year, then turn pale and fade.

We walk back to the car. I feel light with relief. Joshua licks his lollipop. He's been brave, my son. My family is important to me. I love my family. I love my son. The cut will heal, the scar will fade. I love my lover. It wasn't his fault.

Chapter Thirteen

We leave as planned the next morning. Joshua, seemingly unaffected by his trauma, is boastful of his black eye. It took five stitches to close the wound. Five stitches will not stand in the way of our holiday, I know. My father's graver condition had not stood in the way of our holiday two years before. Victor needs his holidays; teaching is a strain. My explanation for Joshua's fall had been simple, acceptable. We had stopped at a playground; climbing on some monkey bars, Joshua had fallen. Just as in all matters regarding the kids to which I react with hysteria, Victor responds with a contrasting calm. Sometimes I want to label it indifference, but I know it isn't true. He is genuinely concerned about his children; he simply reacts to situations the way his parents have always reacted — with dignified calm. Unlike my mother, who translates every cut and bruise into a tragedy. At times, I marvel at how different Victor's upbringing has been from mine, marvel at our having come together at all.

When Victor has loaded the station wagon and we've checked all the doors of the house to make sure they are locked, everyone takes their usual place in the car: Alison and Micah in front with Victor; me in the back with the twins, who become more easily restless and demand more attention. In a duffle bag by my feet, I guard our store of snacks — potato chips, cookies, granola bars — which I will dole out as necessary to appease and soothe.

Outside of the city, the highway stretches out in front of us like an endless satin ribbon, silvery in the sun, dipping and weaving among the trees. The fields are early-summer emerald, luxuriant with leaf. On a hillside, gaggles of geese gather here and there like patches of unmelted snow lingering into spring. Daisies fill the hollows along the road and remind me of my christening — *Margarita*. Nature is beautiful. Being alive is beautiful. Surely, I have noticed all these things before, but I have no recollection of having done so. Valentin has opened my senses, allowing me to absorb everything around me more fully, as well.

Victor is what you might describe as an impatient driver, always in a hurry to reach his intended destination; woe to us when he gets stuck behind a truck. Already now, scarcely twenty miles out of the city, I can see, in the rearview mirror, his brow furrowed against a farm tractor lazily pulling a load of baled hay. "You gotta be kidding me," he erupts. "What's this clown doing on a highway." As usual, his tension transfers to me, making me nervous and apprehensive. He is impatient to pass, but it is a solid line. And it's only a two-lane highway. Victor has taken this route to avoid the cottagers heading north. Driving always seems to involve, for Victor, conflict and strategy. A road game with all the other cars the opponents. *When are we going to get to the lodge?* Jamie once asked on a previous trip, the five-hour drive unbearably long for a three-year-old. Joshua's response: *When Daddy stops chasing the cars.*

The solid line opens ahead of us like a row of stitching running down the centre of the road; Victor quickly passes, casting a dirty look at the farmer and the stiffness instantly leaves his body. The road is his. I look back. A young fellow, dressed in overalls, wearing a baseball cap, is riding high on a tractor. How proudly these farmers harvest their hay. As if it were gold, instead of humble grasses. These bales are green. Clover, maybe, or trefoil and alfalfa — hay, not straw. Hay, fresh cut, is green, straw is gold, but coarser fodder, the hollow stems of grains. Uncle Enzo, one of my mother's brothers, taught me that. He tried to be a farmer once. Didn't get far. Thought he had to do everything by hand like they did in the old country on their sparse, stony acres. Forgot this was Canada. If it was famous for nothing else, it was famous for space. You had to be careful with all that space; you could explode with it. He'd lost everything to lenders, his farm being sold under power of sale.

But I am comfortable in my small space; happy in my kitchen with my family, happy in my small radius that includes Valentin. No fear of exploding. Waiting for Valentin to call, hearing his voice. *Buen día, preciosa.* It is all I need and want. That, and our brief meetings in between. Life is bliss. Whenever I look up to see my face in the rearview mirror, I see myself smiling. A Mona Lisa smile. Enigmatic, my reasons, my own. How had this happened to me, Rita? Being in love made you religious. I could almost believe in fate, believe in a Superior Being who had ordained this. *You make your own reality,* Maddy had said. But I hadn't planned, I hadn't asked, hadn't even dreamed. Let Maddy live within her boundaries of self-inflicted destiny. My life had magic. Valentin had brought it. There was something magic in his touch. Magic? An electrical energy, at least, exuded in the coming together of — what? — our auras? Everyone is surrounded by their own particular aura, their own particular field of magnetism — Victor had explained this to me once. Victor, himself, had had a strange experience. If it had happened to anyone else except Victor, I would not have believed it: one of his students, Victor had said, experienced mild electrical shocks whenever he got close to her. Victor felt them too, something like static electricity, sharp needle pricks on the skin. Victor was baffled by it. But the shocks kept getting worse and worse, until the girl started screaming whenever he got near her. Victor had had her transferred to another class. The incident had been very upsetting for him. Such incidences are the reason he needs his holidays.

Farther north, the highway merges into another that follows the shores of Georgian Bay. The water is deep blue, almost green further out. Cottages line the shore, chalets the opposite side of the road. A mobile sign parked next to the highway advertises: *Skier Jake's. Wind Surfing Lessons. 183 days till winter. Welcome to Biff and the gang.* Winter's skiers become the windsurfers of summer. Who is Biff, I wonder? Who belongs to the gang? The skiing world, a world I had missed. The football world, the baseball world, the hockey brawling world — I was never a fan; Victor was, but mildly, during postseason play. Although I do admire the players' physical challenges — a celebration of their vibrancy. Other worlds, too, I'd missed: the pot smoking, flowers in the hair, free love, hippie world of the sixties and seventies had passed right by me. Even in the era of the miniskirt, I'd kept my dresses at a decent length, wanting to hide the ugly scar on my thigh. I had lived through it all, but it had not touched me, shielded as I was within the protective casing provided by my parents, then Victor. Not a Sleeping Beauty but asleep, nonetheless. Valentin had kissed me awake. He had placed flowers in my hair. He had re-christened me. Now I belong to Valentin. My soul belongs to him. Between Valentin and I, there exists a subtle channel of communication that goes beyond words. Victor cannot pick up my feelings and thoughts as Valentin does.

How can Victor not see my happiness? How can he not guess? Perhaps my field of magnetism differs greatly from Victor's. Even though we are husband and wife, our level of communication remains superficial. I find nothing challenging, nothing enchanting in what Victor says. Our intercourse is one dimensional. What Valentin says so often means much more than the mere words spoken, challenging me to second guess. It is a game, an exciting game, and something else — Valentin makes me laugh. Victor has never made me laugh. I try to recall a special moment in my life with Victor, a tender, sensuous moment, and can't think of one. Was that possible? Surely, I have forgotten, never having had the need to hoard, since there has never been any question of losing him.

The children begin to fidget and complain of hunger. Feeding, takes the greater part of a mother's life. The kids are, actually, being very good and patient. I open a bag of Oreo cookies and give everyone two, including Victor. "Are you getting tired driving," I ask. "Should we stop for coffee?"

"I'm fine."

I fold the top of the cookie bag and press together the wire closure strip. The scenery is changing, the colours becoming muted and monochromatic. Roughly cut granite flanks the highway; there are more evergreens, less deciduous growth. We pass a young fir tree growing sideways out of the flat face of granite. Sparsely branched and stunted, it nevertheless persists in growing in this awkward position, horizontal to the road, and perpendicular to the direction of every other tree, like an absurd arrow pointing to someplace obscure. Gravity, of course, dooms it to a short life. Yet now it is green and healthy and stubbornly thrives. There are gray-green rivers that reflect gray-green foliage, and lakes the same colour as the trees — rivers and lakes and solitude.

Surprisingly, I'm enjoying the ride. Usually, I hate long drives for fear of having an anxiety attack along the way, but I haven't had one of those in months. When did they start? Sometime after I was married. I don't recall having that fear on the lengthy ride with Victor to our honeymoon destination — Disney World. Sitting side by side, Victor had been so intent on his driving, he had not tried to hold my hand or touch me. It was as though the intimacy of the previous night had not occurred — a clumsy attempt at lovemaking for the first time. It was four in the morning by the time we had reached the hotel after the reception, showered, and gotten into bed. My virginity was more of an obstacle than I had expected. We were both exhausted and fell asleep, our marriage not officially consummated.

Along the way, an accident had held us up for two hours. We sat quietly, making polite conversation — who would have guessed we'd been married only a day.

How different it would have been with Valentin; ardent kisses along the way, furtive touching — why, he would have *had* me there on the roadside behind some bushes during the traffic snarl. Victor needed to wait — wait to reach the hotel, to have a shower, to slip into his robe. Everything planned and perfect. Not perfect the first night of our honeymoon, either, slime between my legs, unfamiliar, wet — what was all the hoopla about, anyway? *That* was sex! Our honeymoon was nothing like the romantic idyll I had envisioned.

The children are getting restless again, Joshua is whining that he needs to pee. Victor pulls over to the soft shoulder, and I walk into some tall grasses with the twins and Micah, who wanders further away from us now that he's approaching adolescence and demands his privacy. At the next gas station, we stop once more for my sake and Alison's. Victor becomes irritated whenever there are stops because it renders futile all his skillful passing. It will take another two hours of driving before we reach the lodge, where lunch awaits us. The twins are complaining that they are hungry *again*. There is still a bag of potato chips that we could share, but it would make the children thirsty and we would have to stop for a drink and then another bathroom break, which will upset Victor. The twins' whining continues. I debate for a moment, then tear open the bag.

***

A young woman lies sunning herself on a blanket spread over the stones, sand, and scrub grass in front of the cabin next to ours. I am sitting on the porch of our cabin, the one Victor rents every year, a year in advance, just as soon as our week-long holiday ends. Victor, Alison, and the boys have gone for a walk in the woods. I didn't want to go, ostensibly to read, wanting, instead, time alone to reflect on, to re-enact, and to relish every moment, every word I have ever had with Valentin. I glance up from my book to look at the girl. How lovely she is. She is staying in the cabin with an elderly couple old enough to be her grandparents. But they are her parents — I hear her address them by something that sounds like Mama and Papa, but foreign, Polish, Ukrainian, maybe. Her mother brings things out to her, sunglasses, a drink, a pillow, and rubs tanning lotion on her body as delicately as if she is oiling a newborn. An only child, possibly, spoiled, pampered. When the girl turns to lay on her back, her straw-coloured hair fans out like a shiny halo around her head. She sits up and says something to her mother: *Mama ... ja ... ida ... wade.*" Fragments of the girl's speech reach me, but the language is strange to me. She stands and stretches, her body linear, her arms pointed upward, as if she were about to dive. A white bathing suit, cut high on the hip so that the crotch is a narrow "v", exaggerates the darkness of her tan. She is a sun goddess that Valentin would adore. She rubs the back of her legs where the elastic from the bathing suit has left welts. There is a hint of fullness around the upper thighs and hips that warns of a tendency towards being overweight, later on perhaps, after she marries and has children. But right now, she is perfect. Her body sways lithely as she walks towards the lake. She is smiling — there, that smile again! The Mona Lisa smile — enigmatic, hiding a secret no one has been able to divine through the centuries: she is in love; she is with child; she is da Vinci himself, in drag. No matter, someone surely loves her, but why isn't he here now? Perhaps she has a forbidden lover. Married, perhaps — yet she is his. The girl and I are alike — our smiles are identical.

There is the sound of gravel crunching on the driveway at the back of the cabin, then the voices of the children. "Mom!" Joshua comes running towards me. "Mom — guess what we saw?" Joshua blurts out excitedly. "Some bear scats, in the forest."

"Bear what?"

"It's really poo."

"Yeah, Mom," Jamie adds, "from a grizzly."

"Not a grizzly," Micah corrects, "a brown bear." Micah is the naturalist in the family and opening the book he is holding, shows me an illustration of what looks like a variety of stubby sausages. "See. *Brown bear* — it looked like this."

"Yuck — it grossed me out," Alison says, appearing from behind the cabin with Victor following behind.

"So, stay here next time. No one forced you to come." Victor is treating the experience like a science class, and Alison wants none of it.

"Well, it was *sick*." Disgusted, she sits down on the porch steps and starts flipping through the paperback I have been reading.

"Hey, gimme that. That's adult fiction. Go read Judy Blume."

"Can I read *Forever?*"

"Certainly not."

"When can I read it, then? When I'm thirteen?"

"Older." Alison is twelve. When will I consider her old enough to escape corruption? Will what is happening between me and Valentin corrupt her? The thought makes me nauseous. "You have lots of other books, Alison. Read one of them — but later. It's dinner time. Everybody get cleaned up." I help the twins wash their hands, then we walk to the dining room, which is in the main lodge. The meal offers nothing surprising: vegetable or tomato soup, ham steak or fried chicken, Jell-O, rice pudding or apple pie — made with canned apples, I discover after the first taste. We eat too quickly and go for a walk afterwards.

"Look at this," Micah says, stooping down to pick up something at the edge of the path. "A snake!"

The other three screech.

"Don't worry, it's only a garter snake. It's not poisonous."

"Is that true, Victor?" I ask, mildly alarmed.

"That's right, it's non-venomous. There's nothing to worry about."

"Look, Mom," Micah says, holding the snake up to me. "It's really tame. And look at his eyes — see how they look kind of milky. That means it's about to shed. I read it in a book. You know what else? Male snakes have *two* penises."

"That's interesting. But I think you should let it go now — *please.*"

It is dark when we reach the cabin again. I feel giddy with the exertion, the excess oxygen, and my own happiness.

"Alright guys," Victor says, "hit the sack if you want to come fishing with me tomorrow. You have to be up by 6 a.m. Alison, you coming?"

"No, I'm staying with Mom."

"I'm still hungry," Joshua complains. Could we go for a Dairy Queen?"

"There *are* no Dairy Queens around here, dummy," Micah says.

"Is that true, Mom?"

"Don't call your brother names," I warn Micah. "But no — there are no Dairy Queens. Only raccoons and beavers and chipmunks and..." I hold my hands out in front of me and claw the air. "And ... *grr* ... *grrr* ... *grrr*-owling bears!" The twins scream, laugh, and run into the cabin.

***

At night the stillness of the lake is mesmerizing. The moon in third quarter washes everything around us with silver. The myriad stars against a dark sky seem a loosely woven veil of white lace suspended before it. I sit on a lawn chair with my bare feet up on the wooden porch rail. Victor is sitting beside me drinking a beer. I seldom drink beer, but tonight on impulse, I decide to have one too. I take small sips, noticing, with each successive sip, the bitterness more.

"Great here at night," Victor says, thoughtful. "Hal Weaver — remember him? Teaches art at the school."

I nod.

"I told him about this place and he called in April to reserve a cabin. They couldn't even give him a room in the lodge. Grinning, Victor doesn't seem particularly sympathetic to Hal Weaver's plight. He takes a long swig of beer, which he is drinking right from the bottle. "You always think I'm overdoing it, renting this place the year before. We wouldn't have it otherwise."

"Hmm." I am only half listening.

"Hey — I like your nail polish," he says, reaching over and giving my toes a tweak. "You don't usually wear nail polish on your toenails."

"I do sometimes."

He gets up, tilts his head back, and finishes the dregs of the bottle, then unexpectedly leans over and kisses me. His breath smells beery. "Let's go to bed," he says, his voice husky.

"I haven't finished my beer."

"Finish it later."

I leave the half-finished glass of beer on the porch and reluctantly follow him inside. Before getting ready for bed, I check the children's bedrooms to make sure they're all asleep. The walls are thin particleboard, psychological barriers merely.

"Don't bother with a nightgown," Victor says. The curtains are open and the moonlight filtering in etches each object in the room with a pewter lining, including Victor who is lying naked on the bed. I undress and lie down beside him. Turning towards me, he curls his legs around my thighs and kisses me more ardently than he has in some time. His breath smells very beery; he has had three bottles since supper. His beard feels rough, with a few days' growth. Unusual, since he shaves each night before bed, so he doesn't have to in the morning. But these are his holidays, he allows some slackness. I like the feel of the roughness. It feels familiar: Valentin's face scraping mine, his beard coarse and bristly. Sometimes, the day after we've been together, my chin feels gritty and dry — like it's covered with the residue of dried salt water. I inhale but cannot smell Valentin. Inhale again, eyes closed. There now, the faint smell of cigarette smoke, the muskiness. I seem to taste the slight bitterness of tobacco on my lips and I open my mouth hungrily. His fingers, like the frenzied playing of a harpist, stroke my back up and down. He clasps my buttocks with the palms of his hand, molding them like dough, while he presses his uprooted hardness against my pelvis. With one deft movement, he is inside me. He rocks me roughly back and forth. His mouth finds and suckles my nipples, sending searing sensations downward to a blossoming bud of excitement in my core. The clitoris. I've located it once or twice, mirror in hand. As if divining my thoughts, he touches me there. I feel more irritation than pleasure and push his hand away. He moves his body upward slightly, making his contact angular, persisting like this for several minutes. His mouth is moist and fringed with stubble. Valentin! I almost cry out. My thighs ache. Heat, and an unbearable pressure generate from my vulva. I feel like I'm about to explode. I press my thighs together, tightly, tightly. There is a moaning, an animal sound, foreign and frightening, coming from my own throat. I am swirling in a funnel, dropping rapidly down its eye. A flood of violent spasms, starting at my centre, flow through my body and outwards to my limbs, carrying me away. The moaning becomes distant, receding farther and farther from my consciousness. The room blurs and disappears into complete blackness.

A few seconds later, I am once again conscious of my surroundings. Hysterical, I alternate between crying and laughing, both. Victor looks terrified, which makes me cry and laugh even more, while he apprehensively strokes my shoulders with his hands and stares at me dumbfounded. I calm down finally, rubbing tears from my eyes. Victor untangles himself from me. Has he even come?

"Are you alright?" he asks meekly.

I'm not even sure how to answer, so I don't.

Victor lies quietly beside me, not daring to touch me or to say anything more until sleep, sweet as a newborn's, delivers me from his presence.

CHAPTER FOURTEEN

Early Sunday afternoon, we return from our holiday; as we unload garbage bags full of dirty clothes, pieces of driftwood, shells, stones, and other souvenirs, the telephone rings. It's my mother; she sounds distraught. "*La Nonna*" — the other day she fell and broke her hip, *mischina,* poor thing. She was using the bathroom, got dizzy and lost her balance. The doctor says it's a bad break. They had to operate and put in a metal plate.

"How is she?"

"*Grazie a Diu,* she's coming along. But she'll be in the hospital a while."

"Why didn't you call and let me know. I left you the number of the lodge."

"I didn't want to bother you. I know *Vittorio* gets annoyed. But I wondered if you could take me to see her later. She's at Saint Joseph's Hospital. Your uncle, *Zu* Franco, and *Za* Lina and I were there all day yesterday, but today he has to work overtime."

"Just a minute, I'll ask." Victor is standing next to me, suspecting something is up judging by the expression on my face. I switch from dialect to English. "My mother says my grandmother fell and broke her hip. She wants me to take her to see her at the hospital."

"What, *now*? We just got home, Rita!"

"She's eighty-nine years old, Victor. She's alone at the hospital and she doesn't speak English. Have some compassion. I'll call Sandra and see if she can babysit."

"Rita, my summer courses start tomorrow. I have to prepare for the class."

"Well, I'll go by myself, then."

"You don't even know how to get there."

My stomach lurches; he's hit a vulnerable spot alright. "I — I'll study the road map before I leave. It'll be fine if I don't have to take the highway."

"Well, I'm not gonna let you drive the Mercedes there, so you'll have to wait till I unload. And I guess that means I'll have to get the kids' supper since you haven't prepared anything…"

"There's a lasagna in the freezer," I tell him by way of appeasement.

"So, what time do you think you'll be back?" he asks petulantly, clearly annoyed.

"Visiting hours are till nine, but then I have to take my mother home."

"It's *Sunday* night. I have to get to sleep early so I'm awake to teach tomorrow."

What he really means is: it's Sunday night, another night of the week marked off for sex, and there won't be enough time devoted to that if I come home late because of my grandmother. Without sex, tomorrow he'll be grumpy and take it out on me and the kids. It's always been his MO — his *modus operandi*.

"So, I guess I'll have to get the kids to bed, too."

"Just have the twins get into their pyjamas and make sure they brush their teeth. Alison and Micah can take care of themselves."

Grumbling, he drops the bags that he's carried in from the station wagon at my feet and goes back outside for more.

"Maria Rita … Maria Rita…" My mother's voice calls anxiously from the receiver; she senses Victor's annoyance. "Never mind, Maria Rita. I'll call *Za* Caterina; she said she was going, too, with *Zu* Domenico. I'll ask her to pick me up. It's out of their way coming from the east end, but I'm sure they won't mind this once."

"No, *Mamma*, I'll take you." I give her a time when I'll pick her up and end our conversation.

Victor notices I've hung up the phone and asks, "So — what did you decide?"

"I'm driving myself."

His face takes on a sour expression, but he sees that the die is cast. "If you take the QEW, it'll be much quicker." The remark is cutting. He knows very well I won't take the highway.

"You don't have to worry yourself, I'll find my own way to the hospital." Returning to the station wagon, I pull out a road map from the glove compartment and take it back to the house, spreading it out on the kitchen table. After checking the index, I scan where my two fingers meet, finding the rectangle with the "H". I can go east on Bloor, past High Park, then south on Indian Road — that would be easy enough. It will get a bit more complicated closer to the hospital, the streets winding into each other, but I'm sure I'll eventually find it. I try to convince myself of this.

In our ensuite, I comb my hair and put on lipstick. Victor barges in, as is his habit. I am never allowed my privacy, even in the bathroom.

"So, did you decide what route you're taking?"

"Yes — I'm going to take Bloor to Indian Road. Would you please excuse me while I use the toilet."

He mumbles something as he exits the bathroom.

"What did you say?"

"It'll take you an extra half hour if you don't take the QEW."

***

On the way to my mother's, I stop at the Mac's Milk store for something to take to the hospital. I debate between a box of chocolates with hard centres and nuts or one of their pots of mums displayed outside the front of the store. My grandmother has few teeth and never having bothered with dentures, might have difficulty chewing the chocolates. I decide on the mums, picking a pot with light lilac flowers. When I get to the car, I regret having picked lilac, and go back to switch them for a pot of yellow ones that look more cheerful.

My mother is already waiting at the door when I turn into her driveway. Although I follow my planned route carefully, I get lost twice before finally managing to find the hospital. Still, I feel a satisfying sense of accomplishment, even though it has taken me forty minutes longer than it would have taken Victor to get here, ten minutes longer than he calculated. My mother, who knows my grandmother's floor and room number because she's already been here several times, aggressively leads the way. I smile watching her. It's so unusual for her, she's always followed.

At the end of a long hallway, in a semi-private room, I find *Nonna* sitting up in bed. Her face looks very pale against the white sheets, as white as the nightgown my aunt has brought her from home, along with the white flannel kerchief she always wears to bed. Instead of being wound in a bun, her yellow-tinged white braid is hanging out from one side of the kerchief and almost reaches her lap. I don't think my grandmother has ever cut her hair, at least not for as long as I have known her. There are bars on either side of her bed, like a baby's crib. By the window, *Za* Caterina sits next to her husband; my uncle looks bored, my aunt preoccupied. There is someone else in the room, an old woman, not as old as my grandmother, her gray hair cut short and flattened on one side of her head from sleeping on it. She eyes me curiously as I pass her bed to go towards my grandmother, who, having noticed me, is holding out her arms. "Maria Rita," she says, "*figghia mia.*" I embrace her and kiss the soft skin that drapes loosely, like fabric, on her face. I move aside to allow my mother to kiss her on both cheeks, then ask, loudly, because of my grandmother's hearing loss, "*Comu si senti, Nonna?* I wish I didn't have to yell so loudly and attract attention in order to ask her how she's feeling. I always feel a little self- conscious speaking our dialect in the presence of strangers.

"*Meggiu, figghia mia. A la voluntá di Diu.*" God's will. My grandmother is a trusting child. At home, the mirror of her dresser reflects the plaster statues in front of it: a Sacred Heart with gold bracelets hanging from its neck, a Saint Anthony of Padua, a Blessed Virgin. There are also several pictures of saints in gilded frames, a souvenir someone has brought back to her from Fatima, a container of holy water, and a rosary that hangs on one corner of the mirror. Twice each day, morning and evening without fail, my grandmother prays the rosary and the Litany of the Saints. When I was little and used to stay overnight, my grandmother made me pray along with her.

"I brought you some flowers," I tell my grandmother, holding the pot of mums in front of her face.

"I told Maria Rita it wasn't necessary to bring anything," my mother interjects hurriedly. My grandmother looks at them briefly, then looks away. "*Sì, grazie,*" she says quietly.

My aunt gets up from her chair. "Here, let me put those over here…" she says, "in this corner by the light. It's not good to smell the scent of flowers when you sleep."

My grandmother gives some caressing pats to the sheets around her, flattening them into smoothness. She smiles at me and takes my hand. The skin of my grandmother's hand is thin and semi-transparent, like inferior quality waxed paper, exposing the blue veins underneath. It looks as old and delicate as ancient parchment. "How are *Vittorio* and the children?" she asks.

"*Sì, tutti boni. La salutanu a vossia.*" They said to say hello. The kids anyway, although Victor hadn't said anything. "The nurses won't let the children come to visit, but Victor will come and see you as soon as he can." My grandmother used to take special care in dressing when Victor would come to the family gatherings while we were dating. She admired his fair skin, his milk-white hands and long fingers. But most of all she complimented his ears — he had the cleanest, tidiest looking ears she'd ever seen on anyone, she exclaimed. *Arichhi puliti.* I'm actually not so sure that Victor will come before she leaves the hospital, now that he's teaching summer school. "How long did the doctor say you would be in the hospital?" I ask.

My grandmother strokes the back of her hand under her chin in a Sicilian gesture of bafflement. "*Ma, nun sacciu.* Old bones mend more slowly."

"Two weeks, maybe three," *Za* Caterina fills in.

"They *say* that," says my grandmother, "but then they make you stay longer, much longer. Ask *la signora* next to me. She's been here two months. *Signora*, this is my granddaughter, Maria Rita. Her husband is a high school teacher. She has four children, two are twins." My grandmother mixes dialect with a few words in formal Italian with the elderly woman who is her roommate.

"*Piacere*," the woman says, reaching out to shake my hand. After exchanging a few words with me in Italian, she seems to sense my discomfort and switches to English.

"You speak English so well," I tell her, surprised.

"I've been living here since I was sixteen. I came to Canada with my parents in 1926. I learned to speak English in the basement of the church near where we lived. Nobody else cared to teach the immigrants to speak English then." She pauses to lick her lips, which are coated with a film of white that's clumped at each corner. "It was the Evangelist church we went to. My father said, 'What difference what church you sit in to praise God.' So, we all changed to Protestant. My brother, God rest his soul — oh, he was a handsome, intelligent boy — went to university and studied theology. Then he became a minister and taught the gospel of Our Lord in his own church until he died four years ago, may he rest in peace." Her words pour out urgently, as though speaking is something she is seldom permitted to do and it feels good, like stretching a limb that is stiff from inactivity.

"I'm very sorry about your brother," I say.

"Poor *signora*. She's having a terrible time with her stomach," my grandmother explains, not realizing she is changing the subject.

"Colitis," the woman says, returning the conversation to English. "I've had it for years — awfully painful sometimes. But now they think they have it under control, thanks to Jesus Christ, Our Lord and Saviour who died for our sins."

"I'm glad to hear that," I say. I wonder how I can return to my grandmother without seeming rude.

"Maria Rita," my aunt calls, as though reading my mind, "come and sit a while in the chair. I've been sitting too long." My uncle has already given up his chair to my mother. I accept the offer but not because I feel like sitting. My mother, aunt, and uncle talk reassuringly of others who have suffered the same or similar misfortunes as my grandmother, and how well they have mended. My grandmother, only half hearing the conversation, rests against the pillow with her eyes closed. Both sight and hearing have diminished for my grandmother over the last few years. I always have to raise my voice to speak to her and when I look in her eyes, I can see a milky circle around her pupils indicating the progression of cataracts. My grandmother's head slumps forward and she nods off for a while, her snoring sounding like loud huffing, like she is blowing out a hundred birthday candles. When she wakes up a few minutes later, she seems startled to find herself here, surprised perhaps to find she is still *alive*.

"Should we go and let *Nonna* sleep, *Mamma?*" I ask.

"*Sì, ammunì.*" She approaches my grandmother. "*Mamà,*" my mother says more loudly, using the more antiquated version for "mother", "Maria Rita has to get back to the children." She too betrays an eagerness to escape the pernicious smell of urine and antiseptic, a smell that would pervade no matter how many times the floor was washed or the beds changed, no matter who else used the room. I embrace my grandmother as before, kiss my aunt on both cheeks and my uncle as well, as does my mother.

I stop at the next bed on my way out of the room. "Goodbye," I say, offering my hand. The old woman sits up to take my hand; she clutches it tightly and won't let go. "I told your *Nonna*, she's so blessed to have grandchildren. It wasn't in the Good Lord's plans that my husband and I should have children. Now I'm all alone ... no husband, no grandchildren, no brothers and sisters ... I'm all alone. Except for my nephew, my dead sister's boy. He's looking for a nice senior citizens' residence for me to go and stay as soon as I leave here. He says there's some very nice ones — senior citizens' residences." She flourishes the words *senior citizens' residence* proudly, optimistically, as though she hopes it might be like a resort. She holds my hand tightly still. "I sold my house, you know. The people are going to be moving in in October, so I'm going to move out in September. That's when I'm going to the senior citizens' residence, except I don't know which one it will be until my nephew finishes looking around. It's going to be nice there, he says. They have good meals so I don't have to worry about getting my own supper. That's all I really care about, that I won't be all alone and that somebody gives me something to eat." She stops talking to catch her breath. Her lips are white and crusty from dryness. "I can't expect any visitors," she says thoughtfully, "my family all dead, my friends all gone, no grandchildren..."

"I can come and visit if you like," I say, looking for a way to escape, my hand getting cramped from extending it, but also genuinely feeling sorry for the woman and meaning it.

"Bless you, dear, I would like that. Only I don't know which senior citizens' residence it will be yet. My nephew is looking around. Soon I'll know."

"You can give me the name the next time I come to visit," I say.

"Yes, I can do that. God bless you, dear." I slide my hand out of the old woman's grasp and wave to my grandmother who smiles back weakly, as though she is very tired and wants only to sleep.

CHAPTER FIFTEEN

We had agreed to meet downtown, in front of the apartment of a friend of Valentin's. His friend was away for several weeks and he asked Valentin if he would water his plants. Valentin is working again at Santini's, but only part-time, and today is his day off. I have taken the subway, since I wouldn't have a clue how to negotiate the station wagon on these confusing streets, many of them one way. Not wanting to be conspicuous, I stand next to a bus stop fearful that if I linger around the doorway, I might be mistaken for a hooker, since the apartment is in a "bad" part of town, and I've already noticed several men casting glances my way. It is the first time Valentin and I will be alone together in a completely private setting. Until now our passionate joinings have been clandestine and brief, and very intermittent. I have taken great care with my makeup and in picking out what I would wear: a short pink skirt and a white off-the-shoulder peasant blouse that imparts a continental look. My hair is clean and shiny, my eyebrows evenly plucked, my legs and underarms smooth shaven. It is too warm for pantyhose and my open-toed, slingback sandals display my polished toenails very nicely. Yesterday, in the feminine hygiene section of the drug store, I spent twenty minutes examining douches, vaginal suppositories, feminine deodorant sprays. There were no products, I noticed, manufactured for personal *masculine* hygiene. Didn't men smell? I decided on a floral scented douche and paid for it self-consciously at the checkout counter, thinking the salesclerk was making assumptions.

It is five minutes to twelve. I am to meet Valentin here at noon. The sidewalk flows with people moving at lunch hour pace — professionals with suits and briefcases, students with backpacks and blue jeans.

At five after twelve, I catch sight in the distance of someone tall and slender with a full, wavy head of hair. Valentin materializes among the crowd, an illusory figure at first with the dubious aura of an oasis, becoming more substantial with each successive stride.

He has also dressed up for our meeting; he is wearing a black-and-white, long-sleeved shirt that I have never seen before and black slacks. He walks with a certain pride, a certain disdain of the world around him. As though he *mocked* it. As though he understood it better than anybody else, so it could not touch him like it could them. He greets me curtly, almost with indifference. "Come on," he says, beckoning with his head for me to follow.

In the elevator, we stand in opposite corners, like strangers. I begin to feel uncomfortable. Was this the same Valentin who two weeks ago was declaring his love? While unlocking the apartment door, Valentin pauses, perhaps noticing my uneasiness, to give me a quick kiss.

The apartment is full of plants. Valentin hadn't lied. They are well cared for, lush and green: spider plants and ferns, a Ficus Benjamina, at least a dozen African violets along the windowsill, a long trailing heart-shaped philodendron, an enormous rubber tree. I look around the apartment; disregarding the plants, this is a true bachelor pad without a bedroom. The couch is a low, triple folding foam mattress that opens up into a bed. My parents had one like it in the basement rec room, and once during our courtship, when there was an unexpected snowstorm, Victor had stayed overnight and slept on it, the basement being a safe distance from my own bedroom.

"Have a seat," Valentin tells me, gesturing towards the couch that is, at this moment, still folded together as a couch. "There's some wine in the fridge. Can I get you a glass?"

"Half a glass."

Valentin soon returns, bearing two plastic juice glasses, one stamped with an orange and one with a tomato. "Sorry, no wine glasses — these are all I could find."

I accept the tomato juice glass and think how wonderful it would be to have only this tiny apartment with a couch to sleep on, and juice glasses for wine, and Valentin.

"Should we order something to go with this? I haven't had lunch. A pizza?"

"If you like."

"Pepperoni okay?"

"Sure," I answer, sipping my wine." It tastes slightly vinegary. While Valentin leafs through the Yellow Pages in search of a nearby pizzeria, I walk around inspecting the apartment more closely. It is sparsely furnished; besides the plants and the couch, there is only a knock-down dresser, a metal shelf holding a record player, and, in the dining area, a red Arborite table with four matching vinyl and chrome chairs. The kitchen is a tiny narrow corridor in which Valentin, who is on the phone placing the pizza order, is taking up most of the room. I deposit my purse on the kitchen counter and head towards the balcony door in order to see the city. The apartment is on the twenty-third floor, and from the balcony there is a view of Lake Ontario, the water gray-blue and a bruised purple further out where billowy cumulus clouds block the sun. Below, toy houses with rectangles of green, patches of black asphalt, and Dinky Toy cars. I feel Valentin's body suddenly beside me, and I catch the freshly laundered lemon scent of his shirt? "Great view," I tell him. "Your friend has a nice apartment."

There is a cooling breeze this high up, but Valentin's body radiates heat. Proximity to him always involves a magnetic attraction, a drawing towards, like lying under the warm rays of a sun that surrounds you with its warmth. He slides his hand under my hair and gently massages the back of my neck.

"Is there more wine?" I ask. My voice is slightly tremulous, betraying my nervousness. Hadn't I agreed to come? Hadn't I come willingly?

"Sure. I'll get you more." He returns from the kitchen with a bottle and refills both glasses. "Come inside," he says, "and I'll put on some music." He flips through a pile of albums, choosing one. The music is surprisingly *uncontemporary,* a bouncy Argentinian tango. "Dance?" he asks, reaching for my hand.

I had taken ballroom dancing in university as part of the gymnastic program and vaguely remember a few tango steps. Our instructor was a pompous, gray-haired gentleman with halitosis and a grip of steel, whose commanding jerk of hand would, without fail, produce the desired steps from any student.

Valentin pauses with comic seriousness to get himself into dancing position. Joining cheeks and stretching arms out in front of us, we slink across the room. An abrupt halt, a switching of cheek, and we slink back in the other direction. I laugh, our cheeks vibrating against each other's, making me laugh even louder. Losing track of the steps momentarily, I step on Valentin's foot with the heel of my sandal.

"*Ahoo! Eeeh!* You broke my foot." He bends over clutching his foot, exaggerating his cries of pain.

"I did not, you phony."

He grins and puts on another record, an arrangement of classic guitars, castanets, and other percussion instruments I'm not familiar with. He straightens up, assuming a serious intensity and stamps his feet, his head held high, his arms reaching upward, his fingers snapping in mock clacking of virtual castanets. How handsome he looks: young, slender, vibrant. The ultimate Latin lover. I watch him, spellbound, the way I might watch on a dance floor the partner of another, amazed that he is mine before I can even covet him.

The next song he puts on is a slow one. He reaches for me and I encircle his neck with my arms. His neck is thick and muscular, a *toro's* neck, his shoulders are broad. His hands slide down my back and press me hard against him. His pelvis digs into my hip bones and I feel a fullness there. He lifts my chin gently and looks solemnly into my eyes. "I've never felt this way about anybody," he says simply, seriously, then kisses me meaningfully. Without formality, he guides me over to the couch and unfolds it into a bed, as I stand to the side and watch timidly, as if we've never been intimate prior to this. Then he comes back and takes me by the hand.

I resist. "I want it dark," I say. "I have scars that I don't want you to see." We've never made love in such an open, brightly lit space before. "I don't have a perfect body."

"Who does?"

"I look much better with my clothes on."

"That's for me to judge." He sits me down on the mattress next to him and kisses me — soft, tender kisses, no passion to them, no demands, just kindness — for an unrushed length of time. I feel a throbbing between my thighs, liquid heat. "If it makes you feel better, I'll close my eyes." Eyes closed, he undresses me very slowly, by touch alone, savoring the relenting of each button, and when I am completely naked, he removes his clothes too. Lying me on my back, he lays his head on my chest and I can feel the soft pillow of his hair against my breasts, then he turns his head and, eyes still closed, seeks out a nipple, finding it, and suckles eagerly as a sightless newborn. His mouth moves down along my body, unhurried until he reaches the ropey keloids of my inner thigh, but still he does not open his eyes, merely follows their ragged route, gently, with his tongue, to my swollen *womanhood*. He moves up, and when our bodies come together, I feel a trembling, and in my state of wonderment, think it must surely be me, but it is him. There is a warm wetness between my thighs, and although I am breathless and my nerve endings are exquisitely sensitive, everything comes to an abrupt halt.

Valentin detaches himself from me and looks away, his eyes open, but hooded by heavy lids, the furrows on his brow and the set of his jaw revealing dissatisfaction. "I was too fast," he says.

"It doesn't matter. Really. I just want to be with you. I don't care about that."

"We can try again in a while," he promises.

"Honestly, I don't care."

He comes back to the bed, both of us feeling more relaxed. Self-conscious now that he has opened his eyes, I position my arms to cover as much of me as possible.

"Don't cover yourself," he tells me. "I want to look at you. You have a beautiful body."

I *was*, actually, more fit than I'd ever been. But I'd had four children, after all. "I suppose you haven't noticed my surgical scars, and stretch marks, and varicose veins."

"That doesn't make you less beautiful. It just means it's something you've survived."

I snicker to myself and wonder whether he made that up or heard it somewhere — it sounded too smooth. Perhaps he considered it mere etiquette to compliment the women he bedded. Has he told each of *them* he loves them just to be polite? I look over at him, seeing his body really for the first time, his legs spread unselfconsciously, his genitals unabashedly exposed, meek looking now.

Getting up, Valentin makes his way to the bathroom. Black hair covers most of his body. His chest, his abdomen, his neck, arms and legs are covered with a dark layer of fur, making his nudity less blatant, concealing, almost modestly, the private parts of him. I grab his shirt, which is lying across the arm of the couch, and put it on; it covers me down to my thighs. Valentin has left the bathroom door open and I can see him urinating into the toilet in a long golden stream. Previously, when we entered the apartment, he'd use the bathroom and discreetly closed the door. Sex, it seems, renders impersonal all other bodily functions. But I retain my modesty, and when Valentin exits the bathroom, I slip inside, closing the door behind me.

The doorbell rings. I hear the apartment door open, then shut.

"Pizza man!" Valentin flings open the bathroom door as I'm washing my hands and grabs me around the knees, making my legs buckle and my body collapse across one of his shoulders. I shriek. In the vanity mirror, I see a happy, jubilant, youthful face I barely recognize as mine.

Carrying me into the dining room, Valentin deposits me into one of the kitchen chairs. The smell of cheese and tomato and cardboard leaks out from the closed carton; it billows warmly out as Valentin flips open the lid. He rips a triangle from the circle, breaking the stretchy filaments of cheese with his fingers, and he hands it to me, then detaches another triangle for himself. "Listen," he says, "I forgot my money in the truck, so I had to take some from your purse. The pizza was nine dollars."

I try to hide my surprise that he has taken money from my purse without asking. But I *was* practically naked in the bathroom, after all. Unfortunately, ten dollars was all I had, plus a few subway tokens; I planned to use the money to pay the babysitter, a young girl from our street whom I'd asked to stay with the kids who were home for the afternoon, since it was a teachers' professional development day, but I could owe her, and pay her tomorrow. Problem solved. Yet, Valentin going into my purse without my knowing somewhat disconcerts me. My concern disappears the minute I bite into the pizza. Maddy must have been right about sex expending calories. I devour the pizza slice as if I hadn't eaten in days. Valentin wolfs down three pieces in the same period of time it takes me to eat one, but he takes his focus away from eating long enough to notice what I have on. "You're wearing my shirt."

I am wearing it, unbuttoned, and demurely pull the two ends together in the front.

"You're always covering yourself." Wiping his hands on a napkin, he spreads the shirt open, exposing my breasts. "They're nice," he says.

I quickly cover myself again. "They're flabby. Nursing four kids does that. I'm sure you've had better." Looking at Valentin earnestly, I ask, "Will you promise me something?"

"What?"

"When there's someone else, you'll end it with me."

"Why?"

"Because that's the way I want it."

"*You* have someone else."

"I have no choice. Would you have me leave my husband and risk losing my children to be with you?"

"What am I supposed to do with my weekends if I can't see you? You can't expect me to stay home every Saturday night. Are you saying I can't even go out with friends, go to a movie, or something."

"Girls included?"

"Well, if they happen to be in the group."

"I suppose. But if it turns serious — *intimate*, I mean, we have to end it. Will you promise me that?"

"Alright."

I swallow the last bit of pizza crust and find it tasteless. Without knowing why, I feel annoyance. "It's really not hard to come to this, is it?"

"Come to what?"

"Come to *this*. To make love with someone else, someone new. There always seemed to be such mystery attached to it. But it's really no different than any other physical contact, really, is it? No different than patting someone on the back or shaking hands."

Valentin looks at me, puzzled, and reaches for a cigarette. He lights it and looks at me questioningly.

"I mean, it's the first time we've really been alone together, and you're already making plans to take someone else to a movie. And you haven't mentioned again that you ... *love* me," I add, more softly.

"Geez, what is it with women?" he says, exhaling smoke from his nostrils. "You always have to have proof. You always have to be told. I'm with *you*, aren't I? I haven't *been* with anybody else since I met you. Does that make you feel better? Sometimes a friend of mine and his girlfriend ask me to join them and the girl sometimes brings a friend along so we're a foursome, but she's not my girlfriend."

"What about the last girl you were going out with, why did you break up?"

"A lot of reasons. She had problems … she was … *frigid*."

Frigid. The word always makes me think of an icebox. It was a word I had never really considered. Victor, in all our years of marriage, had never complained about my lack of response; he had never called me *frigid*. Was a woman only frigid when a man felt inadequate? I try not to think about the night at the lodge with Victor; it made me feel unfaithful to Valentin.

"She was frigid," Valentin repeats, taking another puff of his cigarette. "Always giving me instructions — do this, do that, touch here, not so hard — I mean if someone has to tell you what to do…" He gives me one of those puzzle pieces look, trying to guess what's going on in my head. "Alright," he says, "is this what you want? *I love you, I love you, I love you*. There."

It sounds funny, and forced, and insincere. But I love hearing it just the same. He leans over and kisses me, his lips tasting at first of pizza, then becoming warm and passionate and electrically charged. Before I know it, we are lying again on the couch that is also a bed. And he is inside me, and I want him, desperately. He pumps slowly, once, twice. Almost immediately, he arches his back, takes ragged breaths, releases air through his teeth, hissing. I move ineffectually against his limpness, then stop.

"Did you get anything?" he asks anxiously.

"*Yes* — oh yes, Valentin, it was wonderful." We lay quietly together, clasping one another. With my fingers, I stroke his curls, his head between my breasts.

CHAPTER SIXTEEN

The house, when I get home, holds a veil of irreality —
familiar, yet with the foreignness one might feel returning
after a long trip abroad. I dismiss the babysitter with an
apology and a promise to pay her tomorrow. In a semi-
suspended state of consciousness, I respond to my children's
demands: a glass of juice, an empty bottle for bugs, help tying
up running shoes, and in between, I prepare supper. Even
though I've changed my clothes, when the air stirs around me
as I move, I smell Valentin; my body smells of him. I rub my
chin against my shoulder and inhale a lingering muskiness.
We have never been as intimate with each other as today.

Despite my lapses of attention at the dinner table, Victor
doesn't notice any change in me. He hasn't noticed any
changes whatsoever in the last few months, or at least has not
mentioned noticing any. Yet my life has done a complete
turnabout, so that even I am not sure anymore *who* I am.

When dinner is over, the rest of the family goes
outside. Victor is going to cut the grass, and I have not
bothered to ask Alison for help with the dishes as I
sometimes do. I much prefer to be left alone in the kitchen
with my thoughts uninterrupted. There aren't many
dishes, and only one roasting pan, and I'm soon done
stacking them in the dishwasher. I move into the family
room to pick up cushions and toys and comics the kids

have left on the floor. Through the sliding doors that look out into the backyard, I can see Alison up in the tree house Victor built years ago in the Norwegian maple; she is reading a book that has my approval. It is just after Labour Day, but the leaves of the trees are already tipped with yellow. At the foot of the maple, Micah is raking together grass clippings and gathering them into a green garbage bag. I can hear the droning of the lawn mower but cannot see Victor, who is mowing at the far side of the yard. The droning becomes louder as he comes closer to the family room door. Victor's reflection appears in the double panes of the sliding doors as he works. His gray, pallid image moves slowly and deliberately, scanning the surrounding lawn in search of obstructing objects that the children have left lying around. His reflection seems immaterial, a ghost locked between two panes of glass. One of Dickinson's ghosts, there to haunt and reproach me. He had told me once, in the first few months of our marriage, when we were getting to know each other better, that his parents had never been very demonstrative towards him as a child, never hugged him; he never once recalled either of them kissing him. Was that possible? Perhaps that was the reason for the hardness that often enveloped him, the vitriol that sometimes erupted unexpectedly. Knowing that, I had tried to show him more tenderness, tried somehow to compensate. Though not lately.

For months now, I have been piling new experiences and feelings and hopes and joys that exclude him. At night, lying beside Victor, I am careful to leave a space in the middle of the bed so we do not touch. Our marriage bond has become each day more tenuous, while the attachment that links me to my lover, like an umbilical cord, strengthens and pulses with life.

Joshua and Jamie flit into wavery view in the glass of the family room door. In mock aggression, they start pushing and shoving each other. The unexpected force of a shove flings one of them hard against the glass with a startling *smack*, like a bird flying into the window. The blow banishes the ghost. The boys regain their balance and once more take up their playful conflict, shouting raucously.

My children are *real*. Yelling reprimands at the twins, Victor comes into view directly in front of the doors where he stoops to pick up some twigs. He, *too,* is real. Micah picking up clippings and Alison up in the tree house — all *real*. Only Valentin is unsubstantial, a memory, his voice, his touch unreal, a figment of my imagination. I dreamed him up, *dreamed* up this whole messy set of circumstances. *You make your own reality.* Maddy was right! This wasn't just about my life, but my children's lives. What chaos I could bring on them! I curse myself for having relented. How boldly he bragged about his women, his loss of innocence at thirteen. God only knew what debauchery there had been in his life. *You can't expect me to stay home every Saturday night.* Damn! Damn! Damn! What have I been so happy about? He could be with some other woman this very minute, not even thinking of me. Suddenly, I regret ever having met him, ever having spoken to him, touched him, made love with him. He didn't make love, he *took* love. But I was the one who allowed it.

During the night my sleep is fitful, filled with bizarre dreams of Valentin that fuel my anger even as I sleep. Exhausted, irritated, and confused the next morning, I resolve never to see him again. All of Saturday and Sunday, I continue stoking my anger so that on Monday morning when Valentin calls, my fury still flames. It is further heightened by his detached conversation (our Friday meeting never happened, it would seem), and his obvious nonchalance as he relates the events of his weekend: Saturday night, a movie.

"Which one?"

"*An Officer and a Gentleman.*"

"Who did you go with?"

"A friend. Someone I play soccer with."

Liar! Two guys wouldn't be caught dead together at that movie — a tearjerker romance I'd gone to see with Victor.

"Really. What else did you do?"

"Went to a bar, had a few drinks." He changes the subject. "You know, I'm going to be playing—"

I stop him abruptly in mid-speech. "I really don't *mean* anything to you, Valentin, do I? You're perfectly happy to be with someone else."

He doesn't answer, doesn't defend himself.

"Maybe it's better," I say quietly, but resolutely, my voice modulated and controlled, "that we don't see each other anymore, that you stop calling altogether." I am surprised at my calmness. It was what I'd decided I'd say the night before, but my calm, unflustered delivery pleases me.

He asks no questions, is wordless for a moment, then angry. "Alright, if that's what you want."

With a terse goodbye, we end the conversation.

***

Retribution offers relief for scarcely a day. I panic over what I've done the night before. My irritability falls heavily on my children when they get home from school. I shriek at them, order the twins to their rooms, reprimand the older two for not having started their homework. Frustrated, I post myself in the kitchen, close to the phone, as I fight off my frenzy with work, wiping the grimy ridges of cupboard doors — something I've meant to do for weeks — scrubbing burned grease off stove elements, getting down on my knees to scrub every inch and every hidden corner of my kitchen floor, all the while listening desperately for the phone, although I made my bed and should expect nothing.

Alison comes into the kitchen looking very upset. "Mom, I think I broke Dad's stereo."

"What do you mean broke?"

"Well, it's turning, but the needle won't go down and there's no sound. Dad is going to be mad."

"Why didn't you call me to turn it on for you?"

"I don't know. I didn't mean to break it." She starts to cry.

"Oh, stop it." Annoyed, I go into the family room and examine the stereo, which is revolving soundlessly with the needle suspended over the record. I press the power button, turn some knobs, move levers back and forth, but still can't get it to descend. Finally, deciding I might be doing more harm than good, I switch the turntable off and leave it. "I can't fix it," I tell Alison harshly.

Fresh tears quiver in her eyes. "I just wanted to play Megan's album. She lent it to me but only for a day. Dad's going to kill me. I wish I'd never touched the stupid stereo."

"It's too late now. You should have thought of that before you touched it. We have to think of the consequences before we do something." I was hating the sound of my own voice. A throbbing headache pounds in my temple. Passing by the mirror in the hall I am shocked to see myself in it. Where is that sparkle everyone claimed they saw in me lately? My skin is chalky; there are ink-blue splotches under my eyes. My face looks fallen, as if my facial muscles have degenerated. I look *old*. In the mirror I see my own death, and only Valentin can save me.

***

Valentin is not at the store when I call. "Please, do you know where he is? I have to talk to him." I'm put on hold for what seems hours but is actually a few minutes.

"He's in the cutting room. Here's the number."

I scribble it down quickly and repeat it to her to make sure I've got it right. "Thank you." Blessed woman. Kind woman. Compassionate woman — who had recognized my desperation and pitied me. When I dial the number, Valentin himself answers. "It's me," I say. Silence. He doesn't know who *me* is. "It's Rita."

"Oh." An exhalation of surprise. "How did you get this number?"

"One of the clerks in the store gave it to me. I wanted to see how you were."

"What do you care?"

"I do. I do care, Valentin."

"You said you didn't want to see me anymore."

"I didn't mean it."

Silence.

"Are you angry at me?"

He exhales — a long, drawn out sigh into the phone. "Look, it's just, if you don't trust me, what's the use?"

"I'm sorry. I'll trust you. I won't ask questions."

Silence.

"Say something, Valentin."

"I don't know. Is there any point to this, to us?"

"Now you? In the beginning it was *me* fighting this so hard. Once, I asked you the very same thing, what's the point? Do you remember what you said?"

"No."

"You said, 'There isn't always a pot of gold at the end of the rainbow, but we can still have something nice together.' It was such a lovely thing for you to say."

He sighed. "Have you been happy with me?"

"Yes — happier than I've been in my whole life."

Silence. No breathing, no sighing. At the other end of the line, nothing — a stifling of sound. A faint choking deep in the throat. Swallowing. Swallowing again. In my own throat I feel constriction. I want to be there, to hold him, to comfort him, to have him hold and comfort me.

He pauses, it seems, to get back control before speaking. "I feel close to you. You feel like you're part of me. I never felt that way with anybody before."

I close my eyes, absorbing his words like a benediction. Face to face, he would never have been able to say them.

"I feel that way, too. When I'm with you, I feel it's where I should be, that this was all meant to be, somehow. I know I'm not what you want, and maybe you're not what I want, but in some ways, in the deep down, important ways, we're exactly right for each other. It's as though we're two pieces of a puzzle that fit together perfectly but none of the rest of the pieces in the puzzle fit. But I don't want it to end, Valentin."

"Look — we can agree to have something nice together, if you want, but we can't go *crazy*."

He sounds old, wise. "Alright, Valentin, I promise." But I know it's too late. My life has already passed the parameters of sanity. Having tasted the impossible bitterness of ending the relationship, I would promise anything.

Chapter Seventeen

Fall 1986

I'm still not comfortable with driving downtown, so Valentin picks me up at the subway. "You're all dressed up," he says, smiling, seeing me in a dress for the first time. It is a burgundy chiffon with long sleeves and a jewel-studded belt, an outfit that is certainly too formal for a casual lunch. It is November 3rd, Valentin's birthday, the first time that we are seeing each other since the reconciliation. We have come to celebrate both.

"It's a special occasion. I wanted to dress up for you."

"I look like a bum."

"I love the way you look." He's wearing simple blue jeans and a black polo shirt with short sleeves that bulge at the upper arms and has a V-neck cut low enough to reveal the curly black hair of his chest. He reaches for my hand as soon as I am seated in the van, and instantly there is a tangible electricity transmitted between us. If all we ever did was hold hands, I would be happy enough. He has chosen a Spanish restaurant for us, *El Flamenco,* that serves authentic Catalán cuisine and is owned by a friend of his. I take Valentin's suggestions and try colourful chicken and seafood paella and beefy *empanadas* for the first time. For dessert he orders caramelized crème brûlée with *dulce de leche* on the side; it's creamy but crunchy on the top, and the *dulce de leche* is caramelly and delicious. On our shortened European holiday, we had wandered through the cobblestone streets along the harbour of Barcelona. To my disappointment, Victor had eschewed local cuisine and would only dine at steak and potatoes style restaurants, so I never had the opportunity to try local Spanish fare.

Valentin holds my hand across the table through most of the meal, occasionally glancing around apprehensively. "What's the matter?" I ask, seeing how ill at ease he looks.

"Maybe we shouldn't have come here. Somebody might see us."

"You've never worried about it before," I point out. For a brief second, I wonder if he's worried about me or himself. "Anyway, I don't know anybody. I'm invisible. I've been invisible for most of my life. Except to you."

He takes my hand and kisses my fingertips. When he releases it, I dig into my purse and hand him the present and schmaltzy birthday card I have gotten him. He opens the present, a pen inscribed with his name, and reads the card, kissing me afterwards to thank me. "Something else we have to celebrate," he tells me. "I got a second job at Talbot Meat Packers. I need the money. Part time at Santini's isn't cutting it."

Even though I've just eaten, an uncomfortable feeling, like hunger, stirs unpleasantly in my stomach. To me, this news translates to no regular morning call, no looking forward to the uplifting sound of his voice. I stare at our hands resting on the table, mine in his. His hands aren't terribly large for a man. Even so, my hand is dwarfed by his — he covers it, protectively. The waitress brings the cheque and I grab it quickly, just in case he makes any effort to pay. "It's your birthday," I say.

***

We walk languidly back to his van, my hunger satisfied, but not my desire for him. We drive to *our* park and get out to take a short walk, following the path we took the first time. "We should make a pact," I tell him. "Agree to meet at this park each year on your birthday, no matter what, even if you marry someone else. Like the movie, *Same Time, Next Year*." Surprisingly, he tells me he's seen it. "Do you agree? Even if you have to take a day off work?"

"*Sí, mi amor*. And you, even if you have to desert your family."

"Yes. For just one day. For the rest of our lives."

"Even if we have to come in wheelchairs."

"Or with white canes and seeing eye dogs. Do you promise, Valentin?"

"Promise."

I smile at him, satisfied that I've neatly arranged the rest of our lives. When we reach the van, he makes love to me in the spot where we're parked, with people passing by just feet away from us on the other side of the padded metal. We lie in each other's arms, reluctant to return to our other lives. Pensive, a satisfied languidness easing his expression, he tells me, "You come so fast, I can't believe it."

I look away from him.

"Don't be embarrassed — it's nice. It's important to a man — being able to give his woman pleasure."

"I get pleasure just by being with you, just by holding your hand or kissing you."

He chews his bottom lip thoughtfully. "Maybe … someday … we could live together, if you wanted to."

I smile in amusement, taking his proposal lightly, in the manner in which it was intended. Yet his words delight me;

my face flushes with happiness. "And how long," I ask, "would this hypothetical arrangement last? Hypothetical means—"

"I know — made up. Not sure. Years maybe. Or forever."

"Do you believe in destiny, Valentin?"

"Maybe."

"I'm not sure if I do. I know that I don't believe in all the religious stuff they taught us at my convent school. Or one Superior Being, or life after *this*. What do you believe?"

He pauses before answering, his eyes unfocused and far away, someplace regrettable. "I think when it's over, it's over."

"So, you don't believe in God."

"Well — that's different. I mean you *have* to believe in God. It wouldn't be respectful not to. It would be like not believing in your parents or your grandmother."

I laugh and plant a sideways kiss on his lips.

"But, if I'm wrong," he says, gently stroking my shoulder, "and if I get a chance to live another life after this one — reincarnation or something — I hope I meet you again. Before anyone else comes along, so we'd both be *pure*. Of course, I'd have to be thirteen years old," he says with his snort-laugh.

"Your problem," I tell him, "is that you live modern, but think old-fashioned."

He responds with another snort-laugh, then yawns. "We'd better get going before I fall asleep."

Valentin drops me off at the subway and accompanies me inside, holding my hand as I pass through the turnstile to the other side. Then, squeezing hard, he releases me, leaving a delightful tingle on my fingers that lasts until I descend the steps to the trains. For a moment I am bewildered, uncertain whether I am on the right platform. In a subway, direction is always ambiguous. I catch sight of a sign that says *westbound* and relax. Once, I hated the subway, the confinement it imposed with its claustrophobic tunnels. Always, I was afraid that I would miss my stop, or that I wouldn't be able to get through the crowd to reach the door before the whistle blew, anticipation forcing me to get up too early to stand in front of the doorway, only to find when the door opened, that I was facing the wrong side. But I'm enjoying it today, looking at the intermittent views as the subway car escapes from the dark tunnels, studying the passengers — all fascinating to me — who sidle in and out the doors.

I've taken a seat in a remote corner, wanting to preserve the pleasure from my recent meeting with Valentin, afraid it might evanesce from my body if I sit too close to anybody else. It is quiet still on the subway; the after-school rush has not yet begun.

I look away, towards the dark windows that reflect my placid smile. Valentin said he might *live* with me some day — he would actually want to live *together*. Never mentioned the complications that might be involved with four kids in tow, however.

The subway doors open and close in staggered time to the blowing of the whistle and to the happy thoughts running through my head. An Indian woman sitting by herself in another corner of the car smiles at me, as if she can read my mind and knows what I'm thinking. She has a red dot, called a bindi, I believe, on her forehead, and her wrists are decorated with deep gold bracelets. Instead of a sari, she is wearing modern western dress — tight jeans and a lace-trimmed blouse, which makes me think of my mother and my aunts who cut off their heavy buns when they got to Canada.

A man comes and sits on the seat across from me. He slips his black metal lunchbox on the floor between his feet. His cheeks are charcoal with the stubs of an unshaven beard. He wears his heavy work boots unlaced; his khaki pants, hanging over them, are caked with mud. Two stops away, the man gets off, and as he passes, a faint tang of musk and nicotine reaches my nostrils. If I close my eyes it could be, though not quite, Valentin. The train crosses the Humber. The river below is a sickly green-brown colour contaminated by the thoughtlessness of man, and I imagine what it might have looked like in the time when this area was inhabited by the Mississauga Indians and the waters flowed sparkling and fresh. Men seem always eager to deface, debase, destroy, and in confirmation of this, I notice on the concrete of the bridge we are crossing, marring graffiti announcing in large lettering: GOD IS DEAD, then underneath it, almost as an afterthought, OR HE ISN'T LISTENING. Coward. Make up your mind.

The train speeds through a tunnel, blocking out the messages. Studying the map over the door, I realize the next stop is mine. I am standing in front of the *right* doors when they open. I am pleased with myself and terribly content.

"Excuse me…" The browned-skinned lady with the red dot is getting off at my stop, too. "I thought you'd want to know … there's a stain on the back of your dress."

My face flashes hotly.

"There might be a bathroom upstairs," she offers helpfully.

"Thank you," I say, trying to hide my embarrassment.

But there *is* no bathroom. I back into a corner and wait for the few people coming up the stairs to pass me. I gather the back of my skirt and glancing behind me, examine it; a wet spot has darkened the burgundy chiffon. There is nothing I can do to cover the evidence of having been with a man. From the station, I take the quieter side streets to my house, double the distance it would normally take to reach it.

As the dark Tudor of our front façade comes into view, my stomach sinks as I glimpse my neighbour, Mrs. O'Brien, watering her front lawn. I stop in my tracks, but breathe a sigh of relief when she drags the hose towards the sunny side of her house to water her petunias. I take this opportunity to sprint to my front door, where I quickly unlock it and rush inside. There is still half an hour until the children come home from school. I change into my bathrobe and draw myself a bath. The delicate chiffon can only be dry-cleaned, but it would be too humiliating to bring it in. Taking the scissors from the sewing basket, I cut the skirt into vertical strips, the bodice and arms into ragged pieces. When I'm through, I stuff the scraps of fabric into a plastic garbage bag, triple tie it, and hide it downstairs with the kitchen garbage, underneath some dusty potato peels. Then I go up to take a bath.

Chapter Eighteen

Now that Valentin is working two jobs, I can no longer expect his daily calls. Yet, I am reluctant to leave the house to shop for groceries, putting it off until late in the day. Always, he is in the back of my mind. As if to keep his spirit alive within me, I find myself, even when I'm talking to Victor, using expressions Valentin habitually uses, or repeating one of his thoughts, and it gives me the greatest pleasure. Passing a mirror, in the bathroom or entrance hall, I sometimes experience a sudden flash of recognition, as I identify in my own face a common expression of Valentin's. Whenever this happens, I wonder if I am mimicking him, or if this has always been an expression we coincidently share. I have even adopted the languid, loose-limbed way he moves. It would not have surprised me, looking in the mirror, to find my hair black and wavy, my eyes slightly bulging and bright.

In general, I feel content as I wait patiently for his intermittent calls whenever he has a spare moment at work, brief conversations during morning coffee breaks or at lunch. I prepare days in advance for our meetings — short, passionate encounters — usually on Saturday afternoons when he isn't working and Victor is home, making it possible for me to spend time away on shopping errands. During the week, I move placidly around my kitchen, singing along to a

Julio Iglesias album of Spanish songs that I've purchased, trying not to butcher the pronunciation of the words. When I reach up to take a casserole dish from its high shelf, my arms brush against my breasts, awakening a sensitivity left by my lover's ardent kisses. I replay, over and over until next time, the memory of our last encounter.

But now, three weeks after his birthday, there is an unusually long lapse in his calls. I become restless, then worried, then terrified as the lapse stretches into its second week. When the phone rings, I rush breathless, to answer it. "I'll get it," I shriek. Too late in the day to hope, still…

It is my mother. She is crying. "*Nonna*'s gone. She died an hour ago. Her heart just stopped. It was too much for her."

"*Nonna* died?" I repeat, in disbelief. I should cry, but tears will not come. Instead, I start to shake. "Are you at the hospital?"

"We're all back at *Nonna*'s house. People will want to visit. *Zu* Domenico is making the funeral arrangements."

"Should I come to *Nonna*'s house?"

"Do whatever's best for you. There's nothing we can do for her now."

When I hang up the telephone, I realize that the children have been listening; they are standing around me, their eyes wide with fright. "Did *Bisnonna* really die?" Jamie asks.

"Yes, honey. She was very old. She was eighty-nine."

"Are we ever going to see *Bisnonna* again?" Joshua wants to know.

"No."

"Did she go to heaven?" Jamie asks anxiously.

I word my answer carefully. "If there's a heaven, and good people go to heaven, I'm sure that's where she went."

"Are you and Daddy gonna die too?"

"Stop asking stupid questions," Alison says, visibly upset.

How should I answer? Yes, we're all going to die? I answer instead: "Daddy and I are going to live a long time yet before we die." Such optimism… "People who are Daddy's and Mommy's age don't usually die."

"Am I going to die?"

"No, Joshua. Not until you're very, very old."

"I don't want to die. I'm scared," Joshua says.

Jamie asks, "What does it feel like, to die?"

"You just go to sleep and not wake up."

"I don't want to die," Joshua repeats.

"Think of it like this," I say. "There was a time before you were born that you didn't exist on earth. When you die, it's the same thing. You don't exist on earth anymore. You weren't frightened when you didn't exist on earth before you were born, were you? So why would you be frightened about not existing after you die?" Did this argument make any sense to them I wonder? I'm not sure it even makes sense to me.

The children are all silent, pensive. Possibly weighing my explanation against the optimism of other answers, simpler answers.

Victor would need to come with me tonight, but I will have to prepare supper before I go out, so the babysitter can feed the kids. I have to call her right away, and hope she is available. I take a casserole with leftovers out of the fridge, then change my mind and put it back. "I have to go out with Daddy when he comes home," I tell the children, "so I'm going to tell Sandra to order Swiss Chalet for you."

"Can't we have McDonald's?" Joshua asks.

"McDonald's doesn't deliver to houses," Alison says.

"I have to go upstairs and change," I tell them. "Please get along. I don't want to have to yell.

Joshua runs after me as I start to climb the stairs. "What about Pizza Pizza? They deliver." His face is chubby still with the last vestiges of babyhood, his expression too serious for such a frivolous question.

I smile at him, "Maybe Pizza Pizza," I say.

***

Who doesn't dislike funeral homes? Such vulgar display of material things no longer significant to the dead: plush carpeting, mahogany furniture, brocade tapestries, silver candlesticks and grasscloth-covered walls decorating a combination living room–church, the offering not the Body and Blood of Christ, but that of another soul, this time, my grandmother's. I sit on a red satin settee between my mother and Victor. My uncles and aunts and the rest of the relatives sit in the row of settees next to us. People I don't recognize, old friends of my grandmother's, who were unable to come during the previous day, have come early this morning to offer condolences. In a few minutes they will close the casket. A litany is being said; my aunt Lucia, my mother's widowed sister, calls out the invocations in what sounds, because of her pronunciation, like Italian, but is really Latin.

Numbly, I respond: *Ora pro nobis.* The smell of the room bothers me intensely — a vault smell, dusty, with a tang of mould, like our basement. And the sickeningly sweet smell of the inevitable floral tributes, in former times used to camouflage the stench of the rotting body, now merely an ostentatious display. Since my father's death, I have come to hate florist shops and their mummified bouquets. Flowers from the garden are all I can tolerate. But Victor persists in bringing me, on every Valentine's Day, a dozen long stem red roses. I never bother mixing the accompanying packet of preservatives into the water to extend their life. I am grateful when they wither so I can chuck them into the garbage and rid the house of their death smell.

I look over at the coffin. My grandmother looks exactly as she did in life. A placid smile lingers reassuringly on her face, a smile artfully applied to convince all she had died peacefully. She is wearing a brown dress, smocked with pearls, that was put together hastily by an Italian seamstress who specializes in such circumstances. Why brown, I wonder? My grandmother had been a widow all the years I had known her and had worn nothing but black. Perhaps it is another custom I've been kept in the dark about. My mother often does inexplicable things, superstitious things — throwing salt into every corner of the house, tying a red ribbon on a new appliance, taking out a Bull of Holy Places during a lightning storm, without explaining why, afraid of being ridiculed, but more afraid of defying invisible forces. My grandmother had done such things also, but openly, without being ashamed that it was part of her life. I'll miss my grandmother. And my father, and my uncle, and my little cousin who died years ago. These people are all gone from my life. How many people would be left if I lived to be my grandmother's age? What was the point in living to an old age if it was going to be spent missing people you loved?

The litany ends. The men from the funeral home close the casket. My mother and aunts start crying. My uncle, *Zu* Domenico, her only living son, starts crying too.

We follow the black hearse to the church. It moves slowly since the weather has abruptly turned winter-like and driving conditions are hazardous. Rain falls and freezes instantly on the windshield. My grandmother always feared the spring. Years before — twenty, thirty years, perhaps — my grandmother had consulted a fortune teller: she would live to a ripe old age and die in the spring, the fortune teller had said, and my grandmother had never forgotten. But she died in late fall. Fretted needlessly during all those springs. She was ready to go when God called her, she always said. Yet she feared the spring.

The coffin is removed from the hearse. My uncle has arranged for a Requiem Mass. Dispatch the dead in style: dues can be paid for, favors returned, sacrifices thanked for, even after death, if you did it right. Taking my arm, Victor leads me to a front pew. I slide in next to my mother; Victor sits on her other side. He has arranged for a substitute teacher to take his classes for the next two days and hasn't uttered one word of complaint. We listen intently to the priest's eulogy, which is improvised and impersonal. My grandmother, a deeply religious woman, rarely felt the need to go to church, preferring to communicate directly with her God. Organ music peels from the loft at the back of the church, voices sing:

I will never forget you my people,
I have carved you in the pa-alm of my hand...

My mother wipes her eyes, moved by the music, though not understanding the words. Her hands, clutching the tissue, are rough and dry. I remember once when I was nine, lying in bed thinking about my own mother's death. I had started to cry violently, uncontrollably. My father had come into my room trying to find out the reason for my tears, since I had refused to tell my mother. "Someday, *Mamma*'s going to *die*," I blurted finally. He hadn't tried to console me, merely pulled his handkerchief from his pocket and blown my nose. I wonder now whether he'd been hurt by the fact that I didn't seem worried about *his* death. He'd sat quietly by my bed until I fell asleep. A little more than two years ago,

I was burying my father. Now it was my grandmother, and next? I feel weary. The choir sings on:

> *I will never forget you*
> *I will not leave you orphaned*
> *I will never forget my own.*

I long to get away from here, away someplace with Valentin. He said maybe we could *live* together. I would do it if it weren't for my children. *Blood of my blood ... flesh of my flesh. I will not leave you...* If Valentin asked, I would not go with him. That was the truth, though I loved him. I would never leave my children, even if he asked me ... but *ask me ... ask me.*

***

Victor drives the babysitter home. I go upstairs to check the children. Micah and Alison are sleeping soundly. In the twins' room, there is movement in the bottom bunk. Jamie lifts his head. "You're back? Is Daddy home too?"

"Yes. He's just driving Sandra home. Can't you sleep?"

"No. Can you sit with me for a little while?"

"Sure." I sit at the head of the mattress, close to him, one arm reaching around him. He snuggles into the nest of my lap.

"You know what, Mommy?"

"What?"

"I wouldn't be afraid to die if it could be in your arms."

My throat constricts. I look away from him, fighting off the stinging in my eyes, until I get back control enough to speak. "Well — I think we've had enough sad thoughts for today. I want you to put everything out of your mind and try to go to sleep. Do you think you can do that?"

"Yes, I think I'm sleepy now."

"Good." I kiss him and hug him very tightly. "Goodnight, my love. Go to sleep now."

I check the top bunk; Joshua has kicked off his blanket. I smooth it over him and tuck it under the mattress. He is a sound sleeper. His face, placid and trusting, is the face of every sleeping child. Our sweet babies. When we give you *life*, we give you *death*.

***

The telephone rings. Fearing it would wake the children, I hurry to answer it before the second ring. "Hello."

"Hello?" The greeting is a question, uncertain. For a second I think that my ears are playing tricks on me, that the voice only sounds like Valentin's.

"Sorry, I'm calling so late. I've been trying to get you all day, but you weren't home. Is it okay?"

"Yes. It's wonderful to hear your voice. I've been dying to talk to you. These last few days have been awful. My grandmother died, Valentin."

"I'm really sorry, *mi amor*." His voice struggles for sincerity; he didn't know her, after all.

"She was pretty old — eighty-nine."

"I didn't know your grandmother, but back home I have a grandmother that I care about, too, so I understand. I guess you must feel pretty bad."

"I do. Probably because I didn't really expect her to die. I thought I'd have more time with her after she broke her hip. I visited her in the hospital for — how long? Half an hour? You can't talk in a hospital. My grandmother had such a hard life. She was desperately poor when she was young. Suffered a lot of losses. Survived a lot of sickness. Then she dies from a broken hip falling off the toilet. Can you beat that? I only went that one time to see her, brought her a stupid pot of mums ... as if that was the best I could do."

"Mums? *Crisantemos*? You brought them to her in the hospital?"

"Yes. Why?"

"Nothing — except ... you don't bring *crisantemos* to a sick person. It's an Italian superstition — they're flowers for the dead."

"Oh my God! My mother didn't tell me that." Yet I had sensed something was amiss by the worried look on my mother's face as I offered my grandmother the pot of mums, by the tone of my aunt's voice as she spirited the flowers away. "Oh, Valentin, I feel *sick.*"

"I'm sorry, I shouldn't have said anything. I didn't mean to make you feel worse."

"No, I'm glad you told me. How can I know if nobody tells me?" But I think to myself: the last gift I gave to my grandmother meant death. Why hadn't my mother told me? I have to talk about something else, otherwise I am going to start crying. "What about you? How are things?"

"Not too good for me either. Someone stole my truck."

"The van? When?"

"Last week."

"Where?"

"In the parking lot at Sick Kids Hospital."

"Sick Kids Hospital?"

"Yeah, a friend of mine — Tony, he works with me — we had to take his kid brother there because he was really sick, something wrong with his kidneys. We were there for three hours. When we came out, my truck was gone." He sighs heavily in frustration or exhaustion.

"You called the police?"

"Sure. I have my truck back already. The police located it the next day outside some warehouse. But it was stripped. My stereo, my speakers, my tape deck, my ID, everything, gone. And they did some damage. I'd love to get my hands on those bastards."

"Will your insurance cover it?"

"The damage, but not all the equipment. I don't really care about that — some of the stuff was sentimental…"

The World's Greatest Soccer Player figure I had given him?

"…like the picture of my little sister." The one who had died when she was only seven from leukemia, I remind myself; she was only a year younger than Valentin, and they had been close. "I kept the picture with my ID in the front glove compartment. It was the only copy. I can't replace *that*."

Who wouldn't love this man, I ask myself — this wonderfully compassionate man who worries for his mother and spends hours in a hospital waiting room with a friend, this sentimental man who prizes his little sister's photograph more than any other possession?

He exhales heavily. "I've got so many problems right now. The bill collectors are at my mother's throat. I'm working as many hours as I can, but I just can't manage to catch up with all the debts.

"Right now, my mother's got four different notices to appear in small claims court. I told her we'll have to sell the house. That's the only way she can get those people off her back and we can finally have some peace of mind. What I need right now is somebody with dough to burn to lend me a little bit of it. Just enough to get the worst of them off my mother's back. I've been to a few friends, but they're worse off than I am."

"How much do you need?"

"A couple of thousand would really help. I'm working overtime — I wouldn't need it for very long."

I try to think — where could I get ahold of that much money? Victor handles all the savings, writes all the cheques. "I wish I could help, Valentin."

"Yeah — well, what can you do? Money is not important anyway, as long as I have my health, my family."

And *me*, say *me*.

"I'm going to be busy for a while. I won't be able to call you. I'll be working as many extra hours as I can."

Why should he want to? I've let him down. I was close to tears. Frantically, I try to think of a way I can help him out of his financial dilemma. I could ask my mother for the money. She has a few thousand dollars in her account, I'm sure. I could tell her Victor needs it temporarily, that he would pay her back soon.

"I just thought of a way I could lend you the money."

"Look, I don't want you to get into any trouble with your husband."

"My husband won't find out."

"I don't know."

"I *want* to do this."

He pauses. "You think you could have the money for me by tomorrow?"

"I think so. Shall I meet you somewhere?"

"Can you drop it off at Santini's? I'll be working there Saturday afternoon. Would you be able to come after noon?"

"I'm sure I can."

"Alright. Thanks."

Through the open blinds of the bedroom, I see lights flashing in the driveway. Quickly, I say goodbye to Valentin and hang up the phone.

I go downstairs feeling euphoric. It was a miracle! I had needed Valentin, and he had called. Even though he'd never, ever called at night before. He had *known*. Victor comes in through the back door. I slip my arms around him and give him a hug. I feel giddy, high on the thought of seeing Valentin again soon. I think to myself, *I'm so sorry to be doing this to you. I'm so happy.*

***

My mother had received a cheque for twenty thousand dollars from the life insurance policy offered by Cardinale Estate — twenty thousand dollars being the value of my father's life — and my mother had used little of it in the past two years. I know she will lend me two thousand dollars if I ask her. I can tell her we need it to do some unexpected repairs to the foundation of the house where water is seeping in, which it definitely is, so I wouldn't actually be lying.

On Saturday, I put on makeup, style my hair, spray on perfume even though I know I won't be spending any time with Valentin. "Why are you getting dolled up just to pay your mother a visit?" Victor asks.

"I wanted to try out the new stuff I ordered from Maddy," I tell him. "I'm just going to help my mother do some banking. I won't be long. The boys want to come along. Alison is in her room."

My mother will not deny my request, I am certain, and when I sit her down at her kitchen table and ask her to sign the cheque I've filled out with the figure of two thousand dollars, she signs willingly on the signature line in her painfully slow, awkward way that results in florid Italian script. I promise my mother that Victor will pay her back soon. We have a short visit with *Nonna* and are soon on our way again, the boys crunching on the almond biscotti my mother has given them.

"I have to pick up some ground beef for tonight's dinner," I tell the boys.

"It's going to take too long," Micah complains.

"No, it won't. I'll be quick."

"I'm thirsty," Joshua whines.

"We'll be home soon. You can wait. You want some Juicy Fruit gum? It'll take your thirst away."

"Okay."

I take the gum from my purse and hand it over to him. "Share it with your brothers," I tell him.

A shuffling.

"You took two! Mom, Micah took two."

"No."

"Yes, you did. You put the other one in your pocket, I saw you!" Joshua's face is red and angry, the healed stitches over his brow, tiny translucent railway tracks. He's determined not to be made a fool of by his big brother.

I glance back at Micah, whose expression is smug, and know Joshua is telling the truth. "Micah — aren't you ashamed, at your age!" I'm not up to arguments this morning. "Alright, Joshua, you and Jamie can each have another one."

"When are we going to eat?" Micah complains.

"I'll be starting supper as soon as I get home."

"What are we having?"

"Meatloaf. That's why I need the ground beef."

"I don't like meatloaf," Joshua complains. "Can we have pizza?"

"Joshua, you'd have pizza every day if you could. Meat is good for you. It makes you healthy and strong and it has iron and protein."

"This guy in my class," Micah relates, "nobody in his family eats meat. He says that they eat beans all the time. You should see, he's always farting in class!"

"Alright! That's enough, Micah!" I shoot him a warning sideways reprimand with my eyes. "Well, most people eat meat. It has vitamins and iron and makes you big and strong," I add, for the edification of the twins. "Humans are carnivorous — they eat animal flesh." Indeed. My words bring to mind Sister Aloysius, my grade nine religion teacher. "Girls, can anyone tell me what the Eucharist is? Rita?"

"What we receive when we get Communion. It represents the Body and Blood of Christ."

"*Represents*! It certainly does not *represent*!" Sister Aloysius seemed almost to be choking with indignation at the word, her fleshy jowls bulging like sausages from the tight, white linen wimple, while her face heightened to a volatile shade of scarlet and threatened to explode into bloody fragments across the room. "It most certainly does not *represent* the Body and Blood of Our Lord. It *is* the Body and Blood of Our Lord. When you receive the Host, you *are* eating the Flesh of Christ, you *are* drinking His Blood."

So, Catholics are carnivorous, then — even vegetarians.

We are nearing the Canada Packers plant. I can see in the distance the drab, weathered fencing of the holding pens, and inside, the brown and white hides of animals, shuffling against the thick boards, there for the night killing. A pig's snout, pink and vulnerable, pokes through the space between the boards, eagerly sniffing at the air beyond the enclosure. Poor dumb creatures. I would rather not look at what might be my next meal. But this is Valentin's second job — killing and butchering these animals for Talbot Meat Packers.

I arrive at Santini's, leaving the twins in the car in Micah's care. The only other customer inside the store is buying cheese at the other end of the deli counter and I don't bother to take a ticket. There are no butchers serving at the counter at the moment, only two girls in white jackets who don't seem much older than Alison.

"May I help you?"

"Is Valentin here?"

"I think so. I'll check and see."

When the girl returns, she tells me he's busy cutting steaks and I should give whatever I was dropping off to her and she would see that he got it. I pass her the envelope reluctantly and ask for two pounds of ground chuck. She packages the ground beef and hands it to me. "I'd like to you to give the envelope to him before I leave, if you would, please," I say. She takes it and disappears through the EMPLOYEES ONLY door once again. "He says thank you," she tells me when she returns.

I drive home, disappointed that I didn't have a chance to talk to Valentin, but I understand, and the twins are already growing restless in the back seat, in any case.

CHAPTER NINETEEN

Winter 1986

Through the fogged windows of the station wagon, I anxiously watch the approaching and passing of each car. Valentin is late. I hunch my shoulders and press my knees together, rubbing my gloved hands over them to try and keep warm. I should have worn pants instead of a skirt and pantyhose. The rest of me is warm though, inside the mink jacket Victor gave me last Christmas — a week before Christmas — because he thought my cloth coat too shabby to wear to the teaching staff's Christmas party, where the principal and current vice-principal's wives come decked in furs. The jacket has turned up sleeves and a wide collar, and I had tried to show enthusiasm when I opened the gift, although I would have much preferred to pick my own fur if he meant for me to have a fur. Something more youthful, like raccoon or fox. The mink jacket makes me look matronly; I had always thought of mink as an old lady's fur. I hate for Victor to give me presents, for anyone to give me presents, in fact, since it always makes me feel small and beggarly, and after the opening demands a performance. Valentin has never given me a gift, and yet I am certain, whereas with Victor, the excesses seem not to be enough, with Valentin I would be happy with nothing.

But I'm glad to have the coat tonight. It is another biting cold December evening with the night sky clear and the air frosty, hitting the face like ice water. I start the motor again for the third time since I've arrived here, to warm up the car. It is ten past eight. Valentin said he would meet me at 7:30 outside Santini's, instead of the parking lot of the meat plant where he is working today, because it is halfway between the plant and the college where I am taking my real estate course. I'm hoping he'll hurry. The class I'm supposed to be attending ends at 10:30. It is the first segment of a night course in real estate and I'll have to catch up at the next class. The course caught my eye as I leafed through a community college calendar delivered at the door, and I went ahead and enrolled, partly because real estate has always interested me, and partly as a convenient excuse to leave the house two evenings a week. Valentin encouraged me to take it. He too, it turns out, has an ensuing interest in real estate, and hopes to capitulate on future speculative ventures. In any event, the course may serve useful to me. My grandmother has left her house to me, since I am her namesake, as apparently is customary. It is her entire estate; what little money she had in the bank had barely covered her funeral expenses. There is a tenant living still in my grandmother's house — an old woman, but younger than my grandmother, who has for years occupied the third floor of the house. Now that she is alone in the house, she has decided to move into a retirement home, and has placed herself on a waiting list. Perhaps she will end up in the same senior citizens' residence as my grandmother's former roommate at the hospital. I feel a bit guilty that I won't be able to keep my promise to visit her after all, since I have no idea where to find her. If I complete the entire real estate course — and that will take months still — I can list the house myself, once the tenant leaves.

The car has warmed. I turn the motor off. I have been looking forward to this meeting for weeks. Valentin has kept cancelling it because they are busy at the meat plant and he is working overtime. But not tonight. Unless something has come up. I have been watching the passing cars for forty minutes. I will not start to worry until an hour is up. He is always late now. Half an hour, forty-five minutes, not unusual. I've backed the station wagon into a parking space that allows me to see the road in the direction that Valentin will be travelling. The glare of a car's lights hurts my eyes and I lean back against the seat and close them. Only when Valentin arrives, I decide, will I open them again. They are different, the noises of each passing vehicle. Individual, like voices: *swish, screech, purr, grind*; a large truck goes past — *roar, rattle, room-boom*; a small car *squeaks* along. I know I will recognize Valentin's van by its low rumbling, like a coffee pot boiling, an uncertain quaking of metal. I listen for what seems a very long time.

Growing weary of the game, I open my eyes, concentrating on the shape of each approaching set of headlights, trying to make out the vehicle as far as possible down the road, long before it passes me. That one — no, the headlights too low. The next one, perhaps, with lights set wider apart. No, not that one, or the next. Look away then. Don't look at the road. On the right, beyond the parking lot, an eight-foot fence with barbed wire across the top encloses a car junkyard. Rusty rectangles, once cars, are piled one on top of the other: Cadillac or Volkswagen, Buick or Japanese import — all reduced to the same crumpled state. Rust the great equalizer. I try to count the rusted metal blocks, try to imagine what each might have been.

I look again at the clock on the dash. It is 8:25. In five minutes, I will have been waiting an hour. My feet are cold.

Why am I waiting in a freezing cold car for a man who doesn't care enough to be on time? He is *never* on time anymore. And his calls are painfully infrequent, so that sometimes I despair of his *ever* calling again, and then I become hysterical and furious and hate him for making me feel that way. But then he does call, and everything is instantly righted. He is busy at work; they are using him in the killing room now, and he is still working part-time at Santini's, so am I just being selfish? I get so little of him, only the crumbs. But as long as there *are* crumbs, I'll keep lapping them up, rather than face total starvation. Valentin is in me, under my skin, embedded like a hook with barbs, more excruciating to pull out then to leave in.

It is 8:30 now. What if he had had trouble starting his van? The car thermometer reads ten below on the Fahrenheit scale. Here in the station wagon, it can't be much warmer. Again, I start the motor and turn the heater on. I will wait fifteen minutes more. If he just started his van, and waited a few minutes for it heat up, he will be here soon. Yes, I will wait fifteen minutes more. What difference will it make? I will wait an hour, two hours, *more* if it means seeing him.

Down the road, following a lull in the traffic, a set of headlights comes into view, brighter, higher, on a vehicle larger than a car. I recognize the box shape. The rumbling becomes familiar. It is *Valentin*. My heart does an excited somersault inside my chest as he flashes his lights as a greeting and drives into the parking lot. I reach for my purse and after locking the station wagon door, hurry to join him in the van.

"I didn't think you'd still be here," he says, grinning and slightly out of breath. His voice is raspy, as though he's been smoking too many cigarettes. In the darkness, his teeth shine brightly like the teeth of the actors in a Crest toothpaste commercial. But his hair looks greasy, flat against his head.

To me, he looks *wonderful.* "I got tied up at work. I just got out."

Once I'm settled in my captain's chair, he leans towards me and kisses me. I love his hello kisses; they are always eager and warm, not like his goodbye kisses the last thing before he leaves me, stingy pecks that I sometimes wonder whether they betray an eagerness for release. "So where do you want to go?" he asks.

I shrug. "I don't know. I can only stay till ten thirty. We could just sit here and talk."

"And *freeze* to death. Or maybe I'll freeze to death," he says, fingering my coat. "Where did you get *this*?"

"From my husband, a year ago for Christmas."

"Nice of him." He takes a pack of Craven "A" off the dash and pats his chest for matches. "Look, I know a place where we can go, where it's warmer than here, at least."

"Where?"

"A place with a ceiling and four walls — not much of a place, but it'll be warmer than this."

"A motel?"

His eyebrows arch questioningly.

"I don't know, Valentin. If somebody sees me..."

"No one will see you at this place, trust me." His eyes soften into an innocent calf look, a pleading look. It *is* cold and it *is* getting late. I agree.

***

I can smell the lake water as Valentin turns off the Lakeshore into the parking lot of a string of squat white buildings. The neon sign at the entrance flashes Sleepytime Motel and casts a red glow over us as we park next to it. Attached to it is a clock with its hands frozen at three o'clock. The building looks dirty, neglected, the classic dive. Stucco is crumbling off the outside walls. Paint is peeling away on the doors and window frames. I can see, where lights are on in the rooms, that the curtains are so threadbare you can see right through them.

"What do you think?"

"Doesn't look too hot from the outside, that's for sure."

"It's cheap. Twenty dollars if you leave before midnight."

"How do you know?"

"Someone I work with on the killing floor comes here."

"Great. We're in good company."

"We don't have to go in if you don't want to." His voice hints at annoyance.

"No, I'm sorry. It'll do. We can be alone at least — and warm."

He hesitates still. "I'm just a little short—"

"It's fine," I say, reaching in my purse and pulling out a twenty.

He accepts it humbly, not looking at my face, almost as if he were a little ashamed. I wait in the van while he goes into the office. We park in front of the door whose number corresponds to the number on the key tag. The room smells of urine and Lysol. On the wall next to the door, someone has bashed in the drywall, leaving a gaping hole that exposes the wooden studs like a hidden skeleton. The room is furnished with a bed, a battered dresser, a table lamp with a sepia, fly-specked shade, and a green vinyl armchair. The carpet is dirty, the bedspread stained. What kind of people come here, I wonder. Surely not people like me. Yet here I am.

"Well, it's not the greatest," Valentin says. "But at least we can be together. I can hold you in my arms again."

His words strike me as slightly histrionic, almost comical, too smooth and practised. He comes over and puts his arms around me, and I no longer care how many times or to how many women he's repeated these words. He is mine now. His body smells sharply of sweat, which engulfs me like a powerful perfume; I nuzzle against his shoulder, breathing him in. Do human pheromones have a scent? He lifts my face and strokes my cheek; his fingers are rough, the skin tough and dry as leather, his hands, the hands of a working man. "Give me a few minutes," he says, "I'm gonna take a shower."

I nod. When he leaves, I can smell his sweat on me, still. The sound of water trickling in the bathroom is soon accompanied by angry grunts as Valentin bangs on metal with his fist. "Come on! For twenty bucks give me a decent shower head at least!" I laugh in spite of myself, recalling that I've told him more than once that you get what you pay for. But this relaxes me, erasing inhibitions and doubts. Walking over to the bed, I pick up one corner of the bedspread and gingerly draw it back, as if expecting to find, underneath it, a sea of crawling things. To my relief, the sheets are clean. I fold the bedspread and drape it on the armchair.

Valentin comes out of the bathroom rubbing his hair with a towel, a second towel wrapped around his middle. "You planning to wear this all night?" he asks, coming over and sliding his hands beneath my coat. He slips it off me, then, holding it in front of him, he shakes it, stamps his feet and whirls it in a mock veronica, depositing it fur side up on the bed. I giggle. He comes over to me and lifts me high up in the air, then together we fall back on the bed, on top of the fur. He starts to unbutton my blouse.

"Valentin — not on my *fur*."

"Your *husband's* fur. Now — you finish this…" he says, indicating the buttons on my blouse, "…and I'll get the lights."

***

In complete darkness, feeling is more intense than it ever could be in the light. Feeling, it seems, is all there is. Fur silky beneath, fur soft and thick above. I rake my fingers across Valentin's fur, feel the muscular mounds of his chest, slide my hands down the side of his body along his hips. How straight and narrow they are! And his buttocks tight and square; I stroked them lightly, then follow downward, the crevice between.

"What are you doing!"

Passion comes to a halt. Instantly, I feel shame, as though someone has discovered me fondling myself. "Did I do something wrong?" I ask. He detaches himself from me and sits up in the bed. "You don't do that to a *man*."

"What?"

"Touch him back there. Jesus, I'm all soft."

My face flushes hotly. The word *machismo* pops into my head. "Sorry," I say. "I'm sorry."

He turns on the lamp, then reaches for his cigarettes and the complimentary matches from Sleepytime Motel on the dresser. His forehead ripples into folds. He lights a match, and holding it to the end of the cigarette, inhales long and hard, sucking in his cheeks.

Feeling embarrassed, and uncertain of what to say or do, I lie quietly on the bed and watch him smoke, trying to concentrate on nothing more than that — the classic placement of fingers, the rhythm of inhaling and exhaling, the brightening and receding ember at the tip of the cigarette. When he smokes down almost to the filter, he holds the remaining butt between his thumb and index finger, like a pair of pincers, sucking it until every bit of the cigarette paper is consumed. He stabs the filter into the rectangular piece of foil from the cigarette package that he has been using as an ashtray. The furrows have smoothed on his forehead.

He goes into the bathroom to urinate. Turning off the bathroom light, he slips through darkness back into bed. I feel his arms around me again, feel his moist penis grow like an inflating balloon against my thigh. I lie very still this time, taking care not to touch him in any way, letting him touch me, enter me, move against me at his own pace, a moderate ebbing and flowing that too soon becomes frenzied. A wrenching gasp, then all movement ceases. Afterwards, as we lie motionless, his breathing heavy against my ear, I whisper without meaning to, "I love you."

He lifts himself on his arms, then detaches his body from mine, his damp skin clinging, making a soft, smacking sound. He slides over to the outer edge of the bed, sitting up, leaving darkness and the coolness of space between my body and his. "Don't expect too much of me," he says.

I laugh. "What do you think I *expect* of you?"

"I just don't want you to get too attached to me, that's all. I don't want you to do anything crazy."

"What do you think I'm going to do? Leave my husband, bundle up my four kids, and come knocking at your door, *Hey Valentin, you gotta marry me!*"

Sitting up, he turns on the lamp; the shade is so dingy, it scarcely gives off any light. He lights himself another cigarette. Holding it between his thumb and forefinger, he rubs the back of his neck with the remaining three fingers as if to loosen the taut cables of his muscles.

"Valentin, I don't expect *anything* from you. I just wanted to say what I feel. Can't I even tell you?"

"What about your husband? How do you feel about him?"

"I don't know. I care about him, about what happens to him. It's confusing. What I feel for you is so much stronger than anything I have ever felt for him, even at the start. It's you I think about all day, every day."

He lies back on the pillow and forcefully blows out a large puff of smoke, then stares at the ceiling, at the myriad cracks there, as though trying to find in them, like among clouds, a hidden familiar shape. "I never meant to take you away from your husband."

"It's not your fault, Valentin. I made the decision." There is a question I have been wanting to ask but have been afraid to. "Valentin?"

"Yeah."

"What about your friend?"

"My friend?"

"You know, your friend who's *just* a friend."

"Told you … we go out as a group now and then."

"Where do you go?"

"Like I said, to a movie, a party, sometimes visit other friends."

Movies, parties, visiting friends. I feel as snubbed as when, in grade school, kids gave birthday invitations out, but not to me. Why do I ask questions to which the answer, I know for a certainty, will cut like a knife. How I envy this *friend.* "You haven't forgotten your promise, have you? That if it gets serious with her — I mean, if you start getting *intimate* with … *anyone* — it has to stop between us."

"What if I just don't tell you?" His smile is sardonic, teasing. "How do you know I haven't already?"

"Because you made me a promise, and you told me to trust you, and I *am.* I know you wouldn't lie to me about that."

Silent, he begins studying once again the endless patterns of cracks on the plaster ceiling as he inhales and exhales puff after puff of his cigarette. Suddenly, I know, and in the next second also realize that it has ceased to matter, that he has already *broken* his promise.

CHAPTER TWENTY

Christmas is a week away and only five of those days are shopping days. The weather has been cold, but we've had only light dustings of snow that haven't collected. It has made it easier for me to complete the yearly drudgery of choosing gifts, and I have only Alison and Valentin's gifts left to buy. I have had little hope of finding what Alison wants — a Cabbage Patch doll to begin her collection. Alison is too old for dolls, but this one is unique; each one has different coloured hair and eyes, wears a variety of outfits, and comes with adoption papers that identify it by name — Velda Leola, Arnold Jeffrey. Should they meet an untimely demise, the toy company will send you a death certificate. They are this year's fad and destined to become a collector's item. Every store I've tried has sold out. In the paper, I've read of riots in toy stores where shoppers, desperate to get their hands on a doll as soon as a new shipment is put on the floor, elbow and push and trample others in their way. There have been injuries requiring hospitalization. Toy departments have been demolished. At one store, they have taken measures to prevent casualties by starting a waiting list, although the management does not guarantee everyone on the list will *get* a doll. In desperation, I have signed on, and to my surprise this morning, three weeks after putting myself on the list, I receive a call. "Mrs. McEachern?"

"Yes."

"The Bay calling. We're pleased to tell you we have a Cabbage Patch doll for you. Can you come to the store at one o'clock today to pick it up?"

"Yes," I say, delighted.

"Fine. Now please follow our instructions carefully. Come to the camera department counter and give your name. They'll check it against the list and give you further instructions from there."

What was this, espionage? A conspiracy? I only want a *doll*. "Alright," I agree. Amused, I hang up the phone. There are other errands I have to do in any case: get more wrapping paper, buy a present for Valentin, drop by at my mother's, who called this morning and asked what she should do about the furnace — it was making a terrible racket.

I arrive half an hour early at the Bay and head first to the perfume counter. I ask for something masculine. The salesgirl lines up several testers in front of me. I like the Paco Rabanne cologne best; according to the girl, the scent derives from lavender, oakmoss, musk, and Brazilian rosewood. "Perfect," I tell her, and she wraps it up. At thirty-five dollars, it is more expensive than any cologne I have ever bought for Victor. I pay cash.

At precisely one o'clock, I approach the camera counter. After giving my name, a security guard is summoned. "Would you follow me please, ma'am," he says. He leads me up some back stairs and unlocks the door to a small room hidden at the end of a long hallway. *Lo and behold.* A pyramid of Cabbage Patch dolls, stacked one on top of each other up to the ceiling, stands before me. "You may make a selection, ma'am," the guard says.

I pick a blonde doll with braids, sucking a soother; it is dressed in blue jeans and a red blouse. I am not permitted to see what name it has been christened. A salesclerk wheels in a cash register on a mobile stand to ring up my purchase. Instead of a regular bag, the doll is put into a black garbage bag so it can't be seen. There are further instructions from the guard: "Go immediately to your car. Do not stop anywhere along the way. Place the doll in the trunk, out of sight. Lock all the doors. Drive directly home."

Following the instructions precisely, I walk quickly, anxiously eyeing the people I pass, waiting until there is no one around before depositing my doll, nervously, into the luggage compartment underneath the floor of the station wagon. My armpits are sweaty. I am breathing heavily. After getting into my car and locking the door, I leave the shopping mall immediately, glancing suspiciously at the people in the cars behind me through the rearview mirror. It isn't until I have driven into my mother's driveway and played back the scene to myself that I burst out laughing.

***

"You didn't have any heat all night? You didn't tell me you didn't have *any* heat. You only said the furnace was making a racket."

My mother is hunched over at her kitchen table, concentrating on a puddle of dried lentils she's sifting through, checking to see if there are any wayward seeds or tiny bits of stone. She is wearing an oversized wool sweater, balled and faded, that had belonged to me when I was a teenager, and she is wearing the toque my father always wore indoors towards the end because he was always cold. I catch the faint scent of lemon when she gesticulates with her arms and realize that she must use the same laundry detergent as Valentin's mother. "I didn't want to trouble you," she says.

"So, instead you spent the night *freezing* to death. *Mamma, picchì* — why are you like that?" My mother has always been that way. Long-suffering, self-abnegating, never making waves.

"It was too late last night when the noise started. I would have woken up *Vittorio* and the children." Exasperated, I pick up the telephone and call Consumers' Gas. There is a twenty-four-hour emergency number, but my mother could not have found it. Even if she had, she would not have been able to communicate her problem. A representative from the gas company promises to send someone within an hour.

"I'm sorry, *sciatu meu*," my mother tells me. I wouldn't have to bother you if your father were still here. I'm so glad you have *Vittorio*."

Sciatu meu, cori meu, bedda mia — *my breath, my heart, my beauty*; my mother still calls me by the same terms of endearment she used when I was little. But I'm not a child anymore, and I can manage many things without Victor. I want to say, "I *hate* your helplessness. I *hate* your meekness. I don't *want* to be that way, and yet, I *am*. But I think ... I hope, I'm becoming more confident. The real estate courses are helping; it's a start, anyway. "A serviceman will be here soon," I say wearily. I will have to wait to explain the problem to the man.

My mother takes away the lentils, and while waiting for the espresso machine to boil, puts out tiny cups and saucers and miniature spoons that look like playthings, and a plate of *cucciddata* — fig-filled cookies that each year are part of her Christmas baking. They are my favourite. Then she asks, "Would it be too much trouble, *cori meu*, for *Vittorio* to take me to visit *lu Papà e la Nonna*," she asks, "*e lu ziu e la picciridda* — my uncle and the little one too — at the cemetery before Christmas, to bring them wreaths?" The little one is an eight-year-old younger cousin who died years ago.

"*I* can take you the cemetery, *Mamma*." I'm going out on a limb here. It's an hour-and-a-half drive to the other end of the city where the cemetery is located, if I don't take the highway, which I *won't*. A non-Catholic cemetery — but it doesn't matter to my relatives. What matters is that they were permitted to erect an upright gravestone, which is far more impressive than the flat ones the Catholic cemeteries will only allow. My father, my grandmother, and my uncle are all buried there to keep each other company, and my little cousin who was run over by a car.

"We'll need to buy four pots of *crisatemi*," my mother says.

Chrysanthemums — flowers for the *dead*, not the living, I remind myself. Valentin had known. "*Mamma*, why didn't you tell me that time we went to visit *Nonna* in the hospital, that I shouldn't bring her that pot of chrysanthemums? They're flowers for the dead."

My mother's face flushes. She begins gathering up the espresso cups, busying herself so I don't notice her discomfiture. "It's just a superstition," she says, sloughing it off.

"But *Nonna believed* it."

"Your aunt took them away as soon as we left," my mother says, as if that had erased the clumsiness of my gesture.

"Why can't you open your mouth and speak?" I say angrily. "*Say* what you want to say, instead of always being afraid of upsetting someone. Why have you always tried so hard to spare our innocence, to protect us from — *everything?*"

My mother looks at me, bewildered, hurt. "Maria Rita," she says, "you've never spoken to me like that before."

There is a knock at the door, for which I am grateful — the serviceman from the gas company. On inspecting the furnace, he finds a faulty fan belt, replaces it, and quickly leaves. The house, when I leave shortly after him, is already warming. My mother is smiling happily, my previous outburst forgotten. Everything is as it should be, as it has always been. My mother comes to see me off at the front door, watches as I put on my jacket and slide into my high leather boots tucking in my jeans. "With those boots and pants," my mother observes, shaking her head, "you look just like a man."

**

"I have to be honest with you. I think I've started feeling something for my friend."

I want to laugh. Laugh and say: "Hang on a minute, Valentin. I'm on the wrong phone. I should be on the upstairs line, staring at the black spot on the floor, where I've always been when I'm getting bad news." Instead, tears start coming, and I choke up and can't speak.

"What are you doing?" His voice is a gentle whisper, kind. *So* kind. If only he weren't being *kind*. Then I could yell and scream and accuse him — you broke your promise! I knew you had! There *was* someone else! Instead, I struggle to maintain the silent space between us, trying to keep inaudible, my crying.

"Don't," he says. "Please don't do that."

Remorse. At least he feels remorse.

"Do you hate me?" he asks softly.

I can't open my mouth. If I open it, the sob that is constricting my chest will escape — bloodcurdling it will be, inhuman. Phantom hands are strangling me, pinching my windpipe; my larynx is about to burst.

"*Baby*, it had to happen sometime."

Tucking the receiver under my chin, I rub my cheeks, lathering the wetness into my face. "Can I see you one more time?" My voice is a barely audible whisper.

"Whenever you say."

"Tomorrow?"

"Tomorrow."

We agree to meet the next day, Saturday, outside Santini's. I arrive early to pick up some chicken breasts to validate my excuse to Victor that I'm going shopping for meat. In the chrome that lines the glass counters, my eyes look bloodshot and my face pale. A pimple has started to erupt on one cheek; my period is due. Not wanting to see myself, I look away.

After buying the meat, I sit in the station wagon and wait for Valentin. For once he appears at noon sharp, our agreed upon time. We sit together in his van like strangers and find there is nothing to say. I look straight ahead at the people coming in and out of the stores. "You look tired," he says, breaking the silence.

"I didn't sleep last night." Tears start flowing down my cheeks, and I hate myself for letting them.

He exhales, a heaviness in his sigh. The weightiness of guilt. He takes the box of Kleenex from the dash and offers it to me. The same way he offers it afterwards to collect the semen he has spilled deep inside me — so deep it refuses to leave my body for days, having found some secret reservoir where his sperm, like little fish, can swim around, die, grow putrid. Menstrual blood and rotting semen; no wonder there were more hygiene products for women than men. How quickly the Kleenex box disappeared, replaced each time with a new one with tissues of varying pastels. Yet I seldom saw him blowing his nose, but perhaps I'm being paranoid. Ignoring his offer, I wipe away tears with my fingertips.

"Listen to me," he says, "this could go on and on. But what good is it? Don't tell me you expected more than this?"

"I didn't expect *this.*"

"Look — I've got too many problems right now. My life is too complicated."

I sniff loudly, and with the back of my hand dab at the wetness dripping from my nose. "And with your friend, it's not complicated?"

He looks away without answering.

Strange that all these months, I haven't feared *her.* Somebody else, maybe. Somebody new. But not *her.*

"What's your friend's name?"

"Brenda."

Brenda. The name sends a cold chill through me, like a sudden rushing in of tide on bare feet. "Tell me about her?"

"Why?"

"Just curious." Morbid curiosity. Yes, it was that — unwholesome.

"She's a secretary. Works for an insurance company." He seems to take pleasure in imparting this information.

"Which one."

"It's a new one downtown."

"I see. Where does she live?"

"In an apartment, close to where she works."

I'm surprised he's actually telling me this much. "Alone?"

"Her roommate just moved out yesterday to move in with her boyfriend."

"Will she be living by herself now?" I suppose what I really want to know is, does Valentin plan to move in with her.

"Yeah, she got a raise, so she'll be able to afford it."

There is a bizarre unreality to our conversation. Unreal because of the calmness with which I am asking these questions, and the placid indifference with which Valentin is answering them. Inside, I feel as though my vital organs are being slashed with the sharp edge of a knife.

Valentin becomes silent, afraid perhaps that he's revealed too much. He looks at me sadly, as though pitying me. "I'll call you," he says. "We'll get together sometime for a drink. I'll put your number down in my book, so I don't forget it."

I burst suddenly into laughter. "Tell me something, will you, Valentin? I really, really want to know. Did you ever really *love* me?"

He hesitates, unsure how to answer. "I felt something for you — something between like and love."

Something between like and love. I see the distance between the two points as being vast, a long line stretching for miles. Where along that line would Valentin place his feelings for me?

"I didn't *just* like you," he says. "I wasn't only interested in the … sex part. It was more … a lot more. You understand me better than anyone."

"Let me get this straight. If you're only interested in having sex with a woman, that means you like her. If you want to do more than have sex with her, say, have a conversation or go for a walk or something, then you more than *just* like her — something between like and love." I feel my cheeks burning up, my whole body overheating. I am talking more loudly, my words are less controlled. "You told me you *loved* me. You told me there *was* no one else. You chose to have this relationship knowing I was older, married, had kids. But you didn't give *me* a chance to make a decision based on the true facts. She was never *just* a friend, was she? You *lied* to me. You *used* me. You said you loved me because you knew that was the only way you could get what you wanted — the magic words: *open sesame.*"

He bent his head and looked down at his knees like a scolded child who, clearly guilty, has accepted his punishment as justified. Turning to me again, he says, "We still had something nice together, didn't we? Would you have wanted to miss that? You have your husband, your children, your home. I was *nothing* in your life."

"Oh, no, you weren't *nothing*. My life totally revolved around you — when I wasn't with you, I was waiting for your call, and all the rest of my waking moments were spent *thinking* about you. Even my dreams were full of you. Maybe I was nothing in *your* life, but you were something in mine."

"You were something," he says softly, half-ashamed.

"Oh yes — I was *something* alright. One more female you fucked!"

His upper lip curls up derisively. "I never force anybody to do anything they don't want to do. Everyone has to decide for themselves what they want. If I *used* you, then we *used* each other." He is speaking with his lips barely apart, the words slithering out between the spaces. "I'm telling you how things are because you made the terms." He turns away and opens his window for air, as if our talking has consumed all the oxygen. He tilts the side mirror towards him, cocking his head to look at himself, wiping his mouth with his hand, stroking his beard, the beard he's let grow the past month, smoothing his hair — his wavy black hair. It is something I have seen him do before when he drops me off, comb the unruliness out of his hair, scrub his face and mouth with the back of his hand to erase any trace of — what? Sex? Lust? Women? And go home to his mother untainted, the perfect son.

When he faces me again, I see his expression has solidified to hardness, indifference. His eyelids hang heavily over his eyes, which look dull and milky, lake snake eyes when they're ready to shed because underneath they've grown a new skin.

"I gotta run," he says. "I still owe you that money — I'll call you."

"Sure," I say, opening the door and letting myself out of the van. "Oh — I almost forgot." Reaching into my purse for the Paco Rabanne cologne, which I have carefully wrapped in foil and tied with gold string, I drop the parcel on the seat. "This is for you, Valentin. Merry Christmas."

CHAPTER TWENTY-ONE

A black hole. In my dream, I see myself at the bottom of it, an empty well shaft that I've fallen into, a deep narrow hole with smooth, slippery walls of mud and moss and stone.

My knees are drawn up, pressed against my breasts; I clutch them, rock back and forth on the damp earth, grimace with pain. Pain wrenches my abdomen; an unbearable heaviness, like an anvil deep inside, crushing my organs, choking their blood supply. Contractions of pain, in waves. Something I've eaten is causing this distress. Gnawing at my insides. Something is eating *me*. I want to climb out, to get help, but the walls are too slick. So why even try.

"*Mom*, get up."

A voice enters from the opening at the top of the tunnel where a dim light shines.

"Mom, we're going to be late!"

From the soft hollow of my pillow, I raise my head slightly and open my eyes partway. My lashes are stuck together. In the dull grayness that the closed window blinds concede through the open gaps on either side of the window frame, I vaguely see, but more smell, Alison. A fresh air smell, laced with the faint peppermint scent of toothpaste. "What time is it?" I ask groggily, my voice hoarse with the day's first uttering. I twist my head awkwardly towards Victor's night table, looking for the red numbers of the clock radio.

"It's 8:15. Get up, Mom!"

"Alright, I'm *getting* up. Have you and your brothers had breakfast yet?"

"Yes. The boys had cereal and I had a piece of toast."

"Only toast?"

"I'm not hungry."

"That's not enough, Alison. Breakfast doesn't make you fat — don't believe those boys that tell you you're too fat." I realize I sound like my mother. *Troppu sicca,* she's always complaining about Alison. Too thin. "Make sure you eat all your lunch at least," I warn Alison.

I slide from under the covers, reluctantly leaving the warmth trapped beneath the sheets, and press my hand against my abdomen. A cramp makes me wince. I sit at the edge of the bed, waiting for it to pass. With my foot, I circle the floor near my bed, but cannot find my slippers. Pressed against the cold floor, my arches ache. I take a pair of underwear from a drawer and stumble to the bathroom. Light pours in through the white voile curtains, hurting my eyes, and I shade them with one hand. I sit down on the toilet, tear four squares of tissue from the roll of toilet paper and fold them neatly into one square of quadruple thickness. As I suspected, when I wipe, I find a light pink stain. I take a sanitary napkin from a box in the cupboard and peel off the strip from the adhesive backing, and after attaching it to my panties, I pull them up. In the medicine cabinet, I find the Aspirin and take two.

"Mo-om!"

"I'm coming." I splash my eyes quickly with water and rub them hard with a towel. I am sleepy still, although I've slept, what? — twelve hours. Most nights lately, I go to bed when the children do, hours before Victor, yet I can barely generate enough energy each day to keep going.

"Mom. Come on! We're going to be late." Alison's reprimands ring with the justified impatience of an adult, rather than the spoiled petulance of a child.

"Be down in a sec."

In the bedroom, I put on jeans and a pullover, not bothering with a bra. Such uncomfortable things, bras — they must have been invented by a man. Yesterday's socks are rolled in a ball on the floor next to my night table; I unroll them and put them on. Going down the stairs, I notice that my pullover has a spot of dried spaghetti sauce in front, and licking a finger, I dab at it ineffectually. Downstairs, I put on my coat and take my purse from a shelf inside the closet. My keys aren't in my purse. "I can't find my keys. Has anyone seen my keys?" I hate losing things. Losing things means losing control, losing power over my existence; hadn't it happened when I lost my earring? Feverishly, I feel with my fingers along the closet shelf.

"Mom, it's twenty to. We have to *go*."

"I *know* that, Alison. Please help me. Help me look for my keys." My eyes are starting to tear. I stoop to check the closet floor and hear jingling in the pocket of my jacket. "Found them. It's okay. Get in the car."

Looking in the rearview mirror as I drive the kids to school, I realize I have forgotten to comb my hair; it sticks out on one side of my head like a lopsided rooster's comb. I run my fingers through it a few times and hope I won't see anyone I know.

When I get back home, I put on the kettle. The kitchen feels comfortable, safe — the *only* safe place. My cramps have subsided a little — the Aspirin's kicking in. I make myself a cup of instant coffee and huddle in the corner of the breakfast nook. The hot liquid soothes with each gulp, warming my insides. My arms are cold; I rub them. Outside, winter is melting into spring, but inside this drafty old house remains cold. I take another gulp of coffee. How tired I feel. Bone tired; I ache deep inside, deep in the marrow of my bones. Weariness presses on my shoulders like a dead weight. A carcass. Valentin heaves carcasses on his back from the rack to the cutting table — monstrously heavy burdens. What was he doing now? Hacking, cutting, chopping, slicing, and trimming away. No — he'd been moved to the kill floor, he'd said, when we were still together.

Did he ever think of me, I wonder? After eleven weeks, he might have forgotten me. Eleven weeks, three days, twenty-two hours — I haven't kept track of the minutes. I think of him, sometimes with love, sometimes with hate, or rage, or jealousy for each friend or fellow worker with whom he shares a word, a laugh, a touch. Touching. He was always touching. I had seen him the few times we bumped into someone he knew — hugging a friend, kissing a woman on both cheeks, tousling a youngster's hair. There had been tenderness in his touch, tenderness in his kiss. It *had* been tenderness, hadn't it? I sip my coffee. It has cooled and tastes flat. I push the cup away. What time is it? I get up to look at the digital clock on the stove: 10:15. Coffee break time. There is hope — until 10:30, there is hope. Then again from 12:30 until one, Valentin's lunch break.

Picking up my cup, I carry it over to the sink, and fit it among the dirty breakfast dishes. I squeeze in some detergent and turn on the tap to wash them by hand rather than turn on the dishwasher. I walk over to the phone to set the ringer to a louder setting in case the noise of the running water muffles the sound, then return to the sink and turn off the tap. It feels good to immerse my arms up to my elbows into the hot water. Lately, I prefer to do the dishes by hand, finding it soothing. It is one of the few household chores I still enjoy. The house badly needs cleaning. Yesterday, Victor complained of finding dust bunnies under the bed. Today perhaps I'll vacuum, but I feel so tired. This lethargy, it seems, comes regularly at this time, as if my body and my mind want to escape the exhaustive yearning, the hopeless waiting for the telephone to ring, the heart-rending disappointment afterwards. Why does the phone not ring?

Morning is the best chance of Valentin calling. He often eats his lunch on the morning coffee break, and sometimes works through lunch. He's probably eating his lunch right now. The lunch his mama so lovingly prepares for him — the hard-crusted bread with fried peppers, so hot they'd skin any normal person's tongue. Eating there, *there* among the slaughtered carcasses, among the blood and entrails and whittled bones and still warm flesh and quivering hearts: the hearts would still be quivering, he said, even after you cut them out. *Eating.* Not thinking to call me. Living easily without me, while I was *dying* without him. It would not make one iota of difference in his life if I died. He hadn't *loved* me. *Something between like and love.* Then why had he told me he loved me and called me *preciosa*? *I feel close to you. You feel like part of me.* Oh God, had I? Then how could he say he didn't love me? Had it all been a sadistic game? The clock reads 10:35. No chance now that he would call. I hope he *chokes* on the hard crust of his mother's bread.

Leaving the dishes to drip dry on the rack, I slide back into the corner of the breakfast nook. I unroll the sleeves of my sweater, which I rolled up earlier to keep from getting wet. I still feel cold. Shivering, I pull my knees up and hug them against me, catching, as I move about, a whiff of aged cheese; my sanitary napkin needs changing. I should take a bath. Yesterday, I'd meant to, and the day before. Later, perhaps. I have no energy for it now; I feel so sleepy. Pulling my sweater over my head, I drape it over myself like a tepee and rest my head on the pine tabletop. A moment later I'm blessed with the sweet oblivion of sleep.

***

The rattle of the mailbox startles me awake. It had to be 12:40. With amazing accuracy, the mailman — letter carriers, they are calling themselves now — delivers the mail at that precise time each day. I get up to retrieve the letters scattered like fallen leaves across the floor at the front door. All bills. Never any mail addressed to me. Without opening them, I lay the letters on the console for Victor to find when he comes home. My cramps have stopped. I should eat; I can never eat until they've stopped, and now I feel a little hungry. In the last eleven weeks, I've lost fifteen pounds. Food goes down like wads of cotton. At the supper table, I move my food from one side of the plate to the other, and when everyone is finished, I gather my plate up with the rest and toss my meal into the garbage.

At times, I force myself to eat. "Maria Rita, you have to eat or you'll get weak — *ti fai fracca! Mangia!* In high school, I had always been too rushed for breakfast; my mother would stir a raw egg yolk into my coffee each morning and make me drink it. To my mother, there is no such thing as too fat. Now, avoiding my mother for fear that she might look into my eyes and know, I *mother* myself. In the daytime sometimes, when everyone is away, I prepare special dishes just for me. Old favourites my mother used to make that Victor refuses to eat; cream of wheat with tomato sauce, mashed potatoes with sugar, cornstarch pudding with lemon rind. Setting these dishes on the table in front of me, I feel like I'm performing a

Corporal Work of Mercy — feeding the hungry or comforting the bereaved, who in their sorrow refuse to eat.

What should I eat? Opening the fridge, I deliberate with little enthusiasm, finally deciding on a cup of plain yogurt to which I add a spoonful of cherry conserves that Victor's mother put down (or is it put up?) last summer. I pull out a kitchen chair and set it in front of the stove as if I'm watching TV. Scooping a spoonful of yogurt, I stare at the digital clock: 12:50; ten minutes left of Valentin's lunch break. I take another spoonful of yogurt; the conserves are so tart they jar my tastebuds. I stir them more evenly into the yogurt. *He called me during his lunch break while I was eating yogurt with some cherry conserves* ... I will remember later, if he phones now.

I put another spoonful of yogurt into my mouth. An automatic reflex reaction suddenly jolts my teeth apart — a cherry stone. I spit it out. *I was eating yogurt and had just bit into a cherry stone when the telephone rang, and it was Valentin* ... I swallow another spoonful, and another. The yogurt isn't fresh; over the week, it has grown acidic and its sourness tingles on my tongue. I eat it anyway until I finish it all, then rinse the cup at the sink. *I had just finished eating a cup of yogurt with cherry conserves and was rinsing my cup in the sink when the telephone suddenly rang...*

It was one o'clock. Picking up the chair, I return it to its place at the breakfast nook, then go into the family room. Today, I feel like listening to music. I turn on the radio. It is playing a soft, sad song. Moving languidly to the beat, I take out the ingredients I need to make tonight's dinner. Breadcrumbs, Romano cheese, parsley, eggs, salt, pepper, two pounds of defrosted ground beef from the fridge that has been there since yesterday. Lacking the energy to cook last night, I changed my mind about making meatballs and made

fish sticks instead. Victor had complained; I had promised
spaghetti and meatballs, which he actually likes, as long as I
don't add my mother's Sicilian pasta sauce, which he finds
too sweet, but which the kids love. "Tomorrow," I'd
promised. Along with Caesar salad, of course.

After putting everything together into a bowl, I knead the
meat with my fingers, mixing the ingredients thoroughly. I
look out the window into the yard. The grass is starting to
turn green. We are having good weather this March. Mrs.
O'Brien, the widow who lives next door, is wandering around
aimlessly in her yard, as if in search of something. Her cat.
She doesn't have it anymore, though. She came over to the
car one day last week while I was pulling out of the driveway
to tell me Tasha had run away. "A fortnight ago, it was," she
said, looking distraught, her Irish brogue more obvious than
usual. "I don't know if I'll ever see her again. I have a good
cry every day, so I do," she says.

So do I, I want to tell her. But I haven't lost my cat. Tears
spring into my eyes. How easy it is to make them appear. I
feel them running down my cheeks. If my hands weren't
covered with meat, I would go out into the hall and stand in
front of the console mirror and watch myself cry. Watch my
mouth distort hideously, my eyes turn red and small and
ugly. It helps to pity *yourself* when no one else pities you.
Other times, standing in front of the mirror, I try to
remember what it felt like to kiss Valentin, and press my lips
against the glass in the silly schoolgirl way, pretending I
actually *am* kissing him. But Valentin is kissing Brenda. He's
been kissing her all along while he was kissing me too. Not
Brenda's fault; she didn't know either. She was naïve. Like
me. But not in the same way I was. Her experience is vaster;
she has lived with someone before Valentin; *been with* several
other someones before that, Valentin had said, his lips curled

in distaste. Necked, kissed, fondled, fucked them all before Valentin had met her. *That* had been the attraction to me. Who else could he find so virginal? It had been with him, really, that I had lost my innocence, if not my virginity. He had no further use for me once I'd become like everybody else. It was with deceit that he had won me over. *I love you, I love you, I love you, there.* He never really *loved* me. *Something between like and love.* Why did I have so much trouble believing that? If someone is in love, they have no desire to make love with anybody else. I had no desire for Victor. Good. That proves it. He never loved me, only used me. It's good that it's over. It's good that he hasn't called.

The radio plays a song I've heard before; something about words of love rolling off the tongue of her lover.

Forked, like a snake, I add, smacking the lump of meat hard. I roll the meat into balls and stack them on a plate. The phone rings. My eyes fly to the digital clock. A quarter after one; my breath catches in my throat. *Valentin has taken a late lunch!* Hurriedly, I scrape meat from my fingers, then go to grab the phone.

"Hello." A silent pause. I am breathless.

"Hello-o…" It is a male voice, deep, throaty, with the same singsong way Valentin has of saying hello. My heart pulses in my throat. "…I'm calling from Excellence Carpet Cleaning Services to let you know that we will be in the area next week cleaning some of your neighbour's carpets. Right now, we're offering a twenty percent discount…"

"I'm not *interested*." I slam the phone down hard, as if I'm swatting a stinging wasp. My body feels shaken and weak. Too cruel! Too cruel! How I *hate* Valentin for doing this to me. I slide into the bench of the breakfast nook and crumple into it. Covering my face with my meat-smeared hands, I begin to sob uncontrollably.

Why have I let this happen to my life? *Why?* I could have said no when he asked me out for coffee. I could have said no to the whole thing. But how can you say no to the most magical thing that's ever happened in your life. My longing for Valentin will *never* end. What difference does it make if he doesn't call me? What difference does it make if he doesn't love me? I still love *him*.

CHAPTER TWENTY-TWO

Spring 1987

It is four months since I last saw Valentin. Valentin has no intention of ever calling again, I tell myself as I look out the kitchen window. I can accept this now that the air in the kitchen is loose and light and easy to breathe, and each chair and cupboard and appliance seems so peacefully in its place. Four months is enough proof, surely, that he will never call again, that he is no longer thinking of me. That he is thinking only of Brenda. Was Brenda beautiful? How much more beautiful would I have had to be for Valentin to be thinking of me instead of her. I have never *been* beautiful. Now I am neither beautiful nor young. Brenda was young; was she beautiful?

Leaning against the high back of the breakfast nook, I try to concentrate and remember all the random comments Valentin has ever made about her: she is Irish, like Mrs. O'Brien, blonde, big busted, but not pretty, he assured me. *You've got nothing to worry about.* Liar! She had to be beautiful. Beautiful and blonde — naturally. *Naturally* blonde? I splutter, then laugh. The Valium the doctor has given me makes me giddy. He's prescribed it to make me relax so I can sleep. I stopped sleeping at night all of a sudden. I lay awake each night, hour after hour without ever closing my eyes. Even Victor is concerned. Don't worry, Victor. My mother always used to tell my brothers and me when we couldn't sleep: *lu lettu è rosa, s'un si dormi si riposa*; bed is a rose, if you don't sleep, you repose.

Anyway, I have lots of time for sleep during the day now that the twins are in grade one and get out at the same time as the other two. So, don't worry Victor. At least, you have me back. Valentin belongs to Brenda now. Brenda the victor. Victor the victor. "V" for victory. "V" for Victor and Valentin and Brenda, who is not exactly a "V" but close. I giggle, then break into a full belly laugh that doubles me over the table where I lay my cheek against the wood, until saliva drools from my mouth onto the tabletop. Stop! Stop! I'm getting a pain in my side. Pulling myself up, I take a deep breath and try to control my hysterical laughing. Victor and Brenda and Valentin. I should drink a toast to them. Go into Victor's liquor cabinet and pour myself a glass of something strong, straight. Add a bottle of Valium — that would put me to sleep for some twenty years — like Sleeping Beauty. Sleeping Ugly, in this case. Each time I look in the mirror now, I see only ugliness.

What did Brenda look like? What form registered through Valentin's fingers as he stroked and touched. How would her lips feel pressed against his, her hair brushing along his cheek, her hand held in his. What was Brenda like? For so long, I've been wanting to know. Valentin said she worked for an insurance company. Valentin's insurance claims were with Landeau Insurance; he had told me that once. He'd said a friend had helped him out with the claim. She *worked* for Landeau! Suddenly, I feel certain of that. Taking the Yellow Pages from a kitchen drawer, I leaf through it until I come to insurance brokers. I skim down the columns. There it is — Landeau Insurance Company Limited on Elm Street off University Avenue. Was Brenda working there? Picking up the telephone, I dial the number in the directory. "Landeau Insurance. Good morning."

"Hello. Uh — I was speaking earlier about an insurance claim with one of your employees — Brenda, I believe it was. I didn't catch her last name…"

"Brenda Kelly?"

"Yes, that must be who it is. There was something I forgot to ask her…"

"One moment, I'll connect you."

A click. Muzak, slow and soft, audible only to those with good hearing, plays in the background. *Clever.* Oh, so clever, Rita. My body feels light, but my heart is beating like a drum.

"Personal Liability. Brenda Kelly speaking. May I help you?" The voice has an Irish lilt to it, like Mrs. O'Brien, only more pronounced; it sounds professional and assertive. I had expected a voice that was less mature, less confident. "I'm sorry. I think I've called the wrong department."

"Would you like me to give you back to switchboard?"

"That's alright. I'll call again direct. Thank you. Goodbye." I wish she hadn't tried to be so helpful. I didn't *want* to like her. But now, I wanted to *see* her. I wouldn't have to take the car, I could take the subway. If I went down, would I be able to *see* Brenda?

I reach for the bottle of Valium inside the top kitchen cupboard where the kids can't reach. I pour myself a glass of water and take one of the pills, instantly feeling calmer, a placebo effect, of course — too soon for the drug to kick in.

It is a quarter after eleven. Soon Brenda would be going to lunch. Grabbing my purse from the front hall closet, I leave the house and head for the subway, not bothering to change my clothes or put on makeup. I tell myself this is something I *must* do, like having an abscessed tooth pulled, or giving birth. Then I can accept. Then I can rest.

***

The subway train passes the bridge scrawled with graffiti; on the concrete base, GOD IS DEAD still stands out boldly. But the second part, OR HE ISN'T LISTENING, is sprayed over with white paint. Has something terrible happened to the author, completely eradicating his hope? Or has someone equally enraged, but more stalwart, defied the cowardice of the first?

The subway passes into darkness, the windows becoming black mirrors of reflection. I notice my face looking haggard, my eyes dark and sunken. How old I look! Turning away from the glass, I look instead at the advertisement posters above that show long-legged models with perfect skin and bright smiles. Which would Brenda resemble?

The building I want to go to is a short walk from where I exit the subway. On the directory near the entrance to the building, I search under the L's and find LANDEAU INSURANCE, sixth floor. I get on the elevator with several men in business suits carrying briefcases; I must seem so out of place with my jogging pants and windbreaker. On the sixth floor, the doors open to a reception desk with a company name gleaming in silver letters on the wall behind it. I step out, hesitating briefly for the first time, but I'm quickly spurred on by the closing of the elevator doors behind me. Approaching the receptionist, I ask, "Is there a Brenda Kelly on this floor?"

"Down the hall, first right, Personal Liability. You'll see a sign at the end of the hall." A black wire mouthpiece from a telephone headset arcs in front of her face like a second smile. How cheerfully she surrenders the information.

At the end of the hallway, a sign says: Personal Liability. It is a large, open area divided by office landscaping — partitions, plants, desks. At the front, there are two desks at right angles to each other, a short distance apart. Both are empty. The one closest to me has a triangular name plate that says *Gail Weir*. On the desk, there is a half-filled cup with beige liquid that has a scum floating on the top and, next to it, several manila files stacked together. I venture over to the other desk, focusing on the same triangular name plate. *Brenda Kelly*. Bingo! But where is she? To have gotten this far and missed her! There seems to be no one else around, either, although I hear voices nearby. Moving over to look past a bookcase that blocks my view, I see people seated in a circle, all women, except for one man with gray hair and a gray suit, who is standing in front of the group talking, obviously instructing the rest. No one looks my way. I study the women in the group — nine altogether — focusing at length on each one, eliminating the gray-haired ones because they are too old, and the brunettes because Valentin said his friend was blonde. That leaves three possibilities: a chubby pink-cheeked blonde with puffy hair the colour of beaten egg whites; a prettyish girl with a blunt haircut that is really more red than blonde; a woman of undetermined age with stringy, brass-coloured hair that reaches past her shoulders. The chubby one is my first instinct. But maybe not. No one seems to notice me standing there — I am, as usual, invisible. I scan the books in the bookcase. Some of them look like interesting reading material, mostly related to personal injuries and how to cope.

The man's voice echoes in the background but is foggy. I wish the meeting would end so Brenda Kelly would go back to her desk and I could see which one she is. Then what would I do? I hadn't planned that far. My intention was simply to look at this woman who had taken Valentin away from me. Or had I taken Valentin away from her? Brenda didn't know she was taking him away from *anyone*. He would never have mentioned seeing a *married* woman. Whichever one Brenda is, she is blameless. It's obvious I can't stand here all day. Defeated, I turn to go back to the elevator, having failed in my mission. I pass a door marked LADIES, and simultaneously become aware of an uncomfortable fullness in my bladder. Adrenalin has steered my actions from the initial idea and I have ignored any bodily functions. The bathroom is a combination lunch/sitting room with a separate area for toilet cubicles. It has a red leatherette lounge like they had in the nurse's room in grade school, a one-legged smoking stand with a button that opens it like a mouth, a card table, and two folding chairs. Next to the door, there is a mirror with a ledge underneath it and opposite that, a small kitchenette with a few cupboards and a sink. The bathrooms are through a doorway on the opposite end of the room. Inside, I find that one of the toilets is plugged with paper; I move to the one beside it, hovering above the toilet seat, letting my sphincter muscles relax, the release accompanied by a profound relief that borders on orgasmic. I check the seat to make sure I haven't inadvertently sprinkled on it, then, conscious of germs, flush the toilet using a piece of toilet paper. After washing my hands, I stop in front of the mirror near the door to comb my hair. I look dreadful. From my purse, I take out a lipstick and colour in my lips. Better. Valentin had said he liked my lips.

The door opens, and one of the girls from the circle comes in — the stringy-haired one. She is carrying a coffee percolator. A plain girl. Almost plain enough. "Hello," she says, seeing me. "Lovely day, isn't it." Her Irish accent is noticeable in the few words alone. So, this was her, then — this was Brenda. I felt as though I had accomplished an enormous feat.

"Hello," I respond.

Brenda, close up, looks older than from a distance, older than Valentin. She is shorter than me. She wears flat pumps and a conservative gray skirt and thick wool sweater that emphasizes a matronly bust. Her eyes are small and pale, her jaw heavyset, masculine, her mouth insignificant. I feel encouraged.

"Excuse me," I say, "Are you by any chance from Personal Liability?"

"I am."

"I was wondering about the books you have on the shelf at the front — can they be used by the general public?"

"Are you insured with us?" *Inshared.* Her accent is more noticeable with some words than others.

"Actually, no."

"Well, they're really for the use of our clients..."

I watch her lips move as she speaks. What an unattractive mouth she has, circular, her lips lacking totally the classic Cupid's bow. A man would not be tempted by such lips. Kissing her would be like kissing a fish. But *Valentin* kisses those lips. Her complexion is freckled, her skin underneath pale, except on her cheeks where she wears blush, the only makeup it seems she is wearing. Her eyes look colourless, and without mascara her pale lashes give her a sleepy look. There is really nothing about her that would attract a man. Yet she attracted Valentin.

A sudden gush of warm blood rushes up my neck to my face. Why, they might have been together just the previous night, their legs entwined, the whiteness of her fair flesh against the furriness of his. His sperm might still be writhing inside her. And yet she moves among others, seemingly so pure and virginal in spite of all they might have done the previous night. She is a good Catholic, too, Valentin told me once of this *friend*, going to Mass each Sunday without fail.

Wasn't that hypocrisy? Why did she go, to be forgiven for her last joining, or to seek absolution for the next? Strange that *I've* never felt any guilt.

Brenda is still talking rapidly, though I am barely listening. "…but I guess if you're going to use the books here, it might be alright. I'll check with my boss, if you like."

"No, don't bother. It's really not that important."

Brenda takes the percolator over to the sink in the kitchenette to fill it with water. It is a large thirty-cup perk, like the kind people rent for parties, that takes a long time to fill. I turn to face the mirror, where I can still see the reflection of her face, but it won't be obvious that I'm staring. Her hands are resting on her hips and she is standing against the counter, staring down at the floor, immersed in thought. What is she thinking about? She seems preoccupied and sad. She keeps her back hunched, as if she were weary.

When the percolator is full, Brenda takes it to the counter, drops in a pouch of coffee grinds, puts on the lid, and plugs it in, then walks towards the door. How languidly she walks, dragging her feet wearily along the floor, staring down at the carpet. Why does she seem so sad? She looks like *me*! Could she and Valentin have had a fight? Perhaps he has found someone else, someone prettier. There were more than enough women for each man — plain, desperate, lonely women — and always the possibility of *fucking* any one of them.

Brenda looks up and nods to me as she exits the door, as if to confirm our shared misery. I go home, more than a little comforted.

Chapter Twenty-Three

It is 11 p.m. on a Thursday. I sit in my nightgown by the living room window watching the rain as I finish my cup of warm milk, which is supposed to help me sleep. Outside, the street lights cast a gloomy double light as they reflect off the wetness of the black asphalt of the road. The rain marks the golden orb of light atop each lamppost with diagonal pencil strokes.

Il pleure dans mon coeur
Comme il pleut sur la ville...

Tears are falling in my heart/Like the rain that is falling on the town... I had memorized the lines once for a French exam. A poem by Verlaine, if I remember correctly. The poem bemoans the loss of someone — his wife, or his lover, perhaps. He *felt* the way I *feel*. A romantic poet with romantic notions. Imagine a heart *crying.* Imagine a heart *breaking.* So why did it hurt so much right there — truly, right there behind my breast.

Valentin had not called. I had visited Brenda and it had given me hope because I had seen that they were not alike, Brenda and Valentin. It is Valentin and I who are alike. He'd said so once. *I feel close to you. You feel like a part of me.* We are soulmates. One in thought and feeling. It doesn't matter who else we might find in a lifetime, we would never find another so alike. Perhaps Valentin has realized this too.

Perhaps he isn't seeing Brenda (she looked so sad). Perhaps he isn't seeing *anybody*. I long to see him, to talk to him, to touch him.

Victor is a sound sleeper, and he has gotten used to my insomnia. I often leave our bed in the middle of the night to get something soothing to drink from the kitchen: hot milk, chamomile tea, even a shot of scotch sometimes, though I don't really like the stuff. Thursday night. Valentin used to work late at the abattoir on Thursday nights, perhaps still does. I would be happy even to see him from a distance, *without* talking to him, *without* touching him. It's just past eleven o'clock. If he's there, he'll be leaving to go home at midnight.

Without really thinking it through, I put on my trench coat, grab my purse, and lock the front door quietly behind me. The station wagon is parked outside our garage, so I don't have to activate our noisy garage door opener. I reach the meat packing plant where Valentin works at a quarter to midnight. It is dark and raining heavily, but I can hear the *mooing* of cattle and *oinking* of pigs waiting for the kill. I'm glad I'm not able to look at them — poor dumb creatures. But Valentin looks. Looks and murders, indifferently.

There are many cars parked in the parking lot. My heart leaps in my chest when I catch sight of a red vehicle at the far end of the lot. As I drive closer, I see it is unmistakably Valentin's vehicle: the licence plate MEAT ME, the ladder going nowhere, the drops of blood that are windows. I park further back in the parking lot, hiding the station wagon behind an eighteen-wheeler, but with the nose of my car sticking out, so that I am still able to see the van. I wait until half past midnight, listening to the pounding of the rain on the roof of the station wagon, but no Valentin emerges from any of the buildings. He must be working the all-night shift and won't be out till dawn. I get out and walk towards Valentin's van in the pouring rain, keeping to the poorly lit patches of the parking lot, gripping my coat tightly against the rain, while I breathe in the stench of burning carcasses and diesel fuel.

When I reach Valentin's van, I walk over to the driver door, and with the palms of my hand, wipe away the water dribbling down the window glass; the rain runs down my uplifted arms and wets the nightgown I am wearing under my trench coat. In the sparse light of a nearby lamppost, I can see the captain's chairs and the front of the dash with open holes, like gouged out eyes, in places where the stolen stereo equipment had been. I run my fingers over the chrome handle of the door. It is wet and smooth and cold as ice. Valentin's hands touch that handle each day, many times, had touched it, perhaps, only a few hours before. I put my face against it; the cold metal sears my cheek like a branding iron. I press my lips to it; it feels like when at Perpetual Help Devotions every Tuesday at our parish, I would march up to the altar with the other faithful to kiss the cold feet of a metal crucifix. But colder still. Like an aluminum ice cube tray. As a kid, I would press my lips against the frosty tray and my warm lips would stick to it. If it were winter instead of spring, my lips would stick to the door handle, too. I would have to tear myself away and leave the skin from my lips behind. As a gift. Like Van Gogh, who cut off his ear to prove his love. I would give Valentin my lips; he'd said he liked them. Devotions and rituals: I could make this mine every Thursday night.

The front of my nightgown, where the trench coat has opened up, is soaked. Water drips down the ends of my hair, and I keep blinking water away from my eyes to see. The back of the van is in darkness and I can't see if it is made up as a couch or knocked down into a bed; maybe he'd gone camping with Brenda, maybe they'd slept there in each other's arms, his seed spent — wasn't that the biblical term? I could see him humping Brenda there, from behind, like the mating crows, sucking in his breath, half in agony, half in ecstasy, sounds of sex escaping his mouth, as he pumps his sperm into her. The picture becomes so vivid, it physically jars me, and I shake my head until the image fades. The door is locked, but I pull at the handle anyway, making rattling noises. Goddamn you! Goddamn you! Goddamn you! Even though I am freezing on the outside, I feel as though I'm burning deeper inside, my internal organs the kindling. How consuming it is, this jealousy; I have never felt it before, never had cause to. A volatile thing, unlike hate, which only smolders; it is a venom boiling inside, caustic, acid.

Bastard! Fornicator! Seducer of women! Liar! I chant the words aloud like a litany. How could I ever have gotten involved with him? Yes, yes, we pay for our sins, but not in hell. We are all punished, and *justly* punished. The agony equals the ecstasy, precisely. I've caused my *own* destruction. I believed that he loved me, believed there was tenderness in his touch. I had *mistaken* his touch for tenderness, when it was only technique. Yes, technique, I'm sure of that now. And he honed it and honed it. Tempter! Seducer! Fornicator! Ruiner of women!

Shivering and wet, I unlock the rear door of my station wagon. Throwing open the luggage compartment underneath the floor, I rifle among objects that clang against each other, until I find by feel what I want — the tire iron Victor uses for changing tires. I will destroy the evil. Smash the van apart, watch the windows crumble — the blood-red windows — rip the upholstery with my nails. *Destroy it! Destroy it!*

Car lights appear at the entrance to the parking lot. I recognize the white and blue with superimposed black lettering. I pull my trench coat around me and tie it tightly with the belt, just as the police cruiser pulls up beside me. A young officer with a baby face and a thick mustache to make him look older rolls down his window to question me.

"Evenin' ma'am. Are you in any trouble?"

"No — well, just a flat tire." I raise the tire iron in verification.

"Can we be of assistance?" *We* is the officer's uniformed and mustachioed double sitting in the seat next to him.

"Too late. I've already looked after it. Not the first time I've done this," I assure him, smiling and with amazing calmness. "Unless you can call off this rain. I really got a soaking."

The officer smiles back, his cheeks forming a globe that catches the light. "'Fraid I can't do that, ma'am. I guess you'd better get home and get changed. Sorry we couldn't be of help."

"Thanks just the same, officer."

They wait until I get into my station wagon and drive away.

Back home, I have not been missed. Everyone is still asleep. Quickly, I change into a dry nightgown and towel my hair dry. It is still damp, and I am still shivering when I get under the covers.

Chapter Twenty-Four

It is a misconception that people get sick from being out in the cold and wet. They had done studies — sat people on blocks of ice for hours and hours each day, feet dipped in ice water, and none of them had gotten sick. So, my pneumonia could not have been caused by standing out in the rain. Still, I developed a fever the day after going to the meat plant, and I've been nursing my illness for three weeks now. I haven't really been looking after myself, truth be told, so maybe that's why it's lingering. But the laundry still has to be done, my family fed, and Victor has always admitted to anyone at all that he couldn't cook and, therefore refused to do so. Valentin could cook, though. He could cook and wash and sew, and often did, he said, when he had to, to help his mother out, who suffered terribly from arthritis. Valentin could have nursed me beautifully back to health, if he cared. Once, he had taken me back to his house when his mother wasn't home and cooked me a *tortilla,* like his mother made. He'd peeled and cut and fried potatoes, then taken half a dozen beaten eggs and poured them over the fries, cooking the mixture slowly, coaxing it to firmness, turning it carefully until the whole thing solidified into a tasty golden mass. It was scary watching him. He was a better cook than I was! He'd encouraged me to eat, though I wasn't the least bit hungry, lifting food with his own fork into my mouth. The nurturing instinct was strong in him. His innate qualities were feminine. He possessed patience, concern, compassion. Yet, he could be cruel. So why did I still, sometimes, root out the good qualities and overlook the rest?

Sitting at the kitchen table, leafing through the newspaper, I feel weighted with the torpidity of confinement. The children have left for school; they walk home now most days. I am reading the paper and having my morning coffee. In general, however, I am feeling better. The fever has stopped, although I am still getting the night sweats. It is a viral strain of pneumonia. The antibiotics can't cure it, but merely reduce the risk of secondary infection, the doctor said. Continue with the Valium, he said, for the insomnia.

Today, feeling agitated, I flip through the newspaper. The lead stories in the paper are political: The auditor general's report shows that millions of Ontario's dollars are being spent unnecessarily (I think I read the same thing around this time last year); Libyan terrorists had been unsuccessful in a Paris bombing attempt; there was unrest in Gaza. I continue to the Health and Women's Section, which I enjoy more: a study showed that chlorinated drinking water was more pathogenic than untreated lake water (that's just great, *now* what do I give the kids to drink!); a baby had drowned in a washing machine. How ghastly — in a *washing* machine? How could that happen? How could any mother be so negligent? The newspaper never fails to shock me, to remind me of the uncertainty of the world, the unpredictability of people. In China, a father had killed his baby girl by pushing bamboo splinters into her head. Apparently, the Chinese government allows each couple to have only one offspring, and the father wanted a second chance at having a *male* child. The news item makes me shiver. What about the mother, I wonder? Did she know? Did she go along with it? I am grateful to be safely in my own kitchen. Though today, somehow, it doesn't feel as safe — the stories I read haunt me.

Folding the paper back together, I set it to one side. I would rather not read anything depressing today, I feel depressed enough. The coffee in my mug is cold, but I drink it anyway. Glancing around the kitchen, I notice a slip attached to the fridge with a magnetic banana. I get up to see what it says. It is a shopping list left by Victor. He has written: shampoo, deodorant, razor blades. For several days, he has been encouraging me to leave the house. Underneath the items Victor has listed, a final item, *sour gummies,* has been added in a child's sprawl. Smiling, I slip the sheet from under the magnet. I feel well enough to go out again, actually, and resolve this morning to do so. To the list, I add socks and underwear for the boys, and a Mother's Day card for my mother. I wash the breakfast dishes quickly, stacking them on the rack to drip dry. Before leaving the house, I comb my hair and put on lipstick, not bothering to change out of my pullover and blue jeans.

It is a beautiful sunny spring day outside, too warm for a jacket. Yet, I feel no joy, like I used to on such days. When I step outside, the brightness blinds me, as if I have just come out of a dungeon — a dungeon like the one in my dreams. The recurring dreams of the old hag have returned now. But I shake the thought from my mind. Still, I refuse to allow myself to inhale deeply of the day's freshness — the clean smell of cut grass, the spicy scent of hyacinths erupting from the warming earth, the sweet scent of crabapple blossoms, a painful reminder of this time last year. I feel no desire to rejoice in the beauty around me. Without pausing even to admire the profusion of tulips that line the side of the garage, I get into the car and drive away.

The Woolco store is a just a few miles from my house. The store is quiet this morning, with few customers. Here and there, along the counters, store clerks are bent over books doing merchandise checks. Empty and quiet like this, the store seems extravagantly large. I take out the list from my purse and read it through. Shampoo, deodorant, razor blades, sour gummies, underwear, socks, card. Heading for the drug section, I pick up first what Victor requested. Boys socks and underwear are together in another section of the store. I prefer cotton socks for the boys because their feet sweat in their running shoes, but I can only find 80% cotton with 20% nylon blend. It will do; the socks the boys are wearing now are almost worn through at the toe. I take twelve pairs in navy, size eight to ten and a half, which will fit all of them. Underwear is in the next aisle. I choose the same brand, as usual, two pairs for each boy.

In ladieswear, I stop briefly to look at the new spring blouses. What good is it to dress up if there is no one you care to look attractive for? I don't give a damn how I look anymore, though it does shock me, what I see in the mirror, when I can dare to look. In a few months, I have aged ten years, it seems. A woman stops next to me to look at the blouses too. She is tall and neatly dressed, her hair cut attractively short. Would I look better with my hair that short, I wonder? The woman casts a disinterested glance along the aisle of women's clothing and walks on.

In the greeting card section, the Mother's Day cards have been well picked over. The only one that I like has no matching envelope. I hold it against several other envelopes, hoping to find a match, but without success. I'm getting weary now of shopping; my neck muscles are starting to stiffen. The air conditioning is blowing right at me from above, and I feel my nose start to run. Unzipping my purse, I take out a Kleenex and blow it, leaving the purse open in case I should need another. With little deliberation, I pick a card I don't care for, but which has a matching envelope.

Drawn by a sudden whiff of eucalyptus, I move further down the aisle towards a display of dried flowers and gift items of silver, brass, and cut crystal that flash brilliant under the lighted display. An ornamental dove of glimmering crystal catches my eye. I pick it up, admiring the detail on it, the smoothness of the polished finish, the beautifully chiseled edges that refract the light and make it sparkle, the satisfying weightiness within my palm. How long would it last on the coffee table with my rowdy twins, I wonder? Turning it over, I check the price ticket underneath: fifty-nine dollars! Ridiculous, so dear! I quickly put it back on the shelf. It is lovely, though, but Victor would never allow me to spend so much on a trinket. My nose is still dripping; I pull out another Kleenex from my purse and blow it again. Looking at my list, I see sour gummies is all that I have missed. I debate whether to buy four small bags for each of the kids or one large one for everybody to share. To avoid a fight, I decide on the four small bags. Heading for the checkout, I pass the display of gift items again. How truly exquisite it is, the crystal dove. I pick it up once more, feeling its cool smoothness, like velvet, like skin in secret places — the breasts, the buttocks, the inner thighs. I run my fingers along the dove's crystal body. How easily it slides between my palms as I hold it, then just as easily, propelled by its weightiness, through my palms, disappearing like an anchor to the bottom of my purse. My heart starts beating wildly with excitement, the way it had when I was about to meet Valentin. Hurrying, I veer my shopping cart around aisles, speeding past counters, on my way to the checkout. My brow feels damp with perspiration as I hand the girl my Visa card. A flush of excitement rises in my cheeks. Clutching my bags, I walk quickly to the front door, heavy metal and glass barriers that once opened automatically but have been converted to manual for economy, delaying my escape.

Outside, finally. I am safe, but my heart is still pounding from the excitement and the danger and I let out a little laugh. I catch sight of the station wagon and hurry towards it in a walking jog. As I search for the keys in my purse, someone touches my shoulder. Turning, I recognize the tall woman I'd seen earlier in ladieswear with the short hairstyle. It didn't seem to sink in at first what it was she was saying. Something about wanting to look in my purse. Surely, she couldn't mean what she says. Her eyes are the ardent blue of a hot flame rimmed with red; she is full of her own sense of importance. She means to be obeyed. I open my purse.

***

The manager insists on calling my husband. It's either that or the police. I feel like a kid at the principal's office who has seriously misbehaved and is nervously awaiting the arrival of her parents before punishment is meted. Victor is both angry and shocked. I haven't been myself, he explains, been dealing with health issues, unexpected deaths in the family that have greatly affected me, he pleads — been on the verge of a nervous breakdown for reasons doctors have not been able to determine. The manager agrees not to press charges but asks that I not return to the store again. This will be a hardship, since I do most of my shopping for the kids' clothes here. Strangely enough, I do not break into tears during any of this, but look on somewhat stunned, as if I am an objective observer and have nothing to do with the woman they're talking about.

Victor makes sure that I get safely home but has got to get right back to his classes and says we'll talk more about this tonight. I decide I need to take a bath and wash my hair. I fill the clawfoot bathtub with water as hot as I can stand and lay my head back over the rolled rim. When I was little and wanted to be by myself, I would go up to my bed and lie with my head dangling over the edge of the mattress and look up at the ceiling — white, uncluttered with only a light fixture in the centre taking up space. I'd wanted to have sticky pads on my feet and be able to walk on the ceiling like flies. I was happy then, life bright, white as the ceiling. Now it is gray, even though the sun is shining outside. The world's colour is gray. There is no other colour. Gray fog clouds my existence, darkens my thoughts, saturates my brain cells. Dull, gray, and meaningless, my life. Even my insides, the pink flesh and red blood, I imagine have turned gray, like meat turned putrid after being left out too long. I can see no end to my grayness; it would go on and on. I let my head slide under the water and hold on to my breath for as long as I can. Drowning is a pleasant death, apparently. I had come close to it once on our honeymoon, when we stopped for a dip in the ocean, a large wave had knocked me over, tearing me away from Victor's hand; unable to swim or gain my footing, I had floated underwater and realized and accepted, strangely without fear, that I was drowning. Then Victor's hand had found me. He had saved me. Why couldn't he save me now?

Breathe or burst. I breathe. So ignominious, drowning in a bathtub. If I meant to end it, it must be more dramatic. Jump in front of a subway train. No — too messy. But at least it would never make the news — an unwritten agreement between press and police to discourage rashes of suicides. Swallow arsenic like Flaubert's *Madame Bovary*. It had seemed impossibly painful in the book.

I shampoo and rinse my hair and twirl a towel around it like a turban. Wrapping myself in my terry cloth bathrobe, I go into my bedroom where the shades are closed and it is dark and gray. When would the grayness end, and the endless longing? Would I ever get control of my life? Today I had joined the ranks of common *shoplifter*. Bile rises in my throat, threatening to choke me. Doubling over, I break the silence in the dark house with a paroxysm of sobs. I shove my fist into my mouth, but sobs and tears continue to escape from my body simultaneously. I stagger towards my bed. I want to sleep, sleep for a long time, and not think. On the night table there is a glass and a bottle of Valium. I swallow two pills without water and taste bitterness. I lay down on the bed, eyes closed, and wait. Nothing. When I look up, I see a ceiling that's dark gray and pressing down on me like a coffin lid. I reach for the pills and take all that remain in the bottle. I want to sleep for a long time, maybe forever. How many pills have I taken? Have I taken too many?

The clock radio shines the time at me: 2:50. Ten to three. The children will be walking home soon. What if they find me unconscious? I panic. I grab the phone and clumsily dial Maddy's number. "Maddy? I need your help." My voice is sluggish, seems not to be coming out of my mouth, seems instead to be an echo reverberating in a hollowness inside me. "Maddy, can you help me?"

"Rita? I was just on my way out to a demo. What's wrong? You sound funny."

"Maddy can you come over?"

"Now? I'm kinda in a rush."

"I think I took too many pills."

"What kind of pills?"

"Valium."

"How many did you take?"

"I'm not sure. All there were in the bottle. Five I think."

"How strong were they? I take it sometimes, too, when I'm uptight, but mine are pretty weak. Why did you take so many?"

"I don't know."

"Well, look on the bottle and see what strength they are."

I pick up the container, angling it towards the sparse light creeping in between the blinds, twirling the bottle back and forth like a mercury thermometer in order to read the words on the label. "Valium ... five milligrams," I read into the phone.

"Times five — that's twenty-five milligrams altogether. Rita, that isn't even enough to kill a *cat*. You'll get a damn good sleep out of it, though. Lie down and relax. You'll be fine."

"You couldn't come over, just for a few minutes, just to talk? I really need to talk to you."

"I'm already late, Rita. How about next week? We'll have lunch somewhere. I'll give you a call."

"Right. See you Maddy."

I hang up the phone. My stomach feels queasy, but I doubt that I will vomit. My stomach, stubborn and tolerant, usually retains whatever I put into it. If I help it along, maybe. Walking unsteadily to the bathroom, I kneel in front of the toilet and, with two fingers, stab the soft pendulous piece of flesh dangling at the back of my throat — the uvula. My stomach lurches with each jab until, finally, it erupts in a gush of stinking water. I rinse the acidy taste from my mouth and gargle with mouthwash. Then, feeling weak, I return to the bed. I am half asleep when the children come through the front door, Alison having her own key.

"Mom!"

"I'm up here."

From the stairs, comes the thumping of many feet; all four of the children burst into the bedroom.

"Mom, you won't believe what happened at school," Alison says. "It's *really* terrible."

"What happened?"

"At morning recess — this lady *jumped* from the nineteenth floor of the apartment building next to our school and *killed* herself!"

"What!" I lift my head in alarm. "What are you saying?"

"I saw it too," Micah confirms. "Everybody at school saw it. You should have seen the hole she made in the ground!"

"Oh my God! Oh my God! Joshua, Jamie — you saw it too?" Even before they can answer, I see they *have* by the wide-eyed terror on their small faces. Jamie is shaking.

"We heard this *scream*," Alison says, making it sound, by her intonation, like a question. "Then we saw her falling. She hit her head on another balcony on the way down. She made such a loud noise when she hit the ground — like a gun going off. One of the teachers — Mr. Larson — he jumped the fence to help her, but he couldn't do anything. And he was yelling, '*Call an ambulance! Call an ambulance!*'"

"Yeah, Mom, you should have seen," Joshua adds, breathless from the excitement, "she made this *big* hole in the ground, honest. Her head was all bloody, and her top was open like this," he says, pulling a corner of his T-shirt up to reveal his belly button. "And it was all *blue,* and she was lying on the ground like this." He drops to the floor and sprawls out on it with his arms splayed.

A chill goes through me. "Joshua — *no!*" I scream, and jumping from the bed, pull him up. "My God! Are you children alright?" I feel outrage for this woman traumatizing my children's lives, then remorse for being so unfeeling. "Maybe, it was an accident."

"No, she jumped on purpose," Micah tells me. "The police said so. She killed herself."

Why, I ask myself, although I know the answer only too well. Depression was a hole, a deep hole of darkness, desperation, solitude. Couldn't someone have reached out to help her? *Every* man is an island. Everyone dies *alone.*

"Why would someone *do* something like that?" Alison asks.

"No one can say, Alison, what makes people do certain things. Maybe she was sick and her mind wasn't thinking straight."

"But why didn't somebody help her?"

"I don't know." I put my arms around Alison, then reach out to gather in the other three as well, but my arms are not long enough to enclose them all, to protect them always.

CHAPTER TWENTY-FIVE

I am first to arrive at my real estate class this morning, even before the teacher — a stern Englishman with a dour, wrinkled face; the class had nicknamed him Pruneface. He had divided the class into groups, each group working together at a separate table. All but one of the students at my table has taken the previous two segments of the course with me: Jim had rejoined the course after pausing between segments. He is from out of town, cottage country, somewhere in the Muskokas. Cocky and young, with slick blond hair from which a vagrant strand consistently falls on his forehead, he is the class live-wire, an ex-marine whose volume of energy I could not imagine capable of being confined to one ship. The others in my group are Chuck, a former private detective from the time when infidelity was the only grounds for divorce, his job having been to catch the lovers in the act; Greg, an insurance agent for a now-defunct company (Landeau, I wonder); Ian, a soft-spoken Scotsman and retired postal worker who'd managed to get the highest marks in the two previous exams; and Ashley, a recent university graduate with long, copper-coloured hair, perfectly symmetrical features, and naturally glowing skin — the kind of startling beauty that would always allow her to achieve things in life more easily, listings included, no doubt. The other students are transfers from other locations where they had taken their previous course segments.

I am extremely busy now, concentrating hard during the day at my full-time classes, studying at night for our final exam. I have little time for self-pity. Little time to think of Valentin. But I *do* think of him in spare moments. At first, driving to school in the morning, I'd note each red van that passed me; red was not a common colour, fortunately, but there were some. At first, I'd zero in on the faces of the drivers, tradesmen mostly, but so many had unshaven faces that too often my heart lurched in mistaken recognition, leaving a shakiness in my chest that didn't stop until I reached the school. Now, if I see a red van, I first scan the licence plate for the words: MEAT ME. I feel this is forgivable since it is the only compulsive thing I still do. I tell myself I lack nothing in life, except passion, excitement, and *extreme* happiness. In truth, I am content enough, and, if not exciting, my life is at least interesting, and I am learning a great deal. There are new revelations, new experiences, new friends. Even lunch is a daily treat — fried chicken, pot pies, roast beef, scrumptious desserts, all surprisingly tasty for cafeteria food. Someone always joins me at my table. Several of the men, in fact, seem to gravitate towards me during lunch as if they truly *enjoy* my company. One of them, a bank teller who was taking time off to take the course, actually told me I was attractive. He added he was married with two kids. So was I, I told him, mother of four. He had unblemished pink cheeks and perfectly combed black hair, parted on the side with a pale, perfect part. Did I fool around? he asked. Jokingly? Lout. Had something changed about me, I wondered. Had the aura changed around me, like it had around Maddy? Did I exude an essence of promiscuity? Or did longing for a man put women in perpetual estrus that men could sniff out? I made sure to avoid the bank teller after that.

The rest of the class starts to arrive now. Ashley and Greg enter the room, continuing a discussion they must have started somewhere between the parking lot and the classroom.

"How can you *do* that?" Ashley asks.

"If she doesn't like it, she knows what *she* can do."

"What's that all about?" Chuck asks, amused.

"Greg here just divulged how he augments his income each year by twenty thousand," Ashley explains.

"Will you share it?"

"No problem. I go into a new housing development when it's almost completed and buy the last house. We live in it for a year. By then the same model has gone up twenty, thirty thousand, so we sell her."

"You sell her? Doesn't your wife mind, moving each year?" I ask. "All that packing."

"That's what *I* was wondering," Ashley says. "And what about those poor kids, uprooting them over and over."

"What has she got to do all day," Greg says. "That's her job, and I'm her boss and she does what *I* say. Otherwise, she might as well go out and work."

Several more students file into the class, including Jim, who looks particularly chipper this morning. "Hey, guys," Jim says, coming over to the table, "have I got something for you." He pulls out a stack of photocopied sheets from a briefcase. "Looky here," he says, proudly presenting copies of a final real estate exam. He begins handing them out.

"Nice going, Jim-boy," Ashley says. Her delight increases with each turn of the page. "Hey, this comparative market analysis is almost identical to the one we did in class. It's worth twenty points. That'll be a giveaway."

"How did you get these?" I ask.

"I got my ways."

Chuck arrives at our table, and putting down his coffee, anxiously grabs a copy of the sheets. "Help — look at these acts they want you to know. I'll never be able to keep them straight."

"So, are you going to tell us where you got these?" I ask again.

"From this girl I met who works at the board office. It's an old exam, don't worry, but she says it's not much different from the ones they're giving now. Of course, I had to soften her up a bit before she'd give it to me. It's an old trick I learned in grade school. You pick the ugliest girl in the class and tell her how pretty she is. Then you ask her if she'll let you copy her homework. The tough ones — you have to tell them how smart they are too and keep at it until they turn sweet and fluffy as whipped cream."

"You'd better watch it," Chuck warns. "You keep whipping that cream long enough and it will turn into a hard lump of butter."

Everyone laughs. Jim remains unruffled. "By the way, can anyone help me out — seeing how I've made this unselfish contribution? I have to go by my bank at lunchtime but I haven't got enough gas to get me there and I'm flat broke. Anyone willing to lend me twenty bucks till this afternoon?" He is asking everyone hanging around my table, but he is looking directly at me. "I guess I can lend you twenty dollars," I tell him.

"Thanks, little momma."

Later, when I walk into the lounge where everyone goes for coffee break, Jim is circling the room with the twenty dollars looking for change for the pop machine. "Would you believe I haven't even got fifty-five cents for a Coke?" he tells me.

I wrinkle my nose but dig into my purse. "Here," I say, reaching into the change pocket of my wallet and pulling out fifty-five cents. "I wouldn't want you to feel deprived."

He walks over to the vending machine and inserts the money; when the can rolls out, he twirls it once in the air and catches it, nodding at me in a gesture of gratitude. When he pulls the metal tab, the pop spurts out furiously, raining a spray of sticky liquid on him and on the carpet.

I run to get some damp paper towels from the bathroom and help him clean up the mess. Everyone has gone back to class by the time we are finished.

"Coming? I ask.

"Not till I have a cigarette." Reaching in his shirt pocket, he pulls out a package of Craven "A". Seeing the red and white packet sends a shiver through me. It was Valentin's brand. He pats the pocket of his shirt. "You wouldn't have a match?" he asks.

I hesitate. "I might have." I unzip my purse and, from the side pocket, take out a matchbook that says Sleepytime Motel; I had taken it from the motel a lifetime ago. What if Victor found it? I suddenly realize. I hand it to Jim. "Here — you can keep it."

"You sure?"

"I don't smoke."

He rips out a match and strikes it on the friction strip. Closing the matchbook, he studies the cover smiling, then asks, "What's his name?"

"Who?"

He nods towards the matchbook and winks.

I look at him, shaken. "I'm married."

His smile twists derisively. "What's his *name*?"

I shake my head, grab my purse, and hurry back to the class.

At lunch time, instead of going to the cafeteria, I stay behind to study while I nibble on a sandwich I've brought from home. In an hour, I've covered the evening's reading assignment and have reviewed two of the previous chapters.

"What's this, browning off?" Greg says.

I smile and put my book aside. "I was staying away from that fattening cafeteria food."

"They had your favourite today, Rita," Ashley says, brushing her long hair off her shoulders. "Chicken with cashews."

"No — don't tell me that. I can't *stand* it," I laugh.

"I sure couldn't *stand* it," Chuck said. "I was hoping they'd have roast beef."

Jim is the last student to return from lunch. The teacher is about to begin but waits for him to take his seat. Instead, Jim walks over to me and, clamping his cigarette at the corner of his mouth, reaches ceremoniously in his back pocket for his wallet. With a flourish, he deposits a crisp twenty-dollar bill on top of my desk. A smug self-satisfied smirk curls the vacant corner of his mouth. He doesn't bother to thank me, just continues smirking.

I pick up the money and ask coolly, "Was I alright?" Everyone seated nearby starts to snigger. Others look on, amused. Pruneface, out of ear reach, looks wide-eyed at the class, wondering if some joke is being played on him without his realizing it. Jim's face reddens. His confidence faltering slightly, he tells me in a somewhat serious tone, "I still owe you the fifty-five cents, but I haven't got any change right now."

"Forget it," I tell him. "That didn't count. You didn't get your money's worth, the way it came shooting out all over the place."

Chuck is roaring. The others in the class who had witnessed the Coke scene earlier in the lounge are bent over in hysterics.

Jim takes his seat meekly and, after stubbing out his cigarette, buries his face in his book.

CHAPTER TWENTY-SIX

Summer 1987

"The money's *mine*. When it's *sold*, the money will be *mine*. My grandmother left her house to me, according to tradition, since I was her namesake. I want to keep it separate, in my own account, so I can make my own decisions on what to do with it." I hate arguing while Victor's driving. His driving always makes me edgy anyway, and today, as we drive to the yearly summer bash that Frank Farrell gives for his teachers, I feel edgier still, not only because of the driving or the debate we're having, but mostly because I'm going to have to socialize, not only with Frank Farrell and his wife yet again, but all the other teachers he works with as well.

"Isn't this argument a little premature?" Victor says. "You don't even have your licence yet. The house hasn't even been sold."

"I'll have my licence in a few weeks. I want to clear things up *now*. You've made the decisions about every investment since we've been married, GICs and RRSPs and mutual funds and whatever … and I know it's money *you've* earned, but now I have an opportunity to do something on my own, to invest in my own way."

"What way?"

"I told you — add a laundry room and maybe an office for myself where the sunporch is and, later, if I have enough money and a good deal comes along, invest in some real estate for us."

"Real estate? What if you blow it, Rita? You don't know anything about it."

"I've gotten over ninety-five percent on all my exams!"

"That doesn't mean *anything*."

"Really? Look — can we change the subject for now?"

"Fine. Did you bring your bathing suit?"

"What for? I can't swim."

"You could if you'd taken lessons."

He's right. I'd had the chance to take lessons in university. It was one of the options available as part of the obligatory physical education classes my first year. But I had been too self-conscious about my scars — didn't want to be stared at — and, consequently, didn't take that option and never learned to swim. Instead, I had taken ballroom dancing. Remembering that brought to mind Valentin, and the dancing we did at the apartment with all the potted greenery. But I don't want to remember that, and I brush the memory aside. For the moment anyway. Although those memories will always remain part of my life, I have learned to compartmentalize them. My focus now is on developing a career and caring for my family — for Victor, for my children who need me — and looking after myself. Someone *else's* death startled me back to life — the woman whose life ended in a hole in the ground that she *herself* created — a woman I had never known and would never know anything about. Yet, her death had shaken me back to my senses.

"You don't have to swim. Everyone'll be wearing their bathing suits and you'll look out of it. It's a pool party Farrell's giving, for Chrissake!"

"That's too bad. I don't feel comfortable in a bathing suit. He's having a barbeque, isn't he?"

"Yeah."

"All the other years, he's called it a barbeque, now, all of a sudden, because he put in a pool, it's a *pool* party. Anyway, I wore a sun dress." I don't feel comfortable in that either; my body is pale and pasty and has not seen much summer sun.

We drive through a brick entranceway that opens into the development where Farrell lives. It is a quiet residential area in Mississauga, fairly new, but established and in demand. Houses listed here sell quickly. Victor turns sharply into a driveway. Farrell greets us at the door, and Victor proffers the requisite bottle of wine. I address him as Mr. Farrell, but he insists I call him Frank. We follow him through the house to the back where an above ground pool sits, massive in the small backyard. Adjacent to the door, someone's husband is in command of a double gas barbeque; he is lovingly turning sizzling meat and black sausages on the grill. On a nearby table, there is a selection of charcuterie and crudités, artfully arranged on wooden cutting boards that look like two-inch-thick, horizontal slabs of tree trunks, still bordered with their original bark. The barbeque is giving off a wave of warmth and tantalizing aromas laced with the smell of propane gas. Everyone is either in the pool or sitting on lawn chairs on the high deck bordering it, but all are wearing bathing suits. I ignore the sardonic *I-told-you-so* look Victor hurls my way and follow his lead, greeting everyone informally with a wave from a distance.

"What can I get you to drink?" Frank asks, unfolding two lawn chairs for us.

"Rye and ginger for me. Rita usually has Dubonnet, if you have it."

"I'll have a beer, Frank, if you don't mind. Whatever kind you have in the cooler."

"Chilled glass?"

"Out of the bottle's fine."

Judy — the trophy wife — comes sashaying out of the kitchen towards us carrying a tray with a round, dark pumpernickel bread that looks like a cowpie filled with green mush. "Spinach dip?" she offers, bending down to our seated level. Her breasts inside her bathing suit resemble two large grapefruits squeezing into each other at the centre; you can tell by their turgidity that they are implants. "You're supposed to rip off bits of the bread and dip them in the filling," she explains helpfully. Victor and I both try some, and we both compliment her on her culinary prowess, even though the dip tastes like something that's been through the garburator.

Ruth, the school secretary, comes out of a change room, which is really an aluminum storage shed assembled next to the pool. She is tugging at the left leg band of her black bathing suit. I know a little bit about her from what Victor has told me. She has recently been through a bitter and painful divorce. She looks slightly haggard but, all things considered, is putting on a brave front. I say hello and ask, "How are you doing, Ruth?" She is an athletic, wiry woman with skinny, muscular legs and arms that remind me of Miss Hawkins, my high school gym teacher. She is one of the few people from Victor's school that I sometimes talk to when I need to get a message to him. It's easy for me to imagine her despondency. But it seems as though she's making an effort. Tonight, she's brought a date and walks across the deck to sit next to him, a slim, intellectual type with horn-rimmed glasses and Scandinavian blond hair that hangs boyishly over his eyes.

"Victor, you finally made it."

"Nice to see you, Noreen."

I remember Noreen from the last barbeque and realize that the person manning the grill is Noreen's husband, Arturo. It is a second marriage for both of them, and obviously, they have navigated the difficulty of divorce successfully. She's a friendly sort, a little on the plump side — what you might call pleasingly plump — with a frizzy blonde perm. "Well, some people take their time getting ready," Victor tells her, meaning me, of course, which isn't true. I was ready to go before Victor, but he wanted to stop for a better bottle of wine than what we had at home to bring to the barbeque. "I see Arturo is in charge of the barbequing again this year."

She looks lovingly towards the smoking barbeque. "Nothing my Arturo enjoys more than barbequing," she says with a little laugh. She pronounces the "r" in Arturo as a soft "r", purring it out, instead of a hard "r", as it should be pronounced in Spanish. "He's Argentinian, remember — they're practically *born* knowing how to do barbeque."

What is it with men and barbeques? Victor won't let me near ours. It's the only time he cooks.

Frank returns with our drinks. "Well, don't waste time, you two," he says, putting his arms amicably around both of us. "Get into your bathing suits." His hand presses too familiarly on my bare back; my body goes taut. "You're looking really good these days, Rita," he tells me. "What have you done to yourself?"

Insinuating I didn't look good before, I guess.

"Give us a chance to finish our drinks," Victor says, excusing both of us from using the pool just yet. He's watching a young woman with short blonde hair who's about to dive into the pool. She does, effortlessly, elegantly. "Who's that?" I ask.

"Oh, that's Julie, our new gym teacher — joined us this year."

"Well, what do you think of her, anyway?" Frank asks.

"Hmm?"

Frank is gazing admiringly at the shimmering lapis lazuli waters of his newest acquisition. "The pool — what do you think of her?" Victor and I both direct a scrutinizing eye at the above ground pool with its railed surrounding deck. Across from us, attached to the rail, Frank has hung a sign that reads: *Welcome to our 'ool ... You'll notice there's no "p" in it. We'd like to keep it that way.*

Her — his pool. Are all objects that can be possessed feminine?

"Very nice," Victor says. We both try to maintain an expression of interest, as he spouts out technical information about the pool and insists on sharing with us the cost of every stage of the installation. Mercifully, we are released when Noreen's Arturo yells, "*Eets* ready, everbody!" I smile, noticing how he mispronounces some words in the same way Valentin did. We get off our chairs and approach the barbeque, its double lids, like gigantic open mouths, spewing out smoke and saliva-inducing aromas.

Everyone gets a plate and lines up. Noreen's Arturo dishes out flaming slabs of flank steak, and ribs, and ebony blood sausage, which I know is an Argentinian specialty but can't convince myself to eat. Victor does, however, helping himself to mine, slathering it with Arturo's own *chimi-churri* — a savoury parsley and garlic sauce, indispensable to an Argentinian barbeque, Arturo tells us. On a nearby table, there are more salads and cold cuts and cheeses. The lawn chairs are brought down from the pool deck so people can sit on the concrete patio next to the barbeque, close to the rest of the food. Bud Purcell, a teacher friend of Victor's, and his wife, an anorexic looking woman with a flat chest and overbite, sit next to me and Victor.

"Rita, I hear you're taking a real estate course," Bud says while slicing into the blood sausage and disgorging its mushy black interior. I focus on my own plate and answer, "I just took my final exam. I should have my licence in a few weeks."

"Is that right?" Frank is standing next to the barbeque, but within ear reach, and moves in closer to join the conversation. "You know I get a call from an agent at least once a week telling me he's got someone who wants to buy my house."

Every agent uses that tactic, we learned in class. Call and say you have an interested buyer. Not a lie, really. If you were working an area, you always have a prospective buyer.

"Let me ask you," Farrell says, addressing me, his words coming together with the slightest bit of a slur, "what do you think *my* house is worth?"

The inevitable question. They had warned us at the course. "I'm not *officially* a real estate agent yet, Mr. Farrell — Frank. I couldn't accurately put a price on it, since I haven't been keeping up with listings and sales here. But I could do a comparative market analysis for you, if you're interested in listing with me once I have my licence…"

"Oh — I'm not interested in selling. I was just curious, that's all."

"I didn't know you had an interest in real estate," Judy, the trophy wife, says, looking amused, as if she thought the kitchen could be the only possible place for me.

"Oh, yes — architecture in general has always interested me."

Noreen and Noreen's Arturo come and sit opposite to the Purcells; both their plates are heaped with food.

Arturo reaches over and offers his hand to both me and Victor. "I was so busy cooking, I guess we missed each other," he apologizes. "By the way, congratulations, Victor. Noreen tells me you're going to be the next vice-principal."

"Well, it isn't official yet. I've only just found out myself."

I smile, genuinely pleased for Victor, although we don't dare celebrate until it *is* official.

"We're going to need more teachers," Frank says, setting his empty plate at the foot of his chair. "They're extending separate school support for high schools. What do you think of that?"

Ruth's intellectual date, whose name we've learned is Edgar, says, "I've heard that public school teachers are fearing for their jobs, afraid all the Catholic kids will switch to the separate board. A mass exodus of teachers leaving to teach there, apparently. More secure jobs. All those Catholic immigrants. All with kids. They listen to their Pope as if his words came straight from God, as *if* God exists."

"What's this, an agnostic in our midst?" Frank says.

"Atheist, actually."

"Excuse me," Noreen says. "I can see this conversation is going to take a nasty turn. As luck would have it, I need to visit the powder room." She sets her plate on her chair and makes her way through the sliding doors to the kitchen. She's changed into white shorts and a halter top; her *derrière* is generous but not unsightly, and it quivers behind the white cotton as she walks.

"You mean you really don't believe God exists?" Bud's wife, Evelyn, asks, appalled. "How can you *not* believe God exists? The Bible proves He exists."

"That's ridiculous," Edgar says. "Is *'Twas the Night Before Christmas* proof that Santa Claus exists? I mean, what intelligent human being can believe in the myth of creation?

All that Adam and Eve and original sin stuff, with all the indisputable evidence anthropologists have come up with. It's amazing *anyone* still believes in God."

"You can accept evolution and still believe in God," Victor says.

"That's right," Bud agrees. "Okay, even if God didn't actually mould the clay and borrow a rib or two, somewhere along the line He *infused* man with a soul. That's the important thing. That's really what the Bible means about God making man to his image and likeness."

"Of course, there's also the old argument," Edgar persists, "that man invented God to *his* image and likeness."

"Bad news for women, I can tell you," a woman's voice interjects from directly across where I'm sitting. Somebody's wife. The industrial arts teacher, I think.

"God *is* a woman," one of the female teachers — grade nine I believe — argues.

"He's not even a person anymore, is He?" someone questions. "I thought He was a Force."

"If God is a Force," Edgar says, jumping back into the argument, "then he's just gravity, and magnetic fields, and molecular energy."

"Did we just disprove the existence of God?" Bud's wife asks, horrified. Her voice whines like a child's. "I don't know if I should be listening to this. I just went to confession yesterday, and I'm sinless."

"See — that's the thing about religion, in general," Edgar goes on. "It has you in its clutches. It feeds on your fear of the unknown. It teaches us we have a soul, so we can fear suffering even *after* death, and with that fear, it keeps us in line like good little boys and girls. And I don't mean just the RCs, although that old bugger in Rome really knows what he's doing, I'll tell you. Have you heard what he's come up with? No sex for anyone who divorces and remarries, and you can eat the bread and drink the wine; otherwise, forget it. He's controlling the things we think most about in life — death and sex — not necessarily in that order. He's got *everyone* by the balls."

"What have I missed?" Noreen asks, coming back to her seat. She has sprayed herself with a perfume that is nauseatingly sweet.

"I just hope you're not having sex with your husband," Bud tells her.

"What?" she says, looking questioningly at Arturo in hopes that he'll fill her in on what's going on, but Arturo is chewing on his flank steak and just shrugs his shoulders.

"Well, certainly religion isn't all that bad," Victor says. "Look at all the good stuff people have done spurred by their religious beliefs — Ghandi, and Mother Teresa, and, right here at home, Terry Fox. He believed in God."

"That's right," I say. "Terry Fox believed there was good in the world and good in people and that there was hope and love and God. He was a beautiful person — but he was naïve." Everyone looks at me from their lawn chairs as if they are surprised that I even know how to speak. "Everybody loved him, everybody backed him, even the government — building monuments and memorials to him after he died, when it was probably something in the environment, DDT, or dioxin, or budworm spraying, or something that some big company pumped into the water and the government officials closed an eye to, that gave him the cancer in the first place. He was a martyr. A beautiful, innocent martyr. But what do martyrs ever do for *themselves* except suffer and die?"

Victor gives me a long hard glare. The colour has washed out of his face. Everyone else is silent.

"Ouch! I'm getting bitten alive," Bud's wife says suddenly, slapping a mosquito on her thigh.

"I think I'd better light some mosquito coils," Judy Farrell says. "There's still plenty of food. Everybody — help yourselves." Her voice trails after her into the house. She's carrying away the muddled spinach dip, and good riddance.

I add my plate to the pile of dirty dishes stacked on the table. Victor follows me, grabbing my arm roughly and steering me away from the group. "What do you think you're doing?"

"What do you mean? Let go of my arm, you're hurting me."

"I mean contradicting me like *that* in front of everybody. I'm going to be vice-principal of a *Catholic* school. How do you think it makes me look, my wife talking like that?"

"I'm entitled to my opinion, Victor, even if it's not the same as yours, even if it's not the same as anyone's."

"Not if it's going to cost me my *job*."

I free my arm from his hold. "I'm not *you*, Victor. I'm not *part* of you. And I'm entitled to my opinion."

CHAPTER TWENTY-SEVEN

I am meeting Maddy downtown for lunch. Over the last two months, Maddy has made and broken the lunch date three times. Six months ago, she and Stefan sold their house in the west end and moved to the posh Rosedale area. Their house is an imposing Federal style with two massive white columns at the entrance and a front door flanked with sidelights and topped with a fanlight, along with eight double hung windows on its facade. I've seen a picture of it, but I've yet to visit. Driving downtown along Bloor, I feel completely at ease. I have driven this route every day to get to my real estate classes, once I had switched from the part-time evening courses, which would have taken much longer to achieve my goal of becoming an agent. I have just received the results of my exam and passed with high grades. Now that I have my licence, I'm looking forward to listing my grandmother's house, once the tenant, who has been living there for the last twenty-five years, moves to the top of the waiting list for Villa San Giovanni, an Italian retirement home. My absence from home each day from nine until five has required some readjustments for everyone. The children walk back and forth to school each day instead of getting driven. They have had to accept new tasks: make their beds, wash their breakfast dishes, set the table at night, and get at their homework without being prompted. An increase in allowance has helped. Victor doesn't complain too much as long as his supper is on the table as usual.

In other ways there have been adjustments too. With the children, I am less suffocating, I think; I have even let Alison read *Forever*, finally. She is acting more mature, starting to show interest in preparing meals for the whole family on her own.

This morning, a Saturday, the traffic on Bloor is slow, and I seem to be getting all the red lights. Victor is home refinishing his new auction finds and staying with the kids. Unlike Victor, I am not uncomfortable in slow moving traffic and have left in plenty of time. Here, closer to my house, an island divides the road. In the middle of the island, boulders are propped one on top of the other, as if haphazardly, though they are each carefully cemented. Shiny metallic letters are embedded into the stone and blaze: *The Kingsway*. On sidewalks in front of the shops, trees grow out of massive concrete flowerpots. On one corner, an ostentatious red heart decorates a sign that says MABEL LOBEIL REAL ESTATE. WE CARE. Mabel Lobeil has moved from a tiny office in a shopping mall to a much larger office on Bloor and her signs with the red heart are appearing on many of the houses for sale in the Kingsway. She has taken me on as one of her sales representatives, and I'm determined to do well for her brokerage.

It is fascinating to pass the many shops along Bloor to downtown, small cafés and bakeries, antique stores and gift shops, which, getting closer to downtown, metamorphize from upper-middle-class elegance in areas near my house, to immigrant poor halfway to downtown, to filthy rich extravagance closer to Yonge Street. I stop at a crosswalk where a woman signals with her hand that she wants to pass, and I watch the woman as she crosses, her head down as if a weight were pressing on it, a noticeable downward pull to her whole face. I think I recognize the woman. Her son, David, is a school friend of Micah's. Micah has mentioned that David's father isn't living at home anymore. It seems that the faces of despondent women all resemble each other. I want to reach out to her; there is comfort in shared misery. And always, misery in abundance.

It is now six months since I've last spoken with Valentin. I have very nearly relinquished altogether the slender thread of hope of ever seeing him again; with my arms and with my legs, I've let go, but I'm still hanging on with my *teeth*. I am sure eventually, inevitably, the thread will break, but I am being goddamn stubborn about it. I feel desire for him still, and like some prehistoric keeper of the flame, I refuse to let it die; at times falling back on memory, I'm still able to stoke it to a raging blaze.

But since my mind has been occupied with classes, and now the excitement of a new career in real estate, I do think about him less and less. The courses helped to wean me away from my stifling confinement, not only of the past few months, but of my entire married life. The world is opening up to me, like a black-and-white film that turns suddenly to colour. I can see alternatives.

After driving for ten minutes more, I turn down a side street, negotiate several more, eventually passing *our* park, where we'd gone for so many walks, where my whole life had changed. It is a vastness of undulating greenspace, sketched with charcoal trunks of trees. I thought of our promise to meet here each November 3rd for Valentin's birthday, but hold little hope of that happening. My eyes begin to tear, and I press harder on the gas, picking up speed. Further on is the veal sandwich take-out, and two streets over, the Tim Hortons where we'd first gone for coffee. At a red light I stop and, looking into the distance, recognize the high-rise in which Valentin and I had spent an afternoon. How *can* I ever forget him; the whole damn city reeks of him!

Soon I am in the middle of the bustle of downtown. Turning down Yonge Street, I drive to the Eaton Centre where I hurry to meet Maddy. Only a few months ago, I would never have had the courage to drive myself into the centre of the city, but it will be a necessity if I intend to work in real estate, and I'm finding it easier each time I venture here.

***

"I'm just waiting to get my licence mailed out to me," I tell Maddy as I stab my fork into a spinach salad. "I had to retake the first segment because I got sick, but that part was a breeze. The rest of it was tougher, though."

"I'm, frankly, surprised," Maddy says. She's sipping on the wine that I suggested from Cardinale Estate and seems to be enjoying it. I still feel some loyalty to the owners and a little guilty for having relinquished the translating job, which was actually rather enjoyable. "I just never knew you were *interested* in real estate."

"I've always liked looking at different houses, wondering what they looked like inside, imagining what it would be like to live *there* instead of our house."

"Well, naturally, I think it's *great*. I can't believe it, that's all — the way you've suddenly come out of your shell. Although I can't see why you'd *want* to work. I mean you don't really have to. You've got the perfect marriage, you're the perfect wife, the perfect mother — your husband gives you anything you want."

I produce a wisp of a laugh at her statement. "Yes, anything I want — as long as *he* thinks I should have it."

"Do I detect a note of resentment?"

"I see things differently, that's all."

"You know, it's been ages since we've done this, Rita. We really haven't talked. I'm sorry I put it off so long."

"You're very busy. I understand."

"How are you feeling, anyway? You're not still taking those pills?"

"The Valium? No." I force myself to look at Maddy and smile. "I have to laugh when I think about calling you up in a panic because I'd taken a couple too many. *Help, Maddy, I'm dying.*" Maddy laughs. I go back to my spinach salad. "No," I repeat, "I chucked them all out. They gave me nightmares. I kept dreaming that the maple tree in the front of our house was going to fall on my chest while I was sleeping and pin me to my bed. Isn't that weird? For a while, I was desperate to cut that tree down, but of course Victor wouldn't hear of it. The nightmares finally went away when I stopped taking the pills. I feel good now."

"That's wonderful. What's Victor think of your embarking on a new career?"

"He doesn't mind, as long as I'm contributing to the family income. Of course, he still expects me to have supper on the table at the usual time. The twins are in school full days now and Alison walks them home. I make a casserole the night before — Alison puts it in the oven — and I prepare the rest of the meal when I get home. She's a big help; she's even made whole meals herself. She's actually becoming quite the chef." I take a mouthful of spinach salad and feel a crunching between my teeth. Lifting a leaf of spinach with my fork, I find a brown dusty patch on the underside of a leaf. I turn several more leaves and find more patches. "Will you look at this? They didn't even bother to wash the spinach. Excuse me—" Our waitress has just finished taking an order at the table next to us. "This spinach hasn't been properly washed." The waitress apologizes profusely and takes the salad away.

"I can't believe you did that," Maddy says.

"Why? I don't enjoy sand in my salad."

"No. But *normally* you wouldn't have said anything."

"I guess I've changed. A lot of things are different," I say meaningfully, though Maddy could not possibly interpret my words that way. "What I'm *doing* is different, at least. And I *like* what I'm doing."

"Good for you. Good for *you*," Maddy repeats again, as if she hasn't meant it the first time.

The waitress returns shortly with a fresh spinach salad that crunches only from the bacon bits. "What about you?" I ask. "How's the cosmetic business?"

"Really good. I should be getting the diamond bumblebee again this year."

"Congratulations. How's the rest of your life — your *love* life, I mean, getting right to the point."

Maddy looks away with a coy smile. She enjoys dramatics. In the bright light flooding in from the window next to our table, her light green eyes seem washed of all colour, revealing dark flecks within the irises. "Can't complain," she says. "As long as you don't get too clingy, the city's writhing with men who are ready, willing and, *usually*, able."

"And Stefan — I mean, why stay married if you're living like you're single?" I'm not sure if I'm asking Maddy this question, or myself. "Don't you love him anymore, and if you don't, why keep up the farce?"

"Stef is away most of the week."

"That doesn't really seem like a justification. Aren't you being unfair to him?" *Who* am I talking to? Not to Maddy, I think. "Are you still getting heartbroken?"

Maddy lets out a long, derisive breath, almost as if she were exhaling a puff of cigarette smoke, although she hasn't had one since we've gotten here, claiming she's quit. "Are you kidding?" she answers. "All the time. But you get used to it. You never like it, of course, but if you expect it, it's not quite so bad. And the in-betweens can be really nice. Anyway, I have my therapist when I need to work things out."

"I get over things *myself*," I say, a touch harshly. "I handle my problems alone."

"But you have Victor. Stefan is never around, but you *have* someone who's there all the time. You and Victor are like this." She crosses her fingers and holds them up.

"*Physically*, he's there, but—"

"What kind of problems do you have, anyway? The kids broke a lamp and the dog has fleas? Take it from me, Rita — problems of the heart are buggers."

"I *know*. I was…" I pause as if deciding whether or not to jump off the precipice. "I was *involved* with someone for almost a year. It ended several months ago."

A soundless gasp freezes on Maddy's mouth. "You're kidding me, right?"

"No. It's true."

Maddy's frozen expression becomes more startled, as if she's the one coming across a partridge crossing the road in front of her. "A whole year and I haven't *known* about it. I can't believe it. I never suspected a thing."

"How could you? We see each other so seldom."

"Well, tell me about it."

I hesitate to share, knowing the wonder of it could evanesce with the telling, leaving only the mundane. But, it *has* ended, after all. Why treat it as something sacrosanct any longer? I had opened the floodgates and felt compelled to keep going. "It's over, that's all that really matters." But I continue, propelled by some compulsion. "He was younger — a lot younger, but mature. More mature than me, actually. We really cared for each other." (I hope this was true.) "He even suggested we live together." (In jest, I presume, but he did *say* it.) "Impossible, of course, but really, it was special."

Maddy's eyes, searching mine, keep punctuating each of my statements with a widening of her eyes, questioning their veracity. The relating of my secret is now followed by a dreadful feeling of loss. I had felt magic in the clandestine relationship with Valentin; it had been unique, vulnerable, precious. I had destroyed it by giving it away. "I really *loved* him," I offer, in a desperate attempt to lend authenticity to my words. My eyes blur swiftly with tears. "I miss him a lot." Tears drop into my spinach salad. Taking the serviette from my lap, I crumple it against my face.

"My God," Maddy says, "what men do to women should be a crime punishable by law. You must have had it bad."

I nod into my serviette. My throat feels tight, choked with saliva. "You don't know how bad. I wanted to die."

"I had no *idea* what you were going through." Maddy reaches out and puts her hand over mine.

I pull it away, take my serviette and blow my nose loudly into it. "How could you know?" I say with some bitterness. "You've been too wrapped up in your *own* affairs. I thought you were my *friend*. I thought I could count on you when I needed you. When I called you after taking those pills — what did you do?"

"But you didn't say—"

"I needed you. I said I *needed* you." I pick up my serviette again as new tears start. I begin to sob. Getting up from my chair, I hurry to the bathroom. I am bent over the sink washing my face when Maddy comes in.

"Rita, I'm sorry I let you down. I really am."

We are looking at each other's faces in the mirror. Maddy's face looks absolutely aghast. I break into a laugh. "Maddy, you look just like the time we double-dated and your date told a joke, and you laughed so hard you *wet* yourself."

"Yeah. It was so humiliating."

We both start to laugh.

Maddy props herself up to sit on the ledge of the sink. "Oh, no," Maddy says, suddenly jumping down. "Oh, no — I've done it again!" She turns to look at her skirt which has a dark stripe across the light blue serge, and we both burst into belly-bending laughs that hurt so *good* and make our eyes tear up. When Maddy gets control of herself, she asks, "Does it show much?"

"Yes," I answer, still laughing. "Everyone will just think you're a very horny lady."

"I am, but I don't want to broadcast it. I'm not going out like this." She rustles in her purse for a neat little bundle the size of a cigarette pack and starts to unfold it, unwrapping something that metamorphosizes into a nylon windbreaker that she ties by its dangling arms around her waist. "Problem solved," she declares, then pulls out her cosmetic bag and starts touching up her face, where the tears of mirth have made white streaks and ruined her makeup. "There," she says, snapping the compact shut, "Miss Universe. Now…" she says, stooping down to search for legs inside the row of cubicles, "…since we're all alone in here, tell me more about this relationship. Are you feeling any better about it?"

"Better … but still very bad. Half alive, really, like only half the world *exists* for me now."

"It's a big world."

"No, I mean it, Maddy — it's like everything's still there, but I can only enjoy it a fraction as much as I could with him. I feel like I've suffered a death — only it's my *own* death."

"Maybe I should send you flowers."

Without warning, tears reappear in my eyes.

"Shit! I was only *kidding,* Rita. Maybe we shouldn't talk about this anymore."

"No. I have to talk about it to somebody," I say, pulling a Kleenex from inside my purse to blow my nose. "That's probably why I'm such a wreck — I've never told anybody. I don't know … I was thinking about what you said once, about how we actually make our own destiny. Well, if I really think about it, I guess maybe I did *let* it happen."

"What was he like?"

"He was sweet, romantic — patient. I told him I could never become seriously involved with someone I didn't love and who didn't love me back. He told me he *loved* me."

"You gave him the requirements — he made sure he filled the bill."

"I'm not sure anymore. He sounded serious. I really do think he loved me a little. I really thought we had magic. It *felt* like magic. Even when we were just holding hands, you can't imagine how it felt."

"You made the magic up too," Maddy says.

"It felt real," I say softly. "It felt wonderful — so wonderful — everything pales in comparison. My whole *life* pales in comparison."

"Listen, Rita — being in love is as unnatural a high as taking drugs. My therapist explained it to me. Being in love produces all these feel-good hormones in the brain — endorphins and dopamine and all that shit. And when it ends and you stop producing them, the world seems flat and dull to you because you're suffering withdrawal symptoms."

"You felt that way?"

"It goes with the territory, honey. Love and pain and the whole damn thing — is that the way it goes? Anyway, I have a theory."

"Which is?"

"Well — life is like one of those balls inside a pinball machine; it rolls along until it smashes into an obstacle that flings it in one direction or another, then starts rolling along again until it smashes into another obstacle. We flick the arms that send it flying, or it hits an obstacle on its own, but either way it needs to keep getting bashed to stay in the running. Shut up in a safe little corner — that's not living. You might as well be dead. I *understand* how you feel," Maddy says, coming over to put an arm around me, "and the solution for you is the same as it is for me. Find yourself another lover — and you'll be right as rain again. You got any good-looking prospects from that real estate class?"

I shake my head and laugh. "Maddy — you'll never change." I put my arms around my friend and hug her fondly, *sadly,* realizing she hadn't understood at all.

CHAPTER TWENTY-EIGHT

Fall 1987

It was on an unseasonably chilly day in September, a day so wet and dreary that it was unlikely to inspire hope in the most optimistic soul, that Valentin unexpectedly called. There had been days, during this cheerless summer that had just ended, when the air smelled of cut grass and blooming things, that I would rekindle a tiny spark of hope, stirred by past memories of walking in parks hand in hand, of open-mouthed kisses, of lying snuggly in each other's arms, but not today. I was expecting a call from the listing agent for a property I was showing to some prospects, never imagining it could be Valentin.

"*Valentin!*" the name escapes me like an expiration of air from someone who's been punched in the gut.

"How are you?"

How easily pain can be forgotten: torn by labour, a mother looks at her newborn, still attached to her by its umbilical cord, and the memory of the pain instantly vanishes; at the end of the telephone line, an estranged lover's voice is heard and all is forgiven. "Fine. I'm fine. How are *you*?"

"Okay."

"Are you working?"

"Yeah. I still have both my jobs. The hours at Talbot Meat Packers aren't very good — usually three till midnight, but I need the job. Right now, I'm on my break."

"Well, that's good!"

"I still owe you that money, but—"

A commotion. Louder. Shouting in the background. "Listen, somebody here wants to use the phone. I gotta hang up. I'll call you another time. Take it easy."

The phone clicks. Unbelieving, I stand motionless, the receiver pressed against my ear. Suddenly, I laugh out loud. It is no illusion — he *called*. For the rest of the day, I feel light enough to float. And for several more days, I feel confident that he *will* call again, and he does, a week later, when Victor and the kids are all back at school. He wants to meet for coffee and I feel confident enough to say yes. "Meet me outside Santini's," he says. "I have an hour lunch starting at noon."

History repeats itself as I park my car in front of the store and as I shift from my car to his van and we drive together to the same Tim's we'd gone to the first time. We keep casting surreptitious looks at each other during the drive. His face is dark from several days' growth of beard and his eyes look red and irritated. But, incongruously, he is wearing a brightly flowered shirt — the kind men wear so proudly on a trip back from some exotic place, but feel ridiculous in the moment they step off the plane at Pearson Airport. "Where did you get that?" I ask, laughing. I *mean* to keep the mood of this meeting light.

"My shirt? A friend brought it back for me from his trip to Hawaii. You don't like it?"

"It just seems a little out of place here — kind of flowery. People might wonder."

"I like it. I don't care what people think."

"Yes, you *do*. You want to be respected, remember?"

"And they're not going to respect me because of my shirt?"

I laugh — it feels so good to *laugh* again.

Taking his attention intermittently from his driving, he keeps glancing over at me. "You look different," he tells me. With his eyes, he follows the "s" of my body down to my feet. "I like your outfit," and glancing back up, he adds, "and your hair — it's shorter — looks good on you."

I am wearing a nicely fitting pair of black slacks and a white linen top that is cut in at the upper arms, so that it has to be worn with a halter bra; it shows off my tanned shoulders, which someone — a sales lady in a dress shop, I think — said were elegantly boned. I am pleased at this remark and smile in response.

"And you have your same nice smile." He reaches for my hand; I feel once again fire and electricity — and a magnetism I fail to comprehend.

I make an attempt at light conversation, commenting on the weather, which has lately been unsettled, but today dawned warm and bright. I notice that the gouges that formerly marred the dash of his van as a result of the stolen stereo equipment are filled in once more. "You got new speakers."

"*Sí,* my insurance covered the replacement."

Neither of us really want coffee, so instead, we decide to go for a walk at *our* park. He takes my hand again, continues staring at me. "I can't get over how good you look."

"I must have looked *terrible* to you before," I say dryly.

"I mean it," he reaffirms. "Something different about you."

Perhaps — I'm not the shy, insecure creature I was when he first met me. The real estate course has made me less introverted, more confident.

His voice drops to a low, throaty whisper. "I *do* mean it. Can't you tell. You're really getting me excited." The soft voice is a parody of the one he used when we were making love — passionate, urgent, a *purrr* almost. "Look at me, just *look*." He is wearing tight blue jeans and in front, behind the zipper, is an impressive and unavoidable hump, which he proffers, jutting out his hips. His built-in plaything. He adores it, worries about it, bestows an endless amount of attention on it. Do all men? If he could have two penises, like a snake, it would suit him better still. Indignant, I look away. "There are people around," I say coldly, his exhibitionism changing my mood.

"You never used to mind before." A smug, teasing expression plays on his face.

"I'm finished my real estate course," I say, changing the subject. A ploy. Distract the mischievous child.

"Yeah! You got your licence?"

"Just last week. I have a listing already." My grandmother's house, but I don't tell him this.

He whistles his admiration. "Nice going. Hey, look at this." Ahead of us, to the left of the path among the shrubs and trees, are two freshly sawn stumps close to each other. "Seats," he says triumphantly. "How do I always manage to get so lucky?" Of course, he's referring to the first time we were together here, when he really did *get lucky*. Had he shared information about our relationship, I wonder, belittling the most profound and life-altering events of my life?

He reverts to our previous conversation. "Was it tough, the course?" he asks.

"Pretty tough."

"Could *I* do it?"

"I'm sure you could."

He smirks, pleased. Compliments, especially about his intelligence, he greatly appreciates, I know, and there *is* intelligence there, though often hidden behind his puerile preoccupation with sex and his masculinity.

"Why? Are you interested in a career change?"

"Nah. But I'm interested to buy some real estate when I get some money. I told you that before."

Interested to buy … I'd forgotten how endearing I found his small imperfections of speech.

"The insurance claim has been settled, and I should be getting my money soon — twenty thousand dollars. Of course, part of that is from *your* insurance."

"It was also my fault. I caused it…" I remind him. Caused *everything.*

His large, slightly protruding brown eyes focus on me, their black pupils, like nail heads, pinning me down as he concentrates his steady gaze on my face. "Do you regret it?" His voice is husky again.

I won't fall into the trap, I won't answer. "I guess you're rich now," I say instead.

"Not *rich,* but it's more money than I've had in a while."

"What do you plan to do with it?"

The snort-laugh. "Pay some bills. Free my mother. Maybe put some away until I have enough to be able to invest in some real estate. I know this old guy — Sicilian, like you — he owns these two semis downtown, just around the corner from my friend's restaurant, *El Flamenco.* Remember I took you there once?"

Actually, I had taken him, on his birthday. "*El Flamenco* — sure, I remember."

"The houses are dumps, but it's a good location."

Location, location, location, I remind myself, means everything in real estate.

He rents them out, all three floors, six hundred dollars a floor — good money. But he's older now, wants to go back to the old country to be with his parents, who are in their nineties." His eyes light up as though pondering the lucrative possibilities of such an investment. "Not only that — he owns the vacant lot on the corner right next to them. You might be able to demolish them and together with the lot sell it to a developer for a high rise. Anyway, the old guy wants to sell them all and go back home, but he wants to sell privately — doesn't want to pay the commission. Wants two hundred thousand for them, which is good. He wants all cash. I don't have enough to put down to qualify for a mortgage from the bank, but I told him I was interested. I'm working overtime, so it shouldn't take me long to come up with the extra ten thousand I'll need along with some of the insurance money for a down payment ... you're laughing at me," he says, suddenly noticing the smile on my face.

"No. In fact, I'm impressed. You sound so knowledgeable — I can't get over it."

Accepting my compliment, he grins, then concentrates his gaze on my mouth. "Hey, come sit over here," he says, patting his knee. To override my hesitation, he stretches out a hand. "Come on," he says again. I go to him, sit stiffly on his lap, while his arms encircle me, enclosing me in a tight embrace. I resist at first, then relax and mould myself into his arms. Hugging, strangely not a constricting but a setting free, a wonderful unloosening. "I missed you," he whispers into my ear.

When I face him to see if he means it, he kisses me. A long deep kiss that I break away from suddenly, in order to move back to my own tree stump.

"What's wrong?"

"You have a girlfriend. I don't take other women's men away from them."

A snort-laugh. The corner of his lip lifts upward in a sneer, giving an asymmetrical tilt to one side of his mouth.

"You're not taking *anybody* from *anybody*." He looks away, irritated, his annoyance caused more by guilt, I surmise, because with me he hadn't had any such scruples. "For your information, we're not seeing each other anymore."

"Is that so?" I respond, trying to appear indifferent at this shared information.

"We didn't get along. She's too *bossy*."

I recall the wide, mild face with its insignificant eyes and circular mouth. "Something must have attracted you in the first place."

"I don't know. I guess I thought she'd do what I wanted. But she's so stubborn, always criticizing, always on top of me."

It wasn't what he meant, I know, but a painful picture forms inside my head of Brenda straddling Valentin in the female superior position, and I recoil. "So, how was it?" I ask, my cheeks burning hotly, my morbid curiosity getting the best of me. "The *other* part of it, I mean?" The sarcastic tone cuts wide open my words, making it perfectly clear what I mean, but I add anyways, "How did it feel, finally, *fucking* her?" But I'm being deliberately naïve, knowing full well it must have been going on all along.

Obviously vexed, Valentin's eyelids dip over the protruding globes of his eyeballs, leaving only a slit of vision. He spits out his answer: "I'm — not — talking — about — that."

I hadn't, in fact, wanted to know, only to assure myself that intimacy and candour no longer existed between us. His loyalty was to Brenda. I reach down to grasp at the twitch grass that is growing beside my tree trump, plucking a blade, its inner stem squeaking away from the rest, and I press its tender celadon centre between my teeth, tasting its sweetness. "I'd better get home," I say, still chewing thoughtfully on the grass. I had been eager to see Valentin. Now I felt just as eager for release. "I've got some things I need to get ready for tonight. I invited some people from my real estate class over to celebrate the end of the course. Nice group."

"Women?"

"No — mostly men, actually."

"You friendly with any of them?"

"You mean the men?" He's looking at me without answering, yet his jaw and tightly clamped lips confirm it *was* what he meant. "One man asked me out for a drink after class, so I went." Cliff had, one Friday afternoon when the class had been dismissed earlier than usual, because he didn't feel like drinking alone — talked about his grandchildren. "He's just a friend."

Valentin looks sideways, away from me, revealing his handsome profile. The short hairs at the back of his neck stick out visibly from his collar. "What are you trying to do?" he asks. "Be like your friend Maddy?"

"What's *that* supposed to mean?"

"Picking up guys at bars."

He barely unclenches his teeth as he says this. I am amused at these feelings of jealousy. He didn't want me, but he didn't want anybody else to have me either. I may be a discarded piece of his harem, but he considers me still *his*, nonetheless. "Maddy is a free spirit."

"You mean she sleeps around."

Why, I wonder, have I confided things to Valentin that I would not tell Victor? "That's her choice. What is it you've done most of your life?"

"But she's married."

My laugh comes out as a snort, mimicking Valentin's.

"*I* was married. I slept with *you*. That makes *me* whatever she is."

"That's different."

"How is it different?"

"Because…" His voice softens. "You cared."

I know he means *loved*, but *love* for him is a scary word. *I think I've fallen in love with you. Ninety-five percent sure.* I almost want to laugh. If I hadn't required it to be spoken, made the word an absolute prerequisite, he *never* would have spoken it.

"Why did you and Brenda break up? I mean besides what you said, there must have been something."

"We had a fight. She had a party — invited some friends. One of them was a guy she used to go out with. This guy named Peter. I asked her, 'What do you want to invite him for?' She says, 'We're just friends. I can still have him as a friend.'"

"I see — no longer one of her *meaningful relationships*."

"Yeah — I repeated what you said once to me — all those *meaningful relationships* — the first one, the second, the third — when do they stop being *meaningful* and when does a girl get herself the reputation of being *loose*?"

It flattered me to be quoted so accurately. "What did she say?"

"'*My life before you is my business.*' Maybe it doesn't really make any difference. I mean you could marry a virgin and then she goes out and does it with somebody else behind your back. Is that any better?"

Is he referring to me, I wonder, as my face flushes hotly. "But you still stopped seeing her because of Peter. What about when you were going out with her and seeing me?"

"It wasn't just because of *him*." He runs his fingers through his hair; it is in tight curls today and makes him look mean. "We were always fighting about something — I think she was frustrated."

"Frustrated?"

"Yeah — she had trouble climaxing. She always had to do it herself afterwards. She was *frigid*."

Frigid. That word again. A *man*-made word. A woman could be loving and passionate and warm and give pleasure to her man, but if she was unsuccessful in achieving orgasm herself, even if she didn't need it, or if she was too tired or just didn't feel like having sex, she was *frigid. Man*-made, in order to make a woman feel inadequate while taking the guilt off the man's shoulders. Wasted guilt. Sexual pleasure, mostly in the head, not the heart, not the sexual organs. What I had experienced at the lodge for the first time with Victor, had happened because my mind was not with Victor. It was Valentin I was thinking of. It was not a man's expertise or his sexual prowess that achieved results. But let them believe it, the fools.

"I mean — how can a man enjoy sex with a woman who always has to make *herself* come? I never had a problem with you." So secretive before, he's done a complete turnabout, revealing far more than I really want to hear. Obviously, he was oblivious to the fact that his hasty deliverance might have something to do with the problem. Perhaps, like Victor, he was not much concerned with arriving at the root of the problem.

"Well, it's nice to know you were keeping yourself occupied," I say hotly, "while I was crying into my beer, or in my case, my coffee."

"You missed me?" His look is humble, perhaps even remorseful. He searches my face for a response, but I look away. "I never felt for *her* what I did for *you*." I can't be certain his words are sincere, but the serious look on his face adds to the sincerity. "How are your kids, anyway?"

"My *kids*? Why?"

"Just wondering how they are?"

I laugh. "They're just fine. Simply *swell*."

He looks at the ground, pensively rustling his fingers through the grass as I had earlier. "It had to go that way between us," he says, looking at me compassionately. "It couldn't go any other way." He reaches for my hand; his fingers are calloused, but his touch is gentle and warm. He looks away, gazing through the grasses and shrubs and trees, towards something vague, squinting. "Would you have wanted to put that on my shoulders, all that … responsibility?" He looks into my eyes, at my face, which is also pensive, assuming my answer.

He was right. The possibility of living with Valentin, not only me but my children as well, could never, for reasons of practicality, have been more than a whimsical thought in both our minds.

We sit silent for a few moments, Valentin rubbing his thumb back and forth along the back of my hand. "Listen," he says, "Why don't you hurry up and sell some houses, then we can get married."

"What did you say?" I ask, laughing, wanting him to repeat it, not because I hadn't heard, but because I couldn't believe he would say something so utterly ridiculous.

"I said…" He paused. "Let's get married." His repetition is self-conscious, but I find it hilarious.

"But you said you need to marry somebody rich."

"Sell *lots* of houses."

I'm still laughing, feeling something that resembles happiness. We walk back to his van holding hands. Inside the van, I allow him to undress me from the waist up and gasp as he plants wet kisses down the length of my bare back. "We can't make love," I tell him. This morning on the toilet, when I dabbed myself dry, the toilet paper came away attached to an iridescent silver thread; I was ovulating. Presuming nothing, I hadn't worn my diaphragm.

He nestles his head between my breasts, kissing the cleft there. Then sliding his lips over, takes a nipple into his mouth. I expect pain; his fierce suckling has always made me wince. Instead, he is gentle, so gentle I barely feel it.

"She must have told you off about that."

"What?"

"What you're doing. You're doing it differently. You used to hurt me, but I never told you because I didn't want to distract you."

"I'm sorry. You should have told me. Did I hurt you a lot?"

"It doesn't matter." I press myself against the thick fur of his chest. He holds me tenderly, more tenderly than ever before, as if he's afraid he's going to bruise me. He kisses my forehead chastely, then my mouth, reaching down to undo the waistband of my slacks. "No," I warn him, "I told you — it's not safe. I could get pregnant."

"I just want to kiss you, every inch of you," he says hoarsely, sliding my pant legs down. "Just relax."

With eyes closed, I can feel each nerve end to the deepest part of me ache for the pressure of his lips, the slippery wetness of his tongue. I am weightless, totally weightless, floating in midair. What enigmas we are! We don't want to die, yet we constantly long to escape ourselves. That was the curious thing about being in love — it made you feel really alive, yet it let you lose yourself completely.

I feel Valentin's hand, exploring, from memory, the cleft between my thighs. A warm effusion. Then, a floating, a flying, a gravitating closer, closer to his core. Realizing it is already too late, his hardness entering the slick passageway between my legs, I struggle, beating his chest with my fists, an action that strikes even me as histrionic. I let my arms go limp, then slide them around his neck and hold him tight.

"Come on," he whispers in my ear, "come on ... let's make a baby."

CHAPTER TWENTY-NINE

The morning calls from Valentin have resumed once more, and I await them eagerly. I have armed myself with a pager now, which I need for real estate purposes, and Victor never questions my getting paged at any hour and my responding to any page I receive. Once again, Valentin is laid off at Santini's, temporarily, he says, until business picks up again, although he still has his part-time job at the abattoir. And once again, he finds himself in financial straits and humbles himself to ask if I can give him a loan for a short time, since there is no one else he can ask. This time he needs three thousand dollars he owes for arrears on the mortgage; the bank is threatening to foreclose on his house. I feel for him and I can only imagine the fear his elderly mother must be experiencing; I had seen a news item on TV reporting that, with the weakening economy, evictions were skyrocketing, and they had shown a deputy standing by as movers carried out into the yard the belongings of a woman holding a crying baby and a toddler by the hand, an expression of bewilderment on her drawn face. It was heart wrenching to watch, and no wonder Valentin's words held a note of desperation. I simply *have* to help him. But I can't ask my mother again. It would be a simple matter for me to help him, if only I had been able to sell my grandmother's house, but the tenant is still firmly ensconced there. My household expense account, to which Victor contributes regularly and which he monitors closely, is pretty much empty for the month. I have to think of some other way, and the only thing I can think of is cashing some savings Victor and I have in a joint GIC account at the bank. I don't even want to imagine what Victor would do if he found out, so I would have to replace the money somehow, and soon. But for now, there is no remedy for it — I simply have to borrow from that and worry about returning the money later.

***

At the bank, after a short wait in a reception area with green leatherette chairs and a coffee machine, I am escorted into the assistant manager's glass-enclosed private office, where I am interrogated on why I wish to cash a GIC prior to its maturity and given an explanation of the associated consequences, which involve a considerable loss of interest. When I make it clear that I fully understand the repercussions and want to go ahead with the withdrawal in any event, it takes no time at all until I am walking out of the bank with three thousand dollars in large bills in an envelope inside my purse.

I suggest that Valentin come and pick the money up the following day at my house during his lunch break, since the twins are home with the sniffles, although Alison and Micah will still be at school. I have imagined him being here so many times, but now that I know he is actually coming, I feel edgy and nervous. I yell at the twins for getting underfoot while I'm trying to vacuum, brush their questions aside, insist they can get their own snacks. At eleven, though the house is not quite in the spotless condition I like it to be when company comes, I stop to take a quick shower. Afterwards, I try to make myself pretty, then spray on some perfume. When I go down to the kitchen to check the time, it is 11:50. I have a few minutes yet. The twins are watching an episode of *Sesame Street* they have seen before with little enthusiasm. The front yard is littered with fallen leaves from the towering sugar maples that line our street; the neighbours' houses all have large compostable paper sacks full of them lined up on the road in front of their houses, but Victor hasn't gotten around to cleaning up our yard yet.

"Hey, you guys. Want to make some money? I'll give you each two dollars if you rake the leaves in the front yard and put them in some big paper bags. What do you think?"

"Okay! Can we spend it on anything we want?" Joshua asks.

"I suppose."

They scramble to get their jackets from the kitchen coat rack.

"The rakes are in the garage," I yell after them. "And make sure to zip your jackets up all the way and pull up the hoods. It's a little breezy out there. And take Gigi out with you."

When they are gone, I go to sit on the bench in the living room alcove and look through the leaded glass out towards the driveway. There is moisture on the glass panes. It is early October and the temperature has started to drop during the night, although it is a little warmer now that the sun has come out. There is a frost warning for later in the week, but today it is sunny. The trees are losing their brilliant fall foliage. Only the ornamental shrubs — the hydrangeas, the Japanese maples, the cotoneasters — retain their leaves, studding the yards with red and bronze. The twins' laughter as they throw dried leaves at each other on the front lawn filters through the leaded glass and makes me smile. I can remember my brothers and I making high piles of dead leaves and then jumping into them, scattering them all about again. I pick up the sound of a vehicle's rough motor getting louder as it nears the house, and soon Valentin's van rumbles into our driveway. Through the windshield, I can barely see Valentin's face because of the glare. He hesitates before getting out of his door, as if he's uncertain it is the right house, thinking it is too grand, perhaps, although I've given him the address and described the house — Tudor style, red brick and black trim, turreted alcove, although he might have no idea what Tudor style is. I hurry to open the front door as he emerges from the vehicle, to assuage his uncertainty.

"Hello. Come in."

"Hi." He enters meekly.

"It's cool out there, isn't it? Here, let me take your jacket." Obediently, he slips it off and hands it to me. I lay it on the console by the door, so he won't forget it when he leaves. "How long have you got?" I ask, trying to keep conversation going, trying to put him at ease. I've, frankly, never seen him so nervous.

"About twenty minutes before I have to head back."

"Can I get you anything to eat?"

"Thanks. I already ate lunch. Those your kids out there?"

"Yes, my twins."

He peers around curiously at the rooms open to his vision: the living room, the dining room, a section of kitchen. I wish I had had more time to tidy up.

"I have an envelope for you upstairs. Will you come up?"

He nods, following me to the top of the stairs into the study. I have hidden the money behind some books on a high shelf, and I pull them away, exposing a sepia envelope from the bank, bulging with fifty and hundred-dollar bills.

"Thanks." He slips the money out of the envelope, folds it, and tucks it almost too carelessly into his back pocket. "I'll pay you back as soon as I get the insurance cheque." He seems relieved to get the money exchange out of the way. He seems, however, in no hurry to go, having become more comfortable with the surroundings. "No one else is here?" he asks, although he's obviously already come to that conclusion.

"My twins are." I can hear Jamie and Joshua screeching playfully at each other and imagine they are scattering around more leaves than they are gathering together. "They're raking leaves outside. Child labour," I say jokingly. "I promised to pay them."

He nods, then looks around the room. "This is your study."

"Yes — well, my husband's."

He walks towards the door, stopping to run his fingers over the bevelled glass; he peers through it to downstairs. "Nice," he says. Turning to face the adjacent wall, he scans the rows of books on the shelves. "Is that a dictionary?" he asks, pointing to a massive Webster's Unabridged that, too big to fit in an upright position, lies on its side on the top shelf.

"Yes."

"Can I use it?"

"Go ahead."

"There's something I've been wanting to look up." He lifts the dictionary easily off the shelf, not burdened by its bulky weight. Laying it flat on the desk, he starts flicking through the pages.

"What are you looking up?" I ask.

"One of my friends and I had bet about the meaning of the word 'adultery'."

"*Adultery*?" Which friend? With whom had he been debating the nuances of the English language? Had he spoken of me? Had they ridiculed together my transgression? He offers no response, engrossed in his search.

"Here it is," Valentin says. "*Adultery — the voluntary sexual intercourse of a married person with someone other than his or her spouse.*" He seems neither pleased nor disappointed with the meaning, but *my* mouth gapes a little in surprised realization.

Who had won the bet, I wonder? Intercourse of a *married* person. That meant that I was committing adultery, but not Valentin. *I* was the sinner. For loving someone other than my husband. Valentin, who had been with so many women he'd lost count, was guiltless. *Unadulterated.*

He closes the book, leaving it on the desk. I pick it up, wanting to return it quickly to its usual place on the shelf; I feel this inanimate object has somehow betrayed me. With the heavy weight, my arms strain to reach the top shelf.

"Here, let me do that," Valentin offers. He comes behind me, raising his arms over mine, lifting away the enormous burden, depositing it as it was before, flat on the top shelf. He doesn't move away afterwards. Instead, he wraps his arms around my waist and presses his face against the side of my neck. "Turn around," he says. I do, and he kisses me deeply, firmly. "How come you're not opening your mouth? Not into it?"

I shrug, self-consciously. Through the bevelled glass of the study, I can see the twins jostling with each other on the front lawn and even though we are safely out of sight, what we are doing seems terribly wrong. "It just feels strange here."

His smile is teasing. "You could get used to it — if I come here often enough." He kisses me again, slipping his hand under my pullover and pulling up on my bra. My breasts are sore and swollen; my period is due. He squeezes them, too roughly, then lets them rest on the palms of his hand and with his thumbs strokes the nipples. "*Margarita, Margarita,*" he whispers in my ear, his breath hot and damp. "I've been missing you." His tongue searches for mine, hungrily. "There's something I would really like you to do for me, something special, something you've never done." His voice is hoarse, low, his words implore. "It's my birthday in a few weeks. You could give me my early birthday present. I want you to take me in your mouth."

"No. Not here. I can't, Valentin. Please understand."

"You said there's no one here. Your kids are outside. Come on, baby, I really want you to do this for me. It would be something special for me to remember. It would make me happy." His hands move to my shoulders, massaging them gently, then gently pressing down until I am kneeling, my face brushing against his hip. He unzips himself.

A wave of intoxicating smells wash over me: the smell of the sea primordial, of sunbaked earth, of musk — a smell that always seems much stronger when we make love, like the musk exuded by a snake when mating, and a mélange of other less identifiable smells, not good, not bad, just him. He strokes my hair, whispers encouragement. "You're so good, baby ... another minute, keep it up ... I'm almost there." He grasps my head with both hands and begins undulating his hips. His hand flies to the root of his shaft, until very soon I feel a quivering in my mouth, then a warm fluid, released in concentric spasms.

Suddenly, the earth comes to a complete standstill, the blood in my veins turning to ice, my heart sinking in my chest, as I register the screeching of car tires and, in reflex, swallow, almost choking, tasting, for the first time, the bitterness of my lover's seed.

CHAPTER THIRTY

You make your own reality. The words haunt me, and I repeat them over and over in my head. These are dark days, both inside my head and mirrored outside by dark, gloomy weather. Dirty gray clouds suffocate a sun I have not seen for days. Day after day, I have kept vigil at my son's bedside as he lies between life and death in a medically induced coma, while his swollen brain attempts to heal itself. I am not permitted to spend the night with him in ICU, so I have been sleeping in the waiting room down the hall each night for the last week. Somehow, I have tricked my brain into concentrating on nothing, no other thought than that of the survival of my son. No reprimands, no excuses, no regrets. Only a voidness of thought. My mind can concentrate on this one thing only, exist in this one place only, smell and taste and see and hear *nothing* except the sanitized hospital smells, the cardboard cafeteria food, the blinking monitors, the beeping equipment. And recall no past memories, except one, over and over.

I was ten when my cousin was run over by a car. The back wheel had driven right over her chest. I remember trying to imagine what that must have felt like, a car wheel driving over your chest. I remember my mother praying despondently and walking in a daze from room to room, waiting for the phone to ring, and answering my inane questions as my cousin lay close to death in the hospital. "Will we be able to go see her, when she's better?" I had asked? "I'm going to give her my best doll as a present. The one she always liked. The one that wets — she liked that one. When will she be well enough so we can go see her?"

The next day my mother told me and my brothers, with a choking voice, as she struggled to hold back tears, that maybe my cousin wasn't going to get better, that maybe she would die. She was *already* dead.

My brothers and I had never experienced death before, had never seen a dead person. But it was expected that we go to the funeral home to say our goodbyes. My father patiently answered our questions about what to expect. "She just looks like she's sleeping peacefully, nothing more." But that wasn't exactly true. When my father lifted me up to give my cousin one last kiss on the forehead, there was not the warmth of the living girl I had known. I might as well have been kissing a rock.

**

It must have been the novenas my mother attends every week to pray for all of us so we may be safe that must have saved my son from dying, although he came close to it. It certainly wasn't *my* prayers, or as a reward for anything I have done lately. *There are no atheists in fox holes*, Sister Aloysius used to tell us. So, I have prayed — prayed and then thanked whatever Entity or Power or Force intervened to spare my son. He had rushed out between parked cars without looking, while chasing after a squirrel that the boys had been trying to get close to, and been hit by an unsuspecting driver, who, fortunately was not going at a great speed because of the speed bumps the residents on our streets had petitioned, which I, too, thankfully, had signed. Still, he had suffered a broken leg, three broken ribs, and, more seriously, a concussion that kept him in a coma for over a week. When he opened his eyes and spoke for the first time, I felt I had given birth to him all over again.

"When is Jamie coming home?" Joshua asks anxiously. The boys have always been close. They are, after all, twins, even if not identical.

"It'll be a little while yet. In a few days, maybe." I have come home to prepare something for Victor's supper. Ham steak, frozen peas, home fries, a typical Scottish supper, after he complained about my mother's simple Sicilian fare, although everyone else seems to love her *taghiareddi* — rough-cut, handmade pasta in her home-canned tomato sauce, which Victor *will* eat, if you twist his arm, but he's not a big fan. I have even gone to the trouble of making Scottish tablet, which Victor loves, but Jamie does too, and I will be bringing him some when I return to the hospital to spend the night by his bedside. It's a type of fudge made with tons of sugar and condensed milk that is so sweet it makes your teeth hurt. It's a secret family recipe of Victor's mother's, and I was only allowed to have it once we were married.

I have spent most of the last two weeks at the hospital, and nights too. The nurses have been wonderful, and since he got out of ICU, they've allowed me to sleep next to Jamie in a lounge chair that they have brought in for me. I've returned home for a few hours each day to prepare Victor's supper, then left again. If all goes well, Jamie will be discharged by the end of the week.

***

Jamie's return home is not as joyful as I would have hoped, and it's as a result of my doing. Victor has learned about my cashing the GIC and he is livid. I ask him to keep his voice down so as not to upset Jamie who is still in a fragile state, but he is too agitated to care.

"You must be out of your fucking mind! Why would you cash the GIC without telling me? We've lost the interest on it — do you know that — because you cashed it early?" He was at the bank this morning and realized that I had taken the money out. I am standing at the kitchen sink rinsing dishes and calmly sliding them into the dishwasher. Jamie is sleeping on the couch and I remind him again to control himself until we can discuss it in private. He is justified of course, but I know it's not the only reason he's angry; he's finally found a bona fide excuse to expel the anger he has been holding back for months, like the crescendo of lava inside the cone of a volcano that finally spews out its vitriol. For months, I have been resisting his forced schedule of matrimonial sex that has been the norm for eighteen years, and in those eighteen years, any obstinacy on my part has always resulted in coldness, belligerence, and general grumpiness towards me the next day. Whereas I have usually let him have his way in order to maintain the peace, more recently, I have fought back. "Don't force me, Victor — if I don't want to, you wait!" I had never spoken to Victor like this before, and it is only in the last few months that I have vigorously resisted. "Forced sex in marriage is rape too!"

He scoffed at this, his laugh almost, but not quite, a snort I recognized, and he retorted with, "It's your duty as a wife."

To which I responded with a derisive laugh, his words striking me as being so antiquated. "I'm not your concubine, Victor. We'll make love when we *both* want to — I won't be *forced*."

During the months when I believed that Valentin had gone out of my life for good, I had made a genuine attempt to rekindle the intimacy between Victor and me, and I patiently tried to explain to Victor that sex couldn't be penciled into a calendar, there should be no quota, there should be no pressure — it should come naturally. To his credit, Victor had agreed to our seeking counselling, but I soon realized that he believed we were there to *fix* my inadequate sex drive, or to hear confirmation of my wifely duties. Instead, as Victor released his pent-up frustration during our first session, the soft-spoken psychologist, a grizzle-haired, spectacled gentleman with a foreign accent, calmly told him, "You cannot expect your wife to be always in the desired receptive state that you would wish her to be. Therefore, you must lower your expectations and respect her feelings. They are every bit as important as your own."

"Such *bullshit!*" Victor had declared when we left the session, and after that he had refused to go again, and we began to argue almost every day, not just about sex but any small thing.

Now there is this bombshell, which I am hard-pressed to explain away. So, I simply tell the truth. A friend was in urgent need and I had lent him the money. "Which friend?" he asks, naturally wanting to know. The flood gates open and I confess to being in love with someone else, which, to my surprise, is followed by an unexplained feeling of euphoria.

After that, things happen so fast, it makes my head swim. Victor packs his bags and moves out in a histrionic gesture I have seen hundreds of times on television shows and in the movies. I am soon receiving letters from his lawyer. I'm allowed to stay in the house, temporarily, because of the kids. The house must be sold, of course, eventually, and the lawyer I have retained tells me I should expect alimony only until I am able to generate my own income. We will share custody of the children, with visitation rights for Victor every other weekend, and evenly shared holidays and summer vacations. Soon he has rented his own apartment, not far from our house. The kids don't seem as traumatized as I might have expected; they are receiving more attention than they ever had from their father, enjoying more activities with him. It is mind boggling how easily a marriage can cease to be. It takes most couples a year to plan a marriage in the first place, but only an instant to unravel it, because of one drink, one kiss, one moment of illicit intimacy that can change everything. To my very great surprise, I learn that Victor is dating the gym teacher, Julie, the diver. Was he really at school meetings after school? Has he been seeing her all along? Isn't life a tragicomedy?

***

Valentin calls me daily. He has been supportive over this last month, calling me regularly now that there is no forced time slot for him to call. We have even been able to spend our first whole night together here at my house when the kids were staying at their father's. Victor is more part of their lives now than he was when we were all together, helping them with school projects, taking them on trips to the planetarium, the museum, the Toronto Zoo, with Julie tagging along, naturally. Other people have faced these same arrangements and made them work.

I am starting to visualize the possibility of a life with Valentin, patching together different future scenarios for me and my children. I'm not sure how he will react to a ready-made family, how the children will react to him. I don't even know if he *likes* children. But he cherishes the memory of his little sister who died at the age of seven. Shouldn't that tell me something?

I visualize him making *tortillas* for the whole lot of us, or the flan dessert I know the children will love. He'll play soccer with the boys and teach them the techniques of the game. And we can lie beside each other each night and it won't be forced, the lovemaking; I'll look forward to it, eagerly. Or just lie all night wrapped in each other's arms, my head snuggled in the fur of his chest.

CHAPTER THIRTY-ONE

In the shower, I soap myself, noticing as I rub the suds around that my breasts have enlarged, my nipples and areola have darkened considerably. I had forgotten about these bodily changes. My period has always been irregular, but I first suspected that I was pregnant when, on waking, my stomach begun to gyrate, whirling saliva up into my throat, and I had to run to the bathroom to vomit. Something else I'd noticed: a heightened sexual desire. I'd read in childbirth manuals that this often happens to pregnant women. Since my first violent and rather frightening orgasm with Victor, I'd never had another to compare. For a time, after the breakup with Valentin, I'd allow my mind to drift away, conjuring memories of him, even though I was actually with Victor, and let the pleasant spasms that seemed at their root electric, transport me to a different dimension where I could still be with Valentin. But I resented never having been able to reach with Valentin those heights, or was it depths — a sinking, a falling through, a dying; orgasm, the small death, *la petite mort*, wasn't that what the French called it? Even the first time we had made love following our long separation, the time I must have conceived, my climax was counterfeit, his erection waning within seconds. But what of it — we had the rest of our lives to work on that!

Turning off the taps, I push aside the shower curtain and step out of the tub onto a bathmat. From the linen closet, I take a clean towel and dry myself. As I bend down to dry my lower legs, I feel a pressure weighing heavily against my nipples, similar to the feeling I remember when my milk came in. I recall bending like this after a warm shower and my milk would start to flow; being the same temperature as my body, it felt at first like a tickling along my arms. Looking down, I would see creamy blueish rivulets running down to my wrists. How amazed I'd been when once, out of curiosity, I'd licked the milk off with my tongue. So sweet, so incredibly sweet! When my milk comes in again, I will let Valentin taste it. He will be surprised to discover what sweetness flows out of *me*. Our son or daughter, mine and Valentin's, will soon suckle at my breasts. I can imagine myself, pressing my lips into a mass of silky black curls, our son, his son, or daughter; I could just as easily see the same dark curls, but longer, softer, framing a face less round, more delicate.

Valentin hasn't called for over a week, but I know he has to work as many hours as he can. I am anxious to tell him the news, now that I've confirmed it twice with a home pregnancy test I'd bought at the drugstore. No need any longer for the rabbit to die. The results looked vague to me the first time, but my hands had been shaking, perhaps I hadn't done it right. I'd waited five more days, on the fifth day delaying the voiding of my early morning bladder until I'd once more readied the test tube and eye dropper and mirrored stand, and this time, wondrously, magically, there had formed within the yellow circle reflected in the tiny mirror of the kit a definite rusty brown ring of confirmation.

I dress and go downstairs to the kitchen. This Saturday is Victor's turn to take the kids and he's decided they will go to the Science Centre, so they were excited when he picked them up. I have to inspect some open houses and, afterwards, intend to pass by Valentin's house and surprise him; he has mentioned that he is thinking of listing it, and I could show him some comparables from my listings. Today is his day off. His mother is away for a month, visiting her elderly parents in Spain, not knowing how much longer they might be around and how many more opportunities she might have to see them. I can't wait to see Valentin's expression when I tell him the news — pleased, proud — I'm not sure what to expect. What would he be doing at this moment? He told me he likes to sleep in on his day off. Or perhaps he's hanging around the house watching soccer on TV — what did I really know about his habits?

It takes me an hour to carefully make up my face and decide on a nice outfit to wear. When I'm dressed, I gather my briefcase and listings binder and set out.

***

The side street on which Valentin lives is lined on one side with rows of closely built townhouses not wider than ten feet — modestly priced homes owned for the most part by new immigrants. On the other side, there are post-war bungalows — tiny, detached houses built immediately after World War II, when there was a shortage of bricks. People are buying those up these days and taking the top off, turning them into two storeys. I have been here only once before, when his mother wasn't home and he'd cooked me the *tortilla*. Valentin lives in one of the mid-section townhouses. There is no parking immediately in front of his house, so I park further down the street and walk over to his place. I stop in his front yard for a moment, looking into the dark glass of the front bay window, and haphazardly comb my fingers through my hair, giving it some height. His front door is open; there is a glass storm door in front of it that is closed, however. Because the temperature is cooler outside than in, the glass on the storm door is slightly foggy, but I can see someone is standing on the other side. The person's features are unclear at first, but the storm door is suddenly opened, and I recognize standing in the doorway, *Brenda*. She is wearing a white terrycloth bathrobe and bends down to pick up the local newspaper that's delivered free each week in every neighbourhood. My logic tells me: you *fool*, she's wearing a terry cloth robe, and her hair is wet. What else can you assume!

Without hesitating, I walk robot-like to the door. For a moment I am speechless, struck completely dumb, but then the words escape from my mouth. "Is Valentin here?"

She glances down at my official-looking briefcase, which gives me authenticity. "He's just inside. I'll get him for you." She goes straight through to the back of the house and the room that I know is Valentin's bedroom because we had spent time together there after the *tortilla*. In a few moments, I see Valentin walking towards the door. I am standing to the side and he doesn't see me because of the fogginess of the inside glass until he opens the storm door. "Hello, Valentin." My voice is high pitched and squeaky.

He doesn't respond. Not the slightest flicker of recognition does he give away. He is a salt pillar. Perhaps I wasn't there, perhaps this wasn't happening, or perhaps in answer to his probable hope, I will dematerialize and become a puff of smoke. Invisible.

I swallow. My tongue feels dry and thick — so thick, I think I might choke on it. I am losing my sense of the surroundings; everything seems to have faded away except Valentin's eyes on which my gaze is fixed — *lying* eyes.

Brenda comes out from the back bedroom fully dressed in a pair of black ski pants and a pink blouse that pulls across her heavy breasts. Her broad shoulders taper into incongruously narrow hips, square like a man's. She is wearing a blouse with short, fan-shaped sleeves that stick out ludicrously from her thick upper arms like fly wings. When she looks up, her neck stretches, absorbing the slack of her double chin. She slides her hands boyishly into the pockets of her pants, approaches, indifferently, unknowingly. Valentin comes to life; his voice gritty and coarse from recently waking.

"Look, let's talk in the van, where we can have privacy." Brenda is at the door now, her curiosity piqued.

"I don't *want* to go in the van!" Wasn't it the source of my undoing in the first place?

Brenda is confused and asks, "Something wrong?"

"I have to talk to this lady about listing the house."

Saved by the briefcase, or so he thinks.

"We're going to be late, Valentin!" Brenda's lips are clamped in annoyance, her fists on her hips like a petulant child. With makeup, she looks better, her cheeks round and rouged, her fish-lips lined with lipstick. "How long are you going to be?" she demands.

"Just a few minutes."

He waits for her response like a dubious child asking permission to go out and play, although it's raining outside.

"Well, hurry up!" There is a sternness to Brenda I could never have imagined possible in this placid looking woman. I had misjudged Brenda. Brenda was in control of Valentin! The realization comes to me like a punch line to a joke, and if it weren't for the fury that I now feel, I would laugh.

Valentin steps outside, dressed only in jogging pants and a T-shirt he has slept in, and facing the front of the house, gestures directions. "Ok, you can put the sign here," he says.

I look at where he is pointing, bewildered for a moment, until I realize to what lengths he is willing to go to continue the ridiculous charade. Exasperated, I shake my head. "Tell me something, Valentin, have you ever told me the truth about *anything*?" In the reflection of the front window, I catch sight of my face, white, ghostly, a wild look transforming it almost beyond recognition.

"Listen, let's go into the van and talk," he says, taking my arm.

"*No! No!*" Once, when I was six years old, I had wrenched myself from a nurse's grasp because I knew she was going to stick a needle in my arm, promising it wouldn't hurt worse than a mosquito bite. "I want to talk to Brenda," I say, breaking away from his hold. In a frenzy, I march towards the door, flinging it open.

"*Por favor…*" He is supplicating me in Spanish, as if in his confusion, he'd forgotten the English language, or perhaps, as with his words of endearment to me in that language, he is hoping to touch a tender spot.

Without hesitating for a second, a *driven* woman, I yell into the house, "Brenda!"

Brenda comes to the door, surprised to hear me call her name. "Brenda, can I talk to you for a minute!" My voice must sound wild, urgent, for as Brenda comes reluctantly towards me, she is wearing an expression of bafflement or alarm. She steps outside and faces me, expectantly, perplexed. I experience a bizarre sense of irreality, afraid that if I speak, I might find I am talking in my sleep. Brenda looks first straight at me, then, sideways, questioningly, at Valentin. For a long moment no one speaks. The silence becomes farcical. People are walking by staring at us, a trio of mutes. Valentin drops his head, puts his hands in the pockets of his jogging pants, looks up, exhales, and says finally, "She wants to tell you something."

Puzzled, Brenda looks at me. Still, I cannot speak. Not a sound will come out. My lipstick has caked at the corners of my mouth and feels pasty; my lips are stuck together as though glued. I must look terrible, frothing at the mouth like a rabid dog.

Again, Valentin breaks the silence. "She wants to tell you … that we've been *friends*."

It was amusing the way he put it. I look at Valentin in wonder. This man whose baby was growing inside me — my *friend*.

"What do you mean *friends*?" Brenda turns and directs the question at me rather than Valentin. "You mean *just* friends." That qualifier again, the game of semantics.

"*No*." The word falls like a pebble out of my mouth.

"I see." She looks down at the sidewalk. I do too, and notice Brenda is wearing a pair of those jellybean shoes in pastel colours that you can buy even in a grocery store for a dollar ninety-nine. Hers are pink.

"How long has it been going on?"

"Over a year, a year and a half." Why did I *say* that; it sounded silly, a few months more or less.

Brenda nods, looks sideways, away from Valentin, towards the dark glass of the front window, though she wasn't looking at her face. "Thanks for telling me." Turning, she goes back inside, into the bedroom, and I see her reaching for some clothes. Was that it? Was that all the havoc I could wreak? The blood rushes back to my face; I can feel my cheeks burning. I rush to the door, opening it and yelling loud enough to reach the inside bedroom. "I don't think men should *lie* to women and get *away* with it." Brenda turns to look at me as the door clicks shut.

Behind me, although I'm almost surprised to find him there, I notice Valentin still standing, frozen in his spot on the sidewalk. Large beads of perspiration protrude from his forehead; sweat is dribbling down his temples even though it's cold outside. He seems to be in a trance. Without looking at me, he walks toward the door, then turns and gives me a look of pure hate, his mouth twisted in an ugly snarl. He is an *animal*. Sick with rabies. If I had a gun, I would *shoot* him! As his hand reaches for the door handle, I shout, "And you know what else?" I pause in order to consider the ramifications of his knowing what I am about to tell him, wondering if his knowing would be better or worse for me. Impatient, angry, he opens the door. "I'm pregnant!" I scream.

Not wanting to see his response if there is going to be one, I spin around and run down the sidewalk to the end of the block where my station wagon is parked, and there, looking back at the long row of identical row houses, I try to pick out the door of Valentin's house, and catch sight of an elbow in a doorway — a hairy, muscular elbow — and wonder whether the elbow was Valentin's who, unsure, was hesitating between going to Brenda or coming to me, though later I decide, and I am certain this was so, that I had been looking at the wrong door, the wrong elbow.

Chapter Thirty-Two

The fact that I was carrying Valentin's child had at first seemed to me insurance that he would call me. I had been both right and wrong about this. On the Friday following the incident in front of his house, the phone rang, and after picking it up, there had been an uncertain pause with breathing, his *breathing*, his *sigh*, I was sure of it. Then a *click* and a dial tone. It was *him* — I was certain it was *him*. And I was also certain that he would *never* call again. He had tried and lacked the courage. My pregnancy was, on the contrary, an assurance that he would *not* come back, I now realize, due to his fear of involvement in a complicated situation that he was not prepared to handle. Only recently, I'd accepted another reality: I had burned all my bridges; his friends would learn from Brenda what had happened and lose respect for him. Respect was what he cherished more than anything. So, I had eliminated for myself any possibility of absolution. Perhaps there was a silver lining — I might have done something charitable for Brenda. But my motives hadn't been that lofty; I had thought merely to destroy.

My depression returns. The black hole revisited seems hopelessly familiar, no less detestable. Despondent, I root out bitter crumbs of comfort; I find a perverse satisfaction in replaying the Saturday scene, seeing his discomfort, his suffering. Vengeance is sweet. But temporary.

Today, I move lackadaisically around in my kitchen, listening, in spite of myself, for the telephone's ring, staring out the window at a gray, gray day. Last night's wind has almost totally denuded the trees overnight. The neighbour's house at the back of my property leaps up suddenly, claustrophobically, against my kitchen window, so that I feel self-conscious standing in front of it in my nightgown. Lately, I don't bother to dress and go into the office for my listings; I told everyone I had a prolonged flu.

Restless, yet weary, I sit down at the kitchen table, leafing through a *Toronto Life* magazine, setting it aside, debating whether to make myself another coffee. Getting up, an action that lately demands a ridiculous amount of effort, I take the kettle from the stove to the sink and fill it with water. In the shiny oval of its surface, my distorted face looks jaundiced, my eyes depressed hollows with half-moons under each one, purple as eggplants. I look away, outside into the grayness, noticing the flowerbed's withering remains, the trees and shrubs that stubbornly retain their few ragged, withered leaves, although it is the beginning of November. I fill the kettle, settle it on a burner, stand next to it, and wait, listening for it to begin to splutter as the heat evaporates its wet underside. Looking down, I rub my hand over my abdomen, imagining that I can already feel a swelling there, although I know it is far too early. The kettle starts to rumble, then steam, fogging up the glass covering the digital clock on the back of the stove; it is 10:38 a.m. Past coffee break time, not that it matters, except I thought: *perhaps today*. Hope springs eternal. Again, I check the calendar that hangs from a magnetic clip on the fridge just to see the date: November 3rd. Today is Valentin's birthday. Last year at this time, Valentin had promised for his next birthday we would meet again at *our* park, and each year after that for the rest of our lives, no matter what. What a *ridiculous* notion.

But, what if he was waiting for me there now, sitting in his red van, watching for my station wagon to drive into the parking lot? *Where there's life, there's hope ... foolish woman ... he wouldn't be there!*

Turning the burner off, I pour hot water into a cup and add a teaspoon of instant coffee and a splash of half-and-half from a container in the fridge. Taking my coffee back to the table, I sit looking at the haggard reflection in the shiny beige liquid inside the cup. He wouldn't be there. Promises and lies meant nothing to him. He admitted he lied all the time to his mother. Didn't want to hurt her. Loved his mother. Maybe it was alright to lie to someone to spare them anguish. *The end justifies the means.* Valentin had been my best friend, closer even than Maddy, closer than Victor. I had *never* been that close to any human being. Only with Valentin had I ever felt such ease of conversation, a complete unselfconsciousness of words. And I had been totally honest with him in all things — but one. Though the passion had been wondrously real. Did my deceit equal his? Why should it matter to him, if it didn't matter to me. *The end justifies the means.* Wasn't Valentin sparing *my* anguish by not telling me about Brenda? Wasn't I doing the same for Victor by not telling him? How was I any better than Valentin? I take a sip of my coffee; it tastes like poison. I put the cup down, disconsolately. Today is Valentin's birthday. We promised we would meet each year on his birthday at *our* park, even if we were no longer together. I must go to *our* park.

***

By the time I reach *our* park, it is almost noon. The grayness has lifted and the sky looks merely smokey. Pink rays of sun are piercing the clouds like celestial lasers. As a little girl, this same sight never failed to awe me; I thought that heaven had temporarily settled closer to earth. Such fantastic notions. At that age, I believed a great many things that I no longer believe.

At the entrance to the park, chrysanthemums, dried and faded, mar the appearance of the carefully trimmed boxwood backing them; the remaining annuals — petunias, pansies, and impatiens — have lost their colourful profusion, displaying only a few stunted flowers and a great many twisted bare stems. School children wearing windbreakers and carrying plastic grocery bags marked Loblaws or Dominion, or one of the lesser known chains, are being herded by teachers and parent volunteers who laugh and chat together, displaying a camaraderie that would seem blatantly inappropriate in the classroom. Further along the road, a professional photographer snaps photos of models in fur coats who are posing against the rough bark of a giant oak that offers a wonderful textured background. On the hardened earth paths, joggers jog red-faced and Filippino nannies push carriages with their charges. So different from last year at this time, when there had scarcely been a soul, when the park had been ours.

I drive on to the north end of the parking lot near the rest rooms, where Valentin always parked. There is no red van. I scarcely feel disappointment. The air in the park smells of burnt leaves, a sweet, perfumed smell — almost like incense, a smell I have always associated with dark suffocating confessionals and funerals. I decide to go for a walk and follow a side path that leads to a densely wooded incline towards the pond; I recognize where I am now — Valentin had carried me down this same footpath, lifting me in his arms like a child because my shoes kept slipping on the dusty earth. How had he managed it? It was hard enough getting down alone. Who would ever do that for me again! The memories — all the sweet memories I had so carefully preserved to last a lifetime had curdled into sourness and now, whenever I attempt to conjure them up, they are caustic and contradicting and offer no joy.

Several times, going down the path, I lose my footing; the recently fallen leaves are shiny and slick, and I have to grasp on to the dried grasses and straggling shrubs that grow on the incline to keep from falling. Foolishly, I've worn open sandals and no socks, as if in denial of the season's end. They offer no protection from the sharp twigs that scratch my feet, and halfway down the path, not surprisingly, a dried branch pokes painfully into my foot just beside my ankle bone. Stopping to examine my injury, I see rivulets of blood dispersing along the fan shaped bones of my foot. I lick a finger and wipe the blood away until I can see the small red notch of punctured skin, and I press on it until the bleeding stops.

Continuing on, I feel another sharp pain, this time more needle-like. Trying to ignore it, I go on, but the pain becomes worse with each step until it is excruciating. On a patch of grass, I sit down and take off my sandal, raising my toe to inspect it more closely; a slender thorn has pierced the skin between my big toe and the one next to it. Carefully, I grab the end with two fingernails in a tweezer-like pinch, and being careful not to break it, pull it out easily in one piece. Instantly, all pain ceases. I examine the culprit, a hair-fine thorn, scarcely visible in my palm. What incredibly vulnerable creatures we are! It's a wonder we've managed to survive.

At the bottom of the incline, a wide concrete walk follows the pond whose edges are fringed with bullrushes and waters thick with patches of algae. A family of mallards floats composedly on the glimmering teal surface. On the other side of the pond, partially de-leafed trees, as though suffering from arboreal alopecia, expose the well-to-do mansions that have been built behind them. Only the peacefully swaying willows still retain most of their leaves, although they have paled and yellowed like the hair of the very old. The landscape looks sparse, depleted, foreboding of winter. Summer is an expansion, winter a shrinking, an atrophication — like old age.

A gust of wind sends a mound of leaves swirling in front of me. Oak, maple, beech, and elm leaves shuffle through the air like a deck of cards in four suits. Valentin was playing cards when he met the girl who'd had a fight with her boyfriend and gone to bed with *him*. Who is he going to bed with now? Possibly Valentin and Brenda have gotten back together again; he'd asked her forgiveness and promised to marry her. I would never know. It is better that way. But Valentin *knew*. *Knew* and didn't call. Hid his cowardly head in the sand. When I think of him, I no longer see him as tender and warm and compassionate. I think of him, rather, as metallic. Not stainless steel or iron, but of tin — a flimsy metal, hard and cold, but without any great strength. Why was I here on this fruitless pilgrimage? He would not come, would *not*. Why was I here walking alone in this park? Futilely. Anger accumulates in me like trapped gas and vents itself on recreated scenes of what else I might have said to him that last time. Agitated, I try to calm myself, to enjoy the walk. For an instant, I feel a quivering in my abdomen, and my hand goes protectively to cover it in a reflex gesture of pregnancy that I remember from the past; swallowed air, circulating blood, food digesting — it couldn't be the baby. Too soon. Not yet a baby. It's what I *want* to believe.

I feel suddenly tired and sit down on a nearby park bench. An elderly woman wearing a hand knitted ski sweater that has unravelled at the sleeves and balled everywhere else, is also sitting there. She is reading a single leaf of newsprint, so engrossed that she doesn't even bother to glance at me. It isn't even a regular newspaper, I notice, but a piece of religious propaganda of the kind usually distributed on downtown street corners. One headline blares above the others: DYING WOMAN BLESSED BY MIRACLE. Religion, I have heard, becomes more important when you get old, and even aged agnostics often reaffirm their belief in God. *There are no atheists in foxholes.* Close to death, who has the courage *not* to believe?

DYING WOMAN BLESSED BY MIRACLE. If Valentin met me here today, *that* would be a miracle. I immediately feel guilty for having had the thought; there are far more important miracles called for, life and death miracles, and mine is paltry compared to them. Miracles, like the fact that Jamie lived when he might just as easily have died. I have *already* been blessed by a miracle. I don't deserve another.

Getting up, I follow the path again to where it circles around and continues up a hill, back towards the parking lot. I can hear the laughing voices of children around me. Taking long strides, I reach the top of the incline, the muscles on my legs taut with the strain. I stop to get back my breath. But miracles *do* happen, and there is no quota.

Hurrying towards the parking lot, I scan the vehicles again. Nothing. A beige and brown passenger van, a white Rogers service van, but no red van. I look at my watch: Valentin's lunch hour is twelve to one. It is half past one, half past *hope*. Miracles *can* happen more than once, but not today.

My bladder aches painfully from fullness. I go into the public bathroom door marked WOMEN. *Woe*-men. Inside the air smells sharply of urine, even though a small window has been left open to circulate the air; it always seems to me that an open window in a public lavatory only serves to confuse the smell and augment it somehow. I go over to the sink to wash the grass stains off my hands. When I come out again, my heart does a somersault when I catch a glimpse of a red vehicle exiting the parking lot, but there are other vehicles blocking my view so that I can't tell if it's a van or a car. I run across the parking lot, the heels of my sandals slapping the concrete, and reach the vehicle just as there's an opening in the traffic and the vehicle is about to merge into it, and I notice that, even though it's a red van, the licence plate is numbers, not letters, there is no ladder going nowhere, and no red teardrop windows on the side that look like drops of blood.

CHAPTER THIRTY-THREE

Winter 1987

The operating room, I remember, was surprisingly large and brightly lit and walled with windows on one side, as if they were expecting spectators. The whole procedure had taken little more than thirty minutes. I know because the clock hanging on the wall in front of me as I lay on the gurney said two-thirty, and when I woke up at the end of it, it was three o'clock. *Three* — before the rooster crowed, the apostle Peter had disavowed Christ *three* times. Half awake as I was, I remembered the painting of *The Denial of Saint Peter* by Rembrandt that I had seen on our European trip — Jesus with his hands bound, helpless, vunerable, while Peter denied, and denied, and denied... That's what had gone through my groggy head at that time.

***

The phone on my office desk buzzes and I pick it up, glad to be released of my memories. Mrs. Jovanoski calling again. Yesterday she called four times to ask if I'd heard anything on the offer she'd received and signed back, stubbornly, higher than she should have — bartering an absolute must for Europeans. The prospective purchasers were young, hesitant, and I had suggested a forty-eight-hour irrevocable.

"How are you today, Mrs. Jovanoski?" No, I hadn't heard anything on the sign back, but I would call the buyer's agent to find out what was happening. They still had until midnight tonight — remember? Not to worry, in any case, since it had been a multiple offer presentation, and if this couple backed out, the second prospect would come back with another offer, I was sure. I dispatch Mrs. Jovanoski with the promise to call the minute I hear anything.

This is my third listing, although I have been an agent for a full year now — not a stellar performance, but I am encouraged and hopeful, and I really am taking to the career like a duck to water.

The divorce has evolved more amicably than I would have expected from Victor. We had to sell the house, of course, and he has found a cozy love nest for himself where he has settled with the diving gym teacher. Foolishly, I hadn't suspected anything, but when a man doesn't get what he wants, he looks elsewhere. It was not a happy marriage; things had evolved as they were meant to. I let Victor have all of his antiques — they were his babies, after all, and when I toured the empty house for the last time, just before handing over the key to the listing agent (Victor would not trust the house to be listed with me), checking every closet and every cupboard, I noticed with amusement that Victor had ripped out the Caesar salad recipe that I had years before taped to the inside kitchen cupboard door. Sex and Caesar salad — I guess he really couldn't live without them and now he could enjoy them with Julie. I could visualize her, standing at the kitchen sink, washing romaine lettuce for Victor's salad, and marking on her mental calendar the allotted nights for sex.

We are sharing custody of the kids, and they have adjusted surprisingly well; Alison tells me, "It's kinda fun having two bedrooms." I did not end up listing the house my grandmother left to me. It's where the children and I now live, which is conveniently located near my mother's house, so she can easily, and willingly does, give me a hand with the children. The school bus passes right by my mother's house, picks them up, and drops them off, and they seem proud to call themselves latchkey kids, like so many of their friends. I will be receiving court-ordered financial support from Victor until I can generate sufficient income to manage on my own. I am settling nicely into this new life, along with my children.

Sitting at my desk in the Mabel Lobeil Real Estate office, I start tearing listings from the dailies of my area, W08, and a few from W06 and W07, since I have a young couple who have asked me to find them a house meeting their criteria closer to the Lakeshore, which will be challenging since the basements of most of the houses in the area are seven feet high and the husband is six foot six. But I find it interesting dealing with people — interesting and frustrating. Sometimes after months of driving around, trudging from house to house, my clients finally buy with another agent. Most, however, stick with me, trust me, when there are so many ruthless and aggressive real estate agents out there.

The phone rings again. "Mr. Manzoni, good morning. Yes, that house is still available. Yes, I'm certain it's solid brick (*solid-a-brick*). That's all they built in those days, and you can tell because every fourth course of the bricks has soldiers running in the opposite direction... Absolutely not. No urea formaldehyde insulation." The stuff had become insidious, tragically, now that the government had dubbed it a health hazard. Houses in which it had been installed were doomed and sat and sat on the market, and were finally sold for a song. "Yes, I'm certain Mr. Manzoni. *Certo. Non c'è bisogno di preoccuparsi*, you don't have to worry. If they had the insulation, there would be plugs along the bricks on the exterior, and in any case, I will include a clause in the offer where the vendor has to guarantee that the house doesn't contain it." We book a time to meet to write up the offer.

I peruse the day's perforated sheets of new listings, ripping out the ones I want to inspect and filing them in my binder, until I come to a stark halt at an address I recognize. It is Valentin's house, just recently listed. I catch my breath. My hand hovers over the listing; for a brief second I debate whether to tear it from the sheets and include it in my binder of houses to inspect. He had *said* he wanted to sell. Where would he move to after it was sold, I wonder? Who was he with? Was he married now? I run through the scenario of me driving to his address for the agents' open house, looking through his home, gleaning information from framed photographs I might find on display there, or hair pins lying about, or bathrobes hanging in the bathroom.

The phone rings again. A long silent pause. My heart stands still, and seemingly, the turning of the earth. I tell myself, it won't be *him*, don't even think it.

"Rita?"

"Oh, Maddy, it's you."

"Busy *lady* — never see you anymore these days. How's it going?"

"Good. Really well."

"Selling lots of houses?"

"A couple this year. I have a few prospects."

"Good for you. Looks like we've traded places *again*."

"How about you? What's doing?"

"Me? I can't see beyond the Pampers and Pablum right now. The kid's a real breast man, too. I spend three quarters of the day nursing him."

"Try giving him a little more Pablum to tide him over longer."

"I think maybe a steak. He's *killing* me. You'd think he had *teeth*."

"How's the father?"

"Oh my God — Stef has got to be the proudest Dad *ever*."

The biological clock had gotten the better of Maddy. She had cast Mary Kay aside when her short-lived relationships had suddenly struck her as vapid, just as Stefan had confronted her with irrefutable evidence of her infidelity. Counselling had worked for them; she had realized she needed and cared for Stefan more than she realized; he in turn, gave up all his travelling and started working close to home. Stefan Junior came to be shortly afterwards.

"When are you going to drop by? You haven't been over since I brought the baby home from the hospital."

"I know. I'm sorry. I've just been so busy." It was a valid excuse, fortunately. I had been to the hospital to see Maddy's baby. Seeing Maddy looking so motherly with her breasts full and her stomach still puffy beneath her housecoat from recently giving birth, then in the nursery, the rows of cribs, each with a wondrous, miraculous child, had cut me to the heart, and it was only with extreme effort that I had managed to keep from crying. Stefan Junior was broad-faced and pug-nosed with not a single hair on his head. My babies all had hair — straight hair, not curly. I had wanted to reach out and touch the babies, and I had stood a long time with my hands pressed flat against the glass, examining each one, trying to find the one that would most closely have resembled mine — the one that never came to be. Still, whenever a mother pushing a carriage passes me on the street, I am filled with longing. Once, in the waiting room of the twins' pediatrician, I couldn't resist brushing my fingers through the hair of a curly-haired, exuberant toddler that was running around the room. Visiting Maddy, her house smelling so wonderfully with that new baby smell, seeing her with the baby, would be painful for me.

"I feel like a zombie," Maddy said. "I really need to get out."

"Maybe we can catch a show some night. Will Stefan babysit?"

"I think I can twist his arm. He's a little scared yet, but a show sounds *wonderful*. I'm starting to put the baby on a supplement so I can escape now and then." The telephone falls with a thud and I wait patiently during a considerable pause while Maddy retrieves it. "Sorry, Butch here is nursing while I'm talking, and the phone slipped off my shoulder."

I look at my watch. "Listen, Maddy, I'm sorry to cut you off, but I have to get to some agent open houses before noon. Is it okay if I call you back tonight? Then, we can have a good long chat."

"Sure. Anytime. I'm not going anywhere."

"Right then, talk to you later."

I turn my attention back to the listing of Valentin's house and detach it from the others on the page. I study it for a long moment: two storeys, three bedrooms with one of them on the main floor, one kitchen, one bathroom, unfinished basement, close to shopping, transportation, and parks. There are a few other listings in the area I could also inspect. It *is* part of my job. I have gotten to know the streets well, recognizing the flavour of each area, the good qualities, the drawbacks, the streets that back onto desirable green space or undesirable railway tracks and hydro rights-of-way that never sell unless the price is drastically cut. I have Valentin partly to thank for my increased knowledge of the city, but my knowledge has augmented considerably in the past year. My confidence, too. As well, I've made my first speculative venture — the two semis and the lot near *El Flamenco* that Valentin had told me about.

He was right about the owner mistrusting real estate agents, but I'd spoken to him in Sicilian, mentioned Valentin's name, offered him his full asking price. I borrowed against my grandmother's house and together with the income I have generated from my last two sales this year, plus the rental income from the third floor of my grandmother's house, which I have continued to rent, I have managed the down payment and qualified for the financing.

Grabbing my jacket hanging on the back of the chair and my briefcase, I remember before leaving to check the memo pad on my desk: *call Mrs. Jovanoski. Call the third-floor tenant. Call planning department.* The first reminder I amend to *call Mrs. Jovanoski after calling alternative purchaser's agent*, just in case there is no response on the sign back. According to the purchasers' agent, it appears in the meantime, the purchasers have been smitten with another house, smaller but with more gumwood and stained glass. But I feel fairly certain that the second purchaser will be presenting an acceptable offer soon. Mrs. Jovanoski is an extremely nervous old woman; it is in both our best interest to maintain her high spirits. *Call third-floor tenant.* My tenant from upstairs at my grandmother's house is complaining of a dripping faucet and I have called a plumber. I will check if the repair has been done, but I can do that later.

And, oh yes — *call planning department.* My request for rezoning of the properties I have recently purchased near *El Flamenco* has a good probability of being approved for a small condominium or a professional building; if I hang on to the property for a few years, I'll be able to sell it for double, maybe triple, what I paid for it — and in the meantime collect rent. Valentin's speculative hunch had been right.

I still think of Valentin often. And if at times I hate him fiercely, at other times I think I love him just as fiercely, still.

Wives went back again and again to husbands who abuse them; although I have never been able to understand that, I can understand it now. Passion can linger insidiously. I still long for Valentin — the sound of his voice, the taste of his lips, the feel of his body against mine. There is something Valentin had told me once, a saying in Spanish: *nadie me quita lo bailado* — no one can take from me the dance I have already danced. I *have* danced. My memories, if I choose to preserve them, will always be mine.

But driving clients around, I realize the places where we've been together — the Tim Hortons near Santini's, the sandwich shop, the apartment downtown, and, especially, *our* park — are slowly losing the ghost of him, like white-wash on a fence, fading with the persistence of the elements. Eventually my love for him will fade too, grow vague, along with the memory of his face, his voice, his touch — become a *distant* memory I will question the authenticity of.

I like to imagine what Valentin's response might be when he sees the sign for rezoning go up on the investment property I have purchased, when he sees it's *my* name on that sign. Perhaps, he will be irritated that I beat him to it. Perhaps he will be furious. Perhaps he will call and reproach me. "I was the one who told you about that property!"

And I will close my eyes and concentrate on the sound of his voice, its slight gravelliness, its pleasant grating, even in anger, and I will say simply, "*Thank you.*"

I'm still clutching the listing of Valentin's house . I look at the narrow, oppressive row house squeezed between two flanking identical houses, with its front bay window where, in its gray glass, I had seen my desperate, pained, befuddled reflection next to an indifferent Valentin. I hesitate for a moment, then crunch the listing into a ball and drop it into the blue plastic recycle bin next to my desk.

Acknowledgements

Thanks to my best friend, Angela Waugh, who plodded through the first draft of this novel, and to my beta readers Jill Kneller and William Owens, who gave me the thumbs up I was hoping for. Special thanks to my talented nephew, Anthony Catania, for his creative cover design and to my poetry-loving brother, Bart, for helping me create my epigraph. Heartfelt thanks to the rest of my family, who told me to "just go for it."

Thank you to Gaetano Cipolla, professor emeritus at St. John's University, New York, and president of Arba Sicula magazine, for correcting my Sicilian phrases and enlightening me to the fact that Sicilian is not a dialect, but a language that existed in literature long before Italian.

I am very grateful to my publisher, Greg Ioannou, who, like a fairy godfather, suddenly made it all seem possible. Many thanks to my editor Lee Parpart, whose enthusiasm was greater than I could have ever hoped for, to copy editor Amanda Feeney, who patiently made every change I asked for, and to Meghan Behse, for guiding me through the preprint process.

www.ingramcontent.com/pod-product-compliance
Lightning Source LLC
Chambersburg PA
CBHW022005050726
47499CB00002BA/326